The TALES of SPEHROW

Quest For the Moonstruck Mage

E. L. Baldwin

ISBN: 979-8-218-81220-1 (paperback)

ISBN: 979-8-218-81221-8 (ebook)

Cover design by: Miblart

Printed in the United States of America

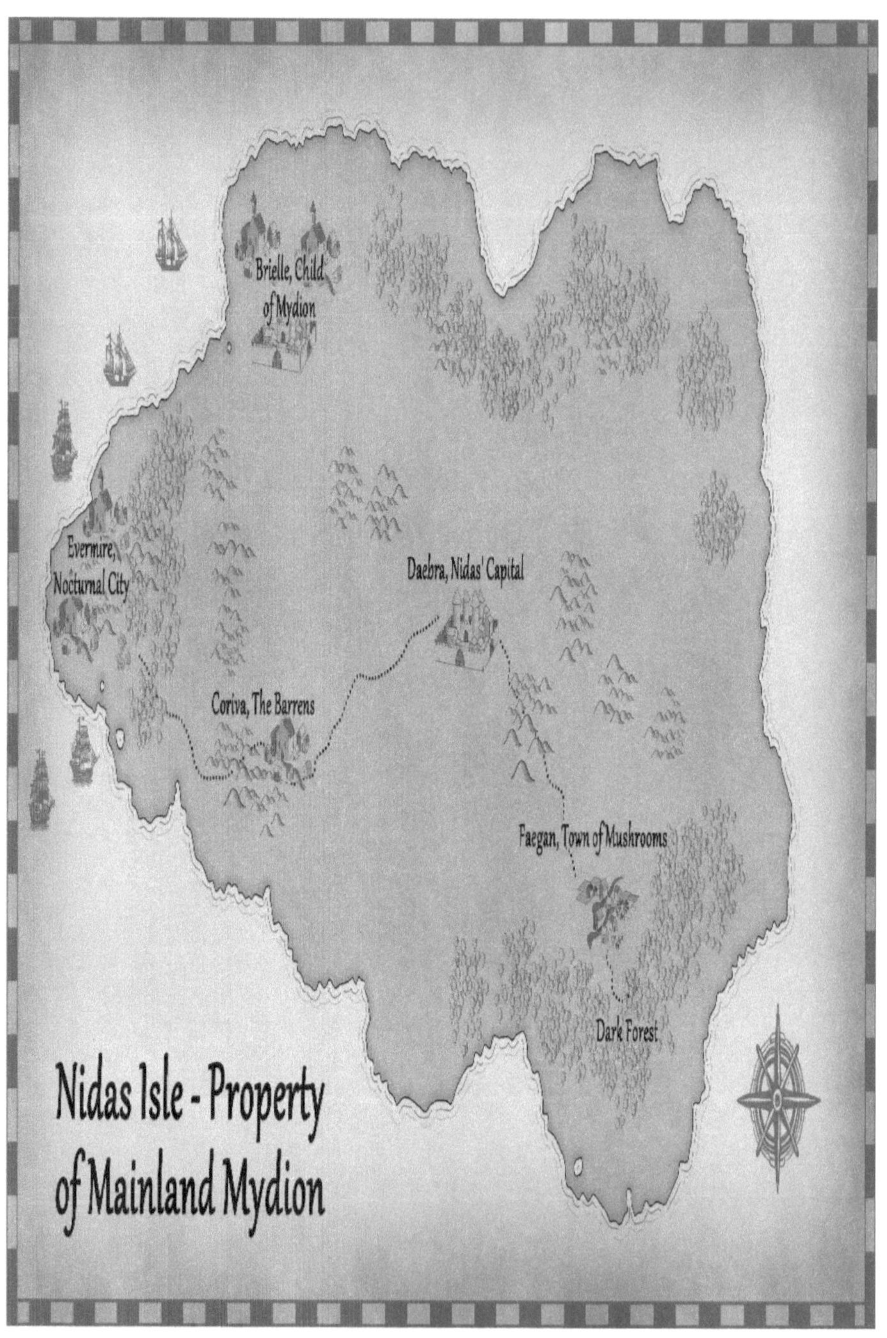

Brielle, Child of Mydion
Evermire, Nocturnal City
Daebra, Nidas' Capital
Coriva, The Barrens
Faegan, Town of Mushrooms
Dark Forest
Nidas Isle - Property of Mainland Mydion

Venari
Land of Mages
Paia
Caelum's Temple
Mydion
Home of Industry
Beltierre   Land of Monsters
Nidas
Isle
The Islands of Pelle

Part One

Prologue

The Spehrow's Eye

Everyone knew Dremos as the Scoffer of Death. A dark, crowded room of villainous monsters could surround the fiendish hunter, and he'd never break a sweat. After all, when he wielded the Blackened Blade and slew his enemies in the blink of an eye, his title reigned throughout Pelle's four islands. Of course, Scoffer of Death was one of the more positive names given to him. He'd take that title over Devil, Impish Traitor, or the worst, Khallus' Spawn.

It was a name meant to spite the fiends of Pelle, condemning the oaths of their treacherous human ancestors. Granted, said-ancestors never expected their offspring to bear the vile deity's features. The curse of wolf-like eyes and large horns made the fiends stand out amongst even the rarest of Pelle's creatures. It prompted the vulgar title to create rumors of their "bloodthirsty nature." Most fiends attacked those who spouted such gossip. But Dremos knew it'd only prove their point. The best he could do was swagger past the rabble and let the words flow off his back. A calm demeanor and a cool head: the well-known traits of the infamous hunter.

So, when memories of certain demons flooded his mind, Dremos' collected nature nearly hurled itself out the window. Thank goodness he had closed his bedroom door, so no one saw him in such a light. He sat in his plush armchair to calm himself down, but it only heightened his anxiety. His heart raced thinking about the monsters of old. The way their decomposed forms preyed on the innocent. Their smell of decay overwhelming his senses. The sight of their darkened blood coating his onyx weapon and rich navy skin.

Dremos couldn't possibly face them again. Not after what happened. Not while he knew what would happen if he slew them.

"Rose, dear," a calm voice purred. Dremos melted upon hearing his nickname. She was here. Of course, she was here. Just the sound of her voice reminded him why he remained a hunter to this day. He lifted his head, and his heart felt at ease. Seeing the love of his life often did that to him, especially when she greeted him with the most radiant pair of eyes he'd ever seen. Warm and comforting, gilded with the brightest shade of gold. Madam Spehrow—his everything, his precious star in the night sky, knelt before Dremos as she squeezed his hands within hers.

"Starlight," Dremos murmured. So entranced by her beauty, he let his nickname for her slip without a second thought. Decades ago, it would have been quite surprising for her to comfort him. In light of her esteemed reputation, most people had thought Madam Spehrow insane. A half-elven woman entertaining fiendish scum like him was completely unheard of. But after thirty years of adventures together, they realized Dremos was just as crazy. She saved his life in more ways than one. The least he could do was settle in the town of Evermire with her and protect her from all harm that might befall. The townsfolk of Evermire titled him "The Spehrow's Eye" on account of his guardin' and spyin', as they called it.

But moments like these, when Madam Spehrow peered up at him with sympathy, were not Dremos' proudest, to say the least. The woman grazed her thumb over his faint facial hair, making him seep back into reality.

"There's my Dre," Madam Spehrow lulled. "You ran off so fast we hardly had time to talk."

He took full responsibility for that. He should've been with her like he was supposed to. Helping to run her downstairs tavern, The Spehrow's Nest, was no easy feat. A break was in order when he received the grave news. Madam Spehrow showed Dremos a letter while he smoked pipes with fellow hunters at the fireplace. When he read the sender's name on the envelope, inner panic took over and he stormed out to think in his bedroom.

He thought he'd dropped that letter on the floor outside, but there it sat at Madam Spehrow's side.

Dremos ran his hands through his raven hair, grazing the skin of his spiraled horns. Perhaps now was the time to talk.

"Forgive me," he lowered respectfully. "I didn't realize my scene would humiliate you."

Madam Spehrow scrunched her eyebrows together. The bedroom light reflected off her pierced one. "You know that if I ever felt humiliated, I'd have Sly scare them off before it could happen."

She'd do it, too. That cheeky snake of hers frightened more customers than Dremos' enemies combined.

His bright red eyes shifted back to the letter on the floor. He noticed the gold wax stamp torn at the center. Did she open it?

Madam Spehrow followed his eyes and gave a half smile as she picked it up. "I hope you don't mind," she said. "You never know with letters nowadays. These newer mages will enchant anything they can get their hands on."

The sender was no new mage. Dremos knew that. As Madam Spehrow stood up, the back of the letter revealed the cursive name of his old comrade. Olivius. The tired fiend bowed his head away, as if its contents were plagued by some sort of curse. Perhaps it was for the best that she read it.

Madam Spehrow exhaled in annoyance as she skimmed through the parchment once more. "Oh, you hunters and your shortness of words. And it's in dwarvish too, no less." She scoffed. It was not her most fluent language.

Great Comrade, she translated out loud.

> *"Make haste to the west at once. The Legion…"* she paused. *"Has made itself known again. Forests of Faegan are where its inqai lurk. Bring your weapons by daybreak and join our cause. We shall pay you handsomely in return. May Caelum and His Children smile upon you.*
>
> *Olivius Hedgethorn."*

Dremos gave a flustered sigh when she mentioned that word. Inqai. The certain demons he'd fought in battles past. True devils, the kind humans often compared him to. He propped himself out of his chair and moved past Madam Spehrow as she finished the letter.

"It's been a while since we've heard from Olivius," Madam Spehrow perked up. "You'd think his letters would be more comforting after so many quests."

Dremos paid her observations no mind and opened the drawer below the large vanity. He pulled out a few sets of clothes, a pair of black socks, and a thick iron rod with bronze engravings.

"You don't have to go, you know." Madam Spehrow tried maintaining conversation. "Olivius has many skilled hunters in Faegan. Surely, he can find others to—"

He cut her off by dropping his things with a heavy thump. "You and I both know that's not true," he bit back.

He moved past her again to the coat rack next to his closet. He sensed her offended scoff as he grabbed the cape and knapsack off the hangers.

"Oh, so the Spehrow's Eye lacks manners, I see," she quipped.

Dremos grunted. "I don't have time for this."

Before he could shoo her away, Madam Spehrow grabbed his face and turned it to meet her own. He watched the stern glint in her eye shine through her golden irises. Even with her severe expression, she never looked more beautiful.

"Don't do that, Dre," Madam Spehrow warned. "Don't shut me out when I try to console you. I only wish to help you think before you make this decision. So, I'll say it again. You. Don't. Have. To. Go."

"I know that," Dremos finally admitted.

"Then why am I still holding your face?"

"Because you love looking at it." He gave her a wink as he smirked.

Madam Spehrow disregarded his advances with a sigh. "Rose, is it because of your oath?"

Dremos paused. She knew better than to ask what they both had the answer for. "It is *exactly* because of my oath. If I don't go now, more innocent lives will be at stake. This town. This island. If I do nothing, who knows how weak our defenses will be?"

"Our defenses are strong enough. Both for Evermire and Nidas Isle," she argued. "Or have you forgotten the battle for her safety?"

Dremos noticed her pointed, pierced ears turn down. They always did when she was nervous or upset. He rested his hand on hers, hoping to ease her mind. "You said you wished to help my decision. Unfortunately, I've made it myself." He planted soft kisses on her knuckles. "But if you desire to help, accept the fate that's set upon me, as I have already."

Madam Spehrow leaned into Dremos' warm embrace and rested her head on his shoulder. He tucked one of her dark brown dreadlocks under her ears, remembering just the thing to comfort her.

"Two days, Starlight. I'll only be gone for two days." He raised a brow at her. "If you're patient enough I might buy you something. What would you like? Flowers? Jewelry?"

"Distracting me with material things? Dre, dear, you know me too well," she said playfully, drawing a chuckle from Dremos. "Hmm…Sly is running out of food. Perhaps you can take him and stop by that bait shop while you're there."

"So, you've reduced me to pet-sitter now," Dremos scoffed.

She looked up at him. "Oh, don't be crude. You know you like him."

"*You* like him. And that's all that matters," Dremos said, intertwining her fingers with his. "Anything else?"

Madam Spehrow rested her forehead on his. "Home isn't home without you, Spehrow's Eye," she breathed. "Be careful and come back safely. Are we clear?"

Moments like this, Dremos never wanted to stay so badly. He planted another kiss on her hand. "Crystal."

The scent of mint burned upon Dremos' lips. He inhaled its flavor through his long pipe, letting the smell linger in his breath. A flicker of heat flashed on his tongue before he bit down on it and quietly exhaled a ring of smoke.

This routine was a must before and after any quest. Most hunters in the field protested his hobby, afraid of being sensed behind enemy lines. But fear was a meaningless word to the Spehrow's Eye. So long as he went about his routine in a dark, high, and isolated area, beyond the eyes of deadly foes. Faegan's forests at moonset were the perfect spot to perch on the tallest tree branch and indulge. He peered with his glowing red irises out from under his black hood. Even with night vision, he barely saw any life stirring down below. But perhaps that was a good thing. With no devils to face, he supposed he could leave early and tell the town of Faegan they had nothing to worry about.

If that were the case, however, Olivius wouldn't be sitting next to him with his short legs dangling over the tree branch or handing his stony friend a sandwich.

Olivius had a warm expression tucked under his hooded cloak: tan, rosy cheeks, a moonlight silver beard, and glowing green eyes. Dremos remained troubled by his smaller comrade's request. He withdrew his pipe and took the snack but didn't eat it.

"It's almost too good to be true, comrade," Dremos prodded. "The beasts don't show for three years, and they just now show up?" He sighed. "Are you certain that you saw them?"

He felt bad for a moment realizing he expected an oral replay, when he knew the dwarf only communicated with his hands.

"I wouldn't forget devils like them even if I tried," Olivius signed, flicking his hand from his chest to his temple as he shook his head.

"How many did you say there were again?"

"Five of 'em," Olivius signed showing the number. "Not many, I know, but Rosie don't wanna risk anything."

Dremos rested his head against the tree. Perhaps there was no running from it. Fate only led him to bring aid to those in need. His thoughts drifted off to home, to Madam Spehrow, to any semblance of having a normal life.

Suddenly, a faraway purple flicker caught his eye. Khallus flames: a sign of destruction in its wake, and a delicacy for his monsters before they took your life. They were close. A distant voice cried above the treetops.

Rowan! the voice exclaimed. Dremos and Olivius sat up immediately.

Rowan, where are you? Another voice called out. Followed by a loud shriek.

The voices were young, helpless, facing imminent danger. Dremos tightened his fists and glared at the stunned Olivius. "You said no innocents were involved," he gritted.

"We never knew of any innocents 'til now," Olivius signed, making a question mark with his hands and pointing to his mouth.

Dremos scowled. Defeating beasts was one thing, but saving innocents was another. One slip-up and he'd be putting his whole oath in jeopardy. He watched the fire flare even brighter; it showed him exactly where they were.

Dremos lifted the black mask around his neck until it covered his nose and mouth. He dug through his cape, taking out an iron rod. He turned its center, broke it apart, and whipped out two black swords.

"Find the innocents, slay the beasts," he reminded Olivius. The dwarf put on his white gloves and gave the fiend a thumbs-up.

"And try not to set everything on fire this time."

Chapter 1

Rowan the Brave

Rowan promised himself that no matter what happened, nothing would explode. He prepared his spells for weeks, making sure he cast them perfectly. There were a few hiccups in his practice, but they wouldn't befall him here. This time his magic would work; it had to. So, with a cape on his back, blue marbles on the floor, and spell book in hand, Rowan made his grand entrance.

"Lady and gentleman," he announced. "Boy and girl! Fiend and half-orc! Thank you kindly for joining me in this… glorious setting for my performance!"

Fine, so the setting wasn't glorious, or even the cleanest. He had only chosen the rooftop because the sun provided better lighting. He noted the moldy brick, the dried-up plants, and the summer humidity heating his mahogany skin. But knowing his two best friends, Selah and Peron, were sitting up front to watch, made Rowan forget all about these things.

"You have seen many of my tricks. How I perfected the art of turning stones into bread. The time I made light appear from my hands, and how I made dolls disappear into thin air.

And now, for the first time ever, I will make these marbles float into the air with clear *acidocracy.*"

That didn't sound right.

"A-accikerky… uh, akera—"

"Accuracy," Peron whispered.

"Thank you, kind sir," Rowan shouted. "With clear *accuracy*! I warn you: your eyes may not be ready for the wonder you're about to behold. Prepare yourselves to be amazed by… Rowan the Brave!"

He gave a dramatic bow and heard simple applause from his audience.

"Woo-hoo! Yeah, Rowan," a cheery voice yelled.

Rowan raised his head to smile at the tall orcish girl with green skin and pale tusks piercing into her joyful smile. Selah was always the first to cheer him on. Peron, however, was a little more stubborn. Rowan thought he didn't cheer because the sun turned his skin and pointed horns from white porcelain to a red-hot sunburn. But no, his expression looked more bored than irritated.

"Peron, come on," Rowan groaned. "At least clap a little, or you'll ruin my whole bit."

"I'm not ruining anything," Peron argued in his lower pitch. "I'm just wondering how long it'll take for this one to explode."

"That last one didn't explode. It just… spread out into a million tiny pieces."

"I kind of like when it explodes," Selah said. "It makes it look like fireworks. Like the ones in those other spells you showed us."

"He'd probably make those explode too. And not on purpose," Peron whispered.

"There are no fireworks," Rowan said sharply. "And there is no explosion! Just floating marbles! Come on, I worked really hard on this. Can't you just please let me finish?"

"Fine, fine," they mumbled.

Rowan flipped through his small spell book and straightened up, clearing his throat. "Now, like I said, prepare to be amazed!"

As he skimmed through the old language in his book, Rowan thought about the day he found it. Dusting shelves in the orphanage library allowed him to explore all the old books. He particularly loved the fantasy section, where all his problems melted away as he turned the pages. Where his dreams took flight. Where he read stories of his favorite mages, both real and mythical.

His favorite stories, however, were about the greatest mage of all time: Linn the Moonstruck. A mighty spell caster with the power of the sky at his fingertips. A member of the most heroic mage party, The Ataxia, and one of the saviors of Pelle's islands. With his scaled scepter, Linn the Moonstruck traveled the dangerous caverns of Beltierre and defeated the evil *mufow* lizard. Or *a muffled* lizard... he never knew how to pronounce it correctly. But he didn't just read one story; Rowan made it his mission to read all ten Linn the Moonstruck books. He had read each book more than five times in fact. The stories captivated Rowan every time.

When he should've been dusting instead of reading, Rowan bumped into a bookshelf, and a tiny book fell off the top. The language was unfamiliar, but the illustrations he understood. They were all images showing how to perform the spells he'd read. He hid the spell book in his room and only practiced in secret, hoping to become a great mage just like Linn the Moonstruck one day. But one day turned into five months. And five months turned into three years, with little to no progress. But today would be different. After so much time, Rowan believed he had finally perfected one spell after failing a thousand others.

Rowan exhaled nervously. "Please let this work," he whispered. Raising and twisting his hand, the young boy shouted a simple word.

Altsum.

Marbled glass flared in the sunlight and lifted off the brick floor. Rowan's toy spiraled up into the sky until they were out of reach. His eyes followed the floating ring of marbles, watching them spin together in perfect unison. They were just what he had hoped for but never saw until that moment.

"It didn't explode," Rowan uttered, forming a smile. "I…I did it!"

"He did it," Peron said, his mouth hanging half open.

"I did it! I did it! I did it!" Rowan jumped up and down, gazing happily at his own work.

"That's amazing, Rowan," Selah cried as she clapped. "You finally got one!"

"Well, let's not be too hasty," Peron said, anxiously staring upward. "Something still could go wrong."

"Per, please," Rowan said. "Can't you be happy for me once in a while?"

But Peron didn't have time for Rowan's whining. His eyes merely widened after seeing a blue flash outline his friend's body.

"Rowan?"

"Stop looking at me like that." But even in his annoyance, Rowan felt taller and lighter than air. "Honestly, it's like you don't want me to learn—"

"Rowan, you're floating," Selah exclaimed.

Then Rowan stared at the floor as he slowly rose and got closer to meeting the marbles in the sky. It wasn't until his book fell, and he'd floated a few yards away, that he realized:

Something went wrong.

"Whatever you do, don't look down," Peron shouted.

Rowan did the opposite, feeling dizzy as he looked at his friends down below. "Ah! It's too high! What do I do! What do I do!"

"Don't worry Ro, I'll catch you," Selah yelled as she held out her arms. "Maybe you can try undoing the spell."

"How am I supposed to do that? I've never gotten this far!"

From on high, Rowan heard Peron's groan and saw him dash over to the spell book. "Hey, hey! What are you doing?"

"Getting you out of this mess, again," Peron said, flipping through the book. "Doesn't this thing have, like, a table of contents or something?"

Who knew how long that would take? His marbles were flying only a foot away from him, so Rowan did the only thing he could think of doing. Somehow, he scooted closer to the marbles and collected them from their flight.

"I think I found the spell! I'm not sure how to pronounce it, though."

"Ooh, let me try," Selah said. She leaned over and squinted at the book. "Alright, so, you point two fingers at the object." She demonstrated for the floating Rowan. "And then you say, uh…Dee-Uh-Sah-Ray?"

"Huh? O-Oh right," Rowan exclaimed. "*Diasare!*"

Rowan and his marbles flashed blue. He fell screaming from the sky, and his toys slipped through his fingers. Fortunately, he landed with a thud right in Selah's arms. She held Rowan as if he weighed nothing at all. "Thanks, Se!"

As for his marbles, a couple hit Selah and Rowan on the top of their heads. The others hit the ground hard and shattered. Only one marble survived, Peron nearly caught it in his hand. But he missed it and hit the floor and rolled away.

"No, no, no, no, no," Rowan exclaimed, breaking from Selah. The orphans all tried to catch the marble in time. But gravity was not in their favor, and the treasured item fell off the roof's edge, seemingly lost forever.

That was until a shrill voice broke through. "Urchins! What are you doing up there?"

The children flinched at the sound; hearing her voice was never a good sign. Of all the hours, why did she have to interrupt their free time? They looked over the edge to see an old silver-haired woman leaning halfway out the orphanage window, frowning at them.

"Nothing, Den Mother," Peron replied. "We were just playing and got a bit carried away."

She held the remaining marble. Rowan backed face away from the edge, hoping she wouldn't notice him.

"Well, playtime is over. Get back here and tidy this kitchen. I'd like to eat my lunch without dust on the counters."

"Yes, Den Mother," the children replied.

They watched her disappear into the building and heard the window slam. Thank goodness she hadn't chastised them. Rowan hated when Den Mother did that. Granted, she wasn't really their mother, but she practically raised them, so calling her that seemed to fit. Rowan never knew his actual mother, but he read stories about how they were supposed to act. Weren't mothers supposed to be kind and loving to their children? Den Mother's love consisted of fire and brimstone. The only kindness she showed was throwing Rowan in the cellar.

Rowan checked on his marbles. The shattered pieces in his hand told him it was too late. His favorite toy, his oldest toy, reduced to blue glass in his fingers.

He felt a palm on his shoulder. "You alright, Rowa?" Peron asked.

Rowan nodded, his face as blue as the marbles.

"Cheer up, Ro," Selah said. "Just think about it. Once we leave this place, we'll get you a new set of marbles. With lots of colors, too. The best money can buy."

He smiled a little, if only to seem alright.

"You remember which one to find, right?"

"Yeah, I remember," Rowan exhaled dully. "Peron, the map. You, the matches. Me, the gold. 'Hide it when you find it.'" He memorized that order about thirty times.

"Great. Now let's get your spell book," Peron instructed, passing him the book. "We'll all go down together. Oh, and make sure to hide it under—"

"Under the tableware closet, I know. You don't have to remind me every time," Rowan rushed. "Let's just get this over with."

He pulled his cape to the side and stomped his way back into his bleak and bitter home. Rowan had had enough. Of the orphanage. Of Den Mother. Of always failing every chance he had. But all of that would end. Because on that day, Rowan and his friends would escape their orphanage once and for all.

●　　●　　●

"Ninety-eight." *Clink.*

"Ninety-nine." *Clink.*

"One hundred. Pieces. Of. Gold." *Clink.*

Rowan smiled down at the weight of the small burlap sack. He'd never carried coins so heavy before. He'd never carried coins at all.

"Quit fooling around, man," Peron whispered. His knees were planted on the wooden floor. "We already knew how much was in there."

"It's a hundred gold! Can you really blame me for recounting?" he whispered, closing the pantry box. "With money like this, we could buy the entire island if we wanted to."

"Of course, you'd want something like that. Luckily, I'm not as selfish as you. I'd be content to buy a few loaves of bread. Maybe even a small cottage to live in."

"And dreams like that, is why *you're* scraping underneath the table."

Rowan decided not to react to Peron's eyeroll. The fiendish boy took the job of map scraping, not by choice, but because of their competition rules. First one to finish breakfast, got the easiest job. And Peron was a slow eater. Good thing too. It took Rowan, the second fastest eater, weeks to steal Den Mother's gold and hide it in pantry boxes. He'd rather do that than have paste fall into his mouth. In a way, Rowan considered it payback for Peron splattering paste on his shirt when they hid the map under the table.

"And that's why *I'll* be holding everything," Selah said. She took the liberty of dusting and sweeping every inch of the floors and countertops. "I wouldn't trust you guys with money, no matter how big of an emergency."

"Right, Sellie. Like we're supposed to trust you with fire," Peron said sarcastically. "Just you wait. I think I deserve a rematch when we get to Faegan. It's only fair since you cheated the last time."

"It's not considered cheating if you're hungry," Selah, the fastest eater, sang. She knelt on the floor and tapped on a few pieces of hardwood.

Tock, tock, tock, went a hollow piece.

Rowan watched wide-eyed as Selah lifted the width of it and pried it off the ground like a simple piece of taffy. He had tried to do it once, but his multiple splinters were no match for her powerful orcish strength. Selah exhaled in relief at the supplies, resting safely on the concrete; a purple matchbox and a little something extra she found on her journey. "Besides, you should thank me." She picked them up. "Because I'm going to get us safely across the forest with these."

She displayed the matchbox, of course. But Rowan grinned the most sinister grin at the set of sharpened wooden stakes clutched in her hand.

Peron's reaction was not as delighted.

"A STA— a stake, Selah? Really," Peron exclaimed, quickly lowering his shrill tone to a whisper.

"Three stakes, actually. One for each of us," Selah returned. "Isn't it cool? I sharpened them myself a couple months ago. I'm so happy with how they turned out!"

"That's a little much, don't you think? Shouldn't we all talk about it before we start carrying weapons?"

"I don't know. Shouldn't you be scraping paste off the table?"

"For your information, I scraped off the map before you even found your stupid spikes." He got up and showed the paper to his friends. Despite the white paste at the bottom, the map was thick enough to make out the old sketches and its title: *Nidas Isle—Property of Mainland Mydion.* Selah found it when it was her turn to dust the library. It was a good thing Den Mother never used those old geography books, or else she might've caught the young girl ripping out a piece of Pelle's most valuable history.

Selah held in a small chuckle, as if his task was hardly remarkable. "Gee Perry, took you long enough. What did it take you, like thirty minutes?"

"Try five, you shameless cheater."

"Ha, I could do it in one," Rowan declared.

"Yeah, if the paste was still wet, you dummy," Peron said, grabbing Rowan and rubbing his fist into his brown coils. The boy demanded he stop but couldn't through his peals of laughter.

"What about you, Selah?" Rowan asked through his giggles. "How many matches do you have?"

She opened the match box and counted. "Um, about three."

Rowan pushed Peron away at her answer. That couldn't be right. Last time, there were eight matches. "A-are you sure?"

"Yeah, I mean, I can count them again if you'd like."

"No, no, it's fine. I just…I thought we'd have enough to make a bigger campfire. You know, in case… the forest is much darker than we thought." Rowan lowered his eyes to the floor, hoping that answer sounded better than the humiliating one in his head.

Peron and Selah glanced at one another, confused. "Well, you said you've seen the firelight before, right?" Peron asked. "That even from the hilltops it'd still be burning by sunrise."

Rowan certainly remembered saying that.

"I think we'll be fine," Selah assured them. "We'll just need to be careful about when we use them, and we'll have all the light we need." She brushed her hand along Rowan's shoulder. "Trust me, Ro. You won't need to worry about anything while we're out there."

That was the problem. As smart as she was, Rowan knew Selah was wrong. He'd never admit it to her face, though, so he gave her a forced grin instead. She didn't seem to mind. In fact, she didn't even see him, as her attention turned to the sound of footsteps walking above the kitchen. Rowan heard them too; the sound made his legs feel like they had turned to stone. Only one person made him feel that way.

Den Mother.

"Quick, hide everything before she gets here," Selah whispered loudly.

Rowan needed no reminder. He raced over to the pantry closet, frantically closing and organizing the misplaced boxes. Out of the corner of his eye, he saw Selah and Peron tossing the broom and scraper to each other, likely needing to hide the shavings and the tool that made them.

Even after setting the boxes in the right order, Rowan had trouble figuring out the dilemma he held in his hands. The bag of coins rattled each time he turned to search for any place Den Mother wouldn't find it. As footsteps came down the stairs, Rowan's pulse raced, and his face turned as green as Selah's skin.

Snap, a sound that jolted Rowan from his daze.

Rowan looked towards the noise to see Selah pushing the plywood back into the floor.

"Rowan, hurry," she breathed. He saw her hide the stakes inside her long, grey boots, and the matchbox behind the purple bow tied to her olive-green dress. Peron folded his map neatly and put it into his white front pocket.

They always had such brilliant ideas. And with the footsteps coming from the hallway, Rowan needed a fast and foolish one. He lifted his plaid shirt and hid the sack behind him.

Like soldiers at their posts, the children stood in a line facing the table. Rowan didn't care if they weren't allowed to look at her meal. If things were his way, he'd scarf the fried potatoes and leave not a trace of lamb before she walked in the kitchen. But he knew if he did that, he'd never see the light of day again, only darkness. As dark as the black gown now fluttering past his vision. And even darker than the two black military uniforms filing by as well.

"Hello, Den Mother," the children greeted politely.

She kept her silver stare of contempt on the children. The guards also stared at them. They'd followed Den Mother like sheep since Rowan arrived at three years old, only there to obey her orders to discipline the children. But how could one perform discipline if they never spoke to you? Or the creepiest part. How could one fear someone's face if they never saw it under the hooded cloaks and crow-like masks?

Den Mother didn't utter a word, merely waiting for the guards to pull out her chair.

"We cleaned everything for you, madam," Peron said.

"We know you hate feeling dust on your fingers," Selah followed. "So, I dusted the counters and the cabinet handles. Just in case they were too dirty."

The old woman sat down and sharpened her silverware, scraping it from side to side. Rowan was waiting for the ear-splitting noise to finish, but Selah elbowed him to speak up next.

"A-also, Den Mother," Rowan began. "I, um…did something without you even asking me to. I organized all the boxes in the pantry. From your favorite food to your least favorite. That way you don't need to worry about—"

"And how would you, urchin," she squawked. "Know which ones are my favorites and least favorites?"

Rowan gulped hard as he inspected the knife in her hand. "I, er…I-I don't know. Probably just by watching which ones you pick up most."

"So, you've been spying on me, have you?" She pointed the knife at him. Luckily, the blade sat far away enough, allowing him to focus on her instead of the murder weapon.

"I should've known. Our lessons have made you far too observant for your age," she huffed, stabbing at her meal in annoyance.

He knew he wasn't supposed to, but when Den Mother ate a piece of her lamb, Rowan almost wept. Selah and Peron were no better. Their stomachs started rumbling even before they did their chores. The woman quickly consumed nearly all her food. Given the chance, Rowan would've gratefully savored every bite, unlike his guardian's shameless devouring.

Den Mother was about to eat a diced potato when she glimpsed the famished orphans. "I can't have anything in this house," she muttered. "Not an hour after high noon and you're already hungry?"

The children nodded, ignoring the heinous insult with starving anticipation.

"Remind me, what are our rules for eating again?" Den Mother asked, chewing her potato.

Rowan hated this game. "Always ask your permission first. It's rude to dine at the dinner table before grownups do."

"Khallus delights in humility, after all," Peron recited. "We'd never do anything to be a burden to you or him."

Rowan buried his sneer. How could his friend say that with the straightest face imaginable?

"So, you really *have* been listening?" Of course, they had. She made them recite it before supper during their reading lessons. "Well, spit it out. What do we say?"

"Den Mother, may we please have something to eat," Selah asked with a smile.

"Shame. I only made enough food for one person." She inspected her fork coyly. "But whom to share it with is the key question."

"If willing," Rowan rehearsed. "Could you let us have a bite from your plate?"

Den Mother's sneer seared into Rowan's brain. He heard her silverware scrape along her plate. She displayed a forked sample of the meat and potatoes to the children with disgust on her face. "Hold out your hands, you little gluttons. This lamb was dry anyway."

Anything sounded better than eating sleep for lunch. Peron went first. Den Mother smeared the piece in his hand, and he carefully picked out each piece to savor. Selah did the same, eating right out of her palm. Rowan went last with his hands out. But instead of giving it to him, Den Mother hit her fork on the edge of the table, causing the food to fall to the floor.

"Oops, apologies," Den Mother hummed. Her smug grin showed off her faux regret.

Rowan's eyes shifted from the food to her. Like always, his dignity would die another day. He knelt to pick up the food, and a familiar noise stopped him from grabbing it.

Shink, the noise went.

The coins. He forgot about the coins. Would she notice if he pretended not to hear it? His widened eyes were glued to the floor, until he grabbed the piece, ate it, and gave Den Mother a nervous smile.

Her glare stayed glued to the children as she prepared her next bite. "Now that I think about it, there was certainly a lot of chatter for children who were supposed to be cleaning. What did you do that was so funny?"

Another rule: never talk while cleaning. Khallus despises lazy servants and only honors the willing.

"Apologies, Den Mother," Peron said. "We didn't mean to be so loud. We'll be quieter—"

"I wasn't talking to you, impish traitor," she interrupted.

Peron lowered his head, but the insult caused Rowan's hands to form into fists. He knew she was talking to him.

Another smile. "Like I said, Den Mother. I organized all the boxes in the pantry. Some had holes in them, so I had to throw those away."

"And how do I know your grimy little hands haven't stolen from those boxes?"

Rowan quickly swallowed his horror and forced a brighter grin. "I wouldn't take anything unless I asked first, madam."

He watched Den Mother stand, towering nearly a foot above him. Her intimidation made him shrink. Her gaze darted from him to her masked guards.

"Hold his arms," she calmly commanded.

Rowan tensed as the two guards rushed at him. He winced as they tugged on his arms, their tight grips digging into his flesh. He looked at Selah and Peron, but they were ignoring him, like he were invisible. Rowan didn't blame them for it. In the orphanage, surviving meant staying obedient and passive, no matter how unfair it was.

Rowan closed his eyes as Den Mother approached him, waiting for the hand to strike his cheek. Instead, her clunking boots walked around until they stopped directly behind him.

She pulled up the back of his shirt, and a small coin bag fell to the ground.

In his head, he screamed *no* a million times over. Den Mother stood in front of him with the bag in her hand.

"Oh dear," Den Mother said. "Not only a thief, but a liar as well."

"I…D-Den Mother, please. I meant to give that back to you. Honest," Rowan explained, vigorously shaking his head. The woman took his face in her hand and yanked him close.

"Do you think I'm idiotic enough to believe that?" Rowan focused on the fitted ring on Den Mother's other hand. Its iron-shaped flame fit right in the center. It was a sign of her allegiance to Khallus, as well as the magic dwelling in her blackened heart. "Look at me when I talk to you!"

He did. Her silver eyes were just as soulless as the day they met. "Where did I go wrong with you?" she said. "I thought at least one of my students would be obedient. Yet here you are again, causing trouble for yourself and burdening your friends. Perhaps some time downstairs will help you remember your place."

"What?" the children cried together.

"Get him out of my sight," she told her guards.

"Wait, Den Mother, please! I'm sorry! I won't do it again," Rowan begged, kicking and screaming as they dragged him away. He didn't care; he was already in trouble. He saw Den Mother blocking Peron and Selah as they shouted his name with anxious regret. "Please, Den Mother! Don't send me down there! I don't want to go down there again!"

At that moment, Rowan almost asked his friends for help. Yet he realized if he did, he'd only be proving Den Mother's point. So, before he turned the corner into exile, Rowan screamed his last words.

"Selah! Peron! I'm sorry!"

Chapter 2

Secrets of Mages

*I*t solved nothing to bang on the cellar door, panicking in the overwhelming darkness. It solved nothing to sit in a corner for three days, wailing for the entire world to hear. Refusing to eat the scraps Den Mother's guard sent down made no difference, either. But his hoarse voice and sunken ribs never bothered him. Not as much as the gnawing guilt he felt about letting his friends down.

It could've been worse, though. Den Mother could have thrown Rowan in the forest, a far more unpleasant experience than confinement. He remembered what Selah told them: *We need to leave through the forest. It's our only chance.* Rowan thought of all the other orphans who tried escaping that way. Den Mother's cruel punishments cut their lives short. Rowan wished he'd gotten to know them before they left. He could've at least said goodbye before those dreadful moments occurred.

Learning spell-casting through Den Mother was the formal way to escape. Everyone in the orphanage knew that. Some were too frightened to try. But not Rowan, of course. After weeks of begging, the then nine-year-old was ready to learn magic with all the other students in Den Mother's class.

His excitement and curiosity outmatched the older orphans with their weary and defeated attitudes.

Those orphans should've been Rowan's first clue. Along with Den Mother calling magic "virca" during his first lesson. But it wasn't until the end of the first month that Rowan knew he needed to leave. He should've left the day Den Mother branded iron into his skin for every failed spell. He should've fled for the hills after three months when she called the orphans "sacrifices" rather than "students." But Rowan took the insults, covered his blistering scars with long sleeves, and remained her student. Even after nine full months, when Den Mother's words became more cryptic the night of that phony graduation ceremony.

"May your sacrifice bring honor to his cause and grant you powers beyond your wildest dreams," she recited.

Rowan should've known that was nonsense. How could one gain power by standing in the middle of a dark forest, especially with a purple match flaming in hand? The other students were in the same predicament, carrying lit matches in fatigue and confusion. When she told them to throw their matches, Rowan almost told her no, a word that, if uttered, led to so many consequences. But soon, violet flames engulfed the trees, a screeching cry pierced the sky, and Den Mother smirked at her students as she disappeared into the forest. Rowan had never felt more afraid in his entire life. All that changed once he saw…*the monster.*

He never remembered what kind of monster. But he remembered running back to the orphanage, and the agonizing screams he left behind.

That was the same night he found Den Mother's matchbox abandoned in the grass. The matches within held so many possibilities. But what, or who, to use them on, remained untested. At eleven years old, a year before he and his friends began planning their escape, Rowan revealed the swiped matchbox to his friends. He told them to keep it safe; he said something like, *It'll give us the light we need to escape through the forest.* Another excuse to hide what really lurked beyond those trees. If he told them about the danger, would his friends truly believe him?

Who was he kidding? Selah and Peron would only baby him. They would dismiss his claims as one of his stories, never taking him seriously. Perhaps it was best Rowan took that secret to the grave.

The cellar door swung open, letting out a harsh light that made Rowan hiss. After his eyes adjusted, he noticed a familiar shape coming down the stairs. A shape that, with each step, exhaled heavy and muffled breaths.

Anything but *it*.

At the bottom of the stairs stood a guard wearing a leather mask and a hooded cloak. A protruding crow's beak hid its entire face, and black lenses hid its eyes. Those masks always reminded him of the early plagues in history books. As if death itself had come to escort Rowan to his fate. He always tried peeking underneath the mask, only to be met with aggressive growls. Which only meant one thing.

"I know, I know," Rowan murmured, heading up the stairs. "Meet her in her study."

When he entered daylight, Rowan went past the empty dining room. It was next to the kitchen they had dragged him out of. He felt disappointed. He'd hoped his friends might've been there to greet him. He noticed less dust floating in the air. That must've been Peron's doing; he was always so meticulous about cleaning.

The guard pushed Rowan forward and gestured for him to keep moving.

Rowan groaned as he went up another flight of stairs to the second floor. No matter how many times he walked the chipped wooden halls, he never felt less uneasy. Looking at the pictures lining the walls sometimes calmed him, but for only a short while. He wondered how the kids seated on the far left next to Den Mother could ever bring themselves to smile. He scanned rows of beaming faces in front of the orphanage, eager to become adopted wards and find a new family. As he turned the corner, the blissful grins turned into hopeless pouts, and the number of orphans declined sharply from one picture to the next. The last photograph depicted only Selah, Peron, and Rowan, the three remaining orphans, staring sullenly into the camera as they stood next to the poised Den Mother.

Rowan and the guard stopped outside her wooden office door. The copper plaque affixed to its center had her name scratched out.

Funny how it had never been fixed after all this time. To this day, Rowan still didn't know her name. He didn't want to. He simply knocked on the door.

"You may come in, *urchin*," Den Mother screeched from behind the door.

Butterflies began to form in his stomach. He opened the door and there she sat across from him, looking bored to tears while stroking the glass dragon on her mahogany desk. At the foot of her desk stood a simple chair.

He sat in the chair and waited patiently for Den Mother to speak. Long ago, he'd made the mistake of speaking first, and their meeting ended with a book being thrown at his head. But waiting allowed him to scan her bookshelves, where he glimpsed at titles like *The Guide to Summoning Fire* and *Spells for the Trained Mage*. Books he'd take much better care of than Den Mother, who let them collect dust over decades of hoarding.

"You realize how disappointing this is, correct," Den Mother said icily.

"Huh," Rowan uttered, his eyes flickering back to her. He bowed his head and nodded in agreement.

Den Mother scoffed as she disregarded her dragon. Her voice grew louder in disbelief. "'Huh?' My last student makes a fool of himself and all he can say is, "huh?' To think that my life is in the hands of someone like you!"

Rowan endured her tantrum before answering her softly. "I-I really am sorry, Den Mother. I promise I won't do it again."

"You say that," she said, fiddling with her ring. "But I'm not so sure if I believe you."

The pit in Rowan's stomach dropped to the floor. He knew what came next once he'd seen the small fire symbol. When Den Mother snapped her fingers, a violent flame erupted from her palm. She beckoned Rowan with her other hand. If he refused, there'd be a bigger price to pay.

His hands trembled as he rolled up one of his dark sleeves. Scattered ember scars ran in a row across his forearm. Rowan slowly scooted forward and set his arm on the desk. His hand wouldn't stop shaking until Den Mother reached for it.

"What are you apologizing for?" Den Mother asked, her eyes glued to him.

"I'm sorry for…not organizing your pantry the right way?"

"Wrong," she said, clenching her branding iron.

Rowan screeched when the bright-red sign seared into his fresh skin.

Den Mother banged his wrist on the desk. "Don't scream! Now, try again!"

He swallowed his pain and strained. "I'm sorry…sorry I lied, Den Mother. About stealing from you."

Another ember branded on top of a duller scar. Rowan bit his lip to stifle his scream, but it didn't stop his tears from falling.

"Closer," she croaked. "Not specific enough."

He lifted his head, breathing hard. She held the flickering emblem over him. One more brand and he'd never use his arm again. "I'm sorry for being a burden!" he hurriedly shouted.

"Go on." She loosened her grip.

His scripted apology was working.

"There's no excuse for what I did. I know my lies never please you. You're…right. I have been a burden. I should've known my place and remembered my purpose."

"And what is that?"

This was it: the sentence that would end his torture. All he had to do was look into her eyes and say it. No matter how painful it felt.

"To always be humble," he exhaled. "To be seen and not heard. And to be grateful for my suffering. For Khallus greatly favors those who suffer for him." The next part almost always made him shed a tear. "Please…forgive me for being a burden to him…and you."

The woman extinguished her fire with a flick of her wrist. She shot him a half-smile filled with satisfaction and victory.

"See, that wasn't so hard, now, was it?" Den Mother said.

"Yes, Den Mother." Rowan lowered his head.

It was done. He had said all the right words. In the end, Den Mother won, like always. After she released him, Rowan slowly rolled down his sleeve, wincing as the thick fabric scratched his raw burns.

"Now," Den Mother said, "you must be wondering where your friends are."

That had certainly crossed Rowan's mind. Where on earth were Selah and Peron?

"They're on the roof again, cleaning up from last night's thunderstorm. You may join them…after you review our previous lesson." From her desk drawer, Den Mother pulled out something that made Rowan grip his trousers. A small, worn book, covered in brown leather and dulled stars. "I always wondered why your *virca* hardly improved. Learning Caelum's wretched magic behind my back? You're truly a fool for possessing this putrid work of filth."

He thought he'd hid it under the cabinet. How had she gotten her hands on it? And why was she tossing it toward him on the desk?

"Cast the spell."

"Which spell?"

"The last one I taught you! What else?"

Rowan remembered. But it wasn't the one from the book in front of him. It was a spell she had taught him in hopes of his magic becoming like hers. He'd rather send himself back to the cellar before letting that happen. "Please, Den Mother, don't make me—"

"I'm sure Khallus would greatly appreciate two more sacrifices to aid his cause," she said, eerily calm. "So, if you wish to become a mage and keep those precious friends of yours, I suggest you remain obedient. Cast. The. Spell."

Casting that spell meant submitting to Den Mother's cruel intentions. Of course, she'd use his friends to get what she wanted. Rowan raised his shaky hands towards the book, turning his head to hide his swelling tears. With a grunt, he cried:

Ulsgat.

Nothing happened. Not a flash nor a spark, only pure anticipation. Rowan thought he was safe until a flicker of purple fire appeared on the cover. The book burst into flames and melted onto the desk.

Den Mother watched the fire peacefully. Rowan wanted to rip the devilish smile right off her face. He hated her. He wished he could snap his fingers, and she'd be gone. He wanted her gone. But the burning book occupied his attention. His tears fell even faster, as the book turned to ash.

"You may leave now."

Rowan didn't care about his tear-stained face. Nor did he care how Selah squeezed him in an embrace, her soft brown curls rubbing against his cheek. He looked out dully above the treetops into the floating clouds far ahead. He wanted to be like those clouds, adrift where no one could catch him. He'd be doing himself and his friends a favor; he'd be out of the way like he was supposed to be.

"I should've been there with you," Selah said tearfully, her arms tightening around him. "None of this would've happened if I—"

"You're fine, Selah," Rowan hushed. "It wouldn't have mattered anyway."

He heard her exhaling as if to say something. Instead, she sighed and said, "Do you need me to hold you a bit longer?"

He nodded into her shoulder, matching her embrace.

"Sellie, if you keep hugging him like that, you're gonna crush his bones," Peron interrupted. Rowan shifted his eyes to see him watering dying ivy in rickety pot holders.

"Seriously, Peron," Selah grunted. "Rowan's spell book just got destroyed. Have a little sympathy, will you?

Peron set his water pitcher down. "I have plenty of sympathy. Watch." He looked at Rowan. "Listen, I'm sorry your book got burnt. But you should've known Den Mother would catch you. Now we have to reshape everything because of last week's incident."

Rowan came out of his daze, catching Peron's dry words with disbelief. "Are you saying it's my fault? It's not like I planned on her finding the money. I panicked."

Peron rolled his lavender eyes. "So what? I panic all the time, but I don't freeze up whenever I do it. If you keep making that a habit, we'll all be in danger."

Rowan evaded his gaze. Peron had a weird way of explaining logic and showing he cared. Yet his speeches always made him feel crummy.

"We're lucky we only lost the money," Peron said. "Think of what would happen if she suspected us too? We'd be stuck here forever, *again*. Do you really want to go through that?"

Of course, Rowan didn't. Why would he go through all that trouble just to be trapped again? Still, the pain of this morning needed more consolation. "What about my spell book?"

Peron ran his hands through his pale, shaggy hair. "Honestly, Rowa, that is the least of our problems. I mean, come on, you realize that just having a spell book doesn't make you a mage, right?"

Something in Rowan snapped; he marched to Peron and tugged him by his grey shirt. He didn't care if he towered inches above him. Peron needed to stop hurting his feelings. "Take that back, or I'll—"

"Do what? Magic me to death? Be serious, Rowan," Peron smirked. Rowan hated that expression as much as he cared for the fiend behind it. "Think about it. If Den Mother found the book days after she caught you, she's bound to figure out something. She probably already has and is just biding her time. But I bet you didn't think about that, did you?"

"Never said I didn't," Rowan gritted, dragging him closer. No matter how smart he was, Peron never knew when to stay quiet. Perhaps a punch to the face would do the trick.

Fortunately, Selah pushed Rowan and Peron away from one another. She always had to intervene to keep them on task. She did that a lot while searching for supplies.

"Both of you, stop it," she exclaimed, then lowered her voice to Rowan. "Peron's right, Ro. You need to be more careful when we do stuff like this. Especially now, when we really to get out of here."

Rowan made himself small, wondering why she always took Peron's side first.

Then she turned to Peron. "And Perry, I love you, but you really need to know when to shut up. Apologize to him, now!"

Silent tension stood between Peron and Rowan. He knew Selah was trying to get them to make peace, like always. But emotion after emotion piled onto Rowan. He simply dragged his feet and sat on the edge of the roof.

"Do you guys really think I can be a good mage?" he asked, watching the grass sway below.

"Uh…where did that come from," Peron asked.

"Nowhere," Rowan mumbled. "It's just…Den Mother said I can't be a real mage if I disobey Khallus or something. I know she wants me to be obedient to…whoever he is. But do I really have to?" He scratched at his long sleeves, the fresh scars itching under his shirt. "I can hardly do magic without anything exploding or floating away. If I can't get it right by now, what choice do I have?"

His friends sat beside him. Peron leaned Rowan's head into his shoulder. "Did you know Den Mother got mad at me this morning?" Peron started. "She told me to water all these dead plants until they came back to life. When I told her that was impossible, she threw a plate at my head. All that is to say we know she's a terrible teacher. Don't base your talent on all her scare tactics."

Rowan wanted to chuckle but didn't have the heart for it.

"We already know you'll be a great mage, Ro," Selah said, twining his hand with hers. "The question is, do you think you'll be?"

Rowan sighed. "With a *lot* more practice."

"Exactly! With more practice. When we get to Faegan, there might be more powerful mages who can teach better than Den Mother." She brought him close as she looked at the clouds. "Think about it! Pushing away bad guys with just a wave of your hand. Using some kind of…magic shield to save people from giant monsters. Ooh! You'd be fighting with Carlita the Stone Crusher! Or maybe even—"

"Linn the Moonstruck," Rowan shot up with glee.

"Right," Selah chuckled. "Even Linn the Moonstruck. Hey, what if we bump into him while we're in Faegan! Maybe he'll teach you a thing or two?"

"That'd be so awesome!" In his excitement, Rowan straightened up into his usual performance stance. "I can see it now! We'd both be wearing our capes as we fought bad guys. He'd use his scaled scepter to blind them while I swoop in like a bird and lift them into the air. I've been working on my animal changing spells, so maybe I'll—"

"Rowan, Rowan," Selah interrupted. "I know you're excited, but you can't just say the spells you want to learn. The important thing is what you'll do with all those awesome powers."

"What do you mean? I just told you."

"She means," Peron put in, "you must want to do something that would prove you're a mage, right? What's one goal you have for wanting to use magic?"

Rowan wondered how to word his answer. Most adventurers in stories either searched for treasure or hunted monsters. But most twelve-year-old boys didn't know where to find gold. As for monsters, well, they were another story. He smiled slyly and put a finger to his lips.

"Can't tell you that," he whispered. "It's a secret."

"What?" Peron and Selah whined. "Come on, tell us."

"Nope. It'll ruin the whole mystery. And even if I did, just know it's something so… *speculating* that it'll finally get us off this stupid island."

"You mean *spectacular*," Peron corrected. "And really, traveling is the most *spectacular* thing you can think of? Everyone wants to leave the island. Heck, everyone probably *has* left the island at some point."

"Well, yeah Perry. Everyone who isn't us," Selah teased. "If we did, we'd be living like kings and queens." She got up and swung Peron in a clumsy waltz. "Just imagine, we'd have enough money to dance in pretty ballrooms and eat a bunch of food. If I had magic, I'd have the power to save big cities from evil monsters. I'd have all the coolest orcs challenging me. Maybe those rich, human mages would invite me to their parties. With them, I could at least be seen as normal for once."

The young fiend flicked Selah's forehead and broke from the dance. "More like *lamer* for once. It's not just about fame and glory, you know. We're talking about magic here. Think about all the knowledge you'd gain. You have the power to create and heal life itself. If I had magic, Pelle would be the healthiest place on earth. You'd never get sick again."

"And you think *my* magic power is lame," Selah said.

Rowan grinned wickedly at Peron. "So, if I sneezed on you right now…"

"Don't even think about it." Peron cried, shoving Rowan's face away with a smile. All three of them broke out in laughter as they lay on the roof.

"You know, you're right, Peron," Rowan said. "I'll make sure my goal is better than what you guys came up with." He shot up again. "Hey! Maybe we could be adventurers!"

"Adventurers…" Selah questioned, raising an eyebrow.

"Yeah, super cool adventurers who go on quests and everything! There's already three of us. Once we leave, we'll find a place that would make us an adventuring party, like a guild or something. I'd be a mage, and Selah, you'd be a hunter."

"Why would I be a hunter?"

"Because. You're a quick thinker, and you're super strong. I mean, remember when you carried me and Peron out of that flooding washroom? You ran so fast, we could've been your rag dolls."

"Yeah, you guys were pretty scrawny. And it was funny hearing Peron scream like a baby," Selah said. "What about him? What would he be?"

Peron's arrow-tipped ears perked up when he heard his name, waiting anxiously to be titled. Selah and Rowan eyed him up and down. "I'm not sure. Maybe a farmer?"

"Yeah, I could see that."

"Hey! No fair, I don't want to be a farmer," Peron complained. "I'm fast enough to be a hunter. Why couldn't I be one?"

"Perry, you're good at a lot of things, but beating up bad guys is not one of them. Ooh, maybe you could be a bookworm. With all the boring books you read, who knows? You might turn into a real one."

Rowan and Selah giggled, while Peron made an expression sour enough to spoil milk.

"As exciting as this all is," Peron said monotone. "We still have to make sure we get to Faegan before any of those adventures happen."

He took out the map from his front pocket and unfolded it to display the faded drawings of Nidas. They looked at the bottom, where a crooked circle held the illustration of the forest. A pencil line extended from the forest to a dot with Faegan's name. "If we measure the points here," Peron explained, putting his fingers on both spots. "It's about a ten-mile walk through the forest. If we run there, that's around… almost two hours."

Rowan and Selah groaned loudly. Impatience always got the better of them.

"But…I think if we leave tomorrow before moonset, we won't get caught."

"Den Mother would be stone asleep by the time we left," Selah said. "But we can't be too sure. We'd have to throw her off balance somehow."

That sounded nearly impossible to Rowan. He never knew how, but Den Mother always figured things out. Every nervous look, every whisper behind closed doors, every small unplanned noise—she'd know where to find them. Unless they didn't leave the building at all.

"Maybe if we just stay here, she won't notice a thing," Rowan said.

Peron and Selah looked at him as if he'd gone insane. "You mean you *want* to stay here?" Peron asked.

"Well, not forever. But…." He felt somewhat sheepish giving his reason. It didn't seem thought-out. "If…I don't know, she might forget about us if we keep doing what we usually do. You know, like doing chores, not talking to each other. All that stuff."

Selah nodded slightly. "I guess I could see that happening. But if we did, when would be a good time to leave?" She addressed her question to Peron. Rowan tried to hide his pout.

"Maybe about a week," Peron said. "A week should be long enough to distract her."

"Would that work for you, Rowan?" Selah asked.

Of course it wouldn't work for him. A week seemed much further away than any day they could've picked. But if Rowan said no, he knew he'd be holding his friends back. *Again.*

"We've been planning our escape for a year," he said. "What's one more week going to do?"

"Are you sure, Rowan?" Peron asked.

"Yeah…yeah, I am. Why wouldn't I be," he asked hesitantly.

"It's just…if we do this, you know what that means, right?" Peron said. "We stay out of the way and keep doing our routine. No more games. No speaking unless spoken to. And especially only practice Den Mot—"

"Den Mother's magic. Yeah, I know," Rowan recited solemnly. "Yeah, I know. But if it means getting to start a new life with you guys, I can wait a little longer."

Selah and Peron observed his forced smile, which curled up ear to ear, displaying the gap between his two front teeth. They didn't buy it for a second. But Selah did what she did best: bring them all together.

"I say," Selah announced, linking the boys between her, "we deserve a celebration for our last days in this miserable place. Peron, would you do the honors?"

"Gladly," he chirped. Like a game of house, Peron passed invisible cups to his friends, making Rowan dissolve into a fit of laughter. They always knew how to cheer him up. "A toast to the best of friends," Peron said, lifting his drink. "For safe travels!"

"For amazing adventures," Rowan cried. Another toast.

"And for finding the best teacher for the greatest mage," Selah said, raising her glass.

Rowan put aside his imaginary glass and looked at Selah in surprise. "Really? You'll really help me find a teacher?"

Selah let go of her own and squeezed him into a comforting hug. "Of course, Rowan. It'll be the first thing we do, I promise."

Rowan felt Peron hug him on the other side. No matter how much he messed up, his best friends truly did care for him, after all.

He didn't deserve them.

Chapter 3

Escape to Faegan

So, a week had passed. As promised, Rowan kept to himself and followed Den Mother's rules, no matter how irksome: doing chores, speaking when spoken to, and accepting the little effort she showed him. Rowan even practiced magic with her in complete silence. But he knew it would be all worth it once he attained his freedom.

Night fell upon the orphanage and the children's escape grew closer. Den Mother lay sound asleep, snoring hideously in her lush bedroom as her guards worked the night shift. The children's room held nothing but a few mattresses and some blankets. *Something urchins like you should be grateful for,* Den Mother often squawked.

Moonlight shone through their bedroom window as the three rested before their long journey. Well, all except for Rowan, of course.

He lay on his back staring at the ceiling, wondering how long before Selah and Peron woke up. Moonset was approaching, and every second they wasted seemed like sand running out of an hourglass. He couldn't stand it any longer.

He turned to his side, which faced Peron, and watched
him sleep. His hair was almost see-through in the moonlight.
His breathing was light and airy, and his white eyelashes
fluttered even while his eyes remained sealed. He looked so
peaceful. That would soon change.

"Per," Rowan whispered loudly. "Peron, wake up."
Restless, he tapped Peron's shoulder, but his friend didn't
budge. Rowan looked at his crescent shaped horns. He enjoyed
tapping the chipped one on his right side. Perhaps irritation
would get his attention.

He extended his finger to poke it. But before Rowan
touched the skin of the horn, Peron's eyes shot open. Like two
purple amethysts swimming in black ink, they glowed brightly
in the dim room. Rowan jumped back. No matter how cool it
was, his friend's night vision always managed to scare him.

"Oh *Cael*," Rowan swore quietly. "I hate it when you
do that."

"You shouldn't have tried to touch my horns then,"
Peron whispered back in a snarky tone.

"How else am I supposed to wake you?"

"Don't touch my horns!"

"Whatever. I've been waiting for you guys all night.
How long have you been up?"

"I never slept. Got too anxious." Peron pulled off his
blanket to reveal not his nightwear but a fresh set of clothing:
white shirt, tan trousers, and black boots.

Peron must have had the power to read minds. Rowan
had the same idea and threw back his covers to display his new
clothes: a dark green long-sleeve shirt with brown trousers and
brown boots.

"I didn't sleep either," Selah called out.

The boys looked over to see Selah resting her hand on her head and looking at them; her hazel eyes possessing the same glow as Peron's. Rowan jumped back again, letting out a soft shout.

"Shh," Selah and Peron hushed. To keep him from screaming again, Peron put a hand over Rowan's mouth. Selah point at the closed door, reminding him about the guards patrolling the orphanage.

Suddenly, Peron removed his hand from Rowan, grimacing at him in disgust.

"GROSS," Peron breathed harshly. "He just licked my hand!"

"And I'll lick the other one if you ever do that again," Rowan retorted.

"Be quiet, you two," Selah commanded. "Peron, you still have the map, right?"

"It never left my sight," he said, holding it up.

"Perfect. Then there are the matches and the stakes. Alright, looks like we're ready." She rose from her mattress, showing off her dark brown dress and boots. She took off the boots and held them in her hand as she tiptoed towards the window.

The boys followed suit, removing their boots, collecting their things, and following Selah. She opened the window. The night air cooled their faces and freshened their stuffy room.

They quietly put their shoes back on to prepare for their next action. As they peeked out the window, they saw the gutter pipe nailed to the outside wall.

"Alright, Perry, just like we practiced. You go down first, I'll go second, and Ro can go down last."

"Why do I have to go last?" Rowan complained.

"Rowan, we've been over this. You don't have night vision. You'd be blind without us."

"He's worse than a bat," Peron said under his breath. Selah heard him and slapped him upside the head. He groaned as he reached for the pipe, clung onto it, and climbed down. When he was halfway down, Selah grabbed onto the pipe.

"Rowan, I'll tap on the pipe when I've reached the ground," she whispered, climbing down.

In the dim moonlight, Rowan watched Selah descend further into darkness. He couldn't tell if she made it to the halfway point or not.

"Selah," he called. "Selah, are you down there?"

No answer.

Unfortunately, his impatience got the better of him. "Selah, I'm coming down." He grabbed the pipe and started climbing.

While concentrating on his descent, Rowan glanced a few times at his bedroom window. He thought about the memories he shared with his friends, like looking outside and counting the stars. Their lively games of throwing objects out the window the farthest, with Selah winning every time. Watching the sunset on the days he went without dinner, which were often.

He'd sure miss those memories. But the orphanage? Not for all the treasures in the world.

Rowan's boot touched the tips of grass. He exhaled; grateful he would never have to do that again. Jumping onto the field, he realized Selah was right: he hardly saw anything at night. Only the moon and the outlines of the forest. A dire situation. He, at least, thought his friends would call him. Instead, all he heard were cicadas and crickets chirping along.

"Selah? Peron?" He walked around with his hands out, hoping to brush against their frames, eventually. "Guys, this isn't funny. Where did you g—"

Backing away, he struck against smooth fabric. He turned around and got a dim view of black clothing. Immediately he was seized by fear. He knew who wore those clothes He followed the seam of the trousers to the hem of a jacket. That jacket led to a dark collar. Above that collar lay a mask with an eerie crow's beak staring down at Rowan.

One of Den Mother's guards, with the other one standing at his side. Which only meant one thing.

"Leaving so soon?" a familiar shrill sounded.

A shiver rolled down Rowan's spine. He turned to see the moonlight highlighting Den Mother's wrinkled face and grey nightgown. He almost cowered before her, but he didn't want to get too close to the guards again. He glanced away from her face and found Selah and Peron at her sides, staring at the ground in shame.

"G-Good evening, Den Mother," Rowan greeted. "It's…It's not like that, at all. I-uh-I couldn't sleep, so I asked them to—"

"Save your excuses," Den Mother bit back. "You've given me enough after all these years. As I have given you far too many chances."

"Madam, I promise. We weren't planning on—"

"Do you really think anyone on this wretched island would barter your wardship from me? For a child like you?"

Rowan fell silent. The harsh truth hit him like a dagger to the heart.

"Even if you wanted to leave, there's no escaping it. Your life is forever in Khallus' hands. He's placed you in my care for a reason, to make sure both of our purposes are fulfilled in his timing. And it saddens me you've forgotten your purpose, yet again. Perhaps another reminder is in order."

Den Mother placed her hand between Peron's horns; her touch made him wince. Rowan felt her smug smile defeat him.

She gave another command: "Now come to bed, 'lest you make your punishment worse."

As she turned, Rowan almost followed, but a moment of boldness struck him. If he went with her, no amount of acceptance or purpose would come from it. The other side of the forest held a brighter future: the chance to become a mage, and for he and his friends to take back their stolen freedom.

"No," Rowan announced. Selah and Peron gasped in shock

Rowan watch Den Mother stop. She tilted her head to view him from the side. "What did you say?"

The darkness in her voice made him stutter, as he also questioned his own words.

"Didn't you hear him? He said 'no,'" Peron said. He slipped away from Den Mother's side and stood next to Rowan.

Den Mother turned around fully with a sharp scowl. "Insolent brats! What is the meaning of—"

"HE SAID 'NO,' YOU EVIL WITCH," Selah insulted. She stepped away and stood beside her friends.

Den Mother's jaw clenched, as she strained to tame the rage dwelling within her. She closed her eyes and inhaled nice and slow. Thick black smoke trailed along her breath as she exhaled, the kind of smoke only the dragons of old possessed, as they sported the same devilish smile Den Mother carried.

"'No,' you say," Den Mother repeated lowly.

Her eyes remained closed as she processed their refusals. It gave Rowan just enough time to notice Selah fiddling with something in her dress pocket. Just what was she planning?

Den Mother chuckled to herself as she peered down at them. "I'm most disappointed in you, children. You all know what happens when I get *upset*." She bared the insides of her mouth again; stained with an overwhelming amount of smog. "Perhaps you should see what happens when I get *angry*."

Den Mother snapped her fingers, conjuring blazing tongues of fire in her palms. Like lightning, she darted for the children, arms outstretched. But before she could lay a hand on them, Selah took a wooden stake out of her pocket and launched it at Den Mother. Rowan hardly had time to admire Selah's marksmanship as he watched the tip of the stake plunge into Den Mother's left eye.

The motion snuffed Den Mother's fire and pinned her on her back. Her shriek shook the earth at its core. Rowan gawked at her lying there helpless, trying to wrench the stake from her eye socket. She pulled it out and sat up, revealing a deep red gash that pooled blood down her face. Bloody remnants remained on the tip, which she pointed at the children.

"SEIZE THEM!" she ordered her guards.

Selah's hand wrapped around Rowan's wrist. "We need to go! Now!" she said. He came back to reality, and they started running.

They hadn't made it even a yard when a guard yanked Rowan by the collar with one hand and Selah's braid with the other. He dragged them onto the grass, toward the orphanage door. Selah tried prying off the guard's immensely strong hand. Unable to, she took another stake from her pocket and stabbed the guard in the wrist. He let go of them both, with a bellow of pain. Selah and Rowan had enough time to help Peron, who was losing a game of tug of war against the other guard for the map.

"I said, LET GO!" Peron strained.

Rowan grabbed Peron's waist and Selah grabbed Rowan's. Selah pulled both boys away; the map ripped between Peron and the guard.

With one guard recoiling from his wound and the other still getting up from his hard fall, the three took no chances by waiting and ran for their lives.

They didn't look back, but they heard the woman's shrill cry one last time before they ran into the dark forest.

"FOOLS!"

"DON'T LET THEM ESCAAAPE!"

One quality Rowan admired about Peron was how fast he could run. What Peron lacked in Selah's strength, he made up for in speed. He won every race, even when his friends tried to cheat. Running through the forest, Peron put his skills to good use leading Selah and Rowan to freedom, with him holding Selah's hand and Selah holding Rowan's. Losing part of their map, however, left Peron confused about where to turn next.

"Which way do we go?" Selah asked breathlessly.

Peron looked around. The fast pace, along with his black and white vision, fogged his thinking. "I-I'm not sure. All these trees look the same. Any sign of them?"

Selah looked behind her, inspecting the trees with her own grey-like vision. "Not yet. But keep going. Who knows where they could be?"

While their battle with the guards was over, Rowan believed a new threat to be near. He tried looking up past the thick, tall trees to the little moonlight shining down on them. He thought it might distract him from the thought of Den Mother snatching him up.

Then Rowan had a thought, a quick and familiar thought. He loosened his grip on Selah's hand and froze in place to think.

"Rowan, we don't have time for this," Selah said, shaking his shoulders. "What are you doing?"

"Selah, give me the matchbox. I have an idea," Rowan demanded.

"Wait? Right now?" Peron exclaimed.

"Yes, right now! Just give me the box!"

Selah gave him a puzzled look, but time was short. She pulled the box out of her pocket.

"Thanks," he said, snatching it and taking out a match.

"Wait, Rowan. Do you even have a plan?" Peron asked worriedly.

Skkrryypp, went Rowan's match. Sparks flew on the first try.

He raised it above his head. A violet bonfire burned through the match head. Selah watched, stunned as the fire illuminated the entire forest. Peron looked equally astonished, only his expression was directed at Rowan instead.

"How did you do that so fast," Peron asked lowly.

Shriek, went the forest.

A familiar, ear-splitting sound, which interrupted Rowan's thoughts. *The monster. It was here.*

He looked at the flame, then back at his friends. "Just take it! Hurry," he commanded, tossing them the matchbox.

Skkrryypp…Skkrryypp, went Selah's match.

Skkrryypp…Skkrryypp…Skkrryypp, went Peron's.

Sparks flew.

They held their matches high, watching the purple hue blaze above them.

"Now what?" Peron asked.

Shriek!

"Now… keep your match over your head," Rowan said, taking Peron's hand. "And run!"

The three dashed forward again with their burning matches. Rowan scanned the forest, waiting for the shrieking sound again. How? How could all this happen so soon? Rowan thought they had a little more time. If only he told Selah and

Peron why he was so apprehensive. Told them what he had really seen out here.

But it was too late.

Another shriek, closer this time, screamed through the forest and stopped Rowan in his tracks. His eyes stayed on the trees in front of him. His heart almost pounded out of his chest as a growl came from within them.

"Rowan, get behind me," Selah prompted, her hand on his shoulder.

"Selah, hold on," Rowan said, as she pushed him aside.

"I said get behind me," she growled. "And don't move until I tell you to." She held her arms out to guard the boys, her match still flaring by her side. She kept her focus on the dark forest ahead, as if bracing for battle.

How could Selah stare fear in the face when she didn't know what reigned within the trees? Rowan wished it was something much different. A bear, a rabid dog, anything would be better than experiencing that horrible nightmare one more time.

His heart sank when *the monster* emerged from the trees. A beast on all fours slowly stalking its prey, a low grumble resounding from it. Its panther-like body was slick with black ink, replacing its fur; a rotten smell exuded from it. Black shards replaced its white teeth and claws, with thick oil dropping to the ground as it snarled.

Another grumble came from the forest, then three more creatures emerged on Rowan and Peron's side. One more came out to face Selah, and soon the five hideous monsters had encircled the frightened children. It had all happened so long ago that Rowan almost forgot what they looked like. But he'd always remembered the eyes. Soulless white orbs glowing brighter than any night vision ever could. The beasts inched closer, pressing the children to retreat until their backs touched.

"Get back," Selah yelled, swinging her match at the beasts. If she had learned anything from stories, it was that animals hated fire. But Rowan knew these were no animals and realized it was a bad sign when they hungrily followed the flames like moths.

"Selah, stop," Rowan said, holding back her arm. "You'll only make it worse!"

"How would you know that," Peron asked.

"I…I don't know," he lied. "They just don't look scared by it, I guess."

"Well, you better come up with a good idea before we're eaten alive!"

He couldn't think as quickly as Selah. Yet a memory swept through his mind, again. The match: that night, they threw it down, and the beasts stepped right into it. Their forms were enveloped in the fire, as they relished the heat. Back then, Den Mother gave Rowan and the other children a thirty-second start before she vanished in the flames and the hunt truly began.

"Thirty seconds," Rowan muttered.

"What was that?" Selah asked.

"We have thirty seconds to…to get out of here." Rowan nodded to himself. He didn't know how it would work, but it was the only solution that could save his friends. "Alright, on the count of three, throw your match and run as fast as you can."

A beast swung its claw at them. Selah and Peron guarded themselves from the ooze that flung onto their skin. "Seriously, that's the best you can think of," Peron shouted.

"Peron, shut up," Selah cried. "Rowan, where do we run to?"

Another monster screeched in Rowan's face. "Anywhere," he yelled over the noise. "Just leave and don't look back."

"Rowan, if we live through this, I swear—," Peron exclaimed.

"Please, guys," Rowan said, his voice breaking. "Just trust me."

Their silent contemplation seemed louder than the monsters themselves. Rowan squeezed his eyes shut, despising the thing in his sight.

"Alright, go ahead," Selah said. "We trust you, Rowan."

Another shriek menaced Peron.

"Yes, yes, we trust you! Just count already," he yelled.

So, they really did trust Rowan. Which only made his plan harder to carry out. But he pulled himself together, knowing it was the kindest thing he could do for them.

"One," Rowan whispered.

"Two." Their matches stood higher in the air.

"THREE!" *Swing.*

The children threw their matches. Selah, with her good arm, threw hers a long way into the forest. Peron's landed just a few feet away from where they were. Rowan's match was the unluckiest of all; his flame went right into a monster's face.

Crash!

They hid their faces until the explosions' light faded. Three separate flames created voluminous bonfires at their landing points. Rowan opened his eyes to see the beasts shrieking and heading for the firelights.

"What are you waiting for," Selah exclaimed, shaking him again. "We have thirty seconds, right? Let's get out of here while we still can."

Peron grabbed Selah's hand, and without a second thought, they started running into a darker part of the woods. But Rowan stayed behind, his legs trembling. Why did he feel so hesitant? This was what he wanted. This was how he would keep his family safe. All he had to do was move.

Slowly but surely, his feet shifted backwards. He turned around, stumbled forward, and ran in the opposite direction of Selah and Peron.

The firelight dimmed further with every step into the darkness, its warmth on his back fading as he sprinted away.

"Twenty-five, twenty-four, twenty-three," Rowan counted, breathing heavily. He scratched against trees and tripped over roots, but it didn't stop him from counting. He swung his arms faster, brought his knees higher, recalling every mistake he made from the last hunt. He'd escaped them before; he was sure he'd escape them again.

"Thirteen, twelve, eleven."

Ten more seconds, and he'd be in the clear. At least he thought he would be, until a familiar voice screamed out his name.

"Rowan!"

"Rowan, where are you?!"

His feet slowed and he froze. Selah and Peron. They called out for him. They were coming to find him.

No.

No. No. No. That wasn't supposed to happen. Why would they do that? They said they trusted him. They were supposed to stay safe.

"Rowan, please! Come back!"

"Selah!" Rowan exclaimed. He spun in circles, trying to find her. But what good would that do? Without Peron and Selah, Rowan's sight was useless. It wasn't until he got dizzy and had to stop that he noticed a pair of glowing white dots fixed on him in the darkness. The dots etched closer, allowing him to perceive the empty gaze and the beastly outline before.

The only defense Rowan thought to do was hold out his hands, and cry out, "Please! Just stay away! Go!"

The beast ignored his desperate plea, hungrily waiting for the moment he would slip up and give in. His heel hit a tree root, and he tumbled backwards, giving the beast the chance to pounce.

Rowan's voice was so choked up he could hardly shout the word "NO." Instead, he lay in shock, waiting for the monster to sink its teeth into him. But once all hope felt lost, it made itself found again. Behind the beast came a fiery orange chain that wrung itself around the beast's neck.

The chain straightened and yanked the monster to the ground. The linked flames quickly set the grass and a tree trunk on fire. The screaming monster lay on its back with the chain searing its mucky skin. The one holding the chain was a small dwarfish man covered in a dark cape with only his luminescent green eyes visible.

The loud crack of a tree branch forced the man's eyes upward. Rowan did the same, although he wished he hadn't. From the highest part of the flaming tree, another caped figure jumped out with swords in both hands. They landed on top of the beast, plunging both weapons into its chest. The monster's anguished cry resounded over Rowan's shocked gasp. He wanted to look away, but he couldn't help watching the person's swords drag down the monster's belly. The beast choked on its own cries as its body cracked and turned into golden ashes.

Suddenly, Rowan felt himself breathing again. If only for a second. These caped figures, holding a flaming chain and two swords, had defeated a monster without breaking a sweat. For a moment, Rowan didn't feel the need to run. Until the person with the swords slowly turned his head, revealing his eyes with their fearsome red glow.

Rowan's mind went blank, and a high-pitched ringing filled his ears.

Chapter 4

Eye-Catching Magic

Rowan should've known Den Mother's guards would come after him. He heard her command them; it was the only possible answer. Why else would two men in dark clothing stare at him like meat on a platter? Perhaps it was for revenge. Selah had the stomach to stab Den Mother in the eye. What if they already took her and Peron out and just came to finish the job? That was probably why the red-eyed swordsman left his swords in the ground, slowly rose from the ashes, and stalked his way.

"No, please. Stay away from me," Rowan whimpered. The swordsman completely ignored him. Rowan's legs somehow scurried back up, his back flushed against a tree.

As the swordsman stomped closer, Rowan closed his eyes and gave one more desperate plea. "Please! I promise I won't leave again! Just tell me what you did with Selah and Peron!"

Rowan expected to be struck with a final blow. But when he opened his eyes, the swordsman's face was only a foot away from his. Rowan flinched at the wolf-like eyes. They were radiant as rubies, rimmed by the black of night. There was something familiar about the eyes. Something similar to the way Peron looked at Rowan when he was most concerned.

"You said there were others?" the man asked in a deep voice. It took Rowan completely by surprise. Den Mother's guards never spoke. The ringing in his ears faded, as he comprehended the frightening man's question.

"Huh?" Rowan uttered breathlessly. Perhaps he hadn't heard the man correctly. The mask he wore covered the bottom half of his face, after all.

"This… Selah and Peron," the man repeated. "Do you know where they are?"

Rowan tried to answer, but his words came out in small stammers.

The man sighed in frustration and pulled down his mask.

"If there are others in danger, child, you must let us know. We're only trying to help you."

Rowan's fright gave way to doubt. Maybe it was the glimpse he'd gotten of the man's sharp fangs, or the way his breath reeked of calming mint. But Rowan did not trust that statement.

"How…" Rowan struggled to find the words. "How do I know you're not—"

A blaring scream and a monstrous shriek collided and pierced through the trees, followed by a voice that shouted, "Selah, stop!"

It sounded like Peron's. Rowan couldn't believe it. They were still alive.

"Olivius," the swordsman said, turning to his smaller partner behind him. "Head south. Find the inqai and the innocents."

The small dwarfish man named Olivius gave a thumb's-up and rubbed his gloved hands together. As Olivius ran past him, Rowan caught a whiff of smoke from the gloves. A bright orange flame emerged from them, consuming them without burning him.

Rowan's mouth hung open. He didn't know how that fire appeared from his hands, but it only reminded him of one thing: Den Mother's emblem. That man was going to burn his friends alive if he found them.

"Wait," Rowan shouted. He pried his back off of the tree and stumbled after Olivius into the forest.

"Don't hurt my friends! Come back!" Rowan would have said anything to make this Olivius stop in his tracks. But the dwarf's short legs traveled at what felt like a hundred steps a second. How could someone so small run so fast? No matter how hard he tried, Rowan's pace slowed and his chest heaved. Realizing he'd never catch up, he panted in place as he watched the dwarf travel farther down the path.

Why had he stopped? He was supposed to keep his friends safe, not admit defeat like a coward. With a groan, he lifted his head to see that the bright orange fire had vanished. All he saw were the dim outlines of the trees before him. Without night vision, that's all he'd ever see. Except for the faint light flaring on the horizon.

Rowan squinted, wondering if Olivius was coming right back. The light was traveling his way, growing larger by the second. Getting *closer* by the second. The closer it came, the more Rowan noticed the color of the light: a luminous purple color that spread along his path, setting the surrounding trees ablaze. Fire. Not light. From within that fire, a hideous sound emerged from it.

Shriek, it cried.

Another inky monster, engulfed in its own fiery hunger, saturated the forest as it bounded in Rowan's direction. Lavender heat reached the tops of the trees. He spun around, trying to outrun the scorching flames. He wheezed and coughed through the smoke, searching for any escape from his impending doom.

Shriek, the monster went again, much closer than last time.

Rowan felt the heat of the creature right on his tail. A burning branch fell in his path, catching him off guard, and he fell. The monster leapt towards him. Rowan closed his eyes, accepting his own fate. But a harsh breeze disrupted his hearing and crashed into his frame.

He braced for excruciating pain. Maybe even a life-ending explosion. But when his eyes eased back open, the life surrounding him already faded into nothingness. Every branch, every leaf, every tongue of fire had been snuffed out, all thanks to that breeze. *How is that possible?* Rowan thought. For about two seconds.

He viewed the fallen beast cracking and twisting its body, jolting forward out of the dimness.

Suddenly, a dark shadow swelled from underneath where the creature stood. It rose above the monster and enveloped it, forcing it down as the darkness floated away. Rowan squinted again. He swore he saw someone within that shadow, someone moving really fast along with it. When the monster didn't relent, the shadow struck the beast again. A clashing sound echoed.

Schring, went the sound.

Followed by the beast being sliced in half. It barely had time to choke before its body dissipated into golden ashes.

Rowan couldn't catch his breath; it came out in short, horrified pants. What exactly had he witnessed? What kind of…magic force had the power to slice a monster in half?

The shadow eased back to the ground, morphing upward and shaping itself to that of a person. The silhouette faded, and the mysterious swordsman revealed himself.

Rowan was speechless. Had that man really taken out an entire monster, yet he couldn't even see him?

The masked swordsman breathed heavily, hardly paying Rowan any attention. He looked at his trembling hands holding the swords and muttered to himself.

"Three more," he huffed. "Only…only three more."

Rowan staggered to his feet and carefully backed away from the distracted man. A single twig snapped under his foot.

The swordsman's eyes to locked with his. Rowan froze. What would he do now?

"You shouldn't be here, child," the swordsman said, flinging the gross ink off his blade. His black boots trudged towards Rowan. "It's far too dangerous to be out and about like this." The swordsman pushed a button on the hilt of each of his swords. They instantly retracted into their handles. He held out his navy-skinned hand for Rowan to take. "If you follow me, we can find your friends and get you to safety."

Rowan noted the length of the man's nails. Also, how sharp they were, far sharper than Peron's, given his age. Rowan peered up into the man's hood for any semblance of fiendish horns. Peron would probably trust him in a heartbeat if he saw someone else like him. Rowan didn't have that luxury.

"I don't need your help," Rowan proclaimed, furrowing his brows. "Just stay away from us; I can find them my—"

"Quiet," the swordsman hushed, gazing back into the forest. As tempting as it was to rail at the swordsman's interruptions, Rowan stopped, when he saw the man's hand hover over his weapon. Was there another monster, or was the swordsman finding another way to silence him? Either thought frightened Rowan. Until he realized why this man wanted him quiet.

He heard footsteps from behind, along with the sounds of heavy breathing still deep in the woods. Between the burnt stumps, pairs of beady eyes— faint purple and bronze— looked up and down. Rowan crept towards the familiar glow and found the outlines of Selah and Peron keeled over in exhaustion.

"He has to be here somewhere," Selah told Peron.

Without another thought, Rowan waved his arm and cried, "I'm over here!"

His loud voice caught their attention, and Selah and Peron scurried towards him, but a pair of soulless orbs gave chase. It was another monster, only a few seconds from slashing them to bits.

"Watch out!" Rowan shouted.

The monster shrieked, and they turned back around as it leapt in attack.

But before it could reach the children, the monster was struck down by a golden ax puncturing its back. Rowan covered his mouth in shock, not only because of the thrown ax, but because of its thrower. Olivius, with his gloves all aglow, held his arm out in a throwing position.

"Well done, comrade," the swordsman complimented. "Were there any other innocents?"

The firelight from Olivius gloves reflected off his rosy cheeks. A long silver beard hung from his chin. For someone who had just slaughtered a monster, Rowan thought he looked way too friendly. Even as he shook his head to answer the swordsman's question.

"I assume you've slain the other three inqai as well?"

Olivius reply was cut off by three more echoing shrieks coming from all around the children. One shriek to the right, another on their left, and the third directly behind them.

Panic overtook Rowan. He remembered the swordsman saying there were only three more. By the looks of the twitching monster on the ground, the battle was not won yet.

Rowan noticed the ax still sticking out from the creature's back. The way the ax faded into little embers made him wonder where it came from. He also wondered why the twitching thing didn't turn to ash like the others. But his friends evidently didn't share his curiosity, as Selah grabbed his wrist to escape.

"Let's hurry before they attack us too," Peron said.

Rowan couldn't have agreed more. But after running only a couple feet away, the three orphans were halted by a line of fire drawn in the dirt.

Rowan saw Olivius on the other side. The flames from his glove created an impenetrable wall around the fighters and orphans, blocking any chance of escape.

"If you flee from this circle, you will die," the swordsman said bluntly. His stern glare heightened Rowan's worry and distrust.

Selah didn't let the fire and brimstone stop her from speaking her mind.

"You can't keep us in here," she yelled, stomping his way. "Let us out now or—"

Another shrieking monster interrupted Selah's demand. When it tried leaping over the firewall, the swordsman flung one of his blades at it. The sword plunged through the creature's snout and skewered it to the ground. Rowan stared past the firewall at the impaled monster. Its rotten debris coated the sword as its mouth hung open, choked by its demise. And yet it still did not form into ashes.

Crack! Crack! Crack! Like the sound of fallen branches.

The children and fighters looked in terror as a long rotten limb from the slain monster contorted and braced itself on the ground. Its other arm did the same, splattering muck on the grass.

"S-Selah, w-what's going on?" Peron quivered.

"I don't know. But just stay close," she said quickly. Rowan could tell she was trying hard to make her voice sound level and unafraid. But her hands fidgeting through her dress pockets said otherwise. She dug around for her last wooden stake.

Rowan hoped she'd find it soon. Once the monster lifted its head, he knew they'd be dead in seconds.

A small click brought Rowan out of his trance. It was followed by the sound of steel scraping out of its sheath. He watched the swordsman brace for another attack, twirling the handle of his sword as he and Olivius looked at each other.

"I'll take care of the outer ring," the swordsman proclaimed. "Ready your weapons. Keep that inqus away from the innocents."

The swordsman turned to face the frightened children. He took a few long strides, then leapt from the ground. Selah pushed Rowan and Peron down as they watched him soar over them and the wall of fire.

Through the crackling fire, Rowan saw the swordsman descend upon the impaled beast and destroy it. He rose and bounded after the others.

The wounded beast behind the children shrieked once more. Its twisting form finally stood on its hind legs. Rowan saw Selah stand back up, still digging for the stake in her pocket.

"Selah, hurry up! It's coming," Peron said.

"I'm trying to," Selah grunted in his direction. "Just shut up and let me handle it!

But there was no handling this situation. The beast was already rushing for the vulnerable orphans. Just before it throttled them, Olivius lunged out and struck the monster with a diamond-shaped shield. Its snout slammed into the heavy armor, driving it into the dirt.

The children froze with their mouths wide open, looking just as shocked as the inqus, which slanted its head toward the dwarf and growled at him. But Olivius paid no mind to its threats, standing his ground while holding the shield close to his chest.

A warm flare caught Rowan's eye. He looked at the glove on Olivius' free hand. As the gold trim along its fingertips glimmered, the caped fighter snapped his fingers. The glove emitted a raging flame which swelled and morphed into a weapon the size of his entire body. The fire dispersed, and a long steel sword appeared in his hand. Selah and Peron were amazed by what they'd seen.

"Is that…" Selah hushed.

"Could it be…" Peron tried to say. But Rowan did it for them.

"Magic," he affirmed. Breathtaking, eye-catching magic.

It was the kind of magic Rowan had hoped to see all his life. Cast by a dwarf with powers similar to Den Mother. However, his fire carried the weight of faith and safekeeping, which comforted Rowan. At least until the inqus clawed its way back up to attack again.

Olivius strode towards the beast. Even on all fours, the brute towered over him by a foot. But that didn't stop the shielded fighter. The inqus tried biting his head, but he dodged it. He swung his sword and the tip slashed the beast's eye. It howled in pain while Olivius smacked it with his shield again. An uppercut to the jaw made the inqus stumble backward. With its head faced upward, Olivius found an opening and slashed the monster in its upper chest.

Even while injured, the beast launched a counterstrike, knocking down the fighter and pinning him with its sharp claws. Olivius' sword fell to his side as the monster reared back again to bite him. Reflexively, Olivius thrust his shield into its mouth, blocking its sharp teeth. As he pushed it farther in, the beast retaliated by dripping its dark slime onto his face.

Olivius put all his might into one final push, and the beast yielded to his strength. It fell back on its haunches while Olivius cautiously rose to his knees. His gloved fingers grabbed the sword handle. He plunged the blade through the beast's chin, choking it as it screamed.

Rowan covered his eyes at the assault. A sword stabbing through a head was the last thing he wanted to see. Even so, he parted his fingers ever so slightly to watch more.

The blade stayed buried inside the inqus. Olivius used the shield in its mouth to hurl its body up in the air with immense strength. The monster's back hit the ground with a defeated thud. He climbed on top of it and stomped along its mucky skin. To finish the job, Olivius tore the sword out of the inqus' jaw and plunged the weapon into its chest.

The beast choked out one last cry as Olivius dragged the blade down to its belly. The same way the swordsman killed the monster from before.

Black ink faded into golden cinders from the top of the inqus' hideous head to the tips of his wretched claws. Olivius sifted through its remains with his sword and shield, which flickered into the same embers that his ax had.

His fire creates weapons, Rowan thought. *Den Mother's magic never did that.*

Rowan thought he heard Olivius emit a long sigh, before he slumped into the ashes and planted his face into the golden mess.

Seconds passed within the wall of fire. Olivius' body still didn't move.

"Is…he dead?" Peron muttered.

Rowan didn't know what to say. If this truly was one of Den Mother's guards, he should've rejoiced. On the other hand, the man had saved he and his friends from certain doom. Who exactly were these people?

Another choked cry echoed outside the firewall, followed by an inqus running through it. It was quickly sliced by another blackened blade. Its ashes fell softly in front of the children. The swordsman emerged from the fire. Flames ricocheted off his cape, leaving his skin and fabric completely untouched.

It was a devilish display, one that Rowan could only imagine from a horror story. He noticed the swordsman's hand trembling again. The monster faded into nothingness before their eyes.

The man turned his attention to the frightened children. Peron and Rowan cowered at the fireproof hunter. Anyone able to walk through fire was bound to make the boys shudder. Selah, however, did not seem so easily swayed. Her hands tightened into fists and the whites of her eyes darkened to a blood red color.

The swordsman approached them, but Selah blocked his way. The orcish girl stood between him and the two helpless boys behind her, brandishing a wooden stake.

"Drop the weapon," Selah growled at the swordsman.

"Selah," Peron muttered. But she only ignored him.

"I said drop the weapon NOW!

Chapter 5

A Magic Business Trip

The orphanage is no place for a child. Another nonsense phrase Den Mother spouted when her children played more than they worked. She included among childish things, anything that kept her orphans entertained: dancing to grainy records on the old record player, winning foot races, or playing dress up. Doing these things got their hair pulled or an emblem seared into their skin. Selah experienced all of these things when she snuck away from her work.

When other orphan boys teased Peron for his "rotten dance moves," she danced all over their faces. And when an orphan girl threw a rock at Rowan during a foot race, Selah threw her body down the cellar stairs.

Rowan had seen it firsthand. Anyone who threatened Selah's friends ended up another victim to her protective rage. But when her rage was accompanied by a sharp stake in hand, Rowan felt clueless as to how things would end.

Her threatening stance had no effect on the towering swordsman. He didn't run and hide like the other orphans, or call her a monster, as many did. But he did bend to Selah's demands. He pressed the button on his iron hilt, causing the steel to retract, then dropped the sword on the ground.

"Who are you? Did Den Mother send you after us?" Selah clamored, still flashing her weapon.

Her question was one Rowan felt too afraid to ask. The swordsman stayed silent, making Selah impatient.

"Tell that witch to go die in a hole somewhere! We're never coming back! Go find some other kids to hunt!"

Rowan wished he knew enough magic to stop this suspenseful standoff. But if he made the wrong move, who knew what would happen to him or Selah. But the standoff ended, when the swordsman leaned forward to meet at her level. Selah's arm flinched a bit, her stake poised inches from the space between his brows. He eyed her up and down, as if assessing her strength and appearance, the way one did upon meeting someone cowardly. His eyes floated back to hers.

"You're holding it wrong," the man uttered through his mask.

Selah blinked in confusion. "What," she spat.

"The spike. You're holding it wrong," he repeated.

She almost looked down, but, likely worried about a trap, she shook off his words and kept her gaze on the swordsman.

"I don't have time for games! Just leave us—"

"If you want to threaten an enemy," he interrupted, "never let your fingers touch the tip of the spike. You'll injure yourself that way. Have it facing out, rather than in."

Selah finally looked down at her stake. Its tip had already pricked her index finger. But the specks of dripping red did not irritate her as much as his remarks did. Her tusks pierced into her sneer.

She fixed her stake position with a quick twist, before lunging with it at the swordsman. He straightened up and dodged her advance. Selah exhaled in surprise, but it didn't stop her from swinging the spike again at his chest. He stepped back, dancing past her attacks.

"That's right. Stay back," Selah grunted through her smile. She hunched over in exhaustion. "You just gave away one of your biggest secrets!"

With a rising yell, she lanced at him, aiming for his stomach. But it was to no avail. The swordsman sidestepped her, grabbed her wrist and gave her a light push into the golden ashes.

"I have many secrets, child," he said. "This is not one of them."

Selah stumbled back up and spun around to wield her weapon again. But when she raised her fist, the stake was gone. It appeared in the hand of the swordsman, who twirled it with his fingers as he raised his brows.

His smug expression made Selah boil over. She raised her fist again, ready to punch him, but Peron grabbed her shoulders.

"Selah, it's alright," Peron assured. "We're safe. We're fine."

He tried keeping her still, but she squirmed in his grasp. Rowan was concerned. He had never seen Selah so angry before, not to the point of being completely uncontrollable. As she jerked around grunting, Rowan held onto her forearm. It hurt to know that was all he could do.

"Se," he softened.

As if hearing a lulling melody, Selah's breathing slowed to Rowan's voice. The red strain around her hazel eyes subsided along with her anger.

Finally calm, her eyes glanced at the swordsman, Peron, and Rowan. Her face scrunched together in regret. "Not again," she mumbled into her hands. She bowed her head in shame. "I-I'm so sorry, sir. I-If I hurt you in any way—"

"Did I hurt you?" the swordsman asked. Rowan sensed sincerity in his tone. He glanced at his friends; the distress on their faces told a thousand tales they'd probably never tell him. Even so, they hesitantly shook their heads. Rowan did the same.

The swordsman sighed in relief. "That's all that matters."

Why would that matter, Rowan thought. *Did Den Mother really want them to bring us back alive?*

The swordsman picked up his sword from the other pile of ashes. He swept the blade out towards the wall of fire, causing a harsh breeze to extinguish the flames all at once.

Moonrise shed just enough light for Rowan to see the swordsman retract his blade and shed parts of his uniform.

"It appears we got off on the wrong foot," the swordsman said, removing his mask. "My comrade and I never meant to frighten you. In our line of work, we defend all innocents who come across inqai, no matter how dangerous the situation might be."

The man pulled back his hood to reveal dark spiraled horns protruding from his forehead. He ran a hand through his long raven hair and cracked his neck while showing off his sharp canines.

"You're a… you're a fiend," Peron murmured in amazement.

"Is that a problem?" the swordsman inquired.

Peron stuttered. "No… I mean… Well, it's just… y-you look like me. B-but you're also a stranger. We've been told we're not allowed to talk to strangers."

"Quite sound advice." He placed his hand on his heart and bowed his head politely. "Dremos. The man sleeping in the ashes over there is Olivius. So, I suppose we know each other now."

Something was off. Den Mother's guards never had names. Why were they just now introducing themselves? And why was Peron recklessly introducing himself as well? He copied this… Dremos' motions before saying, "Peron."

"I'm… Selah," Selah said sounding dazed.

Rowan knew Peron would be surprised to see another fiend there, but he never thought he'd lower his guard so easily. Rowan looked up at Dremos and frowned as he introduced himself.

"My name's Rowan. And we were just leaving."

He turned around ready to leave the smoky forest, only to be stopped by a flickering candle light burning in his face, while he shielded his eyes, Selah and Peron looked past him in surprise.

"You're back," Selah exclaimed.

"You're alive?" Peron questioned.

Dremos had said Olivius was sleeping in the ashes. Yet there he was before them, bearing a gloved hand with flames at his fingertips and waving with the other. Olivius glanced at Selah and covered his mouth slightly. He gave her a rosy-cheeked smile and made different motions with his free hand. Was he casting some sort of spell?

"He says he wishes to heal your wound," Dremos interpreted.

"He doesn't know how to talk," Selah asked.

"Of course he can talk. He just does it differently."

Olivius beckoned for Selah's hand, which she held out hesitantly to him. He put his flaming fingers underneath. Rowan's mind immediately went back to Den Mother.

"Hey don't do tha—" But before he could finish, he watched as the blood from Selah's cut dried and the wound sealed itself under the warm firelight. Selah and Peron gasped as her finger returned to its healed form. A single tiny flame did more for Selah than any brand had for Rowan.

"Not many children come around this way," Dremos said, catching the orphans off guard. "So why are three of them, a human, a half-orc, and a fiend, running around in an inqai-infested forest?"

Rowan glanced at his nervous-looking friends. If they said they were escaping the orphanage, he'd send them back without a second thought.

"We're headed to Faegan," Selah answered honestly.

Dremos raised a brow. "You were headed to Faegan? Alone? A hair before moonset, no less?"

Selah ran her hand through her braid, looking nervous about how to respond. Rowan gulped. He had to get these men off their backs. Then, he had a thought, a tricky yet deceitful thought.

"Well, of course! That's the perfect time," he exclaimed. "We just wanted to do a little…late night sight-*seeking* as we traveled."

"Sight-seeing," Peron corrected.

"Exactly."

"You mentioned this mother of yours," Dremos said. "Something about never coming back and…wanting her to die. Rather harsh way to think about your mother. Just how much trouble are you all in?"

Rowan's eyes went wide as he realized the man really didn't know who Den Mother was. *He really wasn't one of her guards.* Rowan would've been relieved, but he worried the fiend had sensed his deceit. Still, he feigned a smile. "No trouble at all," he said. "It's just…she's so protective of us all. She even has guards chase us around every single day, but they can never do their jobs right, you know?"

"Interesting. And where is your mother now?"

"Yeah, Rowan," Peron said with a squinted glare. "Where is our…mother now?"

"She's in-uh…"

While he could have just said "across the forest," that didn't feel far enough. He should say somewhere farther, far away from Nidas Isle. But Rowan had slept through his geography lessons, and names failed him when he needed them most. All he knew were the four mainlands. He couldn't say Mydion; that was way too easy. There was Paia. There was Beltierre. Then there was…

"Venari," Rowan blurted.

"Venari," his friends repeated in disbelief.

"Um… yeah, Venari," he affirmed. "That's where our mother is! The Magical Island of Mainland Venari! Far away on a… magic business trip."

Even as he spoke, Rowan was internally screaming. He felt Peron's stare of contempt and a monstrous weight of embarrassment. How had it come to this?

"Magic business trip, huh," Dremos contemplated, stroking the hairs on his chin. "From here to there, it's about a two-week boat ride. How long did you say she'd be gone?"

Rowan wished he'd stop asking questions.

"We're… not really sure," he replied confidently. "It's usually a long time before we see her again. Could be days. Weeks. Months even!"

"So, until your guards find you, you're all headed to Faegan for shelter."

If Rowan said another word, the two men would see right through him. He nodded his head slowly instead, holding his breath in hopes that they would believe his horrid lie.

Olivius snapped his extinguished hand and directed several fast hand signs at Dremos. His silent attention worried Rowan. Did they know he was lying? Would they try to force the truth out of him?

"If Faegan is what you seek, perhaps we can show you the way," Dremos told them.

"Why," Selah asked, not even waiting for the request to linger.

Olivius signed another line of phrases to her. Dremos translated.

"He owns a shelter there on the edge of town. We planned on heading back after we finished this quest. If you join us, we'll get you a room where you can rest your head for the night. A room, I presume, *you'll* be paying for, comrade?"

Dremos directed that quip at Olivius. The dwarf simply shook his head as he sighed.

Rowan huffed at the offer. If he thought Selah and Peron would bend to his clever ploy, he was dead wrong. At least he thought so, until he saw Selah and Peron glance at each other reluctantly. They weren't seriously thinking of trusting him, were they?

"Thanks, but we'll be fine." Another lie. "We can find our own way around. We'll meet you there when we see you."

Dremos shrugged. "Suit yourself." With that, he and Olivius walked past the orphans ready to head back.

Peron punched Rowan's shoulder.

"Why would you do that? Are you insane?" he whispered through his canines.

"What did I do?".

"Rowan, without a map, we have no way of getting to Faegan," Selah said. "These guys might be our only hope."

"Come on. No, they're not." Rowan pushed aside their reasoning. "These people fought like, a thousand monsters and put us in the mix. We can't actually believe them, can we?"

"Oh what, like we can believe you?" Peron retorted in disbelief. His response shocked Rowan and Selah. "These men obviously aren't with Den Mother. They just saved us from being eaten alive by a living oil spill, and I'm not letting your little 'hero's ego' stop me from finally getting a new home."

Was that truly how he felt? But before Rowan could ask, Peron stormed off to follow the hunters. Selah almost went with him, but Rowan caught her by the hand.

"You believe me, right Se," he asked. The girl's doubt had melted at his soulful eyes. Rowan believed she would relent.

She sighed and whispered, "We'll talk about this later. Come on." She let go of his hand and went after Peron, but Rowan didn't follow. He stood alone in the fading moonlight.

They wouldn't actually leave me behind, Rowan thought. *Would they?*

His mouth went dry at the thought of walking in the dark alone. He imagined trudging back to the orphanage. All hope being lost. Being back in Den Mother's clutches while he screamed at himself in regret. If he went back now, he'd only be proving her right; that his only purpose was to be with her. He would not let her be right.

"How do we know you won't harm us," Rowan called after the hunters, catching his friends' attention. "How do we know you're not just a bunch of… *kid stealers* just saying they're from Faegan? How…how do we know if we can trust you?"

Dremos nodded, seemingly impressed by Rowan's honest questions. "I have no use for children. *Kidnapping* goes against everything I stand for. You three were just in the wrong place at the wrong time, and I'm willing to help if you'll allow me." He smirked at Rowan before continuing. "Besides, your stubbornness makes you less likely to be kidnapped. Take that as a compliment."

Rowan scoffed as Dremos headed into the depths of the forest. Peron, Selah, and Olivius followed him. With an answer like that, Rowan groaned to himself as he stomped in the same direction.

●　●　●

Smoke from the charred trees had already infused into Rowan's clothing. He thought fanning out his shirt would make it better, but Olivius flame would go out if he did. At least that's what this Dremos told him. But it made everything seem more eerie. The flame never shone past Dremos and Olivius, who led the way to the orphan's safety. Rowan relied only on his hearing to observe his surroundings. Deer snapping twigs in the distance and cicadas shrieking in the trees reminded him of those terrible monsters.

Rowan watched the firelight reflect off Dremos horns. It seemed wrong to ask, but knowing what those monsters were and why they attacked might give Rowan the clarity he needed. Swiftly, he walked to Dremos side, gulping before he spoke.

"Those monsters you fought," he murmured. "You called them *incu* or… *inquae* or something. Where did they come from?"

Dremos kept his eyes on the path before him. "They're called inqai," he finally stated. "They've been around since the dawn of Khallus."

The fiend spat out the name like a bitter aftertaste. The same name Den Mother obsessively worshipped to no end.

"Why did they attack me and my friends?" Rowan asked.

Dremos chuckled dryly at the question, like it was impossible to comprehend. "They were created that way. And you can thank their creators for that. They and their Legion of

Khallus, as they call themselves. Dark mages who use virca to form the beasts and wreak havoc on innocent lives."

"But what do they have to do with-"

"You've had a long night," Dremos interrupted. "Why don't you save your questions for another time?"

"Hmph, it's not like he needs his questions answered," Peron grumbled. "He should know all about those monsters since he kept them from us."

Rowan rolled his eyes. "I thought we were going to talk about it later."

"We will once we get to the shelter," Selah confirmed softly.

"What do you mean? I think this is the perfect time for him to tell us, Sellie," Peron continued. "I mean, it's not like we've been best friends since we were five. Not like we've been planning this for so long and right before-." He didn't realize he was raising his voice until Dremos glared at him. He softened it. "Right before we're attacked by corpses with claws, Rowan here somehow knows how to light a match, knows exactly how to distract them, and abandons us to fend for ourselves."

"That's not what I was trying to do," Rowan argued.

"*You* don't get to explain." Peron pointed at him. "Not until we get to the shelter."

Rowan groaned. "Selah, tell Peron he's being annoying again. Not like that's anything new."

She'd been awfully quiet since her attack on Dremos. Her moment of rage must've really affected her normally cheery mood. Finally, she spoke. "You do a lot of crazy things, Rowan. But this is just... I'm so confused. First you keep secrets from us, then you leave us in the middle of the forest. Now you're lying? Lying to us? Out of all people?"

Her voice, laden with disappointment, filled Rowan with enough regret to last him a lifetime. "I…I didn't mean to—"

"Like we said," Selah said. "We'll talk when we get to the shelter."

Silence dampened their conversation all the way through the forest.

More than half an hour had passed, and the children's legs grew heavier with each step. Rowan might have complained if he wasn't on the lookout for Faegan.

Without warning, Olivius blew out the flame in his glove. Rowan flinched in the sudden darkness, expecting the hunters to commit some dreadful act. Instead, they kept walking.

"Just in time, Olivius," Dremos said. "We should see those lights here soon enough."

"But I don't see a thing," Rowan blurted. "What kind of lights are they? Are they going to take us to Faegan?"

"Yes, they will take us to Faegan," Dremos said reassuringly. "But be on the lookout for any strange lights that appear."

Rowan pouted as he looked into the darkness. "What do you mean by strange? Are they like fireflies or something?"

Dremos chuckled. "Much bigger than fireflies. Just keep looking."

Rowan did as instructed, wondering what good it could possibly do. Soon, though, he saw a few glowing green clumps scattered on tree bark. They passed another tree with even more green patches. Then another tree. And another. And another. Until hundreds of glowing patches were all squished together on each individual tree.

"What are those things?" Rowan asked,

"Spore lamps," Dremos answered. "The dwarven people love their mushrooms. And if you look closely, their light gets warmer when they sense creatures nearby. Watch."

Rowan concentrated on the mushrooms as he walked past, watching them change color from light green to yellow, then back to green. "Wow," he whispered.

"Quite beautiful, aren't they?"

"Uh-huh."

"Well, don't be too mesmerized," Dremos said, then pointed ahead. "You'll ease right through town if you don't pay attention."

Rowan stared up to see what he meant. A shimmer of brightness reflected in his eyes. He looked in awe at the town that would only be the start of his journey.

Chapter 6

Promises by the Fireplace

A mushroom-filled world of Faegan. Rowan's new home. It sounded so blissful in his head. *His* new home. No more living in the darkness. And no more terrible people putting him there. Now he and his friends finally reached the place they longed for. He was free. Like he had always dreamed of becoming.

He scoured each glowing tree to its very tip and observed their intertwining branches arching over the town. Narrow cottages lined the streets of Faegan. Each one was painted with different vibrant colors and decorated with shrubbery and flowers.

Rowan thought there would be more people around, but only a few stared at him before heading into their homes. Then again, it was nighttime, so he'd meet his new neighbors in the morning.

"Whoa," Peron exclaimed, watching the color change. "This is amazing. I can't believe we're going to live somewhere with glowing fungi."

"Fungi?" Rowan asked.

"Yeah, like yeast and mold and stuff. Like the kind we had on the roof."

"Wow! Magic glowing mold," Rowan said with delight.

"If you have any belongings, get them now. We'll be at the shelter soon," Dremos instructed.

"How much longer until we get there?" Selah asked.

Olivius tapped Rowan's shoulder. He pointed to a white house ahead of them. When he saw it, Rowan's face lit with a beaming smile. Its exterior reminded him of the orphanage, except cheerier and only a couple stories high. It was lined with oval windows aglow with warm lighting. Inside, he hoped, were bedrooms, so many bedrooms that he would never have to share again. And unlike the moldy rooftop at the orphanage, Olivius' roof was like a grass field, with blue flowers and ivy hanging off the side. A long gravel path led to a pale-yellow door. Olivius faced the crowd like he had an announcement and signed a phrase with a smile.

"Welcome to Residence Hedgethorn, kiddies," Dremos translated. "I hope you enjoy your stay."

"Wait, I thought we were going to Olivius' house." Selah asked. "Who's Mister Hedgethorn?"

Olivius signed another phrase, followed by a wink.

"You're looking at him," Dremos translated again, before walking down the path with Olivius.

Rowan watched Selah and Peron begin to follow. He rushed in front of them and blocked their path.

"A-are you sure we can trust them," he asked.

They hesitated for a moment until Selah broke the silence. "They saved our lives, Ro," she said. "What choice do we have?"

"I mean, sure, these guys brought us to Faegan, but we're free now. We can find our own place to live."

"Again, with what map, dummy?" Peron sneered. "If anything, all our resources are right here. Food, shelter. This…Mister Dremos led us right to it, while expecting nothing in return. Besides…" He eyed Rowan up and down. "At least he's honest about it."

Peron's icy stare left Rowan in disbelief. Peron and Selah followed the hunters, leaving him to drag his feet after them.

Once Rowan reached front door, Dremos' hand was on the copper handle, but his gaze was locked onto him. Was he waiting for him to join them?

"Looks like we're all accounted for. Go on in," Dremos said.

Ring-a-ling, went a small bell at the top of the door.

The sound hung in the air as the door opened into a cozy foyer. As the group entered, a cheery voice chirped at them.

"Hi, welcome in!"

Rowan wanted to focus on the orange mushroom cap on the ceiling lighting up the room, or how his nose tickled with the room's earthy scent. Instead, he discovered a dwarven woman standing behind a short wooden desk.

"Evening, Miss Abigail," Dremos greeted.

"Mister Dremos and Mister Oli," Miss Abigail announced, waving to them. "I'm so glad y'all made it back safely! None of them inqai devils snuck up on ya, did they?"

"Of course not. Although I can't say the same for your manager here," Dremos quipped at Olivius, who jabbed the fiendish hunter in the ribs.

As they walked up to the desk, Rowan noticed a long row of hooks behind Miss Abigail with keys and hats hanging on some of them. Taking them in, he noticed Miss Abigail staring at him with wide-eyed fascination.

"And who are these young ones," she asked, leaning towards the children.

Rowan was taken aback by her purple-shadowed eyes, rouged cheeks, and red lips, which matched her sideburns and wavy updo. He knew she didn't mean to scare him, but the sight of her makeup made him cringe on the inside.

"They're travelers we found along the way," Dremos replied.

"Well, ain't y'all just the cutest lil trav'lers I've ever seen! I could just eat you up, I could!" She said, scrunching up her nose. Heat rose in Rowan's cheeks, and not in a good way. His friends looked slightly embarrassed as well, Selah playing with her braid and Peron covering his flushed face. "Now you know I'm happy to be of service. Mister Oli knows how I get when I see kiddies. Y'all need an extra room for 'em, I presume?"

"Yes, in fact. Can you place them in the suite next to ours?"

"Mmm, no can do. Just booked that one this afternoon. But I think one of our other rooms just opened up. Hold on now, lemme see."

Miss Abigail placed hands together. Pink dots shone on her fingertips. She lifted her hands, and a pink beam appeared between them. She formed it into a large circle and pressed her finger into the center. It faded into a floor plan of the inn.

"More magic," Rowan murmured to himself in awe. He added it to the list of spells he wanted to learn.

"Hmm. Ah, here we are," she said, pressing a room on the right-hand side. "Some fellas from Daebra just checked out of the combined suite a while ago. It'll be just down that hallway." She tilted her head toward the door beside her.

"Is it possible to add necessities to the room," Dremos asked.

What necessities, Rowan wondered. Did they forget some things on the way here?

"I certainly could…for a lil' extra, of course." The hostess rubbed her fingers together.

Dremos smirked at Olivius, and the dwarf rolled his eyes, knowing exactly what that meant. He took a single gold piece from his pocket and flipped it to her. The hostess caught it, placed it to her ear for a moment, then flipped it again in satisfaction.

"You're too kind, Mister Oli." She placed the coin on her desk. "And here's your necessities." She placed her fingertips together, and they turned pink once more. A cube shape formed from her hands, then transformed into a box with black and white stripes, and a red bow to top it all off. Presents. Rowan had never received a present before. He'd only seen gift boxes in illustrations, and they usually contained toys or lots of money. He wanted to be the first one to open it. But that dream died quickly.

"Here you go, sweetie," Miss Abigail said, handing the box to Peron. "You look responsible enough."

"Me," Peron asked. The fiend looked up at his adult counterpart, who nodded. "Um… alright. Thank you, madam."

"You're very welcome!" She turned back to take a key off one of the many hooks. "Your suite's gonna be number nine on the right," she instructed, handing Dremos the key.

Rowan didn't know what to expect next. Dremos walked to the door beside her, taking out a key and turning it in the lock.

Click, it went.

Dremos opened the door to a long hallway with sprouted lamps lighting the maroon walls.

He and Olivius led the way, the children hesitantly following.

"Bye-bye," cried the hostess. "Y'all enjoy your stay now!"

Slam, went the door behind them.

It made Rowan flinch. But he had more important business to discuss, specifically with Peron. Coming up next to him, he said, "Per, please, please, please be a good friend and let me have a look. I promise I'll share everything that's in there."

"No way," Peron said. "It's for all of us to have. I'm not letting you, of all people, spoil the surprise."

"Come on," Rowan whined. "What if there's food in there? Quit being stingy. Why do you get to hold it, anyway?"

"Didn't you hear her?" Peron explained, perking up his chin. "She said I'm the responsible one, remember?"

"No, she said you *look* responsible. There's a difference." Rowan's hand was only an inch away from the box.

But Peron swiped it away and scoffed. "Like you know the meaning of the word. You can't be responsible with a present, let alone your own life."

Rowan felt instantly deflated. Peron might scold him and annoy him, but that really stung.

"We'll look at it when we get inside," Selah said softly.

Right. Rowan almost forgot that, they still needed to talk. He wondered what would happen if he told them. Would they dismiss him? Blame him? There was so much he couldn't say.

Their room was at the end of the hallway. Dremos opened it and allowed everyone else in before he entered.

"Make yourself at home," he said, shutting the door.

"Whoa!" the children exclaimed, admiring the room. It was filled with good-quality furniture, painted portraits on the walls, and tan curtains hiding the windows.

Rowan heard the faint sound of flames crackling.

"Ooh! A real fireplace," he said. He couldn't help but compare it to the one at the orphanage. While both were constructed from neatly placed brick and cement, this fireplace burned actual fire, not just a pile of built-up ash and dust. He and Peron dashed over and sat on the wool rug, exhaling as the warmth seeped into their skin.

"You'll find a small washroom on the side," Dremos explained. "And there's a cabinet in your room where you can place your needs in."

"So, where is our room?" Selah asked politely.

Dremos opened the door behind the couch. Selah peeked into the room and Rowan followed suit, inspecting all its quaint details.

The bedroom had two full-size beds and a wood cabinet. There was a mushroom-cap lamp on the nightstand and a few others in the corners, all exuding the same earthy smell. It wasn't much, but it was certainly better than what Rowan expected.

"And your room?"

"There's a door on the other side that leads to it. We'll be right by you if you need anything."

"Oh," Selah said quietly.

"If it's not to your liking, we can switch rooms," Dremos offered.

Selah scanned the new room. "Are there any bigger covers?"

"Yes. There are thicker ones down the hallway closet."

"Could you both get them for us?"

"I suppose I could show you where it—"

"You guys know this place better," Selah interrupted. "We'd probably get lost even if you helped us. So… could you get some more covers for us… please?

Dremos and Olivius looked at one another a bit surprised, glancing a few times at the children. Olivius gestured his head toward the door. "I'll keep the door unlocked. We'll be back shortly," Dremos said.

As the door closed behind them, Rowan saw Selah slouch her tense shoulders. She knelt next to him on the rug, quietly watching the firewood burn. He knew what was coming next.

"Talk," Peron spouted.

"I'm not sure I can," Rowan responded.

"Well, then try!"

"Peron, stop," Selah demanded, before calming her voice. "Rowan… how did you know about those monsters?"

"It's a long story."

"Tell it anyway," Peron said.

Rowan felt an itch on his forearm. His long sleeves scraped along each branded scar as he tried scratching away the nervousness. Unfortunately, it only grew deeper the more he thought about that night. Telling stories was much harder than reading them.

He recounted his terrible lessons with Den Mother, which they'd heard a thousand times over. He followed it with a tale of flames, a brief moment with the monsters, and a horrid description of fallen orphans, whose screams had haunted him ever since.

Selah and Peron had experienced Den Mother's endless cruelty but never understood it, not until Rowan spoke of her loyalty to Khallus and the true reasons she taught spell-casting. It took Rowan all his might to tell the whole truth, including what would happen if he or any of his friends disobeyed Den Mother. By the end of his story, Selah and Peron's expressions had melted from doubt, to disbelief, and ultimately to absolute horror at what he'd gone through.

"Sacrifices," Selah said, frightened. "What do you mean, sacrifices?"

Rowan kept his gaze on the crackling embers. It was far easier than answering Selah's question. Still, he answered her anyway. "I mean… we'd already be dead if I hadn't destroyed that spell book," he explained softly.

"'*Your life is in Khallus' hands*,'" Peron said to himself. "So that's why she was so cruel to us. She only saw our worth as offerings to him."

"And if she ever finds us," Rowan continued, "that's all we'll ever be worth."

There was silence as his friends processed the dreadful realization.

"Rowan, why did you really burn your spell book?" Selah asked, the slight boldness in her voice breaking the tension.

He sighed and answered. "Because I knew Den Mother would take you away from me if I didn't."

Selah huffed to herself before scooting closer to Rowan. "Then I understand."

"You do?" Rowan asked, surprised.

Selah nodded. "You were trying to protect us. But Rowan, you don't need to hide all that stuff to do that. If you wanted to keep us safe, you should've told us and stayed with us so we'd have more time to prepare."

"I didn't think you guys would believe me."

"We believe you can do magic, right? Don't put all that on yourself just because you're the mage in the room." Selah placed her hand on Rowan's. "We protect each other. Always have, always will. Right, Peron?"

Peron, looking discontented, didn't reply at first. He sighed and crossed his arms.

"That was a really dumb idea, you know. Leaving us like that," he finally said. It made Rowan feel more guilty. "Even if we were made to be sacrifices, you should've stayed with us, instead of going out and pretending to be Linn the Moonstruck." The young fiend scratched one of his horns and scooted to Rowan's other side. "But I guess I understand. Kind of. Not really. Maybe not the 'keeping the secrets part,' but… everything else."

Rowan gave a half smile as he felt relief wash over him. He rested his head on Peron's shoulder; Selah attempted to wrap her arms around her two best friends.

"I wish I could undo everything that happened, Ro," she whispered. "But please don't do that again. I don't know what I'd do if you guys got hurt."

Rowan rested with that truth. He truly didn't deserve them.

The door creaked open. The orphans stood as Dremos and Olivius stepped in with bedspreads in hand as if their heartfelt conversation never happened.

"Would you like us to make your beds?" Dremos asked.

"Um, sure," Rowan answered straightforwardly. They moved toward the children's bedroom, but before Dremos went in he called him. "Mister… Dremos?"

He looked at Rowan quizzically.

"We, uh, *I* wanted to say… thank you," Rowan said. "For… everything that you did back there. How can…I don't know, how can we repay you?"

Dremos stroked the hair on his chin. "How about for now, you all call me Mister Dre, and we'll call it even."

"Well, then thank you…Mister Dre."

"You're welcome, Rowan. You all have a good night." The bedroom door shut behind Olivius, and the children sat back on the rug.

"I have one condition," Peron told Rowan.

"Name it."

Peron looked at him dead in the eye. "If you want to protect us, that's fine. But let us protect you too. No more of this… doing stuff on your own business. Understand?"

Rowan hesitated, but in the end, he found the right words. "I'll try."

"Can I make a condition?" Selah asked.

"Sure," Rowan replied.

"We finally have a new home. I think we should have a fresh start. No more lies and no more secrets," she demanded. "We tell each other the good and the bad, no matter what happens."

Peron and Rowan looked at one another and nodded in agreement.

"That works for me," Rowan said.

"I can agree with that," Peron added.

Rowan grinned brightly at his friends. Inside, however, he still felt a twinge of guilt. He wasn't sure he could keep both conditions, but he said he'd try. And that's what truly mattered.

"You guys want to find out what's in the box?" Selah asked slyly.

"I get to open it first," Rowan cried, dashing towards the present.

He swiftly undid the bow before his friends could get to it first. Unfortunately, though, Peron was the one to remove the top of the gift box. Selah took out some of the black tissue paper and threw it over her head. They all looked inside.

"Huh, well it's not food, that's for sure," Rowan said, slightly disappointed.

"Are you kidding? This is so much better than food," Selah proclaimed.

"Wow, and I thought *you'd* be disappointed," Peron said. "I think these presents will fit quite nicely."

Chapter 7

A Hedgethorn Luncheon

Rowan found himself in an unfamiliar room. He no longer dwelled within the inn's wooden walls of fur and portraits. Rather, he was in an empty room with walls so white he could barely see the corners. A chill surged through his body, although no breeze swept through the room. As he shook, energy fizzed through his veins. Soon his frame flickered and shined like a thousand light bulbs.

"Cool," he said. His voice echoed through the white room. He laughed a little as his voice reverberated off the walls; he wanted to hear it again. "So cool!"

It did it again.

But this time, his bright flare spread out to every corner, making the room glisten like solid gold bars. Rowan looked at his hands again. Magic. He performed real-life magic. What else could he do?

Rowan wanted to perfect his floating spell, the only one that had ever worked, even if it was just for a second. He took a deep breath and readied his hands, then twirled them, saying the word, *altsum*, with more confidence than he had the first.

His feet swiftly left the ground. And just like his marbles, he floated upward until his body weighed no more than a cloud.

"Not again!" He squirmed and fought, trying to swim to the bottom and undo the spell. "Uh, I'd like to get down now," he echoed. But every attempt made him float farther from the floor.

His heart raced, and his ears rang again with the same high-pitch as when the inqai attacked him. He looked around the golden room. The color from the ceiling started disintegrating into dust; the walls were changing back to white.

"No, no wait! Come back," he pleaded. "What did I do wrong? What did I do wrong?"

The ringing grew louder and louder until Rowan covered his ears and closed his eyes, hoping to stop his own madness. When he opened them, however, a spiral of diamonds and stars appeared before him. He blinked at it, puzzled by the sparkling display. His heartbeat slowed and the ringing in his ears started to settle. Something about this twinkling presence calmed his anxieties. Was this *his* doing?

"*Never fear, child,*" a soothing, feminine voice echoed from the sparkles. A bright light pulsed as it spoke.

"W-what are you?" Rowan asked.

"*A guardian of some sort,*" it resounded. "*If you allow me to be. I am here to guide you in your time of need.*"

"Oh no, it's fine. I can try getting down by myself," Rowan lied.

"*Can you? It appears you cannot even look down without being afraid.*"

"I'm not afraid," he argued. "It's just…this is my mess. I did this. If I want to be a mage, I need to learn to do it on my own. I need to learn how to be brave."

"But you do not know how, do you?"

Rowan opened his mouth to make a polite reply. But a stream of past events flooded his mind, and he realized. "No. No, I don't."

For a moment, the stars didn't respond. Their slow spiral tightened, spinning around until it took another form: a hand. The hand glowed whiter than the entire room and held itself out as an offering to Rowan.

"If you let me, I can show you how," the hand said. *"All you need to do is take hold of me."*

A floating hand asking Rowan to trust it. No other explanation. But Rowan felt assured by this hand's presence. It gave him a choice. No demands. No tricks. A simple choice. A choice where Rowan knew he'd be safe, no matter what he decided.

He stretched out his hand and placed it in the glowing one.

"See, child," the voice hushed. *"It's alright. I'm right here with you."*

The hand's fingertips pressed drops of white light onto Rowan's skin. He watched as they circled up and around his arm. He cringed at the harshness of the spiraling lights, their texture rough like scales. They traveled to his shoulder, up his neck, and then scratched along the side of his face. The last thing Rowan saw was the light shining into his eyes, blinding him until his own sight went black.

Then Rowan woke up. Feeling drowsy, he squinted at the nightstand beside his bed. Its orange mushroom lamp shone across the other bed, where Selah slept on her side. *What a strange dream*, Rowan thought. It was even stranger when he woke up in a safe and cozy room. It should have been his last night on earth, especially after the previous night's events. What a horrible and exciting time.

But today would be a new day. He'd search the streets of his new home bright and early and find a teacher to guide him in magic. All he had to do first was get out of bed.

Rowan couldn't thank Mister Dremos—Mister Dre— enough for the extra necessities. Warm, heavy covers granted Rowan the best sleep of his life. He whined to himself, not wanting to leave the comfortable mattress. He rubbed the sleep from his eyes and heard a sound to his left. It was Peron, he figured, who often snored when he was extremely tired. But it wasn't a loud snoring noise, rather a soft hissing one.

Tsssss, it went.

Peron never snored like that. Rowan opened his eyes fully to find where the sound came from. He looked to his left, where Peron was sound asleep.

Tsssss, it went again.

Rowan's focus shifted to his arm. Wrapped around his dirtied red shirt was a thin coil of silver snake scales. The snake's shape moved around until its head popped out behind Rowan's wrist. Its beady black eyes stared at him, and its tongue slipped out to taste the air. Rowan yelped and fell off his bed.

His thud on the hard wood floor startled Peron from his slumber.

"Rowan, what happened," Peron asked, climbing over to see.

"Peron, help! There's a s-sn—," Rowan stuttered, trying to shake away the clinging reptile.

"Whoa! A snake!" Peron jumped out of bed to study it. "It must've come in while we were sleeping. How did it get in here?"

"I don't care how it got in, just get it off me!"

"Fine, fine. Let me see." The fiendish boy grazed his fingers along the snake's head, making it hiss and bare its fangs.

Both boys screamed, disrupting Selah from her deep sleep.

"Ugh, you guys are so annoying," she groaned, sitting up from her bed. "Why are you—?"

She saw the snake on Rowan's arm. She opened her mouth as if to scream, but no sound came out. Then she jumped out of bed, grabbed a mushroom lamp, and raised it high in the air, ready to swing.

"No, no, no, no, no! Stop! Stop! Stop!," the boys protested, rising off the floor.

"Rowan, buddy, come over here, please," Selah said in an endearing voice. "I'm just gonna bash that thing into the ground."

"Hold on, I can just grab it," Peron reasoned. "We don't want to hurt the snake."

"Uh, we don't want to hurt *me*," Rowan challenged.

"Everyone hush," Selah ordered. "It's moving."

The snake slid up Rowan's forearm. He shivered as its scales slithered along his shoulders. Peron and Selah stared at it in silence.

"Don't. Move," she whispered.

"Trust me, I'm NOT," Rowan said, before dodging Selah's swing. "Hey! Wait, a minute!"

A violent game of tag ensued, with Peron trying to stop Selah from breaking anything and Rowan running away. After a while, they all ended up standing on Selah's bed. "Come back, Rowan! I'm not gonna hit you!"

"We said no more lies, Selah!" He ducked under the swinging lamp once more and spotted the door close to the bed. It led to Dremos and Olivius' room. They would know what to do. The top of the lamp grazed Rowan's shoulder as he jumped off the bed and dashed for the door.

"Mister Dremos," Rowan cried, banging on the door. "Mister Drem—" His plea was interrupted by the door opening. At that moment, the chase finally ceased. He fell to the floor and noted the dark brown boots in his view. He gazed upward to see none other than Mister Dre looking down at him. He wore much lighter clothes than the ones he wore the other night; with a white long-sleeve, tan waistcoat, and trousers that matched his shoes. Rowan never imagined an adventurer wearing circle-rimmed glasses. Or looking so relaxed with a thin stemmed pipe in his lips.

"Uh, good morning, Mister Dre," Rowan said with an awkward smile.

"Good *afternoon*, Rowan," Mister Dre greeted, blowing a ring of smoke. It smelled of fresh mint. "Quite the predicament we're in, aren't we."

"Yes, sir." Mister Dre offered his hand to help, and Rowan gladly took it.

"I see you've all met Sly. I was wondering where he went."

"Who's sly?" He looked at his arm. "Oh, you meant the snake."

"Clingy thing must've snuck out of my bag last night. You have to charm him into letting go. Extend your arm."

Rowan did so, and Mister Dre held his arm out as well, so that their fingertips were barely touching. Sly saw the man's arm and stayed in place. Mister Dre gave two short hisses and beckoned the snake to come to him. The reptile spiraled to the end of Rowan's hand and transferred itself onto Mister Dre's arm, slithering up around his collar.

Rowan stretched his arm, which thankfully felt lighter than before.

"It seems you all got a proper night's rest, considering you have the energy to chase each other." His gaze fell on Selah, who placed her weapon on the floor. He was about to continue when Rowan's grumbling stomach interrupted him. "Right, how could I forget? When was the last time you all ate?"

"Not since yesterday morning," Peron answered.

"Yesterday morning," Mister Dre repeated. "If that's the case, who's hungry now?"

All three raised their hands to the highest of heights.

"Very well. Once you're ready, we'll go together and join Olivius on the roof."

"Why would he be on the roof?" Selah asked.

"One of the Hedgethorn's famous luncheons. They have quite the spread. Get dressed and you'll see for yourself." He took the snake back into his room.

Food. What a glorious word, which sent Rowan's imagination spinning. To finally dine on something other than scraps seemed like a dream come true. But to achieve that dream, the children would need to get dressed, like Mister Dre said. Luckily, their new gifts would come in handy for the occasion.

* * *

On Den Mother's gracious days, mush with parsley was the fanciest meal the children ate. Selah styled her hair down and straightened her salmon-pink dress as if to attend a luncheon for royalty. Rowan sported a new red long-sleeved shirt, tan vest, and brown trousers. But instead of happily skipping down the hall, he groaned softly while listening to Peron's constant droning. He wished he would've talked about his new white shirt and grey slacks, rather than asking Mister Dre endless questions about the snake. But Rowan didn't blame him; he'd ask many a question too if Mister Dre held a magic artifact. Or, in this case, a snake wrapped around his arm.

"But if it *were* venomous, what would you do with its fangs?" Peron asked. "I mean, you'd probably have to take them out so it wouldn't bite anyone, right?"

"Again, that I cannot tell you," Mister Dre answered. His back was to the children as they climbed the dim stairwell. "If Sly were poisonous, which he's not, you surely wouldn't see him on my arm. My *wife* would be the one to answer such questions."

"You have a wife?" Rowan spouted.

"Is that so surprising?" Mister Dre smirked.

"No! Well, kind of." Rowan imagined him to be the loner type of hero. After all, stories never ended in marriage, only victory and conquest. "Why didn't she just come here herself?"

"She knew I'd be in Faegan. So, she asked me to run some errands for her. One of those involved finding food for Sly."

"What kind of food does she feed him?" Another question from Peron. Rowan might've groaned louder if Mister Dre hadn't stopped in front of them. He was looking up at a clear-domed hatch in the ceiling that let in a ray of sunlight.

"Peron, perhaps you should think about what *you'd* like to feast on instead." Mister Dre said, opening the hatch, and disappearing out on the roof. Rowan peered up at the sky. He saw blue, cloudless skies, and a warm breeze blew through. He longed to be in the daylight after hours of nightfall.

He and his friends climbed up, and their eyes adjusted to their bright, new setting. The spore lamps stayed in their regular spot, shading them from the sun and no longer glowing green. Rowan searched beyond the floral roof, observing the simple town in the daylight. A few townsfolk walked through the streets with their families or wagons, some with parasols in their hands, enjoying the beautiful day.

"Wait, where is everybody?" he asked.

Before Mister Dre could answer, a nearby voice cried out. "Well, I'll be. There ya are, Dre," it shouted. They looked up to see a dwarven man with a short brown beard and a worn sunhat. Even as he waved from the inn's tallest roof, he almost looked the size of an ant. "We thought you left us hours ago."

"And leave before seeing Rosie? Never."

"Well, now, you know she'd love to see ya. Hold on, lemme get a ladder." The man left. A few cries of "Whoa," "Be careful with that thing," and "Watch the potatoes" reached the children's ears, until the ladder finally landed on the side of the roof and descended to them. Mister Dre led the way again, climbing up and waiting at the edge of the garden roof.

As the children went up the ladder, Rowan caught a whiff of something delicious. "Guys! I think I smell bread," he exclaimed.

"Great, if you go any slower, we can eat it by tomorrow," Peron quipped sarcastically.

"What kind of bread do you think it is?" Selah asked. "I've always wanted to try something in a book I read. Some kind of bread treat called a 'pancake.' Do they have any pancakes up there, Mister Dre?"

"Pancakes are for breakfast, Selah," he called out. "I don't think you'll find any up here."

"Well, if there's other stuff like that," Rowan said, reaching the top. "I just know it'll be better than—."

"Hoorah," a crowd cried. The cheers made Rowan flinch, and he would have almost fell off the roof if it weren't for Selah and Peron behind him. He composed himself, realizing that the voices belonged to a group of dwarves seated at a long, slender table.

"Hoorah, Spehrow's Eye! Hoorah, Spehrow's Eye!"

Rowan pondered the strange title. Who on earth would name themselves after a bird? He caught sight of Mister Dre, who smiled humbly at the dwarves' praises.

"A surprise party," Selah said. "I thought we were just having lunch."

"I thought so too," Mister Dre murmured. "Friends, you're embarrassing yourselves. You truly shouldn't have."

"Oh, stop all that, Dre," a sweet elderly voice spoke. It was a female dwarf at one end of the table, holding a cane. At her side stood Olivius, who helped her over to Mister Dre. "You know we ain't letting you go without a lil' hero's treatment."

"It's greatly appreciated, Rosalind," he said, crouching down to hug her.

"And of course, ya can't leave without your payment. A hundred and thirty gold, as promised." Out of her white dress pocket, Rosalind took out a small velvet sack. She tossed it to Mister Dre, and it sounded heavy in his hand. The things Rowan would do with a hundred and thirty gold! He could buy Nidas and the mainland with that money.

"And who are these little cuties," Rosalind asked, smiling at the children. Her comment made Rowan grumble in embarrassment.

"They are my guests. Olivius and I met them just a while ago.

"Well, any friend of my baby brother is a friend of mine. And now!" Rosalind waved her cane above her head, and sparklers burst out and popped like firecrackers overhead. "Let's all dig in, shall we?"

At this announcement, the other dwarves joyously applauded. Mister Dre and the orphans sat alongside Olivius and Rosalind. Once he sat, Rowan realized the feast was far beyond his imagination. His own plate was empty, but his teacup was filled to the brim with fizzy red liquid. Trays of fresh bread carved with stars zipped past his nose and were accompanied by blocks of cheese and butter. People poured soup from large pots into their bowls. Plates of vegetables including potatoes and mushrooms piled high above their heads and were seated next to a tray of roasted pig.

But the dish that made Rowan drool was a golden pastry cut into triangles, being passed in his direction. One man took a bite and danced a jig from the flavor. It looked savory. No. Sweet. Rowan didn't care what it was, he wanted one. But if Den Mother were here, she'd throw those pastries in the trash just for looking at them. Would these people act the same way? Peron's neighbor placed the steaming plate in his hand. When him and Selah each took a piece, Rowan stared at them in shock.

"Uh, Mister Responsible?" Rowan whispered to Peron. "What do you think Den Mother would say about you enjoying that?"

Peron scoffed as he swallowed his treat. "Den Mother's not here, remember," he countered softly. "She's in 'Venari' on a 'magic business trip.'"

Rowan sneered at his mocking tone. "Whatever happened to getting permission to eat first?"

"I don't think that's something they practice here, Ro," Selah said. "But if you want your stomach to keep growling, then, by all means, wait as long as you like."

"Oh yeah? Maybe I will," Rowan said, slumping in his chair. He watched Selah pass the treat to Mister Dre. He returned the favor by pouring soup into her bowl. The big helping he gave her could have fed Rowan for days.

For some reason, Den Mother still had a hold on his life, no matter how far away he got. What a waste to just sit there staring at everyone's plates. Even the snake got side of frog legs, yet Rowan sat there looking out of place. All because he waited for permission.

Or maybe he *didn't* need to. The treat was just sitting there unattended. What if he took his own food with no one catching him? He knew just the way to do it, too. Under the table, Rowan lifted his hands, so no one would suspect a thing. He trained his eyes directly on the plated treat. With a flick of his hand, he mouthed the word, *altsum.*

Nothing.

Maybe he needed to be louder. He tried whispering. *Altsum.*

Subtle. But one piece broke away and lifted slowly from the plate.

It had worked, finally. Rowan tried hiding his smile. He was so close to the treat melting in his mouth. Just one more spell, the one to make it float forward. But how did it go again?

Cori…cormaki, Rowan whispered.

"Now what is your plate still doin' empty?" Rosalind asked, tapping Rowan's.

Rowan ceased his spell-casting and sat up straight at the question. He glanced at the pastry still lifting off the plate. Its crisp edges started bubbling like boiling water. That was different. He hoped she wouldn't notice. "I-uh, I didn't know if I was allowed to eat yet."

"Why wouldn't ya be? I said go on 'head and dig in. You're about as thin as a twig. Have 'em pass around that stone soup again. And Oli, make sure this cutie get a tart or two."

Rowan gasped. "Wait, we really get to eat?!"

Boom, went the treat, splattering on Rowan's face.

The exploding dessert made the dwarves groan when it fell into their soup bowls. Selah and Peron ducked down and squealed at the loud noise. Mister Dre clenched his jaw as some of the pastry landed on his cheek. An entire plate exploded all due to Rowan's spell. He licked his lips. It tasted sweet and lemony—his favorite flavor. He tried to remember the correct pronunciation of the spell. When he did, he gulped in regret.

Oh, cori-__mani__. Not cori-maki, he thought.

"What did you do?" Selah mouthed, nudging Rowan's arm.

"Nothing," Rowan returned sheepishly, slumping into his chair. Maybe if he hid, no one would notice a thing.

After a couple moments of silent confusion, Miss Abigail stood up and said, "Well, it ain't a Hedgethorn luncheon 'til somethin' explodes!"

The statement received carefree laughter from everyone except the children. Even Mister Dre chuckled into his drink. Strange. No one had threatened or yelled at Rowan for his mistake. They just sat there… amused. So much so that someone poured a batch of soup into his bowl. Olivius even reached over and placed another thing of tarts on his plate. He winked at Rowan as if knowing his goal.

Rowan could get used to people being amused.

When he peeked at the soup, he couldn't hide his grimace. Who would want to eat soup the color of creek water? With carrots, cabbage, and who knew what else; Rowan thought he saw specks of dirt swimming in it.

"Eat it. Don't be a baby," Selah commanded.

Reluctantly, Rowan took a spoonful, watched the excess drip back into the bowl, and ate it. Surprisingly, it delighted his senses. The green broth tasted of garlic but still warmed his chest. The mixture of spices made Rowan want more.

Disregarding manners, he lifted the bowl to his lips and drank all its contents. When he set it back down, he found a grey stone sitting in the bowl.

"Did they put rocks in your soup, too?" Rowan asked, taking it out of his bowl.

"Pretty neat, huh. I guess it's called stone soup for a reason," Peron said. He tossed his own stone to Rowan. Selah did the same.

"Thanks," Rowan said, before placing them in his pockets. Rowan loved collecting rocks. Besides reading, he spent his free time comparing all colors, shapes, and sizes, hoping to one day make his own marble collection. Perhaps all these stones would have a purpose.

"That little spell of yours caused quite a scene," Mister Dre spoke lowly. He sat across from Rowan, calmly sipping his drink. "If we were in Venari with your mother, you'd be kicked out for inappropriate use of magic."

Rowan gasped. He wouldn't take it *that* far. "I...no, I didn't mean t—."

"Luckily, we aren't in Venari, now, are we?" Mister Dre raised an eyebrow.

"Um…no, sir." Rowan calmed down. He'd stop immediately if Mister Dre gave him that look again.

"I catch myself saving more mages the more I do this. How long have you been practicing?"

"Since I was nine."

"Any teachers?"

"No," he lied quickly. "I've… been teaching myself."

"How odd. With your mother on her 'magic business trip,' I'd think you'd be somebody's ward by now."

At that, Rowan froze, and his friends did too. He remembered the horrid lie he told him last night. Had Mister Dre figured them out already?

"But perhaps that's my experience," Mister Dre continued. "Sound parenting is hard to come by nowadays."

Rowan drew in his breath. "Well, I mean, Den…uh m-mother didn't want me to learn super young. She wanted me to focus on other things. So, I learned in secret." Technically, that was half-true. "And now that we're in Faegan, maybe I can find a teacher of my own."

"Quite the goal," Dremos said. "When you find a teacher, what *oath* do you plan to take?"

"An oath?" No one had ever mentioned anything about an oath. "I guess I never thought about it."

"Oh, hush all that nonsense, Dre," Rosalind scolded. "All that talk of oath-keepin' and breakin' will do nothin' but spoil your lunch."

"It's an important question to ask, Rosie. Something that will affect his decisions for the rest of his life."

Affect my life? Rowan thought. *In a good way or a bad way?*

"Take your brother, for instance," Mister Dre continued. "After fifty years, his oath to Caelum remains intact. To this day, his magic grows stronger every—."

"Ya know, I sure do miss the old Spehrow's Eye. The one who questioned no one about their oaths. Or kiddies' oaths, for that matter. You remember him, Dre?"

Mister Dre shook his head. "That was a long time ago."

"Well, I still miss him. The way he led dozens of adventurin' parties with confidence and flair. Wouldn't hesitate to challenge and fight anyone. Whether an Oathkeeper or an Oath breaker. All while swinging two *hammers* in his hand to boot."

A sad expression crossed Olivius' face. He placed a hand on Rosalind's shoulder, while Mister Dre, with a clipped smile, patted her hand softly. "*Two short swords*, dear. It was two short swords."

"Was it?" She blinked. "Oh, must've slipped my mind. Either way, you shouldn't be botherin' the boy about oaths and such. Just let him figure it out, and he'll be alright."

"Uh… thanks." Rowan felt bashful. He'd never gotten advice before; it felt nice. "Do you think you could teach me anything… Madam Rosalind?" Even with just her one spell, she had more knowledge than him. But he saw Olivius shake his head behind her back.

"Oh, cutie, call me Miss Rosie," Rosalind said. "I'd love to, but my old age and memory will only let me cast so many spells now. Just a few of us in Faegan are akin to magic, and we're not as boastful about our gifts as others. Besides, you wouldn't want some old fogies wasting your time."

He saw Miss Abigail pass by; he remembered her spells. "What about her," he blurted as he pointed. "Could she teach me magic?"

"Sorry sweetie," she said, grabbing dishes from Miss Rosie. "My oath's to the Hedgethorns and the Hedgethorns alone."

He lowered his head. There went the neighborhood.

"I know," Rosalind exclaimed. "What about them Ataxia folks, Dre? I haven't seen them in a while. Perhaps they might be available."

Ataxia? That name sounded familiar. Where had Rowan heard it before?

"This boy's knowledge is still growin'. I wonder if that Clascia Valdi is still doin' music. Or let him train with someone like Thierric of Turphyme, he'll have the world at his feet."

Turphyme? Rowan hadn't read about him in years.

"Now what about the Dreamin' Nova? With someone like her, he'd be the best shapeshifter on the island. I've got it! Send that *Linn the Moon Knight* a message! I know *she*'d love a ward of her own."

Mister Dre sighed. "Moon. Struck, Rosie. Linn the Moonstruck."

That name alone caused all three children to rise from their seats.

"You know Linn the Moonstruck," Selah and Peron exclaimed. Rowan didn't join them, too preoccupied watching Mister Dre massage his brows, clearly irritated. Then a crazy thought entered Rowan's mind.

Olivius hastily signed something to Rosalind.

"Yes, Oli, I remember my appointment with the healer," she replied. "Dremos, dear, thank you again for your help. Your bravery is beyond words." She leaned in to give Mister Dre a kiss on the cheek. "Hope to see ya again, kiddies. And Dre, tell the missus I said hi."

"Anything for you, Rosie," he said, tipping his head.

She created tiny circles around her and Olivius with her cane. Spiraling fireworks covered their forms until they vanished within the bursting explosions, leaving nothing but a pillar of smoke behind them. Applauding crowds rushed over to the side roof, waving down from above. Rowan's curiosity followed them. He smiled in disbelief, as he saw Miss Rosie and Mister Olivius wave back, now standing in the streets.

"What kind of spell was that," Rowan questioned, as he bid them farewell.

"One of Rosie's grand exits," Mister Dre said. He stayed in his seat, feeding frog legs to his snake. "She used to get in a lot of trouble with those smoke-screen spells. Linn forced her to stop after so many times."

Rowan wasted no time. He ran back to his seat, slammed the table and said, "Could you take me to him?"

, "To whom?" Mister Dre said.

"To Linn! Linn the Moonstruck! I want him to be my teacher!"

"Why do you need to see *her*? I thought you were a self-taught mage."

He stammered, thinking of an excuse. "Oh. I-I am, but I think he-I mean *she*— might be a better fit for me. I guess once I find him—*her*, I'd see if—"

"Mister Dre," Peron interrupted. "Rowan's a really big fan of hers. And yeah, he's self-taught, but just imagine if he had someone like Linn the Moonstruck to teach him. You saw that floating food spell; with enough training, he'd be almost unstoppable."

Mister Dre chuckled, showing off his sharp canines. "You should work on your persuasion skills, young one. Think if I did take you to Linn the Moonstruck, I'm sure your mother would be worried sick knowing a stranger took you from her."

Den Mother? Worried sick? That only happened when she needed someone to clean up all her messes.

"I wouldn't hear the end of it," Mister Dre continued. "Frankly, I don't wish to. Besides, why should I help you? Especially when you've been dishonest with me?"

So, he'd known all along. He was just very good at hiding it. But what reason could Rowan give for this hunter to be their guide?

Rowan looked into Mister Dre's eyes, as red as they were brash. "You said it yourself. You have no use for us, right? You're only willing to help if we let you…" Mister Dre sat, unmoved. "And you'd really be helping by letting me meet him, er-her. I learned magic because of Linn the Moonstruck. If I don't meet her now, all my hard work would be for nothing."

Mister Dre thought for a moment, then leaned back into his chair with a sterner and more collected look than his usual smugness. "Tell me everything."

"What?"

Mister Dre shrugged. "A mother traveling to Venari. A story, I presume, you think I wanted to hear. But I've seen many fraudsters try to conceal the truth from me. They either confessed out of their own free will, or with the blade at their throats. All that to say, if you want me to guide you to the Moonstruck Mage, we must use our free will and be honest with each other."

"I don't know what you're-."

"Ro," Selah hushed. "Remember what we promised?" He did. "No more secrets and no more lies. You want this, don't you?" More than anything.

Another itch fell upon his sleeves. He couldn't believe what he was doing. "Alright, fine. I'll tell you."

So, he told Mister Dre everything: about the orphanage, about their escape. Even about Den Mother, the hardest thing to talk about. He almost choked up during his confession, but Selah and Peron comforted him through it. They spoke for him when it got too difficult. When he finished, the uneaten food had turned cold and Sly the snake moved from Mister Dre's arm to his shoulders. Rowan felt drained. He waited for a response from Mister Dre, who sat quietly for a while. Then he ran his hands through his hair.

"If what you say is true," Mister Dre finally said, "then this isn't just a matter of magic. It's a matter of survival."

"Yes, sir," Peron said.

Rowan's confession had seemed to make Mister Dre weary. He sighed, then spoke. "Are you all familiar with the term *bartered wardship*?"

How could they be? Not a single soul outside the orphanage came to tell them new things. "Very little, sir," Selah admitted.

Mister Dre nodded. "If you truly wish to be out of this…Den Mother's grasp, there is truly no one better than the Ataxia to challenge her for your adoption. Most of them disbanded decades ago, with only a few members remaining in contact. Once a quarter they recount their adventures in my town of Evermire."

Rowan pondered his words in silence. In case he needed to travel on foot.

"Linn the Moonstruck, in particular, spends most of her time at the Spehrow's Nest, the finest tavern in Nidas. The only problem is that, to meet her or any of the Ataxia, you must convince the tavern owner, Madam Spehrow. She treasures them like family and deems many unworthy of their presence. You're not the first to try to meet them. Having only one spell might not be enough to convince her."

Wonderful, more conflicts to add to Rowan's plate.

"While I could vouch for you and ease her mind, I cannot assure you it'll be Linn. I am sure, however, at least one member would take you three in. If they proposed a bartered wardship against your Den Mother, they'd have to give up something in return. Should that succeed, one of them would adopt you three, and you, Rowan, would have a teacher who could make you their ward."

Rowan was shocked. "What are you saying?"

"I'm saying if we're going to Evermire, we must leave at once."

Mister Dre had said, *we*. He actually wanted to be their guide. The three children tossed all etiquette aside, as they leaped and hollered for joy. Rowan hung onto Peron's neck and Selah pulled them both into a tight embrace, swinging them around as they laughed.

"See, Rowan," Selah beamed, "I told you, didn't I? Finding a teacher would be the first thing we'd do."

Peron shook out of the hug and grabbed the plate of tarts. "This calls for a celebration!" They each took one and raised them high, with Peron yelling, "To Evermire!"

"To Evermire!" the dwarven crowd cheered with the children.

Rowan felt elated. It was the happiest day of his life. As he bit into the lemon-flavored tart, he pondered his bright

future, which in that moment tasted sweeter than anything he'd
ever asked for.

Part Two

Chapter 8
Stories in Caravans

"*A*ll aboard," the dwarven footman drawled. "Last call for Evermire, right, Sven?"

"You said it, Ben," the coachman bellowed. "These horses wait for no man or creature!" He took his neck-whistle to his lips and made a harsh, wheezing sound.

Storybooks might have captured the sharpness of horse-drawn caravans in their illustrations, but Rowan had never realized how beady a horse's eyes were up close. But he had learned something new: feed the four horses a carrot or two, and they'd let you pet their manes.

The dwarven coach and footman, who gave him the carrots, were just as nice as the horses. The footman had red hair and a top hat, and greeted the orphans from the side door, while the coachman with a black cape and scraggly grey beard sat atop the caravan's ledge and saluted Mister Dre.

Rowan scanned the caravan in awe; living inside of it came to mind before riding it. Its exterior was off-white, with tips of orange swirling around the glassless windows. Below the windows sat a bronze plated sign: <u>Ben and Sven's Caravan</u>

<u>Services</u>, with the heads of a ginger dwarf painted on the left and a grey bearded one on the right.

Rowan heard Mister Dre mutter to the footman. He counted the change in his hand; Sly the snake still wrapped around his arm. Rowan wondered how it didn't swallow Mister Dre whole before the exchange.

"That's four, five, and… six silver should do," Mister Dre said, dropping the coins in the footman's hand.

Ben the footman eyed the coins and stroked his red scruff. "A bit much for a one-way, Spehrow friend. Why the extra three?"

"Consider it for my guests. First time travelers, you see," he whispered, glancing at Rowan, who couldn't help staring at him.

"I *do* see," Ben the footman said. "Well, time's a-wasting then." He swung open the orange door, as if presenting a magic trick. "Step on in kiddos, and we can make it before sunset."

"Rowan, let's go," Selah cried, dashing for the door with Peron.

The children hopped up the caravan step and went inside. Their boots clunked on the pine floors as they scoured the warm-lit bulbs lighting the red velvet walls. But Rowan noticed something extra special. The bulbs lit up a small set of stairs leading up to a longer bench with a scenic view behind it.

Rowan didn't hesitate, rushing up the stairs to the bench where he bounced on the plush seats. Once Selah and Peron joined him, they all turned to the back window. A clamor of voices sounded from atop Residence Hedgethorn. When they looked up, dwarves were waving and bidding the orphans farewell.

"Goodbye! Y'all come back now! Have fun," the lunch-goers exclaimed. The orphans smiled and chuckled at these good tidings.

"Afternoon, everyone," Ben the footman greeted with a cheesy grin. The children turned towards him. Along with his top hat, he wore a fine tuxedo and white gloves with blue trimming. "Thank you for joining us! Ready for your first travelin' adventure?"

The children nodded in excitement.

"Wonderful! Our one-way trip to Evermire will start soon. So sit back and relax, and it'll be smooth travels from here on out." He closed the door behind him and stood beside several thin lengths of twine next to it. A bell rang as he pulled a rope, and he yelled out the window, "All set for thirty, Sven?"

"Miles ahead of you, Ben," Sven the coachman shouted, his voice muffled by the caravan roof. "Hyah!"

With that, the caravan shifted forward, and Rowan looked out the side window, where the townsfolk left his vision as the caravan rode past.

The children resumed looking through the scenic view and waved back at the patrons atop the inn.

"Farewell, everyone," Peron yelled, sticking out his hand.

"Bye! Thank you for the yummy food," Selah said, waving both arms.

"Goodbye! See you next time," Rowan cried.

Rowan prolonged his gaze, slightly saddened as the quaint inn got farther away. Not even a day had passed, yet the dwarven folks already treated him like family. If people in this town were this kind and generous, who knew how Evermire would treat them? But even as he set out to find another new home, Rowan knew this wasn't goodbye for the town Faegan. Not even as the mushroom-filled town faded beyond the rolling hills.

* * *

Faegan got smaller and smaller with every mile. Then, for a while, he saw nothing but bountiful flowers of sun-orange and soft lavender. Eventually, they arrived at another town, one that seemed just like Faegan.

"This here is my lovely hometown of Daebra," Ben the footman announced. "The finest village in dwarven civilization. Gotta pass through here if we want to make it to Evermire." He pointed down to the circular town with a mushroom tree looming over it. In the valley, spherical cottages were placed in neatly aligned circles.

"Guys, check this out," Selah exclaimed

Rowan counted the rows of cottages as they traveled to the center of the village, where a concrete building towered over the twisting branches. Its bronze centerpiece pointed up towards the sky. Little, white-striped ornaments covered the pale surface. Painted tongues of fire decorated the base of the structure. Each flame carried a color of pale green, royal blue, or bright orange.

"Ah, would you look at that! Our very own Temple of Caelum," Ben the footman said. "One of the Crown Jewels in this neck of the woods. Come a long way since the Battle for Nidas, eh Spehrow friend?"

Mister Dre sat on the side bench, writing in a small leather-bound journal. "You speak the truth, comrade," he said dryly.

Rowan's eyes stayed fixed on the mighty tower, even as they traveled farther away from it. He never imagined a temple to be so…colorful. He wondered if Evermire had a temple of its own. Maybe it had even brighter colors than this one. Thoughts of Evermire clouded his mind as they exited the lovely village he planned to explore in the future.

Rowan knew nothing of Evermire, but deep down, he already knew it was marvelous. It would a majestic town where every day was a celebration, a place where magic roamed free, never ceasing, and always creating. He thought of the Spehrow's Nest and imagined the best adventurers boasting of their talents and performing spells much better than his own. He wondered about the Ataxia and imagined them all coming together in one place. For where there were the Ataxia, there was always Linn the Moonstruck. With her as his teacher, Rowan could finally hone his craft and become as powerful as they were.

Once he met the Ataxia, he'd ask them every question. Well, at least the ones he had while reading their stories. The orphanage library only held five Clascia Valdi books. In those, however, she was called by another name: the Stringed Siren. A musical heiress who entertained the masses with her enchanted violin. A mage with enough power to charm or hypnotize her enemies with her song. The gliding melody on her bow lured evil-doers right into Clascia's traps. All it took was a pluck of her strings for the villains to drop dead where they stood. Thus, the name, the Stringed Siren.

Rowan didn't know what a violin sounded like. The only music he'd ever heard was the muffled and scratchy sounds from Den Mother's record player. Perhaps Clascia Valdi and Linn the Moonstruck could teach him something. Maybe a spell to burst the eardrums of his enemies.

There was also The Dreaming Nova. Rowan and Selah had read both of her books in Den Mother's library. The mysterious shapeshifter had the power to copy anyone and anything, so long as they looked her in the eye. Nova's death-like stare at villainous mages, allowed her body to match their appearance and physical abilities. Nova's magic confused, manipulated, and defeated many foes. It drove many of them mad.

Rowan thought about his own shapeshifting abilities. They were as nonexistent as his perfectly working spells. But if this Dreaming Nova ever showed him how to turn into other people, he'd be happy to learn from her too.

Then there was Thierric of Turphyme. Rowan didn't know much about him. His only story in the orphanage library was a mighty tale. Rowan and Peron had read Thierric's book together years ago. He was a kinetic orcish mage who controlled earth with his ear-splitting voice and fists of immeasurable strength. His strength led him to defeat rival tribes, whom he crushed into the dirt. With his hands punched into the earth and a loud bellow, Thierric split the ground in two, forcing his enemies to fall into a bottomless pit.

Meeting an orc with earth magic would be just the way to live, Rowan thought. And living with his friends on top of that? No matter which mage he met, Rowan knew they'd make his life all the more—

"Rowan!" Selah shouted.

"Huh," Rowan stammered. His eyes focused on his view out the window. He must've been daydreaming for way too long; the once bright blue sky had become orange and pink. He shook his head and saw Selah staring at him, leaning on the window's edge. "Sorry. What happened? Are we almost there?"

"Yep! Just a few miles left." She pointed out the window to a wooden sign fixed into the grass.

Now Entering Old Town Coriva

Evermire 5 miles left   **Brielle 30 miles right**

"Ugghhh, Five? Why five?" Rowan groaned loudly.

"What did you expect?" Peron said, slouching on the bench. "We knew it'd take a minute to get there. It's not like you can magically get yourself into town."

He didn't know how, but Rowan would certainly keep that as an option. "Why can't it be one more mile? That feels like forever away."

"Cheer up, Ro," Selah said. "I mean, look at how much road we've covered. Five miles is way less than thirty."

Rowan was still pouting, but Selah noticed and rubbed his coils playfully.

"Did you really mean to make that tart explode?" she teased.

Rowan pursed his lips together as he stared at her. He thought staying quiet might keep him from telling the truth. Unfortunately, Selah had seen right through him. Folding her arms, she said, "You were trying to make it fly closer to you, weren't you?"

Rowan nodded slowly, making himself small. "I meant nothing by it. All I did was pronounce it wrong," he confessed. "Guess I thought no one would notice."

"Yeah, well, they did," Peron interjected. "They clearly noticed how out of practice you are."

Rowan reached over to hit Peron's arm. Peron did the same. But Selah, sitting between them, stopped them from squabbling.

"What if there was a better way for you to practice?" Selah asked Rowan.

"How?"

He watched Selah look around. Then, sporting a devious smirk, she nudged Rowan's shoulder and pointed at the sleeping footman draped over the bench to their left.

"By taking off Mister Ben's hat…without waking him up," she whispered.

Rowan observed the footman's strange sleeping position; his hat was covering his face. Rowan shot Selah a wicked smile, already accepting her challenge.

"This should be fun," Peron mumbled, resting his chin into his hand.

Rowan glared directly at the footman's hat. He'd never tested his spells on clothing before. But after his luck with the tart, perhaps he was far more capable than he realized. He held out his hands, took a deep breath and cast his spell the same way at the luncheon.

Altsum, he whispered.

A beam of blue washed over the hat. It lifted inches off the footman's face, revealing his dreadful snoring.

The orphans exhaled in relief. All Rowan had to do was bring the hat closer. His mind felt heavy. He felt nervous about casting the next spell correctly. Concentrating as hard as he could, he softly pronounced the next spell.

Cori…mani, he carefully breathed.

The top hat rotated as it slowly inched towards Rowan. Selah and Peron watched in amazement, gasping and shaking Rowan's shoulders. He wanted to join in his friends' excitement. But the heavy feeling only ached even more. It blurred his vision of the flying hat and made his breathing shallow.

As dizziness overcame him, Rowan slouched and dropped his arms.

D-Diasare, he strained.

In the same breath, the top hat fell, hitting the footman's face and landing on the floor. The dwarf swiftly sat up with his eyes closed, then lay back down as if nothing had happened.

While ordinarily that would have been enough to make them laugh, Selah and Peron were looking concernedly at Rowan in exhaustion.

Selah carefully helped him sit up. "Is everything alright?"

Rowan had the same question. He had never experienced something like that before, not in all the time since he'd learned magic. Whatever it was, he hoped it would never happen again.

The sound of Mister Dre clearing his throat made the orphans sit up straight. He stood in the middle of the caravan with his brow turned up at them. He retrieved the top hat from the floor and rested it gently back on the footman's face.

"It's best not to wake a sleeping dwarf. They're quite cranky if woken up wrong," he said, sitting next to Ben the footman.

'Sorry," the children whispered.

Mister Dre chuckled softly, clearly amused by the orphan's guilty looks. "In any event, you'll want to put your energy in thinking about what to say."

"To who? Linn the Moonstruck?" Rowan questioned.

"No, Rowan. To that Madam Spehrow lady," Selah answered.

"Oh... right." Rowan rested his head on the velvet wall. That name irritated him more than the weakness in his body.

"It's alright if you're not prepared," Mister Dre said. "But we'll soon step foot in Evermire. So, I suggest you—"

"O-of course I have something," Rowan fibbed. "I just want to save it for when we meet Linn the Moonstruck, is all."

Peron and Selah looked at each other, their keen smiles turning to worried frowns.

"We understand, Ro," Selah said. "But we're almost there and you haven't practiced your speeches like you usually do. You'll want to make a good impression, you know?"

"That's why I'm practicing my spells, aren't I? I mean, maybe if I'm good enough, Linn the Moonstruck will make me her ward. I can just skip meeting Madam Spehrow altogether."

"Come on, Rowa. Just admit you aren't ready yet," Peron whined. "We're here to help you find a teacher, not stop you."

Rowan sneered at his friend. "Do you have any faith in me?"

Peron shrugged. "It's just advice, man. This Madam Spehrow seems like a super serious person if she decides who does and who doesn't get to meet the Ataxia. Like Mister Dre said, one perfected spell won't be enough to change her mind."

"Well, I think it will, thank you very much," Rowan said. "Besides, it takes all the pressure away from arguing with another mean, old lady."

"Watch your tongue, child," Mister Dre asserted. His slight threat pierced through his glasses. "You haven't met Madam Spehrow, so you shouldn't make negative assumptions about her."

Rowan gulped. If he'd known his statement would strike such a chord, he would've kept his mouth shut.

"I just… I thought that's how most serious people are," Rowan said. "Super old and super mean."

"Hmph, if that's the case, I wonder what that makes me," Mister Dre uttered. "If you must know, Madam Spehrow is quite serious, but never hateful. Evermire sings its praises for her generosity and kindness. Who knows? You might enjoy her company. She's quite the storyteller."

"What's that got to do with anything," Rowan asked.

Mister Dre tapped his temple right below the skin of his horn. "Think about it. A tavern owner who knows more adventurers than anyone in Pelle. She's bound to share a few stories. Probably ones you've never heard yet, am I wrong?"

Rowan folded his arms. "That still doesn't mean anything. I can hear all those stories from Linn anyway, when she becomes my teacher."

"Indeed." Mister Dre chuckled and took off his glasses, putting them in the bag around his shoulder. "And what makes you think Madam Spehrow will accept you into her court? Let alone allow you to be Linn the Moonstruck's ward?"

"I… um, well," Rowan stammered, taken aback, "like I said. She'll have to make me her ward once I show her my spells."

"Like the exploding tart spell?" Dremos asked sarcastically.

"Yes. Like the… exploding tart spell," Rowan gritted his teeth. Something told him he'd never live down that spell.

"Then it's a good thing I'll be advocating for you if your spell casting goes wrong."

"How do you know if she'll even listen to you?" Selah asked.

A suave smirk stretched across Mister Dre's lips, and he shrugged once more. "I'm called the Spehrow's Eye for a reason, Selah. Just because I'm her guardian doesn't make our relationship any less honorable."

He said that as if holding some sort of secret. Rowan squinted at the mysterious Mister Dre. He knew he shouldn't pry; his curiosity got the better of him. "How long have you been protecting her?"

Mister Dre slouched arrogantly in his chair. "Since the day our paths crossed at the Battle for Nidas. When Linn the Moonstruck and the Ataxia first came to Evermire. Although that was many, many years ago."

Rowan felt giddy. He sensed a new story coming into play. Not the kind of ink and paper, but one told by word of mouth, by experience. Perhaps a story he'd never find in the library. Where the voices in his head probably didn't compare to the ones told in real life.

. "You're wanting to know more, I presume," Mister Dre asked, ushering them to the other bench.

The children raced down the small set of stairs, leaving their high thrones for the bench across from Dremos. Rowan bounced in his seat, watching Mister Dre contemplate his story in silence.

Mister Dre started his story with a deep breath, "Have any of you heard of the Legion of Khallus?"

That question made Peron swallow hard, and Selah's eyes grew big. Rowan stopped bouncing and clawed his nails onto the bench, trying his best not to sink through the floor out of fear. What a way to start a story.

"N-no sir," Peron stuttered. "We haven't."

"I don't intend to scare you. It's simply an introduction," Dremos said calmly. "They are the mages your Den Mother associates with. Back then, the Legion of Khallus had a greater impact on Mydion and its lands. With their use of virca, 'the forbidden magic,' they terrorized the islands, letting them rot to nothingness for centuries. Nidas Isle was hit the hardest. You travel to these other mainlands like Paia or Venari and you'd see nothing but protection artifacts lining their cities. Their barricades made it impossible for the Legion to invade. Not the case for Mydion and this island. At least, not until the Ataxia arrived."

Rowan's smile slowly returned. Maybe the story would get better, and he'd have nothing to fear.

"The Ataxia's goal was to set up the border they created and make Evermire be the first of Mydion's guarded property. If successful, a piece of the border would go to Mydion, finally protecting the lands from any invading inqai. The search for the border was awful, but fortunately, the Ataxia bonded together over one common theme; hatred."

"So cool!" Rowan exclaimed. "Hatred of what? The monsters?"

Mister Dre shook his head. "For each other."

That can't be right, Rowan thought. Linn the Moonstruck hating people? Stories painted her as caring and generous, a friendly face to all who'd seen her.

"I thought adventurers were friendly in books," Selah said. "Why would they go on a journey together if they hated each other?"

"Shouldn't believe everything you read in stories, child. Regardless, they put their differences aside and journeyed in search of creating the border. Some trials they fought and won, while others fell through, leaving the Ataxia with only hope in their minds. Eventually, they had a spell for the border they needed, and the party brought it to Nidas with only a few scrapes. When they reached Evermire, they were terrified by what they found: a town with flames engulfing the salty air, inqai running rampant in the streets, and the Legion of Khallus awaiting them."

Rowan's heart sank upon hearing those words, believing his big, magic city fantasies were dashed. Why would Mister Dre take them to a city of monsters? He continued.

"The legionnaires, as we call them, knew of the Ataxia's plans and tried thwarting them in advance by terrorizing the largest areas in Nidas. Fortunately, some survived the desecration, but the Legion would not stop there. In a hurry, the Ataxia separated to fight the legionnaires on different parts of the island. Linn, however, stayed in Evermire, fighting within the ruins."

Rowan sat on the edge of his bench, imagining Linn the Moonstruck with her scaled scepter in hand. Bracing for battle like it was the last one of her life.

"Even as Khallus' forces struck her, Linn prevailed using her unpredictable powers. Bursts of energy surged from her weapon. Lightning and streams of light disintegrated inqai and blinded the legionnaires. When the Legion fought with more fury, Linn knew she needed to get them; find enough time to set up the border. But to distract them, she knew she would need one of her most dangerous spells. One that would likely weaken her if she didn't cast it correctly. She devised a quick and clever plan. To cast the—"

Thunk, went the caravan. *Thunk!*

The noise, faint as it was, interrupted Mister Dre's story telling. Rowan jerked his head toward it; it had come from behind the caravan. Dremos paused, eyes darting cautiously from side to side, while his hand hovered over the weapon on his belt.

But there was nothing else but hooves clopping over the dirt road.

Dremos relaxed but still kept his weapon at bay. "As I was saying," he continued, "to cast the spell, Linn ran to the edge of Evermire. She avoided their attacks until the Legion flew past and stopped her where she stood. One legionnaire mocked her; insisting she yield to their battalion. But the Moonstruck Mage never gave in. She lifted her scepter and—"

SLAM, went the caravan.

Chapter 9

Have Sly Be Your Guide

The slam rocked the children off the bench. Selah and Peron fell forward, Rowan crashed to the floor, and the sleeping footman awoke with a yelp and jolted up straight.

"What was that?" Selah exclaimed.

"I have no idea," Ben the footman said, brushing off his suit and picking up his hat. "Don't worry folks, let me see how far along we are." He hurried to the back window to investigate, then let out a horrified gasp and slammed the shutters. When he turned back to them, his pleasant aura was gone, and he stomped back to his seat cursing in dwarvish. He yanked on the twine and as the bell rang furiously, yelled out, "Should've known he'd do this! Having us in *the Barrens* a hair before dusk. Where in Cael is your head, Sven?!"

"Wasn't my fault, Ben," the coachman shouted. "The horses thought it'd be a good shortcut!"

"What are *the Barrens*?" Peron asked.

Rowan knew he shouldn't, but he had to see why wherever they were was called the Barrens. When he looked out the window, he regretted it instantly. Fields of brown and grey grass grew patchily along the dry soil. Abandoned and broken buildings were worn to their foundations. Sparse trees were choked by their branches with little life to spare. The pinkish-orange sky looked smoggy on the horizon with only half its sun left.

Shriek!

The familiar noise haunted Rowan. He slowly turned his head downward. Only to stare at a dripping, muck-secreting beast running alongside the caravan. Another inqus, with several others coming up behind it. *How on earth did they get here?* Rowan thought. He thought Mister Dre defeated them all. Rowan froze. His eyes met the beast, and he watched its neck crack as it stared back.

Suddenly, the beast pounced at him, missing him by a few inches. If Peron and the footman weren't there to pull him back, Rowan would have been eaten alive.

"Stay down, kiddo," the footman warned. "You don't want to be near those things."

Rowan didn't need reminding. Yet, his frozen condition ceased to thaw. The flailing inqus was stuck in the window. For a moment, the monster seemed to give up. Then its rotten limbs stretched out and its claws latched onto the soft velvet cover. It scratched along the seat, popping out pockets of cotton, clawing its way through the wooden floor and headed in Rowan's direction. Its arm came closer, but Rowan still couldn't move. He looked at Selah and Peron, who the footman was holding back from the beast.

Rowan's breath hitched as the monster's claws prepared to tear through his face. Instead, glistening black steel passed through Rowan's vision. It cut through the inqus' wrists, which collapse into ash. Ben the footman jumped onto the bench and struck the monster with his gloves. It screamed again. A jab to the cheek, a right hook to the snout, and a kick to its eyes, knocked the inqus out of the window and crashing onto a brittle grey cottage.

"That should hold 'em off for now," Ben the footman said, straightening his top hat.

Rowan shuddered. It took all his strength to turn his head to see Mister Dre with one of his blackened blades in hand. The other was plunged deep into the pile of ash on the hardwood. They were the same swords he used to rescue him.

Peron lifted him up carefully while Selah checked his face for any scratches. But Rowan didn't have time to say thank you. He was too busy observing the footman's white fabric gloves. No, not white. Silver, and made of steel. Had they always been that way? And did they always have a blue ax on their back? It vaguely reminded him of the golden one on Olivius' gloves. Especially when the footman shook his gauntlets. Blue fire engulfed them, changing them from steel back to the pristine white-and-blue fabric.

"What are those things doing here?" Selah asked.

"It's the Barrens, kiddo. Them inqai devils are more ravenous than a pack of wolves. We're in their territory now," Ben answered.

An entire ghost town full of those ugly things. Perhaps Rowan was safer at the orphanage. But thoughts like that only lasted about three seconds.

"Say, Spehrow friend. Think you can put those swords to good use if I open that hatch up there?

The dwarf pointed at the door in the ceiling. A piece of rope was tied onto its knob.

"That depends," Dremos said, yanking his other blade out of the floor. "How soon can you get us to Evermire?

"With the way Sven's driving, I'd say about ten minutes."

"Make it five, and I'll refer your services to Madam Spehrow."

The footman's eyes widened. Rowan was just as shocked as he looked. Was he the only one who didn't know about this Madam Spehrow?

"It'd be a fine honor, friend." Ben gave a slight bow before heading towards the many ropes. He tugged on another piece of twine. It opened the hatch in the ceiling, rolling out a rope ladder and revealing the sky above. "You got five minutes, Sven!" he yelled. "Man your station and get to it!"

"Gettin' to it, Ben," the coachman yelled. "Everybody hold on! Hyah!"

That single *hyah* sped up the caravan at an alarming rate. The change in pace jerked the orphans back to the floor, while Ben and Mister Dre held on. Rowan smelled hints of smoke coming from the footman as he rubbed his gloves together. Blue fire emerged from them, turning the fabric into steel once again. Mister Dre threw the cape from his leather knapsack over his shoulders, pulled his mask over his face, and retracted his swords into their hilts. Ready to head into battle, he climbed the wobbly ladder onto the caravan roof.

Rowan gaped at the brave hunter walking past the open hatch. Then he had a thought, a brave and heroic thought; fighting side by side with a hunter might've worked in his favor. He could brag about it to Linn the Moonstruck and force that Madam Spehrow to find him worthy.

Tss. Tsss, went a soft sound from the knapsack.

Rowan found Sly sneaking out of Mister Dre's unattended bag. As more inqai slammed into the caravan, Rowan stumbled towards the knapsack. His fingers grazed the brown leather, and he snatched it just as the snake hung by one of its handles. The bag's unexpected weight dragged Rowan down.

"Hey Mister Dre, you forgot something," Rowan yelled, pulling the bag. The footman's cold, metal hand held his shoulder.

"Not so fast, kiddo," he said. "We can't have you getting hurt. It's best you stay here with me."

"But he needs his bag. I was just going to give it to him." His gaze flickered up toward the hatch as he lied. So much for that promise.

"Battlefield's no place for a child. Whatever you wanted to do, you won't be doing it now."

Selah's hand rested on Rowan's other shoulder.

"He's right, Rowan," Selah said. She snatched the bag from his grasp. He couldn't believe she was trying to ruin his fun.

"You won't be doing anything…" she smiled, "…without me."

"What?" Peron and the footman blurted. Rowan almost did the same, wondering if Selah had gone insane. But when she threw the bag over her shoulders and climbed the ladder, Rowan realized how serious she was.

"N-now hold on a minute. This is highly unsafe of you, friend," the footman warned, though hardly took any action.

"Perry, we'll be right back." Selah ignored him. "You can stay here with Mister Ben."

"You don't have to tell me twice," Peron quipped, crouching on the floor.

Rowan started climbing behind Selah. Once she made it to the roof, she pulled Rowan to the top and started rummaging through the knapsack.

Rowan scanned the rooftop below the murky sky. There was no sign of monsters on the roof. To his right, the coachman sat driving the caravan. On his left, with his back to him, stood Mister Dre, holding his swords in a fighting stance.

Shriek, went the creatures.

The orphans flinched and yelped, and Mister Dre turned his head toward them. He rolled his eyes in annoyance, then he gripped both swords in one hand and strode over. His stern walk intimidated Rowan more than the inqai did.

"What are you doing up here," he asked through his muffled mask.

"I came up here to help you," Rowan said.

Dremos pinched the bridge of his nose. "You children really are stubborn. It's not safe up here. Go stay with the footman."

"But I don't see any of those monsters, though," Selah said. "If anything, you should be down there instead of up here."

"I know what I'm doing, child. Both of you are too young to be up here. The Barrens are no place for—"

Rowan knew he probably should've listened to Mister Dre, but then a low growl in the distance caught him off guard. From behind the fiendish hunter, a dripping claw scratched along the wooden roof. Another one came into view, lifting its limbs until the head of an inqus bared its fangs at him. He glanced at Mister Dre, who was still prattling on. The inqus' grotesque body mounted the roof. Selah must have noticed too. Her gaze fixed on the monster while she clenched something tightly in her hand.

"Not to mention your lack of weapons," Mister Dre continued. "You can't expect to be a mage with no defenses."

The monster scurried toward the distracted hunter. Before it attacked, Selah revealed a spherical bottle of green liquid and hurled it over Mister Dre's head. Luckily, he ducked in time, and the bottle shattered in the inqus' face. The liquid sizzled along its skin, making it writhe in agony while its form stayed intact. Dremos deployed his weapons, leapt up high, and sliced the inqus in two.

The beast burst into golden ash and floated into the smog. The fiendish hunter landed on his feet and peered at Rowan and Selah.

"That was my last bottle of acid," Mister Dre said bluntly. The orphans shielded Selah's throwing hand; thinking it might preserve her innocence. And if that didn't work, Rowan hoped his pitiful gaze would.

Mister Dre shook his head. "They'll try to climb up here again. Find any weapon worthy enough in that bag. Have Sly be your guide."

He turned his back on them and readied himself for the next beast. Had Rowan heard him correctly? Let Sly be his guide? As in…*the snake?*

He must've spent a long time thinking about it, because the next thing he knew, Sly had wrapped around his arm. He saw Selah digging through the bag and tried snatching it from her.

"Hey, stop," Selah exclaimed, pulling it back. "I threw the acid, so I get the bag. Why don't you worry about the snake?"

"I'm the one who grabbed it first," Rowan countered. "Selah, come on. I can do this myself! You're not even supposed to be he—"

"Rowan, look out!"

A shrieking cry sounded behind the orphans, followed by an inqus leaping from the ground to attack them. In a flash, Selah swung the bag with a grunt and struck the monster, sending it flying back down to the surface.

"I'm not supposed to be *what?*" she asked icily.

Her gutsy demeanor made Rowan stutter.

"I-um… nothing." Her spirit amazed him and slightly scared him.

"Hmph, that's what I thought," she said confidently. "I take the bag; you hold the snake."

As Selah stomped away, Rowan cringed, seeing Sly still spiraling around his arm. He yelled in Selah's direction. "What am I supposed to do with a snake?"

He flinched as Sly hissed, and he watched it swiftly uncoil and extend itself into Rowan's hand. Sly began to glow white, then its grey scales hardened into a smooth hollow metal. Tiny gold symbols spiraled upward from its tail until they reached the top of its head. Sly's glow dimmed, and the symbols transformed into foreign spells. Spells he only recognized from his old book.

"Whoa, magic snake wand," Rowan whispered to himself. His fingers grazed one of the spells. He squinted at a newer-looking one and tried pronouncing it. "*Stree-aht-si?*

Striatsi? What's that supposed to mean?" As soon as he said it, Sly's jaw creaked open, and tiny flickers of lightning came out of it.

Rowan held Sly away from his face as the lightning grew bigger and brighter, bright enough to break through the dense air. Bright enough to shine on a one-limbed inqus clawing toward Rowan's left side. The footman must have done a number on it. The lightning beam, now the size of Rowan's head, fired towards the squirming beast, blasting it off the roof.

Rowan's eyes widened at the stripped wood in front of him, the effect of the shocking spell. He eyed the snake in amazement as hints of smoke rose from its fangs. He had just used a magic wand. A snake wand, but a real magic wand… and nothing exploded or floated away when he used it.

He looked back at Selah, who swung at another monster with fighting fury. But Mister Dre was nowhere to be found, only the blade of one of his swords attached to a bronze chain. It wasn't until Rowan heard monsters in agony from down below that he investigated. He peered over the roof's edge to find Mister Dre leaping on top of the ravenous beasts. His swords punctured their forms, as he jumped from one beast to another, leaving them defeated with shrieks and ashes drifting through the Barrens.

He's so cool, Rowan thought.

Mister Dre's slaying had reduced the number of inqai after them. Five… eight…nine left. They could still make it out. Perhaps, using Sly, Rowan could cast his spell again.

"Uh…*striatsi*," Rowan chanted uncertainly. But Sly's jaw produced another lightning sphere. It grew enormous size so quickly, Rowan almost dropped the snake. Fortunately, he gripped it tight enough and aimed at the farthest beasts.

Zooom-CRACK, went the snake wand.

The beam shot out with such strength that Rowan almost lost his footing. An explosion landed between two inqai, incinerating both and causing damaged to others in front. Rowan couldn't believe his eyes. He'd done nothing like that before.

Rowan aimed the wand again. "*Striatsi*," he said confidently.

Another inqus leaped towards him as the lightning appeared. Another blast and the monster crumbled to ash. He chanted the spell again and again until the wand felt warm in his hand. *Striatsi*, he kept saying, even as fewer inqai were in view.

Another explosion slew his target, and Rowan shouted from the exciting thrill. He turned to Selah, hoping to gain her praise as usual. Instead, he gasped when he saw her laying on the roof, struggling to keep a ferocious inqus. She was pressing the knapsack with all her strength into the monster's throat, grunting and straining. The inqus' black saliva was dripping on her face.

"Stay away from her," Rowan cried, filled with fear and rage. He grabbed both Selah and the monster's attention, as he directed the wand at them.

"Rowan, wait," Selah yelled. "Don't aim it at—"

"*Striatsi!*"

Out of nowhere, Mister Dre's shoved the wand away from Selah and the inqus, and out towards the Barrens. The blast vaporized an abandoned building on the side of the road. Mister Dre unsheathed his swords again.

He pushed another button on the hilt, and a blade with a chain lunged forward. It struck the inqus right between the eyes; it screamed as Mister Dre pulled the chain back with one hand. The swift movement turned the inqus to a pile of ashes. Selah scooted away from the remains before they fell into her mouth.

Rowan ran over to help Selah to her feet. "You alright, Se?" he asked, feeling guilty.

Selah's face briefly twisted into a scowl but changed into a smile straining along her tusks. "Yeah, Ro. I'm perfectly fine," she affirmed sarcastically.

Something in Rowan's gut told him she was definitely not fine.

"That was quite foolish of you both," Mister Dre said, walking towards them. His steps were slow and menacing as he retracted the blade into its hilt. "If I had known you'd put yourselves in danger, I would've sent you back."

As he stopped in front of them, Rowan felt the air leave his lungs. He glanced around, trying to think of an excuse. As he did so, he realized he couldn't hear any more screeching. Which must have meant one thing.

"Well…good thing you didn't," Rowan said, nervously smiling. "Or… or else we wouldn't have defeated those…inqus things."

Mister Dre almost argued, but then his eyes scanned over the dry stillness of the Barrens. He pulled his mask down and sighed. "Perhaps you're right, child."

Rowan exhaled in relief. At least he had done one thing right today.

"So…we actually defeated them all?" Selah asked.

"No. They're still out there. But we defeated the ones that were around." He grabbed his bag from Selah and lifted it over his shoulders. He took Sly from Rowan and watched the spells on his scales trickle away into stardust. Its solid, silver form softened into its scaly one, as it spiraled up Mister Dre's sleeve.

"Thank goodness Sly's a charitable familiar," he continued, gently placing the snake into his bag. "If Madam Spehrow found anyone else using him, you wouldn't hear the end of it."

Rowan scrunched his brows. *Why would she need a familiar?*

HONK!!! went an interrupting noise.

It had come out of nowhere. Soon, it made itself present, a faraway low, blaring sound. Rowan jolted when he heard it, and then his eyes looked to the sky. The dense smog melted to reveal a royal blue with hints of maroon at the base. Only a sliver of sunlight left.

HONK!!!

Rowan squinted past an upcoming forest, wondering if that was where the sound was coming from. Perhaps it came from beyond the lush trees they had almost driven through. The thin grass patches slowly but surely thickened as the horses clopped along. Soon, the travelers left the ominous Barrens behind and were enveloped in vast green forest.

HOONKK!!!

The sound blared again much louder this time than the last, followed by Sven the coachman's voice. "One minute 'til arrival. Slowing down."

Rowan had forgotten how fast they were actually going; it was quite a relief to slow down after all that had happened. Still, he had to admit it really was quite an adventure.

The group heard footsteps on the roof. Ben, the footman came up from the fight below wearing a rosy smile. His steel gauntlets had turned back to regular gloves, and he straightened his suit as he walked over to Mister Dre.

"Sounds like the ferry's arriving a bit earlier than usual," he said.

"It appears we will also," Mister Dre agreed.

Rowan didn't know what a *ferry* was. The way he said it, it probably wasn't like the ones in storybooks. But he figured that wherever that ferry was, so was the town of Evermire.

"Is it safe to come up yet?" Peron asked, poking his head out of the hatch to inspect the scene.

Rowan and Selah ran over and helped their cowardly friend. Once he stood with them, Peron stared at his new surroundings— the ruined caravan roof, the strange forest. He looked at Rowan in disbelief.

"What's that for?" Rowan asked.

"What on earth did you do?"

"Peron, you should've fought with us. I had a wand! A magic wand, well… a snake that turned into one. But it also gave me lightning spells! Ooh, there was this one monster with no legs, and I blasted it out of nowhere! And then Selah, she used Mister Dre's bag to bash their heads in!"

Peron looked wearily at Selah. "Not you too."

"What did you expect, Perry," Selah shrugged coyly. "Someone had to keep him from hurting himself."

Peron simply ran his hands through his hair in defeat. "Great. Now both of my friends are insane."

"Reaching the border, Ben," the coachman yelled.

"Ride on through, Sven! Evermire straight ahead," the footman replied, stepping forward.

Rowan walked around the roof, searching for this shining town of Evermire. But he saw no streets of gold, nor magic on every corner. Just trees. More grass. Some more trees. And a couple out-of-place hills on either side.

The only majestic thing he saw was a wide stone archway reigning from on high. At its peak, loomed bold, curly letters around its arch — *E V E R M I R E*— with bits of green shrub between its crevices.

"I never tire of this part," Dremos exhaled, looking at the archway.

"What part," Rowan interrupted. But his question was soon answered. Once the horses passed through the archway, a mix of lavender rays swirled inside the entry. Then the coachman made it pass by. When the light went through Rowan, it sent shivers down his body.

Rowan saw Mister Dre smile after the light passed over him. As if a storm had settled in the back of his mind.

"You didn't finish your story," Rowan said.

"Pardon," Mister Dre asked.

"Your Linn the Moonstruck story. You left off somewhere between him...*her* running away and almost using her scepter."

Mister Dre smirked and relaxed on the roof. "That's quite the memory you have, child. It'll serve you well one day."

He patted a spot next to him, requesting Rowan to sit. A welcoming gesture that made Rowan feel…safe. Only a few grownups made him feel that way. He sat beside Mister Dre.

"Very well. Yes, she was at the edge of town with a scaled scepter in hand. She prayed a silent prayer, plunged it into the ground, and a force of the border pushed the Legion down. It disintegrated any inqus or Legionnaire who dared to touch it, preventing them and the inqai from entering Evermire's borders. So, the Legion of Khallus fled from the town into the outskirts of Nidas we call the Barrens. It's the only place those devils can roam freely and not jeopardize our safety. All thanks to Linn the Moonstruck and the Ataxia."

Rowan looked back at the gate they'd come through and finally understood.

"Wow," he whispered. "That's amazing! So, they saved an entire island and finally got the praise they deserved, right? The celebration for them must've been huge!"

"Quite the opposite. Some parts of the island were far too angry to have a celebration, especially in Evermire."

"What? Why," Rowan asked, disappointed.

"Some citizens wanted to banish the Ataxia for life. Something about ruining Evermire's reputation and what not. Fortunately, through the efforts of one woman, Linn and the Ataxia were praised and welcomed by the people."

Madam Spehrow, Rowan thought. Who else could it have been?

"She became enamored by the Ataxia's bravery and skills. So much so, she even persuaded their skeptical town leader to reconsider a better solution. One that didn't involve banishment."

"What did he do?"

"He made a deal with Madam Spehrow and the Ataxia, *'If you can promise me the border stays in place, you are welcome to come and go as you please.'* And so, the Ataxia entrusted the border to Madam Spehrow in Evermire, preventing the townsfolk from any danger caused by the Legion of Khallus."

"So that's why she's so famous? She keeps everyone safe."

"Perhaps. Or maybe it's just the tavern that everybody loves her for," Mister Dre said sarcastically. "Still think she's old and mean?"

Rowan almost said something but clamped his lips tight. He wanted to avoid that argument. He would keep that question in mind, however.

As Rowan pouted, Mister Dre rose and looked out beyond the forest. "I'm sure you'll be the judge of that. Whether it be Madam Spehrow's comforting light or the lights coming in from the streetlamps."

That's a weird way to end a sentence, Rowan thought as he stared at him. Suddenly, he felt warmth on his skin. It wasn't like the heat of the sun, it made him feel at ease. His eyes glimmered upon the town that lay ahead.

"Selah, Peron, and Rowan. Welcome to Evermire."

Chapter 10

The Spehrow's Nest

*E*vermire, Rowan's town of magic and victory, had
the strongest smell of fish in the air. He hadn't expected it and
he tried hiding his scrunched-up nose from Mister Dre. He
looked around hoping to distract himself from the smell and
found something that caught his attention.

Streetlamps. Long, black street-lamps with bulbs at the
top. Bulbs filled with soft, warm lighting shining everywhere on
the brown cobblestone. It was the kind of light Rowan could
sleep under, and they made the dark less scary than before.

Rows of lamps lined down a short hill, shining on the
town's many homes and buildings. Most were older buildings,
made of worn wood and grey brick, with circular windows. The
townsfolk impressed the orphans with ornamented paintings
and decorated shrubs on their balconies.

In Faegan, the townspeople stared at the giant caravan
like hair out of place. But in Evermire, the people ignored it, as
if a nearly destroyed caravan on the road was an everyday
occurrence. Instead, the people were more focused on each
other, gathering in work and conversation. Dwarves spoke with
orcs, humans laughed along with goat-legged men, and many

other creatures walked the pavements as if they had been there their whole lives.

Rowan did, however, spot a particular creature at the edge of a building they passed by: a frozen stone figure with wings, slanted eyes, and snarling teeth. He saw the same creature on the ground. And another on top of an apple cart. And one in front of a large tent being set up. Evermire certainly wasn't majestic, but so far, it was pretty weird.

"Well, what do you think?" the footman asked.

"This is Evermire," Peron asked, gawking at the shining city. "It looks so different from what I imagined. You made it sound like it was all destroyed, Mister Dre."

"Oh, that was a long time ago," the footman answered. "Ever since the Battle for Nidas, this town's been putting in a lot of effort to clean it up." They turned a corner, and the footman pointed down. "For example, you see this bridge we're on?" The children looked, noticing the ocean flowing below it. "Wasn't always here a couple decades ago. People would've tried jumping across and take a mighty deep dive. Now it's a path everyone can use, all thanks to Ataxia members like Spehrow friend."

He motioned to Mister Dre, who chuckled at the praise. Rowan's eyes grew wide while Selah and Peron looked at Mister Dre in awe. It all made so much sense now.

"So that's why you know so much about the Ataxia," Rowan connected. "You were one of them all along."

"Would've helped if we knew that beforehand," Selah said. "I could've asked you to tell me stories about the Dreaming Nova."

"As I said, Madam Spehrow is a much better storyteller than me," Mister Dre said. "You'll just have to ask her yourself."

Rowan didn't know why Mister Dre hated the attention. If he was the fiendish hunter, he would've asked for more praise. But all of that would come for him some day, Rowan believed; he'd just have to be patient and train his hardest with Linn at his side.

The caravan turned another corner, where the dark blue ocean met the gaze of the awestruck orphans. A sliver of sunset reflected off the water as it finally dipped below the horizon. A large white ferry with a spinning light sailed towards the shore. Rowan had never seen a real boat before. It might be fun to ride one day.

"Well, thank Caelum, friends! The Spehrow's Nest is in our sights," Ben the footman cried.

Rowan shifted his view to the beautifully lit tavern to his right. As he studied it, the surrounding buildings became nonexistent. The tavern's polished wood glistened under the bright torches burning on either side. Its wide shingled roof contrasted with the other buildings' extra housing.

When everyone climbed down the hatch to exit through the caravan door, Rowan ran out in front, if only to be the first to step foot on Evermire's soil. He noticed two double doors at the entrance. One door swung open to reveal a small dwarf leaving the tavern for the striped tent right beside it. A different group of people entered through the other door, and they weren't just any people: they were adventurers and mages alike.

He had to go in. He needed to go in. But before he could step towards the entrance, Mister Dre tugged his shoulder back. He almost protested, until he turned to his left to see the ferry docking at a bay downhill.

HONK!!! went the ferry boat.

Scores of people traveled up the bay. Some carried fish in nets and wore grungy overalls, while others wore fine clothing and hunting gear as they walked past the Spehrow's Nest. As the crowds pressed through, two male elves in overalls and sun hats locked eyes with Mister Dre.

"*Pera Kal*, Spehrow's Eye," one of them said in their language. "Say, wanna share any hints on Madam's new quest?"

New quest? Did Madam Spehrow run some sort of guild as well as a tavern?

"You know she never tells me anything," Mister Dre said. "*Auergo*, I'll be seeing you."

"Say hi to the missus for us," the other one teased, before walking through the tavern doors.

Once the traffic died down, Mister Dre and the children walked to the front entrance, where a hanging sign below the roof read **THE SPEHROW'S NEST** in big, bold letters.

"Well, is there anything we should know about first," Selah asked.

The fiendish hero crooked his neck to the children and knelt to their level. Rowan noted his expression. No sly looks, no mystery behind his eyes; only seriousness, which worried Rowan even more.

"Forgive me, children," Mister Dre said. "I will not be joining you all."

"But you said you would go in with us," Rowan whined. How could this hero go back on his word so quickly?

"And I would have, if an emergency had not come up at the last second. To answer your question, Selah, there are a few things you should know before going inside." Rowan huffed at his excuse. But he supposed some support was better than no support. "The first thing, be careful around the patrons in the tavern. While some are hospitable, there are those who let their arrogance get the better of them. They can be quite unruly. Especially around newcomers."

Rrring, went the tavern bell.

The double doors swung open to reveal a skittish human holding a broom and a large orc gripping a wooden pipe.

"Well, well. If it ain't good ol' Red Eyes, come to grace us with his presence," the green orc bellowed in a thick accent. "Hey, Spehrow, tell this little shrimp here I ain't no cheat. I paid good money for me and my table."

Mister Dre massaged his brows, as if this argument had happened one too many times.

"We know that sir," the skinny man trembled. "But M-Mistress has strict rules about *s-smobac* fumes in her tavern. Either s-sit at the booths or-."

"I didn't even ligh' it yet!"

"Thank you, Toby," Mister Dre greeted the human, before looking back at the orc. "You know her rules, comrade. Take it outside until you're finished."

The orc growled at Toby before stomping away. The human swiftly fled back into the tavern. The orphans looked back at Mister Dre, stunned by the scene.

"Try not to engage in their behavior," Mister Dre continued. "Second, treat Madam and her staff with the utmost respect. You wouldn't want to make a bad impression right off the bat. I'd suggest having your friends guide you with that part."

Rowan frowned. What was that supposed to mean?

"We'll help as much as we can, sir," Peron said.

"In that case, I wish you all the best," Mister Dre said, rising to leave.

Rowan's nervousness softened his frown. Many questions plagued his mind. But one stuck out the most as the fiendish hunter turned his back on them. "Mister Dre, wait," Rowan cried.

The hunter turned his head.

Rowan nervously itched his arm before speaking.

"Do you…do you think she'll find me worthy?" He let the question linger for a moment. "I just…what if I mess everything up? What if I came here just for her to send me away?"

Mister Dre stroked his chin, seeming weary at the questions. "I cannot tell you whether she will or won't. That's not for me to decide." He paused, and Rowan felt disheartened. "But I know it only takes one step to do the hard thing first," he continued. "So, face your fears with dignity and respect, and you might find yourself in the situation you desire."

He's so cool, Rowan thought. All while nodding his head and whispering, "Yes, Mister Dre."

A soft smile curled Dremos' lips before he took out a folded up piece of paper and gave it to Peron. "Give this to

Madam Spehrow when you see her. It is for her eyes and her eyes alone, understand?"

Peron nodded, looking serious.

Mister Dre fluffed Rowan's coils gently and walked off with one last greeting. "I'd go in now if I were you. Mages hate to be kept waiting."

The children waved farewell as he roamed through the townspeople, leaving them gazing at the large door.

Rowan tried swallowing the frog in his throat, and his hands shook as he reached for the door.

"You think you're ready, Rowa?" Peron asked, holding the doorknob.

Rowan let out a brief sigh. "I think so."

Selah grabbed his hand with a bright grin. "We're right here with you," she affirmed.

With that, Rowan opened the double doors; ready for whatever adventure waited for him.

Although they didn't know it, their caravan had taken off just as they went inside. Ben the footman and Sven the coachmen sat beside each other, and Ben yelled out towards the tavern. "Good luck, kiddos! You're all gonna do great things someday. We just know it!"

Rowan, Selah, and Peron became entranced by the large chandelier hanging from the ceiling. Soft firelight reflected off their eyes, and radiant candles lit the entire tavern from above. Walls plastered with red and brown brick complimented the wooden accents spanning from the first and second floor. Green vines with smaller bulbs decorated the wooden pillars down to the stained hardwood floor.

"Watch where you step," Peron said, grimacing at the some of the stains.

"Can't you let me have a moment for once?" Rowan groaned.

"I'm just saying. You don't want to end up with some mystery under your shoe."

Rowan rolled his eyes. Of course, Peron would complain about something like that. Compared to the orphanage, this was the second-tidiest place he'd ever seen; the first being the Hedgethorn Residence. Besides, sometimes a messy floor meant more adventurers celebrating their victories.

The children maneuvered through the scattered round tables, observing the different parties in their natural habitat. And oh, there were many. Both floors were decked out with creatures from all walks of life. Rowan saw a table of five indulging in ruthless card games on the second floor. Their defeated yelling didn't seem to deter the other patrons, like the female party of mages who shamelessly flaunted their spells and artifacts. A blue-shirted woman on the ground floor cried out, "Order down," as she walked around with a massive tray of food. She set it on the coffee table next to the fireplace, where a party of seven cheered as they smoked their pipes.

Rowan drooled over the plates of cooked fish and meat pies crowded around every table. The scent of each savory dish overloaded his senses. He found a dwarven woman ready to eat an enormous piece of chocolate cake. She spotted Rowan staring and frowned at him as she chomped on it greedily.

He shrunk in embarrassment, as the rest of the woman's table gave him and his friends strange, jeering looks.

Soon, more sets of eyes were cast in his direction, making Rowan feel like a mouse in a den of lions. In a place where he should have felt more confident, he only felt anxious. Especially once the murmurs started.

What are children doing in the Nest? Not a place for tykes like them. Is Madam running a daycare now?

"I hear them too, Ro," Selah said quietly, still holding his hand. "Just don't let them get to you and you'll be fine."

He took Selah's advice to heart, advancing toward the wooden counter in the middle of the tavern. Empty high stools sat in front of it. Three men dressed in white lounged about as they chatted and sipped hot drinks. The orphans sat on the empty stools, their seats swiveling as they rested. Rowan resisted the urge to spin in his chair. They began eavesdropping on the three men's conversation.

"Hah, Spehrow's Nest, indeed. Torrence, I still think we should've gone to the Council for this. Even the guilds would've been tolerable," the long-bearded man complained. "Why come to a tavern for a quest when the owner herself won't even tell us what it is? Where is she, anyway?"

"Patience, Avion," the purple-skinned fiend named Torrence corrected. "It might seem strange, but Madam Spehrow has ways of revealing what you most desire. The highest guilds are aware of her reputation. I'm sure even the Council hasn't outmatched her yet."

"Still, only giving the quest to one party," the golden-haired one added. "That seems highly unreasonable, considering how dangerous I heard it is. It seems wrong making us go through such lengths to claim it."

The laid-back Torrence shrugged. "When has danger ever frightened us, Heziah? Besides, I find her little competitions to be intriguing. I suppose we'll find out soon enough."

Rowan stopped eavesdropping and contemplated the conversation. What kind of quest was she preparing for them? He thought about it until something different and more fascinating caught his eye.

He squinted at the polished countertop and traced the knife engravings scattered throughout.

THE AXEBREAKERS WERE HERE

Here Lies the Band O'Bards

The Elven Arcane

The Underground Live Among Us

Rowan recognized those names; he'd read them a hundred times in the orphanage library. He turned to the purple-skinned fiend just to be sure.

"E-excuse me, sir," Rowan said. "Are all these names different adventurers?"

"Of course, young man. The finest parties of the past," he affirmed. "Signatures of those who've served alongside Madam Spehrow and her causes."

"Rowa, look up there," Peron whispered as he pointed.

Rowan followed his finger to the top shelf. On the wall hung a framed black-and-white photograph of The Spehrow's Nest exterior with stoic adventurers standing in front of it. An antler-crowned elf gripping a wooden staff. A tall, muscular orc with grey trousers and a boulder under his arm. A dark-skinned woman with bubble-like hair wearing a fancy dress and holding a violin. Another woman with long, wavy hair, an eyepatch, and a flowing robe. And a familiar fiend with a dark cape, holding a pair of black short swords.

Rowan recognized those swords; he knew their owner too. His eyes skimmed to the bottom of the frame, where a gold plate read *In Honor of the Ataxia*. He spun in his seat, smiling wide.

"The Ataxia! It's the Ataxia," he exclaimed, startling a few customers. Peron and Selah were just as shocked as he was.

"No way," Peron said.

"Do you know what this means, Ro?" Selah asked, smiling.

"It's the Ataxia," Rowan repeated. "It's Linn the Moonstruck! I'm about to meet Linn the Moonstruck!"

"Who's meetin' who now? I can hardly work over this racket" a voice said behind them.

Rowan's chair suddenly stopped twirling on its own. Or at least that's what he thought before a hand spun his stool around, where he faced a frowning woman with a mole on her pale cheek. He flinched in disgust at the bird's-nest hairstyle, long tan skirt, and striped, blue top. It was the same woman who served food at the fireplace.

"Sorry, madam," Selah said. "We didn't mean to disturb anyone. We were just really excited about—"

"To-BY," the woman screeched. Soon, the skinny boy from outside rushed to her side with his broom. "What have you been doing? Who let them in here?"

The children cringed at her squawking tone. Surely this wasn't Madam Spehrow.

"A-apologies, Miss Amori," Toby said shakily, smoothing back his shaggy brown hair. "I guess I s-should've told you this. Master D-Dremos brought them h-here earlier."

"Did he now?" Miss Amori looked taken aback and dropped her scowl. "We don't allow children in the Nest after dark. You dearies lost or something? Where are your parents?"

Selah and Peron pushed Rowan forward to answer her many questions. *Traitors.*

"Um…we don't have any, madam," Rowan said under his breath. "We…we heard that Linn the Moonstruck would be here so—"

"So, you wanted to see Madam Spehrow," Miss Amori finished in a snarky tone. "That's what they're all here for."

Rowan shot up. "No, I'm here to meet Linn the Moonstruck. She's the answer to my problems."

"Madam Spehrow's the one you go to, dearie. No getting past her. Either accept that or go home."

Rowan's anger almost boiled over. He could feel his friends trying to calm him, but it didn't work. "That's not fair! We came all this way and you're just gonna kick us out?"

"If that's how it has to be. Or are you gonna make me choose for you?"

Rowan grumbled at her bitter words. He hadn't escaped some awful place just to be thrown out of this one. He climbed up on his stool and stood on the counter, looking down at the unmoved woman and raised his voice in a tantrum. "I'm not leaving here until I meet her! Tell your stupid Madam Spehrow lady to bring me Linn herself!"

"My, my, my," a voice purred behind Rowan. A chill ran down his spine. He'd never heard a voice so soft yet so menacing. Curiosity forced him to turn around and view a new face.

"You must be a new seafarer in town," the voice said again. It belonged to a bronze skinned woman dressed in a green blouse and a long black skirt. Long brown dreadlocks adorned her crown in a low bun. She rested her head on the back of her hands while gazing at Rowan amusingly through the gold coins of her eyes. Her coy smirk ate at Rowan's fiery facade.

"A what?" Rowan scoffed.

"A seafarer. Like a sailor, dear," she repeated in a poised tone. "Or maybe I'm mistaken. A boy like you, must think he's some sort of prince; a *little* prince at that."

The woman's eyes glinted brightly at the word *little*. It made Rowan frown even harder.

"I'm not a prince or a…sea-sailor or whatever. I'm a mage. A really powerful one at that."

"A mere child, a mage? Well, that just can't be."

"What's that supposed to mean," Rowan said.

The woman tucked her locks behind her ears, displaying the pointed tips. "In my tavern, you need to be one of three things: an adventurer, a nobleman, or a seafarer. For those are the only men who can speak disrespectfully to me and face…limited consequences."

Her smirk faded into an eerie stare, while Rowan's frown melted into shock…and a bit of embarrassment. He swallowed a giant lump in his throat. Selah and Peron's eyes widened as they realized who Rowan had just yelled at.

"You… must be Madam Spehrow," Rowan finally uttered.

She bowed her head in affirmation. "And who, might I ask, is demanding to see Linn the Moonstruck?"

Rowan froze at her question, then glanced over his shoulder to see dozens of patrons glaring at him. After the meltdown he'd had, Rowan didn't know whether to hide or beg on his knees for forgiveness. Instead, his voice cracked as he made his case.

"I-I…my name is Rowan, Miss…Madam Spehrow," he started terribly. "Rowan the Brave is what they call me. I'm a mage who wishes to learn more about magic." As he continued to speak, he felt himself growing taller with each word. "And I think the only way for me to improve is by getting help from the Ataxia; Linn the Moonstruck, *statistically*."

"Specifically," Peron whispered.

"Specifically," Rowan said quickly. "I…I've read all her stories and think she is the best in all of Nidas. In all of Mydion. All of Pelle, actually. I want her to be my teacher, and I want to be her ward. I was told that I had to go through you to get to her, but the thing is… I don't want to."

"Is that right?" Madam Spehrow asked. She lifted a pierced brow, like she wanted to know more. It boosted Rowan's confidence.

"Yes, it is," he exclaimed in full volume. He rolled his shoulders back; sure he was giving the best performance of his life. "And so, oh Tavern Spehrow Lady, I request you move aside and take me to see the Moonstruck Mage herself! For I, Rowan the Brave, am ready to follow in her footsteps and learn her ways of spell-casting!"

He ended his speech with a bow, like he did in all his performances. Selah and Peron were usually the first to applaud, but instead he heard both of them groaning softly. The rest of the room had fallen silent enough for crickets to chirp their grating song. Not a single adventurer gave even the most modest of applause.

"I see," Madam Spehrow murmured. After a slight pause, she raised her voice. "Then rise, oh Rowan the Brave." He did as she asked and studied her. Her face and perfect posture displayed elegance. "I've heard your words, young mage. Have no fear, for the end of your quest for knowledge and power is nigh."

Rowan read the word "nigh" in one of his stories before; he thought it meant "almost there." She smiled at him, so he must've been right. He grinned back brightly.

"But before I 'move aside,' I must ask you a question."

"Of course," he said with a hero's posture. "I'll answer any and all questions."

"If you wish to become a mage, what oath do you plan to take?"

Rowan's eyes widened with the smile still stuck on his face. "A-an oath?"

"Yes, dear. What shall your oath be?"

There was that oath again. He'd read so many stories; why was he just hearing about it today? He looked at Selah and Peron, who shrugged. "Um-well," he started. "It'd probably be... to use magic for the greater good!"

"Interesting," Madam Spehrow said. "The greater good of the innocent or for yourself?"

"The innocent...I think." Rowan muttered that last phrase to himself. As he stuttered awkwardly, a sea of groans targeted his back.

"Well, boy, which one is it?" a gruff voice shouted. Another customer, Rowan presumed.

"I... it's not... I don't know... I just didn't think about—"

A smack on the counter cut off his response.

"Do you hear this child, brethren?" Madam Spehrow called out to the crowds. "He insults my tavern and my workers, demands I take him to the Moonstruck Mage, and can't even answer a simple question concerning his oath." She placed her palms on the counter and leaned towards him. Even though he was looking down at her, Madam Spehrow's sharp gaze made her seem twenty times taller. "I'd be all the more offended… if you weren't so hilariously cute."

Rowan heard a stream of laughter. He finally turned to watch in horror as the patrons howled in his direction. He saw Peron and Selah, holding back their laughter as well.

"Hey! I'm not cute," Rowan exclaimed in frustration. "Stop it! I'm not cute! I'm a brave mage adventurer! I'm not supposed to be cute!"

"Even if you're not supposed to be," Madam Spehrow said. "You're acting more like yourself now."

He turned back to her, irritated. "Oh yeah, and what's that?"

"Like a child." She chuckled. "A child… with large amounts of ambition. Just the adventurer we need nowadays. You'd fit right in with these fools. Isn't that right, brethren?"

The patrons' cheering howls and banging mugs echoed around the spacious tavern. Where was this kind of applause when he made his speech?

"Listen, lady—"

"Oh, relax, dear. We do this with every new soul who flies into the Nest. We mean no harm in our words. Just ask Toby. Now, why don't you sit down before you hurt yourself, and I'll make you some tea."

Rowan almost launched another response, but tea sounded really nice. He returned to his seat next to Peron, grumbling to himself, while Madam Spehrow and the patrons went about their business.

"Cheer up, Rowa. You'll get 'em next time," Peron said, patting his back. Rowan heard him stifle a snicker.

"Shut up," Rowan spat.

"We said we're here to help if you needed it," Selah said as she smiled. She looked like she just finished laughing."

"Alright, sure. I should have asked for your help." He bumped his head on the countertop in shame. "Ugh, I can't believe I just did that! I want to crawl under a rock and die."

"Surely, you won't do that. Not without having your tea first," Madam Spehrow said. She displayed a tray of wooden mugs on the counter. Rowan watched the steam fog up the green trim around it. How did she make it so fast?

Selah and Peron gladly took drinks from the tray. Rowan grimaced at Madam Spehrow's politeness. He was still not over how she embarrassed him like that. He took the drink anyway.

The children sipped their tea. One sip became two. Two sips became three. Until the children set down their empty mugs, satisfied with their warm drink.

"Well," Madam chuckled.

"You must be a mind reader," Peron said. "How did you know strawberry was my favorite? I didn't even know they made that kind of tea."

"She didn't make strawberry tea," Rowan argued. "She made lemon tea. Yours must've been too sour."

"Please, you're both wrong," Selah said. "She obviously made it with chocolate. Why would she mix lemon into it?"

They couldn't all be right. "What kind of tea did you make," Rowan asked.

"I made nothing," Madam Spehrow said. "Your minds are the ones who desired such cravings. I simply put a bag of tea leaves into hot boiling water. But if you like it so much, I'll have to use it again."

"So, like, it's some sort of magic… mystery tea or something," Peron asked.

Madam Spehrow tapped her tea kettle and winked. "House specialty, dear. I'm glad you enjoyed it."

A magic mystery tea. This woman couldn't possibly have made something so tasty. But if Linn the Moonstruck made these tea leaves, it'd be a much different story. He gladly held out his cup for more.

"Now, I've officially met this Rowan the Brave, but not his companions," Madam Spehrow said as she poured more tea. "Pray, what are your names?"

Selah hesitated before she spoke. "My name is Selah, Madam. This is Peron. And of course, you've met our friend, Rowan. A pleasure to meet you."

"Well, the pleasure is all mine. What a lovely greeting you gave, Miss Selah. You must've been raised to be quite the young lady." Selah hid her smile as she bashfully twirled her curls.

"So, Selah, Peron, and Rowan," Madam Spehrow said, wiping an empty mug, "tell me, how old are you three?"

"We're all twelve, madam," Peron answered.

"And already you've been told exciting tales about Linn and the Ataxia." She held the mug at eye-level, but her eyes darted right at them. "What have you heard?"

Rowan finished the rest of his drink. But her curious stare made the tea in his stomach evaporate.

"We, um... heard about how they found the border," Peron said. "And that Linn the Moonstruck fought an entire inqus army by herself."

"Unfortunately, everyone and their familiar has heard that story," she proclaimed sarcastically. "Come now, there must be more riveting tales to tell."

Rowan watched Peron's ears turn red from embarrassment. What story could Rowan tell to pique her interest? "Um…there was one story about a giant… *muffled* lizard. The one Linn the Moonstruck defeated with her scepter."

She smiled at the counter for a moment. "If memory serves me right, it was a *mufagio* lizard that changed shape to its surroundings. Expose it to enough light and it cowers away, much easier to defeat."

"So, it *is* true," Peron exclaimed. "What about Thierric of Turphyme? Did he really split the ground and make his enemies fall to their deaths?"

"Who, Terry? Goodness no! That story is highly exaggerated. Sure, he buried them under a trench, but he only kept them in there for a day or two."

"And Clascia Valdi? What about her?" Selah added. "I read that her music could hypnotize people. Is she here now?"

"Oh, I'm sure she's out wandering her way across town. Shame she hardly visits with her tour and all."

Mister Dre said they visited each other. *Good, at least one of them was there. All I need to do is look for the right person,* Rowan thought gleefully.

"I know the Ataxia has many stories written about them, but I must say," Madam Spehrow said, "you all know more information than any admirer I've met. Were there any books ever written about the border?"

"No, madam, we just heard about that story today," Peron stated.

"Really, from whom?"

"The man who brought us here."

"There are many men on this island, dear. You'll need to be more specific."

"Oh…alright." By the looks of it, Peron didn't know how to respond. "He's, uh, he's a fiend…kind of like me. Only uh, his skin was darker. A-and he wore darker clothes too, I think. What else?"

"His name was Mister Dre. At least that's what he said we could call him," Selah added.

"Mister Dre," the woman repeated. "As in Mister Dremos, I presume?"

"Yes, madam," Peron answered before grabbing something out of his pocket. "He said this note was for you and you only."

Peron gave it to Madam Spehrow. When she unfolded it, she read it with a few smirks and scoffs, every so often glancing at the orphans. When she finished reading, she sighed a long and tired sigh.

"Of course, he'd do something like this," Madam Spehrow mumbled. She placed the note in her black apron pocket and straightened her posture. "You said you wish for Linn the Moonstruck to be your teacher?"

"That's what I've been telling you," Rowan confirmed.

"Has he told you everything about the Moonstruck Mage?"

Rowan almost replied, but the more he thought about it, the more he realized that all his information came from stories. "Not quite…everything," he murmured.

"I see. So, he must've left out the part about *her* oath."

The children shot glances at one another. "What was her oath?"

"In short, if you wish to become her ward, she will only refuse you."

Rowan was shocked. Mister Dre never mentioned that. "What are you saying?"

"I'm saying," Madam Spehrow replied. "Linn the Moonstruck took an oath to never take up a ward for the rest of her days. I'm sorry, Rowan, but I'm afraid she cannot be your teacher."

Chapter 11

Stories from a Lady Bird

The earth stood still. Or at least that's how Rowan felt after hearing Madam Spehrow's news.

"I don't believe it," Selah said softly. "A mage never teaching magic? But she's a mage; why would she make an oath like that?"

Madam Spehrow sighed, as if it were a hard question to answer. "People make oaths for different reasons."

"What were her reasons?" Peron asked.

She paused again. Another hard question. "She doesn't like to talk about it." She put away her tea set and cleaned the counter, not giving any further explanation.

A thousand thoughts scrambled Rowan's mind. If Linn the Moonstruck didn't adopt any wards, then why was he here? He could've stayed in Faegan with the dwarves if he had known about her oath. But based on all the books he read of Linn the Moonstruck's trials, what Madam Spehrow said didn't make sense.

"No," Rowan said softly, shaking his head.

"Pardon?" Madam Spehrow overheard.

He said it louder. "No! I don't believe you. A mage like her wouldn't just give up something like that. That's not the Linn the Moonstruck I know."

"How can you know a person when you've never met them, dear?"

"I just do, alright! And I'll know even more once you take me to her."

Madam Spehrow chuckled at him in disbelief. "What makes you think I'm going to take you to her?"

"What?"

She tilted her head again, as if she had called him naïve without saying it. "I meant what I said back there. You're awfully ambitious. But ambition can only get you so far, thinking you can demand to see the Ataxia after the scene you made."

"If I didn't have to meet you, I never would've made a scene in the first place," Rowan grumbled.

"Rowan, stop," Peron whispered. "You're not helping yourself. You know, Mister Dre said this would happen. Don't mess it up now." He looked at Madam Spehrow and said, "Madam, please. What if he could meet another Ataxia member? Maybe after you see his magic, you could judge whether he's worthy or not."

"Oh, I don't judge mages based on their talent. I judge based on their stature, how they present themselves." She locked eyes with Rowan. "And you, dear child, have not presented yourself worthy at all."

Words like that would've easily made Rowan weep. But he didn't. He merely thought that if he stared her down, it would make him more intimidating.

She didn't seem to be intimidated, though, as she said in her pompous voice, "Take my advice, Rowan the Brave. Before you learn an inkling of magic, learn to have some manners like your friends here. Now, if you'd excuse me, I have a tavern to run."

Madam Spehrow politely greeted the men in white before she left the distraught children behind.

"Don't worry, Ro," Selah said disheateningly. "We'll find you another teacher around here."

"Yeah, and maybe an actual home," Peron grumbled.

He and Selah stood, ready to head for the exit. They couldn't just leave yet. Not before getting the chance to impress Linn the Moonstruck. If not his speech or his story knowledge, how else could he prove he was worthy? Then Rowan had a thought, a crazy and desperate thought. He saw Madam Spehrow greeting guests at a few other tables. If he wanted to do it, he had to do it right then and there.

He got up from his stool, stomped over to her, and gazed at her back in determination. The next thing he knew, he was falling prayerfully to his knees and yelling,

"Please! I'll do anything just to even look at her!"

His exclamation once again startled the customers. Peron and Selah's jaws dropped in surprise. Rowan didn't care. He merely watched Madam Spehrow's short-pointed ears twitch at his plea.

She turned to stare at him like she was questioning his sanity. Rowan also wondered if he was going mad.

"What do you mean *anything*?" she inquired.

"*Anything*," he repeated loudly. "A never-ending quest, a giant, evil monster, I'll even do housework for your tavern." Correction: he knew he had gone insane. "If you really think I'm not worthy, then give me any kind of test. Show me how I can be a worthy ward for Linn the Moonstruck."

Rowan saw Madam Spehrow look around the room, probably wondering if anyone else saw this desperate display. Then she sighed.

"Stand up, child," she said, holding out her hand. "You don't want to make too much of a scene, again."

Rowan stood up by himself, finding her charity insulting. She strode back and stood behind the counter, while Rowan and his friends sat back on their stools. Her manicured fingers drummed along the countertop, as she braced herself to speak.

"These adventurers," Madam Spehrow said, "they're not here just for the good food and drink. Many come to the Nest seeking a greater purpose, in the same way you are."

Rowan didn't know where this was going. What did she plan to do?

"You see, apart from my tavern, I am a quest broker. Someone who shares information about quests that would likely grant adventurers more riches and glory than they could ever imagine. But know this. Once you fly into the Nest, who knows what trials you'll go through just to gain what you seek? So, I am offering you the same thing."

"By giving us information?" Peron asked.

"By giving you, Selah, Peron, and Rowan, another way to meet Linn the Moonstruck. If you're ready to pay the price."

It sounded too good to be true. But Rowan was still hesitant, especially about the price part. "Uh-um…what kind of price is there?"

"Psst, Madam," Miss Amori interrupted in a loud whisper. "You better start talking now. Your public awaits."

"Really? How can you tell?" Madam Spehrow inquired.

Most of the adventurers only shouted when necessary. Moments later, their clattering protests started to ring together. All until a table on the second floor started slowly chanting a ridiculous name.

"Lady Bird! Lady Bird!"

It started off as just one group, slapping their table as they cheered. Then one became three, and three became ten, until cries of "Lady Bird" swelled throughout the tavern.

Madam Spehrow? Lady Bird? She had crazier nicknames than Mister Dre, Rowan thought.

"You're not gonna tell *that* story again, are you?" Miss Amori groaned. "I'll say it 'til I die, Madam, but the more you tell it, the whinier they become."

Madam Spehrow turned her back on the waitress, rummaging through the glassware on the middle shelf. She carelessly waved off her concerns. "Ye of little faith, Amori. I assure you they simply adore it."

From the back of the shelf, Madam Spehrow retrieved a silver ladle. She held its long handle and delicately tapped the cup-sized bowl on three glass cups in front. Each glass chimed a bright musical tone.

Ding. Ding. Ding.

The tone was faint yet resounded throughout the room. Enough that all the patrons let their chanting subside. Staring at her, they patiently waited for her next few words. One thing was for sure: she knew how to command a room.

With her hands flat on the countertop, Madam Spehrow gave her patrons a playful smirk. "*Peravo Kalai*, brethren."

"*Peravo Kalai*," the patrons repeated in unison.

It was the similar greeting Rowan had heard Mister Dre give earlier. How did she get a whole tavern to greet her at will?

"Let this be a reminder to you all, that our Nidas of Old must never be forgotten." A few adventurers nodded or mumbled in agreement. "Seek comfort in this truth: that the battles of your forefathers were not fought in vain. In a time when the Legion of Khallus." Madam Spehrow paused as the adventurers hissed and booed this villainous mention. Then she proceeded. "The Legion of Khallus and their allies plagued our lands; they stood strong even as despair struck them down. Luckily, our Battle for Nidas swiftly ended as one infamous party came to our very rescue. Rescue that took the form…of the Ataxia."

The crowds erupted in boorish groaning. Many started yelling at Madam Spehrow from their seats. Rowan was shocked to see them acting out over a story. What made it so upsetting?

Clash, a glass cup shattered on the floor.

Startled, the children turned toward the noise and found the culprit, an angry, burly man with bullhorns and a ringed snout.

"If I hear this story ONE MORE TIME," he snorted, before lifting a table of screaming patrons, "I SWEAR ON EVERYONE IN HERE—"

"You'll do no such thing, Master Raegar! Unless you'd like to pay *extra gold* for my repairs," Madam Spehow raised, still remaining poised.

The man named Raegar growled as he lowered the table. The rest of the customers calmed their tantrums thanks to Madam Spehrow's demands.

"Told you," the smug waitress sang, walking away from the counter.

"Thank you, Amori" Madam rolled her eyes. She smiled her most professional smile and continued. "Brethren, I know you're all here for the quest. Trust me, I'd never tell you this story again without good reason. Think of it as making a good impression for our newcomers in the Nest."

The woman glanced at the orphans before looking back into the crowd. "Now, let us set the mood for our tale," she said. "Pay very close attention, for within it lies what you'll need for your adventure."

Rowan squinted at her, curious. What did she mean by "setting the mood"? What else did the story need?

Apparently, it needed the same ladle she used to silence her patrons. Madam Spehrow picked it up and used the handle end to trace a large circle on the countertop. A line of light appeared in the sketch. She placed her ladle in the center of the circle. Rowan heard a faint click, as she pushed the circle into the countertop. Chandelier candles extinguished, bulbs around the pillars dampened. Every source of light turned off in an instant. Rowan yelped in the darkness. While everyone exclaimed in amazement, he bowed his head and covered his ears. Darkness like this only reminded him of his previous confinement, something he never expected to remember in a place like this.

That is until Madam Spehrow's voice brought him out of his fear.

"Nidas and her Evermire of Old," her voice echoed. *"Many seem to forget those days. Not me, of course. No, I remember the crimes committed by the Legion of Khallus."*

Rowan heard the crowds booing again. A river of lava flowed along the hardwood floor and streamed around the counter. He looked up into a black, cloudy sky that had replaced the glorious chandelier. Floating ash and brimstone turned the air thick and muggy. It landed on his clothes, but when he wiped off the ashes, not a single grey speck stuck to his fingertips.

"Their forces terrorized our people to near extinction. From the dust of the undead, to the dreaded inqai, and to the allied nocturnal beings of legend."

A bony hand leapt out of the lava, startling the orphans. It continued rising to reveal a rotten, burning skeleton that crawled toward the patrons. Many of them laughed or cheered as more skeletons arose and approached them. A few winged figures came out of nowhere, zooming past Rowan and the other customers. All at once, the shrieks of inqai resounded throughout the tavern, as a dozen of them appeared on each floor. An inqus faced Rowan and lurched at him.

"These nocturnal beings were the worst of them all."

Rowan blocked his face from the upcoming attack, only for the figure to fade into black sparkles at the sound of Madam Spehrow's voice. The lava and monsters disappeared, and the room went black again. His heart raced at the speed of light as she continued.

"An insidious race of the night. One that haunted Evermire ages before the Legion. The inqai were horrible, yes. But they were

nowhere as clever and unpredictable as the Nocturnals. Creatures who stole, attacked, and preyed on the innocent at every turn."

Rowan blinked and spotted a few hints of lights. No, not lights…eyes. Small, beady, and embedded along the second floor. High-pitched growls and snarls sounded all around. He had never wanted to leave so badly.

"Those who survived left town in fear, believing no one could tame these once wretched beasts. That is…until the Ataxia came."

Five glowing white figures appeared in the tavern, walking past the tables to stand right in front of Rowan. He couldn't make out their faces, but they were all similarly bright shadows. He looked at the picture of the Ataxia on the shelf. Suddenly, he didn't want to leave anymore.

"From their long and weary journey, the party arrived in Evermire. Great pity befell them as they walked the tattered streets. Wondering how they could prevent these nocturnal beings from terrorizing Evermire once more. And by chance, they met a man as old as Nidas herself. An apothecary who knew how to defeat the Nocturnals."

Rowan remembered Mister Dre telling this story, but he hadn't mentioned any other characters. Why would he leave all these parts out? A hunched, glowing shadow stood in the tavern's corner, as if waiting for the story to introduce him.

"Isolated on the skirts of Evermire, the man lived his life making potions that would boggle one's mind, and he always spoke in verse. They say his rhymes cursed all who approached him, so the people were frightened by his presence. Except for the Ataxia. The party requested something that would stop these foes once and for all. Fortunately, the apothecary agreed to make something that would solve their problem…at a price."

The green silhouetted apothecary conjured some type of energy with his hands. Rowan didn't know what it was, but he knew it was purple, and it lifted with the sway of his hand. It flew around, illuminating the room, until it came across Madam Spehrow and softened into mist.

"And the price," she continued, *"to grant the man what he desired most; three ingredients devised to create his potion. And what's more, he made his desires known in the form…of a riddle. One, he gave the Ataxia little time to decipher."*

The black surrounding walls changed into a bright morning with puffy, white clouds hanging from the ceiling. A bird flew past Rowan's ear and soared into a set of snowy mountains that looked like something out of a fancy painting.

> *Where dragons reigned in Paia's peaks,*
>
> *I seek a crest of creatures' bleak.*
>
> *But never fear their awful scowl,*
>
> *For the beasts, all deceased are more or less foul.*
>
> *They've denounced their ways of fiery affairs,*
>
> *With only their ashes in the mouth of their lair.*

The bird traveled into the mouth of a cave. The snow inside of it turned into grey ash. It looked so realistic that Rowan braced himself for a dragon to awaken from his den. But it didn't. Instead, Madam Spehrow's softened her dramatic tone.

> *Once their ashes stick to the snow,*
>
> *Wait in the lair 'til the moon shines aglow.*
>
> *Under its light, watch its beauty bear fruit.*
>
> *A gem that will form from center to root.*

The wall's morning light faded into a starry night, and a closeup of the cave. Emerging from the ashes was a green gem glowing in a silvery moonbeam. But suddenly the room went dark again, and a flowing pink light appeared, as if capturing the entire image entirely. It floated all around the tavern until it was close to Madam's face.

> *"Brethren, some things remain to be seen. Will you decipher the riddle as quickly as the Ataxia? Would the ingredients for the potion actually work? And most importantly, did the apothecary truly rid the town of the nocturnal beings? All these questions will be answered, once you walk out those doors."*

Suddenly, the tavern bulbs and chandelier candles faded back in, brightening the dark space. Rowan hissed as the lights nearly blinded his retinas. Once his eyes readjusted, he saw the patrons thunderously applauding the charming Madam Spehrow. Selah and Peron joined in, trying to out clap all the customers combined. But Rowan hesitated, his mind clouded by the thought of danger outside the tavern.

"Now then," Madam Spehrow said, after the cheers died down. "Before your quest begins, I'll give you a chance to answer the riddle. The three ingredients for the potion, what were they?"

The room collectively paused for a moment, as if trying to rethink the riddle after that marvelous display. Rowan tried recounting as well. He knew they needed some kind of crest or something, but she hadn't ever mentioned any other items, had she?

"A foul creature's crest," someone shouted.

"Well done," Madam Spehrow complimented. "What else?"

Alright, that one was too easy. But maybe if he just thought hard enough, he could answer before—

"Dragon's ashes, Madam. Dragon's ashes," another person blurted out.

"My, what bright thinkers we have tonight. That's certainly a first." Her sarcasm made the crowd chuckle. "There's just one more. What do you think?"

Rowan's mind went back to the last part of the poem. She mentioned the moon, and she mentioned a gem. Maybe a moon…shaped gem?

"I know, I know," Rowan cried, raising his hand. "It's a jewel shaped like a moon, right?" He looked around for approval from the other adventurers, but they looked just as confused as he was.

"Hmm, close. Gemstones can be found in this ingredient. But not quite. Anyone else?"

Rowan slumped his shoulders. That was all he could think of what else could there possibly be? The riddle mentioned something bearing fruit under moonlight, but only plants could bear fruit. If it made sense, he could try, although he wasn't too sure.

"A moon… flower," he said in a low, uncertain tone.

"Yeah. Yeah, that seems right," Peron declared. "I think I've heard about moonflowers before. They usually only grow in tropical places. Their petals open at night and close during the day. Remember, Rowan? We used to read about them in our textbooks."

Of all the times Peron taught Rowan a lesson, he finally saved the day.

"I think so," Rowan said, trying to remember. Although he never read it in a textbook. "They, er… when they open, there's some kind of gem in it. Like a pearl or emerald or something, right?"

He looked up at Madam Spehrow to see her expression ease into a grin.

"Quite impressive," she told them. Rowan tried to hide his smile. "A foul creature's crest, dragon's ashes, and a moonflower. Brethren, these are the artifacts you'll need to find. The first party to bring them here will receive the unknown quest they desire."

The patrons responded with warrior cries as they banged their mugs on their tables. Anything to excite themselves for a little competition.

"The horn of the ferry will blare once every hour. Bring these items to me by the time the third horn sounds. Last but not least." She took a breath before she continued. "When you leave these doors, you abide by those who bear these artifacts as well. If I hear of any disrespect outside these walls… well, let's just say we don't want another banishment on our hands. You honor their rules, you'll be honoring mine. Are we clear?"

All the patrons mumbled in agreement, except for the long-bearded man seated at the counter. "Hah," he scoffed.

"Master Avion, is something wrong?" Madam Spehrow asked. His disgruntled noise had caught everyone's attention. They paid even more attention when he rose from his stool, tipping his drink.

"The way these cretins gawk at your feet is what's wrong! A quest within a quest? What a ridiculous idea! All you care about is gaining more riches and buying our admiration. You waste our time with this nonsense! Why on Cretia's flawless earth should we trust another greedy broker like you?"

Avion searched the crowds after his speech, hoping for the masses to agree. But the murmuring adventurers laid low, as if they knew the correct answer to his interrogations.

"An excellent question," Madam Spehrow said, gently taking his cup off the counter. "The same question Linn the Moonstruck asked all those years ago." She wiped the counter with a loose rag and answered him honestly. "I will not deny my love for riches, however, we have a saying here in Evermire."

"What you desire in gain, you must give in return.

"If you wish to know more about the quest, you must do something for me first. You may try the guilds or even the Council, but I assure you they do not possess the same information I do." She smirked at the doubtful man as she dropped the rag in front of him. "So, in simple terms: No artifacts, no quest. No quest, means never getting to brag to your guilds about how you can pull your weight… in platinum. Two hundred to be exact."

The entire tavern erupted in gasps and yelling galore. Rowan's eyes widened, Selah's jaw dropped, and Peron covered his mouth in shock. A quest worth two hundred platinum. That could buy way more than Nidas; it could buy all of Pelle and then some.

Madam Spehrow peered down at the shocked children, ignoring the excited adventurers before her. "The same goes for you, children."

They snapped out of their daze to listen closely. "No artifacts, no Linn the Moonstruck," she continued. "No Linn the Moonstruck, means…"

"I won't be worthy enough," Rowan uttered.

"So, Rowan the Brave, are you willing to accept this challenge?"

He thought to himself: was he really worthy or did he just want to be? Well, he couldn't say something like that out loud, so instead he leaned closer to her.

"A foul creature's crest, dragon ashes, and a moonflower," he said confidently. "Yeah, I can find those faster than anyone on this island. And once I meet Linn the Moonstruck, I'll be the one to wipe that smug look right off your face!"

HONK, the ferry horn blared. As soon as it did, Rowan saw dozens of adventuring parties dash out the door to start their quest. He already felt himself losing time.

"Don't worry. I never count that first horn," Madam Spehrow said. "But you better hurry. Mages hate to be kept waiting."

Rowan took that to heart, as he stood up and copied the rushing parties. He didn't even check whether Selah and Peron were behind him. He squeezed past the adventurers, no longer caring about the dangers outside the Spehrow's Nest. He made it outside, where he realized he was not in the same Evermire as before.

Chapter 12

The Foul Nocturnal Market

Selah and Peron made it out the door ready to scold Rowan for running off. But when they got outside, they marveled at the same scene he saw.

"Are we still in Evermire?" Peron asked.

"I think so," Selah affirmed. "It looks so much brighter."

The brightness was courtesy of the endless string of lights hanging from the tall street lamps, stretching for miles along the cobblestone pavement. It was funny; Rowan looked to his right and saw the small tent pitched next to the tavern. Beside it was a circus tent with polka dots. A line of countless different tents flowed down to the dock. Rowan saw more tents on the other side of the street. Curious, ignoring the dozens of people strolling through, he walked out into the street. Selah grabbed his hand.

"Really, Se," Rowan said, annoyed.

"I'm not letting you get trampled out there," she said, taking Peron's hand as well. "If we do this, we do this together."

"Fine," he groaned as they walked hand in hand. He grumbled to himself as they maneuvered through the streets. Rowan went the opposite way from most of the others. He thought he should try to be different from the crowds; it's what any real adventurer would do. Then a question formed in his mind about Madam Spehrow's story.

"Hey Per. What does *nocturnal* mean?"

"It means something to do with the nighttime," Peron answered, making himself small under the crowds. "Why're you asking me?"

Rowan watched the sky above for any stars to creep into view. "Madam Spehrow said there used to be nighttime creatures all over the place. She made this town sound super scary like Mister Dre did. But maybe it's not. Maybe that apothe-, uh…p-potion person got rid of them all."

"Well, there is only one way to find out. I'm just not sure this is the right place in town."

"What do you mean?"

"We should be out someplace daring and mysterious. There's no mystery about this place. I mean, haven't you seen what they sell here?" He pointed to signs hanging outside the tents. "Pickled frog legs? Hair removal cream? Apple scones?"

"Apple scones!" Selah exclaimed, finding the vendor. She ran up to it with the boys still in hand. When they made it to the cart, someone was waiting in front of them. Selah craned her neck to see.

"They look like pieces of heaven," she said with a beaming smile.

"See what I mean?" Peron said. "How are we supposed to find dragon's ashes in a town like this? I haven't seen one dragon."

"Well, it's like she said in her riddle, right? I think she said they're all gone, so we probably don't need any actual dragons."

Peron raised an eyebrow at Rowan as if questioning his intellect. "I… guess so. But what about the crest? Do you even know what that is?"

"Obviously not. But there are all these signs and tents and stuff, we can just find out another way."

"And what if we can't find it that way?"

Rowan rolled his eyes; he knew what he had to do, he just didn't want to say it. "I guess we'll have to ask somebody. But there's so many people here. What if no one wants to help us?"

"Well, Mister Dre wanted to help us," Selah chimed in. "And everyone else so far has been super smart and super nice. They'd probably be willing to help. Most of these people are adventurers; I bet they'll know what a crest looks like."

Selah had a point.

"Alright, I guess I'll try. But if that doesn't work, we find it ourselves."

If Rowan wanted to ask, he'd need to find someone quickly. He observed the person waiting in front of them. They seemed to be a small dwarf wearing a maroon cap with long black tassels. Shyly, Rowan tugged on one of the tassels. No one turned back. He tried again, harder this time, until a slight "OW" slipped out from the person.

The person in front turned around to be not a dwarf but a little girl around Rowan's age. A frown was pasted on her ebony skin as she rubbed the back of her head. Rowan's eyes widened as he realized; they weren't tassels, but braids. Long braids with ornaments of gold and silver.

"What did you do that for," the little girl exclaimed.

"Sorry," Rowan said, startled. "I-I thought you were a dwarf. I mean, the back of your head—"

The little girl scoffed. "I most certainly am not a dwarf. I'm a young lady. Didn't your mama ever tell you not to pull on people's hair?"

This little girl obviously did not know who Den Mother was.

"I just… I've never really seen hair like yours before. It reminded me of a decoration. I guess it just looked… nice?"

The little girl straightened herself up. She dusted off her tan trousers and flipped her hair back looking almost satisfied by his response. "You didn't answer me yet? Why did you pull on my hair?"

"What do you mean; I just said why," Rowan answered, confused. "Your hair looked like a decoration, that's all."

"Hmph. If that were it, you would've stopped talking to me after you apologized. You need to be more specific."

The little girl's attitude almost made him forget why he had spoke to her. But he gritted his teeth and said, "I wanted to ask you a very important question. Something that would really help me tonight."

She folded her arms across her maroon blouse. "Go on."

Rowan let out a harsh sigh; this already seemed pointless, stupid almost. "Look, there's a really powerful mage who I want to be my teacher, *and* there's also this Madam Spehrow who wants me to get her some artifacts. If I don't give them to her, I'll never become her student, which means I'll never become a real mage."

"Wait, wait, wait, did you say Spehrow? As in Madam Spehrow?" the girl asked in shock.

Rowan nodded.

"No way, you've met Madam Spehrow? I've been wanting to meet her for years! The Spehrow's Nest is the best place to meet new adventurers with all kinds of stories. But Mama says I can't go in until I've made my own story." She squinted at the children. "In fact, no kid has ever gotten into the Nest this late. How were you able to get in?"

"Um…we know a few people," Selah said. "But they aren't here to really help us right now. We were wondering if you could."

The little girl's eyes went to the ground as she reached for the cat pendant on her necklace. Rowan waited for her response; he could already tell it wouldn't be good.

"These artifacts. What were they exactly?" the little girl asked.

Rowan blinked, surprised.

"Um… she told us we needed a moonflower," Peron said.

"And we also need to find some dragon's ashes," Selah added.

"But first we need to find a crest from some foul creature," Rowan finished. "You… wouldn't know what that is, would you?"

"Hmm… Mama says it's like fur on an animal's body. Either that or something at the top of a hill, I can't remember which. But if there's any place to find it, the *Nocturnal Market* is the best there is. I can show you around if you'd like. It's going to cost you, though."

Rowan grumbled at her sly smile. "Fine. What's the catch, huh?"

"When we find the artifacts, you take me to see Madam Spehrow."

Well, that likely wouldn't happen. Rowan didn't plan on seeing the girl again this. Still, he questioned her charming yet demanding expression. "Why exactly?"

"You guys seem like the perfect people to write a story about, and I'm going to be the one to compose it. If I share it with my mama, she's bound to let me into the Nest. It'll be my finest creation, my grand opus for all time!"

How could someone be so dramatic and so annoying at the same time? Rowan thought.

"Your scones, little lady," someone announced from behind the booth. The children followed the voice and yelped at its speaker, a creature with stone-colored skin and clothing. Engraved on its face was a mouth with thick fangs and bulging green eyes. Rowan gawked at the bat-like wings on her back; they were the size of two of him combined.

The only person who didn't scream was the little girl, who calmly took the bag of scones from the creature's granite claws.

"Thank you, madam," the little girl said. She took a small pebble from her dress pocket and handed it to the stone merchant. She turned around to see the children, Rowan was confused by her fearlessness. *What on earth is that?* he thought.

"What? Never seen a gargoyle before?" she asked, taking a scone from the bag.

Rowan's face twitched in surprise. Why on earth did she give the gargoyle a pebble? A puff of air passed by him. He looked up and saw another flying gargoyle that landed at another tent. A few more walked or flew past him.

He finally realized. "Nighttime creatures," he muttered. "So that's what she meant."

Shaking off her confusion, Selah went up next and asked the gargoyle for the freshest treats on the counter, leaving Rowan and Peron with the little girl.

"So, what's your name, by the way?" Rowan asked. "I mean, if you're gonna help us, we should probably know who you are."

"Really, you don't recognize me?" she asked, confused. Her smile faded as the boys shook their heads. "The little girl with the tambourine? Tiny Bard of the Band? Mother's Little Prodigy? Nothing?"

The boys offered mumbled apologies.

"Oh," she realized. Then she sported an even brighter grin. "Well, I'm Ahria V—." She stopped to correct herself. "Baroq. Ahria Baroq. But you can call me, the Brilliant Bard!"

Rowan squinted at her suspicious correction. Still, he had to ask: "What kind of name is Baroq?"

"Hey, it's a very prestigious name," Ahria bit back. "And what's your name, mister smart-aleck?"

"I am Rowan the Brave," he announced. "This is my friend Peron, and my other friend, Selah…is walking back over here?"

She strode back to him with no scones in hand.

"That lady said I can't have any without a treasure or something," Selah pouted. "Do you guys have anything?"

Peron ran through his pockets. Nothing. Rowan went through his and took out a stone. He remembered getting it from the stone soup in Faegan. Selah must've figured out she could use it as payment, because she swiped it before he could hand it to her. He remembered what Madam Spehrow said about how things ran here in Evermire.

What you desire in gain, you must give in return.

The stone must have worked on the vendor because Selah merrily skipped back with a pile of scones in her hand. She offered one to each of her friends.

"So, how are you going to write this story?" Rowan asked, grabbing a scone from Selah.

"Allow me to demonstrate," Ahria grinned proudly. There was that sly charm again. She handed her scones to Rowan like he was her servant. She placed a thumb on her cylinder cat pendant and chanted a small phrase,

Repmarchis parc braazi

Ahria's pendant glowed a light teal. Soon, the little girl's whole body glowed the same color, and her frame copied itself. When the silhouette wore off, two Ahrias appeared in front of the orphans; one holding a brass trumpet, and one with a snare drum attached to a white strap around her neck.

"Whoa," the children exclaimed.

"Follow me, everybody," Ahria said. Her drumsticks tapped complex rhythms on her snare, while she and the orphans marched through the crowds. All eyes were on them, forming a straight path as the two-man band entertained them. After a few measures of drumming, the other Ahria blared a heroic tune on her trumpet. The bright and proud melodies entranced Selah, Peron, and Rowan, making them feel like royalty as they walked behind the cloned duo. The magic was so creative. How could Rowan learn something like that?

When they made it through the applauding crowds, the girl spoke another phrase to end her spell and song.

Phinivenic.

Both Ahrias glowed teal again. Her instruments and her clone dispersed into little musical notes and spiraled into the cat symbol on her pendant. Once they disappeared, the real Ahria shook off the teal hue and revealed her original form with a smile.

"What kind of spell was that?" Rowan asked in excitement.

"Just a simple lure spell. Something small enough to make it through traffic without pushing," Ahria answered modestly. "I've been practicing with my brass instruments for a while now and—"

"No, I mean how did you…make another version of yourself?"

"Oh, well, that's something my papa taught me. I just add another instrument to my spell and then *poof*, another me!"

"I want to learn how to make another me," Rowan said. "I could be twice as magical and twice as powerful. One me could make things float, and the other me could blast lightning at people."

"Maybe you should focus on training the 'one you' before you add others," Selah said.

"Yeah, one Rowan is enough already. I can't even imagine what two Rowans would be like. Probably twice as annoying," Peron teased. Selah smacked the back of his head.

"So, a new mage, huh," Ahria said. She turned to meet Rowan's gaze and walked backwards. "I can't remember the last time I met a new mage. You probably know tons of spells already, don't you?"

"Yeah, of course I do," Rowan lied. "I guess you could say I'm kind of a natural."

"That's awesome! Can you cast one for me?"

Rowan looked at her wide-eyed amusement and was confused. "Wait, right now?"

"Sure, why not? We have time."

Rowan was tongue-tied. He didn't expect someone to actually want to see his spells. For the first time, he felt nervous, making himself small before Selah straightened him up.

"We actually don't have much time. He can probably show you after he meets Linn the Moonstruck though," the orcish girl responded. Selah always knew when to step in.

The little girl shrugged. "Seems fair enough. What about you two? Are you guys mages?"

Selah and Peron shook their heads, uttering every word they could in protest.

"That's alright. You certainly don't have to be," Ahria giggled, spinning on her heels to walk forward again. "But that's the best part. When you're a mage, you get to learn whatever you want. I remember when I cast my first spell. I was three years old and still making stuff explode. But I've been practicing since then and look at me now!"

Did she say three years old? That was amazing…and a little upsetting. Rowan had just started practicing, and he still made things explode. Jealousy formed a lump in his throat and his walking slowed.

As they ventured on, the children ate almost half the scones from each bag. The three orphans decided to visit other vibrant tents once their quest ended. Selah and Ahria marveled at a bunch of jewelry stands, with Ahria raving about Pelle's latest fashion. Peron and Rowan wanted to visit the passing book carts, arguing about whether they should look at the fantasy or science books first.

Soon, Ahria led them to the town square, where the cobblestone pavement formed in a circle surrounded by tall buildings and winding roads. A high stone pedestal stood in the middle of the pavement. Usually pedestals supported stone statues of very important heroes remembered for generations. But this pedestal was empty. Perhaps Evermire had too many heroes to count. *Maybe I'll become a statue one day*, Rowan thought with a smile.

"This'll be the perfect place to find it," Ahria confirmed.

"How do you know?" the children asked. All Rowan could see were more and more tents in front of the buildings.

"I said that a crest might be fur on an animal. If you're looking for a foul creature's crest, this is where we'll get it.

The children looked around to see several tents and carts selling white and brown fur coats, leather shoes, and even large fur rugs.

"Ugh, do we have to go? All that just looks so wrong," Peron said, holding his stomach and looking queasy.

"Come on, Perry. We'll be with you. Don't be a baby," Selah said.

"Yeah, Per. Don't be a baby," Rowan repeated. "It's probably not even that bad."

It was that bad, actually. Bad enough for Rowan to grimace at the backs of townsfolk lined up at the unsettling tents. It displayed an array of fur rugs with animal heads still attached. The merchant, a short and stubby gargoyle, took one off the linen wall, rolled it up, and handed it to the man in front of the children. When the man walked off, the eyes of the flattened raccoon followed them. Rowan shuddered, but he mainly felt bad for Peron. His friend's skin had turned even paler than it already was. So much for never freezing in fear.

"Next," the merchant croaked.

Trying to keep their composure, the children walked up to the gargoyle floating several feet off the ground.

"H-hello sir," Rowan uttered, trying not to look at the rugs. "W-we were wondering if you had a crest from a foul creature. It's for Madam Spehrow."

"Ugh, again with the foul creature's crest," the merchant groaned. "You're the seventeenth party to request that from me tonight." Rowan shrunk back at the response. He didn't need to be so rude about it. "I'll tell you what I told the others. All I've got are deer, goats, and a bunch of raccoons I dug up last week. Doesn't seem too foul to me, now does it?"

Maybe the animals aren't foul, but your attitude is, Rowan thought.

HONKK!!!

The sound made everyone stop what they were doing and turn towards it.

That isn't what I think it is? Rowan thought as he walked away from the line. But unfortunately, the noise blared for a few more seconds. It was the first horn of the night, resounding across the Nocturnal Market. It seemed too early for the first one, and Rowan still hadn't found the crest.

The boat horn ceased, but Rowan's racing heartbeat didn't.

"What do I do? What do I do?" Rowan muttered. Absently, he scratched his wrist, wondering what he could do before time ran out. Peron came over to him.

"Rowa, I think we need to keep moving," Peron said, placing his hand on his shoulder.

But Rowan shrugged him and cried, "I know that! I just…" His head felt like it was spinning off its axis as he, tried to dredge up some semblance of hope. He staggered and bumped into what felt like cold fabric on his back. He broke out of his daze as he heard a brief yelp and a feathered coat drop to the ground. He looked up to see a lion-headed gargoyle sighing with a hand on his chest.

"Cael on High," he said in a posh accent. "You scared me, young cub."

Rowan's eyes flitted to the tent behind the gargoyle. Its felt display laden with feathered coats like the one that fell. He picked it up, smoothed out its black and grey feathers, and handed it to the gargoyle.

"Sorry, sir. Hope I uh…didn't ruin this for you," Rowan said. It wouldn't be the first time he had ruined something.

"Oh, you're alright. You have nothing to apologize for," the gargoyle said, taking the garment. "In fact, you're the first kind soul I've met all evening. Thank you." The gargoyle nodded and carried on with his business. "Last chance, gentlemen! Last chance to pick one of my claw-crafted feather coats. I have raven. I have a brown owl. I even have coats made from the giant repha in Paia!"

Although the well-dressed gargoyle shouted, everyone walking by avoided him. But Rowan didn't He and the rest of his group looked at his tent's display.

"So, why are you selling coats," Rowan blurted.

The gargoyle looked down at him. "Well, young cub, I make these coats myself, you see. I'm giving customers a chance to wear the latest trends from the mainland."

"But it's the summer," Rowan said. Peron elbowed him.

Anger briefly flashed on the gargoyles fast before he said, "Weather should never get in the way of good fashion."

Rowan knew little about clothes, so that made absolutely no sense.

"Say, to show my gratitude, why don't you try one on?"

Rowan almost protested until the gargoyle cast a spell on the coat beside him which had puffy white feathers. The gargoyle made the coat rise from the display and come down to Rowan. After a spell like that, he had to try it on.

The children applauded the gargoyle's trick. While Peron and Ahria helped Rowan put on the coat, Selah spoke to the gargoyle.

"What kind of coat is this again?" Selah asked. "Is it from a really foul creature?"

"It's a repha-crested coat. My finest creation," the gargoyle said. "And yes. It's one of the rarest *fowl* known to man. They used to be—"

"Fowl," the children said together.

"Yes. F-O-W-L, like the bird. Anyway, when I went to Paia, I had—"

Rowan ignored the gargoyle's explanation. He never knew there was another word that sounded like "foul." That's something that Peron would usually know. "Why didn't you tell me about this?" Rowan gritted at Peron.

"I didn't know they had another name," Peron explained. "I just call them birds."

They started to argue, but Selah shushed them so they could listen to the gargoyle's ceaseless talking.

"And their feathers. Ugh, the process," the gargoyle said. "You don't know what I had to do to gather from those baby birds!"

The children remembered the gargoyle's lion face and stared in horror. "And h-how did you…gather them?" Peron gulped.

As if reading their minds, the gargoyle shooed away their evil thoughts. "Oh dear, no! No, I simply collected the feathers during their molting season. Besides, they're too expensive to eat, anyway. So, what do you think?"

On Rowan, the coat was about five sizes too big. It stretched past his arms and ankles. But that wasn't the worst part. "It's, uh…it's a little itchy," Rowan said as he scratched his neck.

"Ah, yet it suits you! Very high class! And I wouldn't worry about that too much. That's the enchantment taking effect!"

"Enchantment?" The children said in unison.

As they asked, Rowan felt a breeze flutter off his coat. He looked at the feathers and realized they were flapping rapidly. A moment later, Rowan slowly lifted off the pavement.

"Whoa, whoa, whoa! What are you doing?" Ahria said, trying to pull him back down.

"I don't know," Rowan cried, floating above his friends. "Selah? Peron?"

Selah grabbed his ankle and pulled him back down to the ground. But when she let go, Rowan rose right back up again.

"Rowan, seriously. Come down," Selah said.

"How can I do that," he asked. "I don't even know how I got *up*!" As he said that, the coat flew Rowan higher into the air, above the coat tent. He screamed so loud that the shoppers took notice.

"Ah Cael. Not this again," Peron groaned, as he watched Rowan's display. The gargoyle looked a bit too ecstatic for comfort.

"What did you do to his coat," Selah shouted, sounding demanding and anxious.

"Ah, I give all my creations sky charms, young cub," the gargoyle replied. "Isn't it marvelous? It gives some of these tasteless adventurers a boost in their flying abilities."

"Can you undo your sky charm?" Peron asked.

"Well, no. Not anymore. Once someone else wears my creations, the power's out of my claws. Your friend's the one in control now."

"How does he do that?"

"Simple flying directions, really. You know, up, down, stop. Things like that." He glanced upward. "And definitely not by taking off the coat mid-flight."

The two looked up to see Rowan trying to do that exact thing and rushed over to stop him.

"I tried to tell him," Ahria said.

"Rowan, keep the coat on!? Selah shouted up at him. "That's not how you get down!"

"I don't have any choices *left*, SelAAAH," Rowan cried as the enchanted coat's pace accelerated. It jolted in all different directions, leaving him defenseless.

He flew above the street corner, swerving from tent to tent and nearly destroying them. The coat took him past the pedestal, where Rowan almost ran into two flying gargoyles. They swiftly flew around him, but they gave him an earful. Finally, the coat stopped him high above the street center.

Rowan stared at the ground, although he knew he wasn't supposed to. It felt all too familiar…and so incredibly high.

"Hey, Rowan the Brave," Ahria called out. "You need to control the coat first if you want to get down!"

"I think the coat is controlling me," Rowan screamed.

"She means give it directions," Selah added. "Up, down, left, right! Anything!"

He looked at the coat's flapping feathers, worried about what would happen if he tried to control it. But he had to test it out; he hated being up this high.

"Uh…left," he said. The coat shifted almost too quickly. "No, no. Stop!" It stopped. He tried again. "Right!" Shift. "Stop!" It stopped.

Thanks to his friends, Rowan now knew exactly what to do. He took a deep breath and gave a final command. "Slowly…go down," he said.

And the coat did just that, lowering Rowan at a steady pace. He looked around at the gazing shoppers applauding his safety. He landed atop of the stone pedestal and for a moment, he got a taste of what a hero's statue looked like. He saw his friends dash over to the pedestal.

"Rowan, don't you ever do that again," Selah commanded.

"Are you sure you're alright?" Peron asked.

Rowan took off the coat, smiled at it, and said, "I just found our fowl creature's crest. I'd say I'm the happiest mage alive."

He jumped from the pedestal and accidentally toppled Selah and Peron. But they went in for a hug anyway, laughing and teasing him. When they got up, the well-dressed gargoyle walked up and applauded.

"Marvelous! Absolutely marvelous, dear boy! You don't know how much you've made my night. But you'd make my night even brighter if you brought the subject of payment." The gargoyle presented his paw.

Rowan went through his pockets and grabbed the black stone soup rock. Once he handed it over, the gargoyle, he placed it on the collar of his grey suitcoat. The stone absorbed into his clothing and became an ornament of its own.

Looking satisfied, the gargoyle asked, "Would you like to buy another?"

"No," the children exclaimed.

"Um, no thanks," Rowan said calmer now. "But thanks anyway! Good luck with the coats!" He waved the gargoyle goodbye and hugged the coat tightly. And with that, he and his three friends went on their way in high spirits, ready to find the next piece of their mysterious puzzle.

Chapter 13

He's Never Not Here

Rowan didn't know whether to be impressed or annoyed by this Ahria Baroq. After they left the coat stand, the little girl couldn't help but conjure a dark brown lute from her pendant. When she said she'd write their story, Rowan didn't realize she meant *singing* their story. Not only that, but she and Selah ate the last two scones, which only frustrated him even more. And the worst part was that she couldn't stick to a single melody. She changed the words every ten seconds with exaggerations and dreadfully gloomy tunes.

OOOH, I tell you a tale 'bout the bird of the night.

He preys like a buzzard from the highest of heights.

"Oh please, I didn't *pray* to anybody," Rowan scoffed.

"Well, a lot of people thought differently," Ahria teased. "They couldn't stop talking about you. 'A flying child! He almost destroyed my beautiful tent and my beautiful merchandise! Oh, the humanity!'"

Correction: he was annoyed. He rolled his eyes at the musical girl. The way she said it, it made Rowan sound like a villain rather than a hero.

"They were probably just as worried as we were, Rowan," Selah said. "Don't think too much of it."

She ran a hand through his coils to reassure him. Sure, Selah would say that, and yet Rowan saw her and Peron fully entertained by the little girl's singing.

"Ooh, I know! How about this one?"

Ahria changed the key again as she strummed her lute in a more cheerful, brighter tone.

"*Oh, Mighty is he who flies the scoring skies.*

Mighty is he as he soars before your eyes.

Alright it was starting to sound better.

Mighty is he, the repha in disguise.

Rowan the Brave! Oh, what a knave!

*Mighty to…*save? Cave? I don't know, I'll think about it later."

And just like that, the moment was gone. But it didn't matter too much, as Rowan smiled at the soft coat in his hands. He'd done it; he actually did something good without messing it up. He'd never felt prouder of himself.

He thought about what would happen after he met Linn the Moonstruck. Especially when he became an older mage. Not only would he have a statue, but maybe his own song too. At least one that sounded better than calling him a *knave*. He knew he was not a knave.

"So where to next?" Ahria asked as her lute faded away.

"We have to look for some dragon's ashes," Selah said.

"I still think this is the wrong place for it," Peron said. "Shouldn't we be going through some creepy cave to find a dragon?"

"She said we don't have to find the actual dragon," Rowan said. "Just its ashes. But hey, we found the crest thing, so maybe our luck will keep going."

With the first item being retrieved, Rowan had more positive thoughts about the journey ahead.

"Yeah, I guess so," Peron said with doubt in his voice. "What do you think, Miss Ahria? Have you seen any dragons fly around here?"

"Mmm, I don't think so," she said. "Mama and I aren't really here that often."

"Really? But you know so much about this place," Rowan said.

"Well, kind of. We're from Venari, and we only come here, like, once a quarter. We'll do music tours on the mainlands, then visit here. But in all that time, I've never seen a dragon."

"Madam Spehrow said they were all gone. Something about *for the beasts all deceased* and ashes in their lair. It was a really long riddle."

"*Beasts all deceased*...Oh, I remember Mama telling me that riddle! It'd be part of our history lessons sometimes."

"Did you learn anything that's not from your mama?" Rowan murmured.

"Shut up! Anyway, she told me they used to be the wisest and scariest beasts in the land. They trained other mages how to breathe fire and ice, or even how to turn into one of them."

Rowan thought about turning into a dragon. That'd be more awesome than blasting lightning.

His thoughts were interrupted by a woman passing by. He noted the paleness of her skin and the black seams of her dress. Rowan only knew *one woman* with those two traits. Fear filled his mind, and he hoped not to see her face even as he glanced at her. The woman had long, black hair, and younger features rather than older ones.

Rowan sighed in relief, but then another thought entered his mind. What if she followed them all the way here? Certainly, she wouldn't do that. Would she?

"Is everything alright?" Ahria asked, waking Rowan from his trance. He looked up to see her, Selah and Peron staring at him, concerned.

"So…um, we only need the ashes, where do you think we'd find something like that?" Rowan asked, desperately trying to change the subject.

Ahria narrowed her brows confused. "Uh yeah, I was just getting to that. Are you sure you're—"

"Yeah, we're fine," Peron said, sensing Rowan's discomfort. "Where do you think we'll find the ashes?"

The little girl still looked befuddled, but she shrugged it off once more. "I know someone around here with that carries ashes. We could go find him if you'd like."

"Great, let's do it," Rowan said, stomping forward. Cutting off Ahria's story was rude of him, but he made it his mission to leave the road as soon as possible. He would not let Den Mother control his thoughts. Not after she had already controlled so much of his life.

·   ·   ·

Ahria took the group through an area of town smelling of savory and sweet dishes at every tent. The meals overloaded the children's senses and made them almost forget about their journey. But they kept going until Ahria stopped them in front of a hazel-brown building with a large window and a red door. At the top was a sign that read,

Tawnwell's Toys

"Are you sure we're at the right place?" Selah asked. "Finding ashes in a toy store seems a little dark, don't you think?"

"Trust me, we're not here for the toys," Ahria said as they approached. "There's someone here who I know can help us."

Rowan stifled a sad sigh. He and his friends had never been to a toy store before. He'd only seen one on the cover of a book; a really boring mystery book. They looked through the window, only to see how dark it was. The only toys were on the display counter in the window. They were new toys, the kind that made any child who had one the envy of all other youth.

Rowan counted the jacks and marbles, wondering if he could finally get a new set.

"I wonder if I should get a new doll," Selah said, eyeing one in the window with long, flowing hair and an elegant princess gown. Rowan remembered Selah's old doll had thin yarn for hair, clothes made from rags, and one eye that hung by a thread.

"Hey Rowa, how far do you think that red model train can go?" Peron asked excitedly. His old one at the orphanage was missing several wheels and gave him splinters every time he used it.

Rowan tore his gaze from the window to the red door. A piece of parchment was nailed into the wood with a note that read:

On the Mainland. Will return in 3 days.

—Tawnwell

"We might have to keep going, Ahria," he said. "Whoever this guy is, I don't think he'll be here for a while."

"Who, Mister Tawnwell," Ahria asked. "Oh, I knew he wouldn't be here."

"So, we came here for nothing," Peron asked.

Ahria ignored him. "The owner travels around the mainlands every few months, but he never leaves the store unattended. He puts my friend Truegug in charge of guarding the store while he's away." She looked at the sign and crossed her arms. "And he should've been here by now."

"So, what's the problem?" Rowan asked.

"He's never *not* here."

Rowan narrowed his eyes at Ahria, questioning her sanity. He was about to ask Ahria where else they could go when a voice called out in fear.

"AHRIAAAAAA! Ahria, help me!"

Rowan and his friends turned to encounter the owner of the desperate plea, a younger gargoyle in a brown vest with short green hair running in their direction. Rowan noticed Ahria glaring at the gargoyle as he tripped over his own feet. Once he made it to them, the young gargoyle took a moment to catch his breath.

"*This* is the friend you want us to meet," Peron asked.

"Yeah. This is Truegug, and he's late," Ahria huffed.

"It's not… It's not my fault," Truegug panted in his nasally voice. "I'm…not used to…runnin' all the time."

Rowan noticed a white bandage tied around one of his wings. Truegug stood up straight, revealing his form. He was the same height as Peron when he wasn't slouching.

"I mean, you try flyin' with one workin' wing with Nyx and his friends chasin' after ya."

"Those idiots again?!"

"I found him! There he is! Get him," a trio of voices cried. Three elvish-looking boys ran towards the tired Truegug. One boy a gray cap and blue clothes as dark as his skin. The other two boys had identical mahogany skin and frayed raven dreadlocks. Twins, Rowan presumed. They bore the power of fire and lightning at their fingertips as they ran. It was magic Rowan always dreamed of attaining, but he would never use it for harm.

"Quick! You gotta help me! Use your barrier or somethin'," the gargoyle exclaimed, crouching behind Ahria.

"Ugh! Truegug, come on. Doesn't Uncle Rog tell you to stand up for yourself?" she cried. "What are you going to do when I leave in a couple days?"

"Easy! Invent my own barrier… once I find all the parts."

With the three boys aiming at them, Rowan thought it perfect timing to use the spell from the caravan. Rowan recalled how it went, then wrapped the coat around his waist and imagined a long snake staff in his grasp. As the boys drew closer, he shouted out,

Unfortunately for him, Selah blocked Rowan and the others from the boys. Her steaming frown made the bullies slow down their advances. Then the boy with the blue clothes shoved through the twins with an annoyed sneer. He had bright, luminous dots on his skin, like pulsing stars in the night sky. He squinted his pale eyes at Selah blocking his path and snorted at her attempts to stop him.

"Hey greeny," Nyx called in a cracking voice. "Move aside, will you? Us and *soft rock* were playing a game."

"Oh, really? You call throwing magic at people playing a game?" Selah demanded. "Ahria's right, you three must be idiots if you think I'm going to let you hurt him."

Rowan looked at Selah in surprise. He'd never heard her call anyone names before. What had changed?

"We weren't doing nothin', were we, Sailo?" Nyx smugly asked of the lightning twin. The twin shrugged, hardly concealing a devious grin. "Tell 'em *soft rock*. We were just…testing some things with our new magic and we wanted him to see."

"Sure! 'Tested'," Ahria said sarcastically. "Like that time Loka 'tested' Truegug's skin in the sun and nearly burned him."

"Stay out of this, *princess*," Loka demanded in a low voice. He went back to intimidating Truegug again. "Hey, *soft rock*, you gonna let a bunch of girls speak up for you?"

"Yes," Truegug said quickly.

Rowan knew how this Truegug felt, too scared to do anything. So, he got in front of Selah, looked the boys straight in the eyes and said, "Why don't…why don't you just leave him alone already?"

Nyx and the twins blinked at him, then snickered at his heroic stance.

"Oh yeah? What are you gonna do about it, dunce?" Sailo asked in his strained voice.

"I'll…I'll use my magic to stop you!" Rowan held the pretend snake wand in his hand. With all his might he cried,

Striatsi!

But he didn't see any lightning. No glow appeared in his grasp. Not an ounce of magic in sight.

The three boys laughed in his face. It stung more than the crowd's laughter at the tavern. *How can I be brave if people keep laughing at me,* Rowan thought.

"What a joke. Kid can't even cast a spell," Nyx jeered. Rowan lowered his head in shame. "Say, how 'bout we go through you first? You and your *mutts* can join our 'game' later."

Nyx cracked his knuckles while the twins prepped their spells. Selah got in front of Rowan and blocked their path again. She punched Nyx square in the face. Rowan and his friends exclaimed at the motion.

While she didn't knock him out, Selah sent the boy tumbling to the ground. He winced as he touched his bloody nose, completely stunned. Rowan glimpsed Selah's face, seeing the rage she bore in the forest. Her tusks bared with intensity, and the whites of her eyes as red as the blood on the ground. If he and Peron didn't quickly jump in to hold her back, Selah would've killed Nyx for sure.

"What is wrong with you?" Loka and Sailo sputtered in disbelief.

"That's right! Get back up, freak," Selah yelled. "See what happens if you threaten him again!"

With the twins' help, Nyx stumbled up. The stars across his skin flared a flushed red as he covered his nose. "You losers better watch your backs," he proclaimed. "When my father sees this, you'll be in for a world of hurt." He and his twins ran away from the group, in embarrassment.

Rowan looked back at Selah, who was still in her trance, eyes red and breathing heavy.

"Se," Rowan called softly.

Just like that, her breathing slowed and the redness in her eyes faded back to white. She looked at Rowan with her hazel eyes and covered her face in embarrassment. "I'm sorry," she mumbled. Before placing her hands on Rowan's face. "Did I hurt you or anything?"

"Selah, you're fine. I'm—"

Before he could finish, she hugged him tightly. Out of shock, Rowan hugged her back. It only heightened his concern for her. Even if he thought Selah had looked really cool.

Rowan faced Peron and Ahria. He blinked at the pair of grey wings sprouting from the little girl's back. Then he remembered who hid behind Ahria.

"Is he gonna be alright?" Rowan asked.

"Yeah, we're good," Truegug affirmed, as he stood. "Thanks a lot back there. No one's ever stood up to Nyx like that. You've done so much for me and I don't even know your name."

"Truegug, these are new friends I made. I'm showing them around town," Ahria said.

As they waved hello, Truegug eyed Rowan. "Oh, I know you! You're that flyin' coat kid, from earlier, right? Really impressive stuff back there. I could've sworn you were a gargoyle too."

Rowan flashed a fake smile and gritted through his teeth, "Nice to meet you. My name's Rowan. This is Peron and Selah."

"Nice to meet ya," Truegug greeted them cheerfully, not taking the hint. "Say, you could really do somethin' with that punch of yours. Ever thought of bein' a hunter?"

Selah realized he was talking to her. "I've been told I could be one," she said, playing with one of her curls.

"Well, if you're interested, I got a bunch of inventions I've been dyin' to—"

"We don't have time for this," Ahria sang. "Truegug, these guys are on a Spehrow quest."

"A Spehrow quest? As in a Madam Spehrow quest? How were you guys able to meet her?"

"It's a long story," Peron said. "But Miss Ahria here said you could help us."

Truegug looked surprised. "Me? Why do you need my help?"

"Because we're running out of time," Rowan said. "We need artifacts that'll help me be Linn the Moonstruck's ward. For that, we need something with dragon's ashes."

Looking skeptical, Truegug mumbled to Ahria. "You realize there are no actual dragons here, right?"

"Yes, I know. We've discussed that," Ahria said, rolling her eyes. "But we were wondering if you had something that's a little more… dragon-like."

228

Truegug looked at the orphans rubbing the back of his neck. He seemed nervous; like he knew the answer but was scared to tell them.

"Well, I do know a place, but… I'm not sure if he'd like me bringin' you over there."

"Truegug, why wouldn't he?" Ahria said. "He lets me visit sometimes. What makes them any different?"

"Because they're the super-new kids he hasn't met before, and you're…well, you're Ahria. He's fine when you're around."

Rowan could tell his friends were just as confused as he was. "Wait a minute, what's this all about," he asked.

"It's my uncle," Truegug replied. "He works in the smithin' district close by. You could probably get all the ashes you want. But he's… let's just say he's not the friendliest you'll ever meet."

"Why not?" Peron asked.

"Because of kids like Nyx, and because of every other adventurer who roams through this market. All they ever do is bully us gargoyles and try to ruin our trade. He only allows a few people around. But Mister Tawnwell's gone, Sid's visits get fewer and fewer, and he barely tolerates Ahria and her mom."

"Excuse me, I'm very tolerable," Ahria called.

Rowan sensed resentment in Truegug's tone. He knew what it meant to be picked on, so he could understand mostly. Then he got to thinking.

"Does your uncle tolerate Madam Spehrow," he asked.

"Who doesn't?" Truegug said. "If it weren't for her, our community would never be what it is today."

"What if we told him we're with Madam Spehrow? Do you think he'd budge and give us what we need?"

"That old excuse? Nah, not gonna work. Adventurers only use her name to get whatever they want."

Rowan scowled, then looked at Selah. She looked run down after her intense confrontation. Then he had another thought: an interesting and rather smart thought.

"Maybe *she* can be your reason," Rowan said. Selah snapped her head at him like he'd just said something insane. "If you tell your uncle Selah saved you, we could be one step closer to getting the dragon's ashes."

"Rowan, stop it," Selah said through gritted tusks.

"Why? I'm telling the truth. Protecting Truegug from getting hurt? That was super heroic."

"I wasn't being heroic," Selah countered. "What I did got someone else hurt too. It was violent, dangerous, and… not normal at all."

Her hesitation caused Rowan to wonder: was that how Selah truly saw herself?

"You just broke some bully's nose and gave him a fear of finding out," Peron explained. "If that's not saving someone, I don't know what is."

"So do you think it could work?" Rowan asked Truegug.

The young gargoyle rubbed the back of his neck again, clearly feeling unsure at these strangers' request.

"Probably not," Truegug said. "But if we never try, then we'll never know. At least that's what my uncle says." He pointed to the sky. "You see that black smoke up there?"

The three orphans turned to see rolling smoke coat the navy sky.

"That's where the smiths are comin' from. His tent isn't really that far, so we should be there pretty soon."

Rowan scanned the smoke trail, wondering how far it would take them. It led down from the other side of the long path. Turning at the next street corner would immediately engulf him in smoke. No way. It was just across the street.

Rowan grinned brightly, tightened his coat, and sprinted down the path saying, "This is amazing! You won't regret this!"

Truegug and Ahria watched him weave through the people in the street. They had a look that asked, *Is he always like this?*

"We're sorry about…him," Peron said to Truegug. "And yes…he's always like this."

"What he meant to say was 'thank you,'" Selah said.

"Hey, if it means I can repay you for saving me, I'll help you find all the ashes in town," Truegug said.

Selah gave the young gargoyle a warm smile, before she, Peron, and their new friends chased after Rowan.

Chapter 14

Ashes from a Dragon

Rowan had only been near billowing smoke twice: once in Faegan, where the light smoke trickled off the tongues of fire; second, when he held that purple match in his hand.

This kind of smoke garnered his attention. It was tinted with the smell of burning metal, Rowan coughed as it rumbled thickly through. He practically made a handkerchief out of the feathered coat.

They gazed upon the smithing tents Truegug had mentioned. They were open tents and booths, all black with identical wide dimensions. They weren't as colorful as the ones at the market, but the creatures in them were a different story. More gargoyles flew about the smithing tents than any place in Evermire. On the ground, one hammered a hot steel plate. Others flew past Ahria's head carrying works of iron, brass, or copper.

Rowan had read a book with a blacksmith who made all the best weapons for the heroes. Maybe Truegug's uncle was one of those. He could make Rowan some of the greatest weapons of all time. But he couldn't think about that now, the dragon's ashes were his goal, then Linn the Moonstruck. After that, he'd get his weapon.

Selah and Peron eyed the tents as well. Selah moved past a duo, fighting with heavy blades. She had to dodge slightly as a small dagger flew across the street into a wooden dart board. The creatures groaned when it didn't hit the center.

Peron was watching his footsteps, trying to avoid contact with the creatures. He almost walked into several people cheering a gargoyle who breathed a huge tongue of fire. Or at least, it looked to Rowan like he breathed it. When the creature did it again, he spat liquid over the open flame. They watched it soar high in the air across the entire smiths' district.

The mesmerized orphans stopped in place, and Ahria and Truegug had to pull them out of the way.

"Hey, what are you doing?" Rowan whined.

"You need those ashes, don't you," Ahria reminded him.

"Then you're gonna have to keep moving," Truegug said. "Besides, you don't want to draw too much attention to yourselves. Not in this part of town."

"Please, we've been doing that before we even came here," Rowan said.

"Oh yeah, and what exactly were you doin' before all this?"

Rowan glanced at his two friends, wondering if he should explain who they really were. But these new friends weren't grownups, and they'd probably never seen an orphanage in their lives.

"We've... mostly just been running away," Rowan answered.

"Running away," Ahria repeated. "From whom?"

"From evil monsters," Selah answered.

"From an evil, old woman," Rowan added.

"Basically, just running this entire time," Peron concluded.

Ahria and Truegug exchanged confused looks. Rowan didn't know why, though: the orphans had actually told the truth this time.

"Well, please don't say weird things like that in front of my uncle," Truegug begged. "Or else he's gonna question you. And if he questions you, that means he doesn't trust you. And if he doesn't trust you, then you won't get your ashes. And if you don't get your ashes, then we gotta go with our second plan."

"What's the second plan?" Rowan asked.

"Me! Tamperin' with his oven! Which we're not gonna do. Uncle Rog already took my toolbox for messin' with it a month ago. Do you want my toolbox to get taken again? I don't want it to get taken again."

"Goodness, you're so jumpy. No one's taking your toolbox, alright?" Selah said. "We'll stick with the first plan so that doesn't happen."

. "Sorry," he sighed. "I want to help you guys, I do. It's just my uncle can be a little…intense."

"Is that a bad thing," Peron asked.

"I mean, not really. He's a lot better now, but he used to be this really scary creature before I was crafted. He'd roar at humans, scarin' them half to death. He even carried adventurers by their shoulders and dropped them to the ground."

"I heard he even turned evil mages to stone," Ahria interjected.

That caught Rowan's ear. "S-stone," he asked hesitantly.

"Yeah, if he smelled any *virca* on townspeople, he would turn them into stone right then and there."

Rowan gulped. That did not sound good.

"That's just a rumor," Truegug assured them. "Just make sure you get on his good side when you meet him, alright?"

If Rowan had known he was meeting someone crazy, he would have just turned around. But before he could, another puff of smoke brushed through him and his friends. It wasn't until after they finished coughing that they saw Truegug standing sheepishly outside of a large smoky black booth. The booth had long shelves on either side reaching its canopy laden with ornate plates, vases, and bowls.

"I'm home, Uncle Rog," Truegug said, through the smoke. "You were right. Mister Tawnwell wasn't there, so I came back early."

Once the smoke cleared, the children laid eyes on a tall, bulky gargoyle adorned in a black apron, fanning the smoke with a rusted tin tray.

"I told you he wouldn't, you lil' devil," the gargoyle scolded in a deep, gravelly voice. "Next time, listen before blindly—"

He froze in the middle of his sentence when he saw the children staring at him in awe. His expression changed to a fanged frown.

"What business have you, you lil' brats," he growled. "Care to stare down death while you have a chance? Unless you're here to do trade, keep away from my nephew!"

Rowan, Selah, and Peron backed away from Uncle Rog. Truegug was right; he really was intense. Perhaps too intense, as his large bat-like wings spread out, and he held the tin tray above his head.

"Uncle, wait," Truegug interjected. "You remember Ahria, don't ya?" She smiled brightly and waved at the older gargoyle, surely friendlier in comparison to the orphans' horrified looks. "These are new friends we found in the market."

"Hmph! Friends, eh?" Uncle Rog huffed. "Like that shifty moon elf's son. I told you, if he keeps—"

"No, sir. Friends like Ahria. Friends who… actually saved me from Nyx when I met 'em."

The uncle lowered the tin tray onto a long, wooden table beside him, but his wings were still on display. His yellow eyes stared them down, and he didn't utter a single word. Selah curtseyed awkwardly, while Rowan and Peron waved with their heads turned away.

"I-in fact, Uncle, they were hoping to meet someone like you when they found me. Something about a Spehrow Quest."

"Hmph, how did this come about," Uncle Rog interrogated them.

After a moment's hesitation, Peron stepped up to speak. "Actually sir, my friend Selah was the one who saved your nephew."

"She did more than stand up for him, sir," Ahria interjected, placing herself between the frigid Rowan and Selah. "This young girl…and young boy stood up against Nyx and those bullies, making them run away in terror."

She touched her pendant again and whispered another spell. Her lute, crafted with carved swirls over the chipped paint, emerged from her hand. She strummed a bright and cheery key, making Rowan groan aloud as she sang:

She fought those fellows.

Who bark and who bellow

At the hands of the meek and kind-hearted.

With fury, she defended

And struck them heavy handed.

Knowing 'twas a fight that they had started.

Rowan looked up at Uncle Rog once more. Would that song be enough to change his stony expression?

Oh, mighty is she,

Shall you ever come to blows.

Mighty is she,

Who attacks the fiercest foes.

It sounds nice, Rowan thought. But something was missing. Where was he in all this? Sure, he hadn't fought them, but he stood up to them first.

And mighty is he,

With his magic, he did show.

He did his best.

All is at rest.

Rowan grumbled at her. What did she mean "did his best"? He noticed Selah twirling her curls again, bashful at the attention.

Uncle Rog glanced back at Truegug, still looking quite doubtful. "Do the fiend and bard speak the truth?"

Truegug nodded.

The silence grew thicker than the black smog. But Uncle Rog soon shed his intense expression; the lines of his sneer smoothed out as he rubbed the back of his neck.

"Well, speak up then," he demanded. "You're here for the Madam, so what do you need from me?"

Rowan felt uncomfortable stepping toward the gargoyle, but he made his requests known anyway.

"We um… Madam Spehrow says she needs dragons' ashes if we want to meet Linn the Moonstruck. If I want to become her ward, I need to get these artifacts. Ahria and Truegug said you might have an oven that carries a bunch of them. Would you have something like that?"

Uncle Rog looked behind him, then his wings folded back to their former state. He stepped aside, and a sweltering heat warmed Rowan's face. A wide, heavy contraption made of rusted iron sat atop a long matching cabinet. Crafted scales rippled thought its rectangular frame and a pair of hind legs rested on each side. At its top was an iron reptilian face with bulging eyes and a long snout. At the center, an orange flare was hidden behind a closed rusted gate.

A light went off in Rowan's mind: the oven they'd been searching for was shaped like the dragon in Madam Spehrow's riddle. He and Truegug looked at each other and smiled, subtly celebrating their minor victory. Suddenly, Rowan caught a whiff of a sweet aroma coming from the oven.

"The Madam hasn't been here in a couple weeks," Uncle Rog sighed, pulling on an oven mitt. "Don't know how she tied *me* into her ridiculous stories, but I'm sure this will work as well as anything."

Truegug gasped. "But Uncle, Madam Spehrow didn't say she needed our food. She said they needed—"

"Hush up, boy, and trust the process," Uncle Rog interrupted, opening the oven. "If there's one thing everyone knows about the Madam, it's that her stories are good for business."

Had Rowan heard that correctly? Did Truegug say "food"? But they didn't need any food. He wanted food, sure, but didn't need it. But before he could protest, the oven door opened. He squinted at the fiery light and for a moment was impressed.

Like an actual fire-breathing dragon, he thought and chuckled to himself.

Uncle Rog retrieved a grimy black tray from the dragon-like oven and rested it on the wooden table. He fanned it for a minute, picked it up, and displayed it to Rowan and the other children. On the tray were grey spheres with blackened sticks on the ends, smelling of chocolate and burnt sugar. Rowan and his friends looked at them puzzled.

"I'm not sure this is it," Selah murmured to herself.

"Um, aren't these ashes a little too…spherical, sir," Peron asked skeptically, adding "sir" no doubt in an effort to be respectful. He didn't want to risk being turned into a stone like Ahria had said.

"These are molten truffles, little wiseacre," Uncle Rog spat. "Ash-covered ones, if you will. They're all the rage in Beltierre. Just take one and tell me what you think."

Rowan, Selah, Peron, and Ahria looked at each other nervously, before taking truffle skewers from the tray. The only time Rowan tasted ashes was when he cleaned the orphanage fireplace. The last thing he wanted was to taste chalk and metal. But he had to understand why Madam Spehrow thought these things so desirable.

He and his friends took their first bites together. Rowan's eyes widened as he tasted it. He was pleasantly surprised. The chocolate taste overpowered the chalky ashes. He took another piece off his skewer, one with caramel syrup oozing out of it. Peron was grinning after he ate his. Selah and Ahria hummed in unison as they took another piece from their skewers. They had forgotten all about their scones from before, wondering if they could live off these molten truffles for the rest of their lives.

"Well?" Uncle Rog said.

The children looked up at his grumpy face, forgetting he was still standing there.

"Thif if really gud," Rowan said, mouth full of truffle. "Do you haff anymore?" He went to grab another skewer, but Uncle Rog snatched the tray away.

"Save the rest for the Madam, you little sneak," he chided.

"This is insane," Peron said. "Out of all the ways to use ashes, I never thought they could've been for something so… delicious."

"How do you even make something like this, sir?" Selah asked, her truffles already gone.

"You'll never know in this lifetime, dear," Uncle Rog said dryly. He replaced the tray on the table before wiping his hands. "Nephew! Fetch me my toolbox and those small sack cloths! Under the oven! Left drawer!"

He gave his orders so fast, Truegug hardly had time to stand at attention. He scurried over to grab the ash-wood toolbox and sack cloths. He returned, thumping the things on the table. Uncle Rog grabbed a brown piece of cloth and placed the truffles in the middle; carefully gathering them up for travel.

Other townsfolk must've smelled the delicious treat, because a few customers came in pretending to admire the pottery but really asking for truffles. Uncle Rog was right, Madam's stories sure brought in business.

"Wait your turns, you swine," Uncle Rog growled. "Take a look at my work! Another batch won't be ready for an hour!"

The new customers stayed in line, a little shaken but still waiting patiently.

Has he ever just thought about smiling, Rowan wondered.

As Uncle Rog picked a spool of twine from his toolbox, something fell out that caught Rowan's eye: a few small spheres which he picked up before they rolled off the table. Marbles. They weren't like his old ones, but their vibrant colors made up for it. He rubbed one between his fingers; it had the texture of dried clay. He'd only ever seen marbles made of glass. He turned to see customers admiring the plates and vases on the shelves in the front.

"Don't blacksmiths usually make weapons," Rowan mentioned. "Why do you have a bunch of marbles, vases, and truffles lying around?"

Uncle Rog finished tying the cloth with the twine. "Just because I'm nocturnal doesn't make me a weapon maker," he grumbled. "I'm a potter by trade. The truffles are to bring people in for the good kind of business."

"What's the bad kind of business?"

Clash! Clang! went some metal pieces.

The sound had come from a coppersmith tent across from theirs. A party of mages were throwing copper contraptions onto the street. Uncle Rog growled at the mages as he gave Rowan the bag of truffles. "The kind those blasted adventurers bring. Should've banned them from the district decades ago."

Rowan gulped. It reminded him of Mister Dre and all his mysterious warnings. But despite a few mean adventurers and a smug old tavern lady, maybe the town of Evermire wasn't such a terrible place after all.

"Well, sir, if you and Truegug aren't using those marbles, do you think we could have them?" Selah asked, placing an arm over Rowan's shoulder. "My friend's gonna need a big reward after he becomes Linn the Moonstruck's ward."

Rowan looked at her wide-eyed. "You mean it?" he whispered.

She affirmed him with a wink.

"Well, he better be a good ward," Uncle Rog said, digging through the toolbox. "Or else he'll never step foot on my property again."

It was another ominous warning, but it didn't stop him from giving Rowan a sack cloth bag full of marbles.

"That means he likes you," Truegug whispered.

"Don't worry about paying for it," Ahria said. "Kids get stuff for free all the time."

"No, they don't," Uncle Rog and Truegug countered dryly. The uncle held out his hand to exchange payment.

Rowan handed the bag to Peron and reached into his pocket. The last stone from his soup. He placed it in Uncle Rog's cold palm and watched him bite into it like a piece of hard candy.

"Two down, one more to go," Peron reminded Rowan. "Where do you think they'll have moonflowers around here?"

"Mmm, we could try going back to that forest again," Rowan said. "You know, the one near the entrance gate."

"You sure could," Uncle Rog said. "If you like searching in the dark without night vision."

Rowan deflated. He didn't want to spend the last of his quest scrambling in the dark.

"However, there are some florists who sell those weeds every summer. That is, if you don't mind traveling to the beach."

HOONNNKK!! blared the second horn.

The sound turned Rowan's head once more. But this time, its anxious ringing didn't rush through him. Frankly, he didn't mind the trip at all. He merely smiled at the deafening noise, ready for the last half of his journey.

"Thanks for the tip, freak," a snorting voice said.

Rowan and his friends turned toward the voice and looked up at a burly figure with bullhorns, a ringed snout, and a menacing smirk. *That one angry guy from the tavern. What was his name again?* Rowan thought.

"Raegar, you piggish pile of scum! I thought I banned you from my tent last week," Uncle Rog howled, pointing his toolbox at him. "You better start walking, or I'll call Red Eyes and tell him-."

"Call him all you want, you old canyon," Raegar snorted. "I have what I need, anyway." He snatched the sackcloth out of Rowan's hand.

"Hey, what are you doing," Rowan exclaimed, trying to snatch it back. He managed to get hold of it, but the burly man wouldn't let go. They grappled for the sack.

"What does it look like, kid?" Raegar grunted as he pulled. "I need that 200 platinum. Let go!"

He ripped the bag from Rowan's grasp, sending Rowan falling to the floor. Raegar turned to walk away as if nothing had happened. Peron, Selah, and Ahria came to Rowan's aid, but he didn't notice.

"Those are my ashes! Go find your own, you…you thief," Rowan demanded.

Raegar turned his head slightly towards Rowan. "Who are you calling a thief?" he asked in a low voice. Rowan's fright intensified when Raegar leaned in and grunted sharply in his face.

"Want to try that again, runt?" he threatened.

Rowan didn't dare utter another word; he merely shrunk back, staring at Raegar's nose ring rather than the glaring heat in his eyes.

Raegar chuckled at Rowan and off to another tent, leaving him cowering without even a trace of dragon ashes in his hand.

All that effort, all those people who helped him find the artifacts, just to have it stolen right in front of him.

Peron placed the bag of marbles in Rowan's hand, hoping it would console him. But Rowan held onto them limply.

"Don't worry about it too much, Rowan," Peron said.

"Yeah, I'm sure we can ask Uncle Rog for some more ashes," Ahria suggested.

Rowan hated how that was the last resort. But the line of customers threatened to delay his chances further.

Uncle Rog harrumphed as he put his toolbox away, ignoring the customers. "Like I said, it'll be a while before another batch. But if it were up to me, I'd show that coward what happens when you steal from me."

"What do you mean, sir?" Rowan asked.

"You're Linn the Moonstruck's ward, aren't you?"

Rowan nodded. It wasn't true, but it sounded nice out loud.

"Well then, show 'em what happens when you go up against her mages. Stand up for yourself and fight back. It's what I'm teaching the lil' devil to do now."

"Uncle," Truegug whined, covering his face in embarrassment.

Rowan remembered Truegug trembling before those bullies. Clearly, his uncle's words had little impact on him.

"But… what if something goes wrong?" Rowan asked.

"It might. But if you don't try, you'll never know if it works out in your favor."

Rowan spotted the bull-headed man at a blacksmith tent, holding a sledgehammer in one hand and the small bag in the other.

Then Rowan had a thought, a brave, dangerous, and possibly insane thought. He only had one hope: that he wouldn't end up dead before meeting Linn the Moonstruck.

"Well, I guess that makes sense," Rowan said smiling lightly. "Is there any way I can repay you?"

"Mmm…not right now," Truegug said. He rubbed the back of his neck again and spoke more softly. "But if you become Linn the Moonstruck's ward, show me some magic and I'll give you all the truffles you want."

Rowan liked the sound of that. He took a deep breath and began to march towards the man, but Selah, Ahria and Peron stopped him.

"Are you sure you want to do this?" Ahria asked.

"What exactly are you planning to do," Selah inquired.

"Hopefully not getting yourself killed, are you," Peron said.

Rowan had to agree with Peron on that one. "Just…when I tell you guys to run, run." He walked away. He never meant to hold back the truth, but his idea was so crazy, he'd rather not say it.

The thieving Raegar met Rowan's determined eyes and snorted.

With a light squeak in his voice, Rowan said, "You… you, sir, need to hand over my ashes right now. Or else I'll make you sorry."

Raegar rolled his eyes and faced him, items still in hand. "And I'll ask you again. What are you gonna do about it runt," he said with a sneer.

Rowan gulped. He needed to do this, no matter how foolish it might've been. When his gaze landed on Raegar's muscular calves, a distant fantasy crossed Rowan's mind; it was something he'd wanted to do to Den Mother for years.

Rowan swung his leg and kicked Raegar in the shin. The adventurer fell to his knees in pain, dropping both his hammer and the bag. Rowan snatched it off the ground and turned to his friends.

Selah and Peron looked confused, but Ahria's jaw had dropped. Rowan heard heavy breathing behind him, then the thief rose in a fit of fury and yelled at the top of his lungs.

"Run to the beach," Rowan exclaimed swiftly. "Go now!"

Chapter 15

Barrier to the Beach

Rowan knew it wasn't the best plan. Frankly, it wasn't even a good plan, but it was the only one that had gotten Rowan back his ashes. He expected a lot of things when he kicked the adventurer. He knew he'd get angry, and most definitely chase him around.

"Come back here, you brats!" the bull-headed man roared, striding after them.

Rowan's mind raced as he, Selah, Peron, and Ahria zipped past the townsfolk. Rowan looked at the bag in his hand. They weren't stealing from him. If anything, Rowan just took back what was rightfully his. Although, Selah might've taken his hammer as they fled. *It's for our protection*, Rowan thought.

He looked behind him and saw the raging adventurer push past an unsuspecting family with his horns and charge after the children. Rowan looked forward again, looking for any sign of the nearby ocean.

"Quick, follow me," Ahria said. The orphans did just that, but Rowan regretted it immediately once she took them toward a dark, narrow alleyway between two large buildings. Rowan was questioning her methods as the thief stumbled toward him. The children ran into the alley just before they met with the man's horns, which got stuck on the buildings. Raegar tried pushing through into the alley, but he couldn't. He reached out, almost grabbing Selah, but she struck him with the hammer. With a cry of pain, he pulled his hands and horns back, then fled from the alley, allowing the children to finally catch their breath.

"We should…be safe for now," Rowan wheezed. "Maybe he won't come back for-OW!" His thoughts were interrupted by Peron punching him in the shoulder.

"You are so dead if we finish this quest," Peron muttered through his fangs, pacing nervously. If Rowan had enough time, he'd say the same thing. But he rolled his eyes at the empty threat.

"I should've known you'd try to get yourself killed. But I didn't think you'd drag us along with you."

Rowan scoffed. "What was I supposed to do, Peron? Miss my chance to meet Linn the Moonstruck just for another thing of ashes?"

"Yes," the children shouted.

If Rowan truly had his spell book, he'd make them say the opposite.

"Well, we can't just stay in here forever," Rowan reminded them. "Who knows how much time we have left?" Before he could run out of the alley, Selah yanked him by the shirt.

"Oh, no you don't," she said. "That guy might still be out there waiting for us. If we want to get that moonflower, we need a plan."

"I *do* have a plan. Keep running until we get to the beach."

"We need a real plan, dummy," Peron criticized. "One that involves us staying alive and not being hunted by a giant bull-person! Selah, do you think you can use your hammer again if we see him?"

"I guess I could," she responded. "But you saw him run; it probably won't stop him. If we're gonna make it down to the beach, we'll need to find…"

Listening to his friends conspiring, dredged up memories he thought he'd left at the orphanage. He'd gotten in the way again. Perhaps Uncle Rog's advice couldn't change Rowan's history.

"I've got it." Selah snapped her fingers. "Ahria, when we were helping Truegug, he said something about a barrier. Do you think that's something you can do?"

Ahria seemed shocked by Selah's memory. "I mean, I can. I just learned that spell a couple months ago, but it's one of my weaker ones. Papa says not to cast it unless there's a big emergency."

Rowan felt his presence became that of a spying insect. Selah and Ahria discussed their defenses, while Peron peeked out the alley to watch for the thief. He observed the others do better than he ever could. Ahria interrupted his thoughts by snapping in his face.

"Hey, Rowan the Brave. Are you even listening?"

"Uh-huh," Rowan lied.

"Great! Peron, do you see him out there?" Selah asked.

As soon as she said it, Peron pinned his back against the wall. He gestured out of the alley, where Rowan glimpsed the bull-headed man still pacing angrily.

"Tell your papa, that this is a big emergency," Peron whispered to Ahria. "Because we'll need the biggest, strongest barrier we can get."

"I'll use it the first chance I see him," Ahria affirmed. She held her pendant and whispered a spell. *Soteriparc*, and a pair of cymbals appeared in her hands.

"I guess we're really doing this," Selah murmured, putting her hammer in her dress pocket. "Peron you let us know when to run. Ahria and I will stay behind in case he comes, and Rowan, you stay in between us. You just focus on making it to the beach."

Rowan couldn't help but feel offended. He never got to be part of the action. He groaned, put the small bags in his back pockets, and stood close to Peron, who watching the thief's back turned away from them.

"We run on the count of three," Peron whispered.

"One." He grabbed Rowan's hands.

"Two." Rowan grabbed Selah's.

"THREE!" The four children rushed out of the alley and ran away from the thief as far as they could.

After running from their pursuer for about five seconds, Rowan and his friends heard a loud, "Ha! Caught you!"

Ahria faced the thief, who stamped toward her. Just before his horns charged into her, she slammed her cymbals together.

Clash! Clash! Clash! they went.

Upon each loud sound, a teal ball expanded until it surrounded the children. The transparent wall blocked Raegar's attack; his horns bounced off the teal base and he stumbled to his feet.

"*Phinivenic*," Ahria whispered, her cymbals fading into teal sparkles.

Rowan tapped on the barrier's interior, following its spherical shape all the way to the top. *So cool*, he thought. The teal tinted Raegar let out a loud snort and slammed his fist into the wall. The strength of his strikes knocked the children to the ground. To their surprise, the abrasive motion caused the barriers color to fade in and out.

"The barrier's fading! Why is your barrier fading?" Peron asked in a panic.

"I told you it's one of my weaker ones! He could break through at any time," Ahria reminded

SLAM, went the barrier, making the children fall again.

Ahria got up and braced herself the fading barrier. "Quick, place your hands on the wall and lean forward."

"What's that going to do," Selah asked.

"It's going to take us to the beach faster, is what it's going to do. Now come on."

The three orphans almost questioned her, but another SLAM made them decide in an instant.

"Now, lean forward and keep running," Ahria instructed.

They all pushed and ran forward, causing the sphere to move down the street. It barely escaped Raegar's grasp as they sped away.

The children inside the barrier heard the thief's muffled bellowing once more, but they never stopped running.

The sharp twists and turns made it difficult to maneuver in the giant sphere. It nearly crashed into several tents and townsfolk, though some people managed to dodge them completely. The children got an earful of complaints, following it up with multiple "sorrys" and "excuse mes." Fortunately, Selah thought of a way to pass everyone with minor scratches. She leaned back on one side of the barrier to dodge a wheelbarrow of books. The others followed her lead, leaning together on the other side to evade a vegetable booth. They almost crashed into a crowded tent, but with all their might they turned sharply and rolled safely past it.

However, their trials continued. They heard Raegar's war cry behind them. Rowan saw the man sprinting down the hill.

"He's coming back! Roll faster," Rowan exclaimed.

"We're running as fast as we can, Ro," Selah said.

Apparently, they weren't fast enough. Rowan observed the next hill, which they were fast approaching. It wasn't terribly steep, but their speed decreased as they ascended. It gave the thief more time to catch up. The children tried to run faster, but they only got partway up before rolling back down.

"Wait, I think I have an idea," Peron said, struggling to get up. "Don't move the barrier yet."

Peron stood his ground as the thief got closer.

"What are you doing?" Ahria said. "He's going to destroy the barrier if we don't do anything!"

"With how fast he's going, he'll make it go farther if he runs into it. Trust me, it might work. I read it in a textbook once."

Rowan remembered that science textbook, but it had mentioned nothing about thieves ramming into barriers. Peron's theories were usually right, but what would happen next?

Raegar's horns slammed into the barrier. A loud crack came from the side wall as the children flew up the hill.

They screamed as they leapt through the air, their barrier fading in and out again as they soared. They landed abruptly on the path and started rolling out of control. The sphere dissolved mid-motion, causing the children to fall flat on the cobblestone.

Ahria fell on her stomach, knocking the wind out of her. Selah and Peron landed on their sides, hard enough that bruises appeared almost instantly. But Rowans was the unluckiest, crashing down directly on top of one of his small bags. He slowly sat up and pulled them out of his pockets. He opened one: the truffles inside were mostly still intact. So that must mean the other bag held…

"The marbles!" he exclaimed, remembering the last time a set of marbles shattered because of him. He opened the bag and sighed in relief at the colorful toy. At least a few good things had come out of this night.

"Just wait 'til I get my hands on you," the thief growled, stomping toward them.

Rowan didn't dwell on his soreness, nor how his legs wobbled like gelatin. He simply scampered upward, ready to flee the scene once more. He grabbed the bags and tightened the coat around his waist. His hands paused on the coat's arms.

He had another thought, an insane and high-flying thought. They'd tried running and rolling away, with little success. What if this coat took them farther than ever before? Rowan quickly donned it and helped his friends up.

"I think we might need to use this coat," Rowan said.

"I thought we agreed you'd never use it again," Selah recalled.

"No, *you* agreed I'd never use it." He glanced at Raegar approaching them. "I think if we all use this coat, we'll finally be out of this mess."

His friends looked at each other, still confused. "How would we do that? It's not like we can all fit inside that coat," Ahria said.

"No, but if you guys hold on to me, we could all get out of here. I can just give the coat directions."

"Rowan, that's gonna be really heavy," Peron explained. "Are you sure you want to do that?"

Crash, went the sound of breaking wood.

Courtesy of Raegar. The large wheelbarrow he shoved into a building cleared his path toward the frightened children. Rowan saw Peron looking concerned. He handed him one of the bags.

"No," he said. "But if it's the only way to get to that moonflower, then I've never been surer in my entire life."

His friends sighed at his determination; but they knew they had no other choice. Selah and Ahria linked arms with Rowan, while Peron stood behind him and locked his arms around his neck. Rowan already felt weighed down, and he wasn't even in the air yet. But the charging thief made Rowan erase his inner complaint. With his entire voice, he yelled, "Fly up!"

Rowan's white feathers began flapping slowly, lifting them off the cobblestone path. His friends might be reducing the speed of the coat, but they didn't affect its flight pattern. They were finally escaping their pursuer. For about two seconds.

"You get down here, you little thieves," Raegar cried, unexpectedly leaping at them. His meaty hand grabbed Selah's leg and yanked it. She squealed as he tried to drag her away, but she got a hold of Rowan's ankle. It made Rowan dip lower; his feathers strained to fly upward. Ahria and Peron caught their friend by the sleeves, lifting him for dear life.

"Are you insane?" Selah yelled. "Just stop already, or you'll get us all killed!"

"I'm not having you steal my 200 platinum, girl," Raegar said, climbing up her leg.

Selah's fingers started to slip from Rowan's heel. "We don't even want your stupid platinum! Please, just let us go!"

"I'll let go when the runt gives me those ashes!"

Selah pulled the stolen hammer from her dress pocket and brandished it at Raegar, striking him on the knuckles. He shouted in pain but still didn't let go. She hit him again, scolding him inbetween blows.

Strike. "I!" *Strike.* "Said!" *Strike.* "Please!"

Rowan swore he heard bones crack with each hit. After one final swing, Raegar's bloodied and bruised hand released Selah's leg, and he fell back into the streets. A cloth tent broke his fall, as his burly form crashed through it and trampled its remains.

"Are you alright, Selah?" Peron said.

"I'm fine, Peron," she said. Swiftly, she placed the hammer back in her pocket and fastened her arms around Rowan's leg. "Rowan, whatever you do, don't look down. Just keep flying."

Rowan ignored Selah's warning, but when the ground began to look even further than before, his eyes shifted to look onward. A gasp left his lips. He gawked at the high moon reflecting off the majestic water. He took a deep breath, ready to face his fears and find his next destination. Proudly, he commanded the coat. "Fly forward!"

As the coat pushed the children through the sky, Rowan realized he'd never actually seen a beach before. Sea adventure books told tales of fearsome ships, raging waves, and hideous monsters. But on the beach below, apart from the giant ferry, there were only fisherman boats lit by soft lanterns gliding along the peaceful waters.

He peered down at Selah, who was staring at the vast body of water while still clinging to his leg. The young girl sensed his spying and smiled at him. He looked at her with such pride.

"That was awesome what you did back there, Se," Rowan complimented her.

"It was nothing, Ro," she replied. "I mean we'd all do the same thing for each other."

"Oh, don't be so modest, Miss Selah," Ahria said. "Truegug's right. You could really do something with that strength of yours."

"Once I become a mage, I'll ask Linn the Moonstruck if you can be her ward too."

"Well, we shouldn't go that far, Rowa," Peron said. "We need you to be her ward first."

"I mean, yeah, but think of us doing adventures together. With my magic and Seah's strength, we could take all those bad guys *down*!"

And on that simple word, the coat flew Rowan and his friends back into Evermire at a rapid speed. They screamed as they soared past buildings and dodged a small cliff. Finally, they crashed into a large bed of flowers. The children groaned as they emerged from the bushes, only to be met by a gargoyle couple yelling them. Their growling language sounded like crashing boulders and confused the children. The angry couple gestured at the damaged flowers they were sitting on and pushed them out of the way.

"Sorry! Sorry about that! Our apologies," the children sputtered.

Rowan brushed pieces of flowers off his coat. He watched the gargoyle couple fly back to a rectangular wooden booth with flowers adorning its side. He looked around and found strings of warm bulbs hanging over the many flowerbeds laid against the bottom of the cliff.

"You really need to be careful with your words, Rowa," Peron criticized, brushing the leaves off his pants.

"But look on the bright side; we're finally at the beach," Selah said, removing a stem from her hair.

"Yeah, with a ton of flowers that we have to look through now," Ahria added, straightening her cap.

"They shouldn't be too hard to look for," Peron said. "All moonflowers have fuzzy white petals, green stripes in the center, ooh, and they even glow sometimes. But it only happens when there's a full moon."

I guess all his textbook facts are finally useful now, Rowan thought.

"Good thing that part is already covered," Selah said, pointing at the moon in question.

"Don't they have gems in them or something?" Rowan asked.

"That's more of a legend than a fact," Peron continued. "I wonder how this island even gained this kind of flora. Moonflowers are extremely rare. They usually get confused with other white flowers. But what are the odds of them planting similar flowers right next to each other?"

"I'd say those odds are pretty high," Ahria replied, a twinge of worry in her voice.

She pointed at the flowerbeds cascading along the stone wall. White flowers. More vibrant ones were peppered in between, but it was nearly all white flowers as far as the eye could see.

Why does it have to be this difficult? Rowan thought. But perhaps it could be a good thing too. If he found the last artifact, he'd officially have all the pieces to Madam Spehrow's irksome puzzle. He just needed to make sure he had them in his sights. The itchy crest around his shoulders, which was covered in thorns and petals, the moonflower he believed to be somewhere along this shore, and the ash-covered truffles he…didn't have in his hand.

The bag of ashes. He had them in his hand. Why weren't they in his hand? Rowan looked over at Peron, remembering how he gave him one of the bags. Maybe he had the truffles instead. Alas, the young fiend had nothing in his hands either.

"Per," Rowan uttered softly. "Where's the bag I gave you?"

As if a memory had escaped him, Peron frantically checked his pockets.

"What happened to the bag you already had?" Peron deflected.

"You lost them," Rowan yelled, stomping towards him. "Peron, one of those bags had the ashes in them! We were so close! How could you do this?"

The young fiend backed away with his hands up, defending himself from Rowan's statements. "Hey, it's not like I lost them on purpose! They must've slipped out of my hand when we fell."

"Oh, so Mister Responsible can quote a textbook, but he can't hold a stupid bag for five minutes?" Rowan shoved Peron's shoulders.

"Look who's talking, Rowan the Knave," Peron taunted, pushing him back. "Last time I checked, this was your quest, not mine!"

The boys almost raised their fists at each other until Selah and Ahria separated them.

"Seriously? You guys are fighting about this now?" Selah scolded them, showing off her tusks. "You guys must've just dropped them somewhere." Rowan hid his grumbling; she never took his side first. "But we can't go to Madam Spehrow empty-handed. So, we'll split up. Rowan, you and Ahria find the moonflower. Remember: glowing white petals and green stripes. Peron, you and I will find the ashes and the marbles, and we'll all meet back here. Understood?"

They all avoided meeting Selah's fierce glare. "Understood?" she repeated sternly.

"Understood," the boys mumbled with little enthusiasm.

"Understood," Ahria added, a bit shaken by Selah's commanding presence.

They walked off in their pairs. Peron and Selah scoured the sand for the two bags. Rowan and Ahria searched for the moonflower beyond the damaged flower bed. They combed through each white flower, hoping to find something that matched their description. Rowan plucked one with white petals.

"The center's supposed to be green, not red," Ahria said.

Annoyed, Rowan set it down. He found a dim glowing one and went to pick it up.

"That one's not white. It's off-white," Ahria corrected.

Like he could tell the difference. He sneered at her as he let go.

"Hey, I'm just trying to help you," Ahria scoffed. "You don't have to be all snarky about it."

"Ugh, you sound like Peron," Rowan uttered, scooting away to the next bed of white flowers. "Just because you know everything, doesn't mean you can boss me around."

Ahria pursed her lips but held back whatever she wanted to say and scooted farther from Rowan. "I never said I knew everything. I'm just trying to help you. If you showed Madam Spehrow an off-white flower with a red center, she would certainly know the difference."

"Then quit talking and keep looking, since I'm too stupid to understand," Rowan snapped in frustration.

Ahria shook her head as she rummaged through the flowers. "Whatever. You're not the only mage who wants to prove their worth, you know," she said.

Silence hung between them. Rowan spotted a fuzzy, orange flower buried in the bush. When he went to pick it up, he noticed his two friends digging through distant flowerbeds for the sackcloth. Peron quickly glanced over at him, before walking to the shore and continuing with Selah.

"You know, I don't live with a lot of people my age," Ahria started. Rowan turned to see her searching through the thorny bushes. "When you're an only child, you tend to rely on yourself a lot." She picked another orange flower from the bottom of the bush. "But if I had siblings, or just really good friends, I'd be grateful for the help I got. Even if we all make a few mistakes along the way."

Rowan lowered his eyes. It wasn't that he was ungrateful; he just wanted everything to go smoothly. Perhaps trying to prove himself made him forget about the people who had gotten him this far.

"I guess that makes sense," he mumbled, running his hands through the bushes. A thorn pierced his finger, and he immediately pulled his hand out.

He went to wipe the blood away, but Ahria offered her hand to help. Hesitantly, Rowan placed his hand in hers. The young girl placed her pendant on her lips.

A high-pitched musical phrase came out, followed by teal musical notes spiraling towards his injury. One of the notes landed on the cut, making it glow and sealing it. Rowan ran his thumb over where the cut used to be; it was like it was never there.

"I know it makes sense," Ahria stated. "I just hope you don't take them for granted."

Rowan took his hand back in awe. As he did so, he noticed a light flashing out of the corner of his eye. He turned and saw one of the flower beds glowing at the bottom.

He and Ahria looked at each other hopefully and rushed to the glowing bush. They dug through it, being mindful of the thorns and beamed at the glowing flowers, which had fuzzy, white petals. Ahria delicately plucked one and showed it to Rowan. He examined the green stripes running from the center all the way to the tips of the petals. But the one thing he admired most was the moment of legends. He lightly tapped the green emerald embedded in the flower's center.

"We…we found it," Rowan whispered with a smile. His smile reached Ahria, and she grinned even brighter. "We found it! We found the moonflower!"

Rowan's cheering reached Selah's and Peron's ears, and they ran over to join them. He and Ahria showed them the flower, beaming with happiness.

"Incredible," Peron said, wide-eyed at the emerald. "But t-that's impossible. No one's seen emeralds in moonflowers for centuries. How on earth did—"

"You did say they were extremely rare," Ahria argued. "Perhaps we just got lucky!"

Peron's lip curled in half a smile, still stunned by the discovery. He couldn't argue with that logic. "I…guess that's a possibility."

"I knew it was more than a legend," Rowan proclaimed. "Besides the emerald, does this look like the flower in your textbook?"

Before Peron answered, he went through his pockets. "Depends," he replied. "Do these look like your artifacts?"

"Where did you find them," Rowan asked.

"One of those gargoyles found one in her booth," Selah answered. "And the other one almost washed away with the tide before we caught it."

Rowan noticed his friends' soaked trousers and boots. He truly didn't deserve them. *Linn the Moonstruck, here we come,* he thought.

"Watch out," Selah cried, pointing at the sky. A wooden case of flowers had been hurled in their direction. Selah dashed in front of her friends, placed her arms over them, and lowered them into the sand. The case crashed a few feet away from the children, the wood and flowers splintering into smaller pieces. Rowan looked over Selah's shoulder, where he saw the heated Raegar stomping towards them through the sand. He noted the hand Selah bruised and saw Raegar's other one curled up into a fist.

"He's here," Rowan whispered. "He's here. Why is he here?"

Selah shook his shoulders to keep him focused. "Rowan, listen to me. You and Ahria go back to the Spehrow's Nest. Peron and I will take care of everything."

"But—"

"No, buts," she interrupted. She snatched the two bags from Peron and pushed them in Rowan's hands. "Just get out of here and become Linn the Moonstruck's ward."

Rowan watched Selah take out her hammer and stand beside Peron, awaiting the approaching thief. Ahria scampered off with the flower in hand and waited for Rowan to join her. His feet shifted backwards, and he ran with both bags in his grasp.

"Follow me. If we head for the docks, we'll be there in no time," Ahria said as they ran up a sand dune. Soon, though, Rowan stopped in his tracks; he was worried about the fate of his beloved friends. He dared not turn around, yet he did anyway. The burly thief towered over them. From afar, Rowan saw Selah swinging her hammer. Raegar caught her by the wrist, lifted her up, and slung her across the sand.

Rowan shuddered as he heard a faint thud. Selah, his best and strongest friend, had gotten hurt. He had done this. He was the reason she got hurt. He heard Den Mother's voice in his mind.

You should've just stayed in your place, urchin, the voice whispered.

No. No, he needed to fix this. If he stayed in place, then his feet wouldn't have moved forward. He wouldn't have carelessly dropped one of his bags. Nor would he have ignored Ahria's shouting as he ran towards the thief.

He glimpsed Selah's limp body lying along the shore. He shifted his gaze to Peron and Raegar and heard their conversation as he drew closer.

"I told you, I-I don't know where it is," Peron stammered. "Even if I did, I'd never tell you anyway."

"Then you can kiss your life goodbye, runt," the thief growled. But just before he slammed his fist down on the young fiend, Rowan slid between them.

Rowan stared at his attacker, but his body still shook in terror. Raegar lowered his hand and chuckled at him.

"Please…please don't hurt him," Rowan gulped. He lifted a shaky hand that held the other bag. "Here. You win, alright? You can have your ashes, just please…leave us alone."

"Rowan, no," Peron said.

The thief grinned at the sandy sackcloth. He lowered himself to Rowan's level and grunted in his face.

"You runts have been a pain in my neck all night," he growled. "How do I know you won't do any funny business?"

Another voice echoed in Rowan's mind. *Face your fears with dignity and respect.* Rowan remembered Mister Dre's words, thinking his next actions more foolish than brave. He furrowed his brow, stepped closer to the thief and said, "You don't."

The thief huffed at Rowan, preparing to call his bluff. But his gaze shifted past Rowan, and his proud expression changed instantly. His orange eyes dilated, and his smug, toothy grin sulked downward. Rowan recognized that look; it was the same as one fearful of Den Mother's consequences. Rowan wondered whom or what made this bold adventurer turn into a timid child. But he stopped himself from turning around, if only to escape the same fate.

Raegar grunted in Rowan's face one last time. "Fine," he said, snatching the bag with his good hand. "Thanks for aiding me in my victory, boy."

Out of annoyance, the thief plucked a few feathers off Rowan's coat. He must've forgotten to get the crest. Rowan didn't care; he just lowered his head in embarrassment. The man put the feathers and bag within a crate of moonflowers. He scooped them up and placed them on his shoulder.

The thief smirked at Rowan's disappointment. "Oh cheer up, boy. Just because you're a coward doesn't mean you didn't give me a good workout." Rowan balled up his fists. "Who knows, maybe I'll even split the money with you."

He sauntered off with a burst of laughter all the way up the sand dune. As Rowan watched him go, the thief clipped shoulders with a scowling but familiar fiend. One with spiraled horns, navy skin, and a snake around his shoulders.

"Mister Dre!"

Chapter 16

Linn the Moonstruck

The toll of their journey made their last time seeing Mister Dre feel like ages ago. Apart from shedding his cape, which he now had neatly draped over his arm, not much had changed in his appearance. Had he been watching that entire time? Was Mister Dre the one Raegar was afraid of? What other abilities did he have to make such a creature tremble?

Rowan saw Ahria at Mister Dre's side with the moon flower in hand. He thought she'd be in the tavern by now. Instead, she walked with Mister Dre down the sand dune.

Rowan and Peron heard Selah groan as she tried to stand. They ran over to her without hesitation. They checked her for scratches as they pulled her up.

"Guys, I'm fine," Selah said in a chipper tone. She brushed the sand off herself like nothing ever happened. Which worried the boys even more.

"A-are you sure, Se?" Rowan asked.

"That was a pretty nasty fall back there," Peron said. "We can find someone if—"

"There's no need," Selah shrugged them off with a smile. "I was just in shock. It's not like he threw me that far. Besides, you know I've got a pretty hard head."

Peron and Rowan knew of her strength, of course, but perhaps she had hit her head too hard.

"It appears we meet again," Mister Dre greeted them. He and Ahria came up to them. The musical girl gave them an unusually small wave, while the fiendish man casually smoked a pipe that smelled of mint.

"How did you know we'd be here, Mister Dre?" Selah asked.

He took out his pipe and blew a puff of smoke before saying, "I didn't. But when I saw a group of children flying and screaming across the sky, eventually you three crossed my mind." The orphans looked away embarrassed.

"Although it seems you've brought a new friend to join in your endeavors." Mister Dre peered down at Ahria, who refused to make eye contact with him. "You don't remember me, do you, Miss Valdi?"

The charming girl shyly fiddled with the glowing petals. "It's... good to see you again, Mister Spehrow."

Miss Valdi? Mister Spehrow? Rowan repeated in his head. He knew Mister Dre was called the Spehrow's Eye, but he thought that it was in Madam Spehrow's name. Why would Ahria call him that, unless...?

"I assumed you, Rowan, would have been someone's ward by now," Dremos said. "Considering you're on this quest; I take it Madam Spehrow's judgment was not in your favor.

Rowan looked away. "It's uh... it's kind of a long story."

"Indeed." Mister Dre shrugged off his reply and took something out of his pants pocket. "Either way, I believe this belongs to you." He presented the bag Rowan dropped on the ground.

The bag of marbles; the one slice of hope Rowan had this entire journey. He almost snatched it from Mister Dre's hand. But he stopped himself. He couldn't accept such a prize. Not after everything that had happened. He simply bowed his head and slumped into the sand.

Peron and Selah went down with him, worried if he had been injured. In a way, yes… he was.

"I tried, Mister Dre," Rowan pouted softly. "I really, really tried. But Madam Spehrow was right. I'm not worthy enough to be Linn the Moonstruck's ward."

"How did you come to that conclusion?" Mister Dre asked.

Rowan paused for a moment, trying to find the right words. Yet when he spoke, he felt his voice starting to break. "From the moment I opened my big mouth, she said I wasn't worthy. I went on this stupid quest just to prove her wrong. I thought if I got the artifacts myself, it'd be something that would impress Linn. Even when I had people help me, I only put them in danger. Den Mother was right; I really am a burden. I should've stayed in my place, or else I wouldn't have come all this way just for nothing."

Shame ate at Rowan's insides. The way he shared his thoughts, like he'd always wanted to, only made him hide his face to cover the wave of emotion. Not a single comforting word came from the surrounding crowd. It was silent except for the sound of Sly's soft hissing.

Tss, tss, it went.

For a moment, Rowan smelled the scent of burnt mint. He raised his head and saw Sly and Mister Dre, who held a notebook and a pen.

"Do you want to know why I had to leave you all earlier?" he asked as he wrote.

Rowan didn't know where this was going.

"Apart from slaying beasts, I maintain order for the Spehrow's Nest. I protect Madam, her patrons, and the adventurers who stay in her tavern." He ripped a piece of paper from his notebook. "During our quests, I observe their behavior to make sure they follow the rules. You'll never see me, but I'll always see you. If anything is out of order…" He fed the piece of paper to Sly, and the snake glowed white as he swallowed. "…I report it all to Madam."

So that's why the thief was afraid of Mister Dre. Did that mean he'd been watching Rowan, as well? The heroic fiend wrote in his notebook again and continued.

"Let's see. We've flown across town just to obtain a few artifacts, not giving up. We've defended our friends from foes both big and small, even if it meant giving up our own desires. And last, this conversation; realizing our mistakes and knowing when we're in the wrong." Mister Dre finished writing, ripped out the paper, and showed Rowan the words:

<u>Rowan and company</u>

Determination

Bravery

Humility

Observed and signed by,

Mister Dre fed it to the glowing snake again, making Rowan grimace slightly. How would Madam Spehrow receive his message if it was already in the snake's stomach?

"These are the qualities she looks for, Rowan," Mister Dre stated. "The artifacts are important, but they are not life-threatening. Whether you present yourself with or without them, trust me, she will admire your willingness either way. Which is why I believe this *does* belong to you." He revealed the sack cloth bag from behind his cape and passed it to Rowan.

Rowan sensed a hint of pride in Mister Dre as he smiled along his pipe. Rowan sighed, grabbed the bag, and opened it.

When he looked inside, he gasped. Confusion rendered him speechless. His hand sifted through the bag and lifted a small gray sphere, still scented with hints of chocolate.

"The ashes," the children said.

This makes no sense, Rowan thought. But if it truly didn't, why did he feel his lips curling into a smile? A foul creature's crest, dragon's ashes, and a moonflower.

"But if Rowan has the ashes," Ahria connected. "That means the other guy has the—"

"WE DID IT!" Rowan shouted, jumping up. "WE FOUND THE ARTIFACTS! WE GET TO MEET LINN THE MOONSTRUCK!"

Selah and Peron joined in his celebration, the orcish girl hugging them both and spinning them around until they were too dizzy to continue. In the midst of their joy, Mister Dre cleared his throat, and the three orphans stopped to listen.

"You'll want to hurry and present these to her back at the Nest," Mister Dre stated. "She hates to be kept waiting."

"Yes, sir," the orphans said, still beaming with happiness.

Mister Dre led the way up the sand dune; the children walked along with a skip in their step. Rowan marched through the beach, his smile as bright as the moon above. When Peron came up by his side, Rowan resumed a normal pace and lowered his gaze.

"Thanks for saving me back there," Peron uttered, giving Rowan a shy smile.

Rowan returned the same smile. "Thanks for helping me with the artifacts," he said. They both looked forward as the awkward silence filled the gap.

"Hey, Per?"

"Yeah," Peron responded.

"Do you really think I'm a knave?"

Peron's gaze softened at his question. "No," he quietly replied. "Actually, I don't even know what that is."

Rowan couldn't help but chuckle. Peron joined him, tousling his friend's coils as they laughed at their own naivety.

Mister Dre led Rowan and company back safely to the streets of Evermire through sandy beaches, over destroyed flower beds, and past the sailboats on the horizon, until they stopped at the ferry dock. Rowan ignored the wooden structure's loud creaking by recalling their adventures and the people they met along the way, nearly talking Mister Dre's ears off. But the fiend peacefully listened as he guided them to the Spehrow's Nest.

"So, you've discovered that Mister Golorog is not as abrasive as he seems?" Dremos asked.

"Well, he gave us food, and he told us to come back anytime we wanted. I guess he wasn't so scary after all," Rowan said.

"Oh, Truegug just says that," Ahria interjected. "If you ask me, Uncle Rog is hardly the scariest creature I've ever known."

"*Miss Valdi*, where does your *mother* think you are right now," Dremos asked Ahria. She simply winced and twiddled her thumbs at hearing the words "Miss Valdi" and "mother."

"She thinks… I went shopping with the band," Ahria answered hesitantly. "Which is kind of true! You wouldn't tell her I left, would you?"

"Well, I have to tell her something," Dremos shrugged. "Once we finish this quest, we'll go about town and find her."

Rowan watched the young girl groan while dragging her feet behind Mister Dre. Her expression piqued his curiosity.

"Hey, Ahria, I thought you said your… *preciseness* name was Baroq or something. Why did he call you Valdi?"

Ahria folded her arms and rolled her eyes. "It's pronounced *prestigious*. And that's because… it's part of my name. Ahria… *Valdi*-Baroq."

Rowan remembered how she corrected her last name earlier. He only knew one mage with the name Valdi. "No way," Rowan called in gleeful surprise. "You're Clascia Valdi's—"

"Clascia Valdi's daughter? Yes, I am," Ahria affirmed. Her voice still held the hint of a groan. "I was hoping you wouldn't find out."

"What's wrong with us finding out?" Selah asked.

"Why should I tell you guys? You didn't even tell me Mister Spehrow was helping you."

The orphans stammered before answering. "We weren't sure if we could trust you yet," Rowan said.

The little girl huffed. "Not a good enough reason. You had every opportunity to tell me."

"Oh really? Would that've been before or after we almost got chased out of town?" Peron asked sarcastically.

Ahria scoffed, knowing his statement to be true. "Mama's fame brings a lot of attention. Whenever I try to make a new friend, they usually just stick around until they meet her. I never see them again once they do. I thought if you found out, you'd only want my help because of my famous family."

Rowan had to admit that he found her abilities to be similar. But after all that happened, he knew that didn't matter. "You have music magic that makes another you, a barrier that saved us from crazy bull-people, and a flute that can heal all kinds of stuff. I probably would've asked for your help before I knew who your mama was."

Ahria looked taken aback by Rowan's response, as if no one had ever said that to her.

"I guess it won't matter, anyway," she said. "I'll never hear the end of it when Mama finds out."

"Well," Rowan uttered. "You can just tell her you wrote a good story. One good enough to impress, I don't know, Madam Spehrow."

Ahria gasped. "Are you serious?"

"You helped me with my artifacts, right? I guess I can keep my promises too." Rowan snuck a peek at Selah and Peron, who were smiling at him, proud of his charitable actions.

Soon, they arrived at the Spehrow's Nest. Rowan wondered if anyone had succeeded before them. He saw a trio of dwarven mages sob their way out of the tavern. Another group ran through the double doors with artifacts completely different to the ones Rowan had. He didn't see the burly thief, however. If he still had the marbles, Madam Spehrow must have dismissed him already.

Guess there's only one way to find out, Rowan thought. He went to open the door, but his hand stopped on the handle. Of all the times to have a million questions raid his mind at once. What if Madam Spehrow still didn't find him worthy? What would happen if Linn the Moonstruck didn't want them? Rowan shook that thought away. He didn't want to go back, not until he was prepared.

Rowan took a breath and turned the handle.

Ring, went the tavern bell.

Rowan opened the door fully, expecting some sort of recognition from the other contenders. In stories, adventurers were always praised after their quest. Instead, the sound of gruff shouting echoed through the tavern.

"HOW DARE YOU MOCK ME!"

Raegar was scowling at the calm and composed Madam Spehrow in the midst of his heaving rage. Shattered tableware, overturned tables, and a tipped crate of flowers offered evidence of the thief's childish tantrum. Madam Spehrow's servers, Toby and Miss Amori, had scurried with the other patrons to the corners of the tavern, staring fearfully at the man trying to intimidate Madam Spehrow.

Raegar and Madam Spehrow turned to see Mister Dre and the children at the entrance. Rowan gulped at the thief's horrifying glare.

"THERE THEY ARE," the thief yelled, pointing at the children. He strode towards them, continuing to rave. "These are the ones who cost me my victory!" He pointed to Rowan. "This one attacked me and switched out my ashes for some stupid marbles. And this one," he pointed at Selah. "This one broke my hand with a hammer!"

He kept his damaged hand at his side, barely able to clench it on his own.

"W-we wouldn't have done that if you just gave back what you stole from us," Rowan yelled back.

"I'm sorry," Madam Spehrow interjected. "What's this about stealing?"

"That guy's been stealing all over town," Ahria loudly explained. "He didn't even pay for those artifacts!"

Raegar tensed up at Ahria's words. Madam Spehrow stood behind him, awaiting more answers with a twitch of her pointed ears.

"Yeah. He just snatched the ashes out of Rowan's hand," Selah exclaimed. "Then he chased us until we gave it to him!"

"He threw Selah across the beach when he attacked us," Peron added. "Then, when we didn't give it back, he said he'd kill—"

"YOU SHUT YOUR MOUTH, RUNT," the thief cut him off. Madam Spehrow gently placed her hand on the thief's tense back, keeping him from causing further damage.

"Now, now. There won't be any of that," Madam Spehrow said softly. She took out two pieces of paper from her dress pocket. Both bore Mister Dre's signature. How had his notes traveled from Sly's belly to her hands? "This report from my Dre tells me all I need to know, comrade. Incorrect artifacts are one thing. But stealing from the market? Causing harm to other parties and our nocturnal allies? Why, that's more than not receiving a quest; that's banishment from the Nest. For both you and your guild."

Frightened voices murmured at her announcement before she unveiled the silver ladle from her black belt loop. "Not to worry, I'll write to your guild master and inform him once you leave."

"It'll be a bright day in *thra'ill* before you breathe a word to my—"

"Ah, ah, ah. Language, Master Raegar. We mustn't speak that way in front of children," Madam Spehrow cooed with a smile, as she placed her ladle on the bridge of his snout. "Rest, dear comrade. *Siliituum.*"

The golden glint in her eyes shimmered at the word, which also made gold chains sprout from the floor. They wrapped around Raegar's neck and wrists and pulled him to his knees. His injured hand shook as he braced it on the shattered glassware.

"Why… why can't I move?" Raegar strained.

"Don't worry, dear. That spell won't trap you forever." Madam Spehrow knelt down to his level. "Just long enough for you to feel the weight of your actions. Consider it a mercy I don't send you to the realm you so casually threatened me with."

A chill went down Rowan's spine. He had never heard anything so ominous, yet so compelling. Madam Spehrow yanked the chain around Raegar's neck to pull his face close to hers.

"Now, let's try this again, shall we," she purred. "I'll inform your guild master of the damages as well as the banishment. And should you ever set foot in my tavern again, rest assured, these chains will bind you for the rest of your days. Do I make myself clear, comrade?"

The man wrenched his neck upward and stared at her kind face. In a weary voice, he mumbled out, "Crystal… Madam."

Madam Spehrow placed the ladle on the thief's snout again, and with her other hand, put two fingers on his forehead. She whispered a word that Rowan and his friends recognized.

Diasare, she said.

Rowan didn't even try stifling his gasp when she cast the spell. He understood she was powerful, but he never expected her to do magic. The golden chains shattered and vanished from the thief's body, and he slouched in relief. He scanned the room, watching the patrons gossip louder than a whisper. The thief turned to Rowan. He almost looked away, but seeing his attacker defenseless and afraid made him seem…quite pitiful.

Raegar scampered up off the floor, shoved through Rowan and his friends, and ran out the door, beginning his early banishment.

As the door slammed, the tavern patrons erupted in applause. Rowan didn't even care if the applause wasn't for him. He couldn't help but stare dumbfounded at Madam Spehrow. Her stature, her authority, even the brief magic she displayed, just what kind of mage was she? Once the applause died down and the patrons returned to their chattering, Madam Spehrow came over to the children.

"If it isn't Selah, Peron, and Rowan the Brave," she announced. "My apologies to you all. Brazen behavior is unacceptable in these parts. I can only hope the rest of your journey wasn't too stressful."

The children glanced at each other; their faces told a different story to her claim.

"It was no trouble, madam. Thank you," Peron said.

"And it seems you found a guide along the way." Her gaze shifted, and she smiled at Ahria. "Last time I saw you, dear girl, you weighed nearly nothing in my hands. Did you help these children the entire time, Miss Ahria?"

Ahria looked at Madam Spehrow starry-eyed. "Yes, Madam," she grinned. "I absolutely did. You… you know who I am?"

"Of course, dear," Madam Spehrow affirmed. "If you really are Mother's Little Prodigy, I'm sure you did a fine job guiding them."

Her smile flattened, but she still looked satisfied.

"Dre, dear," Madam Spehrow cooed, holding out her hands for his embrace. The smirking hunter pushed past the children and let her plant a kiss on his cheek. "I'm so glad you came back safely, my love. Those notes you sent me were timely as always."

"Haven't let you down yet, have I, Starlight?" Mister Dre teased as he kissed her hand.

Rowan knew Mister Dre and the tavern owner were close, but he didn't realize how close. The two seemed to ignore Rowan and his friends as they held a brief conversation. Mister Dre carefully placed the snake over her shoulders. Madam Spehrow revealed her ladle again and she whispered another word.

Flonatvi.

The damaged objects throughout the room glowed white and levitated. Plates repaired themselves, tables flipped over, and the crate of flowers delicately turned itself upright. Madam Spehrow's spell received thunderous applause, and the fearful patrons sat back at their tables.

Rowan squinted at the curious spell; its sound felt almost familiar. He tried making a connection. He heard Madam Spehrow hiss twice and watched Sly slither past her shoulders, down her arm, and onto the handle. His silver scales spiraled up and onto the edge of the bowl, blending into the cutlery until he stayed completely frozen. Strange: the way Madam Spehrow held it, it almost looked like a... scepter. A...scaled scepter.

"Peron, she's Linn the Moonstruck! Madam Spehrow is Linn the Moonstruck," Rowan whispered, hitting his friend on the shoulder.

"What! No, she's not," Peron said.

"Why would you think that?" Selah asked.

"Her scaled scepter! The snake is the one with the scales! That's her scaled scepter!"

Peron and Selah paused briefly, observing the couple. Madam Spehrow took Mister Dre's cape and knapsack and handed it to her skinny server, Toby. Sly slithered from the silver ladle back to her shoulders.

Still, Peron shook his head. "That's just a coincidence," he countered. "Just because she has a scepter doesn't make her the real thing. I mean, you used the snake as a scepter, and you're not Linn the Moonstruck."

Rowan inhaled sharply, realizing he used her scaled scepter. Not very well, of course, but he used Linn the Moonstruck's scepter. The sound of Madam clearing her throat interrupted his thoughts.

"Now, that's settled. Why don't you all follow me?" She and Dremos went toward the counter.

Rowan followed willingly, and his friends trailed behind. He couldn't believe it. He was walking behind Linn the Moonstruck. Linn the Moonstruck was in front of him the whole time. He was in Linn the Moonstruck's tavern. Linn the Moonstruck sent him on a quest. Now, he was finally going to be Linn the Moonstruck's ward.

His starstruck thoughts repeated until they sat across from Mister Dre and Madam Spehrow.

"Well, Rowan the Brave, I believe congratulations are in order," Madam Spehrow told him with a smile. "No child has ever won our Spehrow Quests before, have they, Dre?"

"Afraid not, Madam," Mister Dre answered, fixing something behind the counter. "But I suppose there's a first time for everything."

When Mister Dre winked at them, the children beamed at each other in excitement. It felt nice to finally win something in life. Even as they celebrated, Mister Dre finished his task. He brought out a heavy wooden tray with a variety of utensils and placed it in front of Madam Spehrow.

"Oh thank you, Dre. This will be perfect for creating the potion," Madam Spehrow said. Hearing this, the children stopped their jubilee. Did Linn the Moonstruck make potions as well? Rowan furrowed his brows at the utensils. He understood the stone grinding bowl. But what kind of potion required a green tea pot and four teacups? "The artifacts, if you please."

Madam Spehrow's voice forced Rowan to focus. "Oh! Y-yes, Madam," he said. Still confused, Ahria and Selah placed the moonflower and ashes on the counter. Rowan removed his coat and folded it next to the wooden tray.

"Now, let's see," Madam Spehrow mumbled, noting each artifact. She lifted the moonflower to her nose, letting its sweet aroma linger. Then, she placed it in the grinding bowl and recited a poem.

> *"A dash of repha both flight and fowl,*
>
> *The ash from Beltierre's peaks.*
>
> *And precious stones near Venari's gates.*
>
> *Alas, you've found the things I seek."*

Rowan recognized her rhyming style. It was the same style the apothecary used. Madam Spehrow shook her head, clearly remembering something, while dropping a handful of truffles into the grinding bowl.

"That crazy apothecary revealed those ingredients to us only after we found them all," she continued. "We thought they'd destroy the gargoyles for good. But it seemed he had other plans."

Madam Spehrow plucked some feathers off the coat's collar. With her stone club, she ground the ingredients into a paste. The children gawked at the mixture in disbelief. Why would she need the artifacts just to destroy them all?

She chuckled at their confusion and scraped the artifacts into her teapot. "Unlike the townsfolk, the apothecary pitied the savage gargoyles. He believed them to be just like the rest of us: victims of the Legion of Khallus. I suppose, with no greater allies, what choice did they have but to do their villainous bidding?"

Rowan thought about Truegug and Uncle Rog. He couldn't imagine such thoughtful creatures terrorizing the streets of Evermire.

"So, the apothecary proposed an idea," Mister Dre interjected. "Turn the Nocturnals against the Legion. Evermire had no repha for them to feast upon. And no citizen in their right mind would dare feed their carnivorous ways."

"Except the Ataxia, right?" Selah blurted.

"Exactly," Madam Spehrow affirmed. She beckoned the children to look into the teapot. The ingredients rested on a porcelain filter inside. There wasn't a single drop of water in sight.

Madam Spehrow whipped out her ladle from behind the counter. She tapped the side of her teapot twice.

Tap, tap.

At the sound, a pool of boiling water spiraled into the teapot and over the filtered ingredients. Rowan's jaw dropped as the artifacts and water infused, creating a caramel-colored liquid that smelled of chocolate and flowers.

"Who would've guessed that a simple tea recipe would satisfy the gargoyles and their malnourished young?" Madam Spehrow said. She closed her teapot and poured the tea into cups. "Touched by the Ataxia's peace offering, the gargoyles fought alongside them against the Legion and aided in the victory for Nidas. This partnership later led to the Nocturnal Market, where our nocturnal allies vowed to protect Evermire and all its citizens. And will continue to do so for decades to come."

The children sighed at Madam Spehrow in relief, satisfied by the peaceful end of her story. All Rowan could do was stare at her in amazement. Seeing her work up close was better than he ever imagined.

"You really are Linn the Moonstruck," Rowan blurted.

His friends looked at him in shock. But Mister Dre and Madam Spehrow merely laughed to themselves at this truthful revelation.

"I was wondering when you'd figure it out," Madam Spehrow said, laughing. "Tell me, what is it that gave me away?"

Rowan nearly spun in his chair. He couldn't believe he was right. "Oh, um…your scepter," he replied. "In stories, you always use your scaled scepter to cast spells. I guess I didn't realize it was an actual snake that made it scaled. That's a pretty 'sly' thing to do, huh?"

Rowan screamed at himself internally. He had never made a joke like that. Why would he make a joke like that?

Mister Dre looked impressed at the young boy. "Few admirers notice that detail. I'm glad your stories have made you so observant."

Rowan peered smugly at Peron, who'd once doubted his remarks.

"Well, don't let your tea get cold," Madam Spehrow said, setting down her teapot.

The children looked at their drinks. The sparkling green liquid swirled in their cups. They all took a sip. With hints of chocolate and the sweet-smelling moonflower, the warm tea made them feel like they were walking on air. It relaxed all their senses.

"So, since Rowan gave you the artifacts, that means he gets to be your ward, right?" Ahria said.

Madam Spehrow scrunched her brows together. "Who said anything about him being my ward," she asked.

Rowan's smile faded quickly. What did she mean?

"But… we thought Mister Dre said you'd be his teacher once we met you," Selah said.

Madam Spehrow fixed a stern stare onto Mister Dre. "Dremos, did you really tell them all this?"

The fiendish hung his head humbly before her.

"Forgive me, madam," he said. "I told him either you or other Ataxia members would barter for the children's wardship. I assumed we could make some sort of…arrangement."

The tavern owner wrinkled her nose at Mister Dre and sighed. "I'm sure we can find a teacher for Rowan somewhere. But this is not the place. You know my oath still stands on the matter."

Rowan remembered that oath. He'd hoped she would change her mind. But perhaps oaths couldn't change that quickly. The thought, however, didn't stop him from slouching in his stool.

"Did I… did I do something wrong," he asked sadly. "I-I got all the artifacts. I got here on time. I even tried saving my friends from a bunch of bullies, just to prove I could do it. Am I still that unworthy of becoming your ward?"

Madam Spehrow squeezed her eyes tight, leaned on the counter, and looked at him sympathetically. "I'm sorry for my rash words, Rowan," she softened. "From the notes my Dre left me, you certainly have the capabilities of a good mage. It's not that you're unworthy. It's that you're far too young."

Rowan lifted his head. That didn't make any sense.

"But… Ahria's been doing magic since she was three," he countered. "And you. Weren't you born into magic almost a hundred years ago? What's the difference if I learn magic at a young age?"

She gestured toward her patrons. "You see all these adventurers in my Nest?"

He did, but he didn't want to acknowledge them.

"They come from all over just to get a taste of the life you desperately want. And you're correct. Many of them found their purpose early in life. But that doesn't mean it didn't come with challenges."

"What challenges?" Selah asked.

"The kind that bring unwanted enemies," Mister Dre answered bluntly, clearing the tea set from the counter. "The kind that make you look over your shoulder and make you lose sleep. All for the sake of finding your purpose."

Scary, Rowan thought.

"Not every mage's journey ends happily, Rowan," Madam Spehrow continued. "Magic is a wonderful gift, but if doing it means risking your life, maybe it's time to find another purpose."

"But…I don't have any other purpose," he proclaimed. His response made Madam Spehrow blink. "I was always told that I should be grateful and stay out of the way and not be a burden. I thought that if I learned magic, then all those things wouldn't be true. That I could actually be something better than what I was told to be."

"Something better," Linn the Moonstruck challenged, tilting her head to the side. "And what, pray tell, would that be?"

Rowan thought about it. Mister Dre called him determined and brave, but he still didn't know what that meant. He thought about the countless times his friends had saved him from his own mess. But what if they weren't there? What then? "I may not be the smartest or the strongest person alive. But I want to learn how to be brave. And I think the only way to do that is by learning from you. All I ask is that you teach me."

Madam Spehrow and Mister Dre gave each other approving glances, then she locked eyes with Rowan. She held up two fingers and said, "Two lessons. One lesson tomorrow and one the day after. No more, no less."

Rowan offered his widest, most victorious smile. His friends sighed in relief and smiled back at him. That is until Peron asked, "Um, madam, since you are giving him lessons, maybe you could find us somewhere to sleep for a night or two?"

Rowan had forgotten about that. Shelter was important.

"Now that I can arrange," Madam Spehrow affirmed. "What do you say, Rose?"

"We'll get their rooms ready once I take Miss Valdi home," Mister Dre said.

HONK!! went the last horn.

It startled the children before they remembered, they already made it in time. The bell rang, and the door swung open. The men in white stood in the doorway catching their breath. The purple fiend held the dragon's ashes, the blonde one carried a vase of moonflowers, and the white-bearded man wore the feathered coat over his suit.

"Master Torrence, Master Heziah, and Master Avion: Members of Emphyrea's Lights," Madam Spehrow said. "Grant them your praises, brethren, as the first official party to complete the Spehrow's Quest!"

A roar of cheers and drumming mugs were aimed at the bowing gentlemen. The children added their own applause, sharing their victory with another party.

"I'll be with you all in a moment," she told the party, before addressing Rowan. "As for you, I hope you're hungry for breakfast. You'll need a healthy one when we meet first thing in the morning." From her pocket, she drew out a small bag and pushed it towards him. "I also believe these belong to you."

Rowan snatched the bag and opened it to find the marbles safe and secure. That thief must've given them to Linn before he got here.

"Come along, Miss Valdi," Mister Dre said, leaving the counter.

Rowan snapped his head at Ahria, whose charming smile vanished at Mister Dre's call. She hopped off her stool and dragged her feet behind the heroic fiend.

"You're leaving already," Rowan asked, getting off his stool to stop her.

She turned around with a flat smile. "It was bound to happen," she said plainly.

"But… didn't you want to tell Madam Spehrow your story about me?"

She waved off his statement. "Oh please, I have plenty of time. I'm just glad I got to see her. Besides, your story's not done yet. You're just getting started. But don't worry, you'll see me again and then I'll let you know when I'm finished."

She said it so boldly. Rowan brought out his hand for her to shake; a silent way of saying "thank you." Ahria swept in for a hug instead. Even though he accepted it, he understood how Peron felt.

"Thanks for keeping your promise, Rowan the Brave." She went out the door with Mister Dre.

Rowan turned around and smiled brightly at his friends. He rushed over and gave them the biggest hug imaginable.

"I told you, Rowan," Selah said. "It'd be the first thing we do."

Rowan had new friends, a new town, and another new adventure to look forward to. He would finally become the mage he always wanted to be, and he would try his hardest to live out his purpose.

And yet, in the back of his mind, Rowan couldn't shake the uneasy feeling. One that made him nervous about facing new challenges and confronting frightening circumstances.

Part

Three

Chapter 17

You May Call Me

Rowan hoped to wake up to a new room, with a firm mattress and soft bed sheets. Instead, he found himself in a familiar space: the room with white walls. It looked just as empty as it did the last time he dreamed it. Why would he dream this dream again?

"Hello?" Rowan called, his voice echoing throughout the room. No one answered. "Selah?... Peron?... Linn the Moonstruck?" Silence.

He remembered that glowing hand, the one that offered to help. Rowan scanned the room, finding nary a trace of it. If he didn't want the dream to be boring, though, he needed to find something to do. That floor chain spell Linn the Moonstruck used—maybe he could try that before his first lesson. He stood up, pretended to have a scaled scepter in his hand, and tried his best to pronounce the spell.

"Sil…sildrum? No, that's not right. Um… sill… siliiphum?"

"Siliituum," a voice echoed.

Rowan yelped and turned around. A sparkling hand glowed a foot away from his face, still in its outstretched form. He straightened himself up and cleared his throat.

"Oh, you scared me," he said. "Why are you in my dream again?"

The hand took a second to respond. "*I am your guardian, remember?*" it said, pulsing as it spoke. "*That is, if you will still allow me to be.*"

This was the second time it had said that.

"I mean, I guess you can be," Rowan said. "But don't guardians usually protect you, like… in person?"

"*There are many ways in which one can protect and guide. One being how to pronounce spells correctly when you start your journey.*"

Rowan squinted at it. Had he just been insulted by a hand?

"*I've come to give you a warning.*"

"A warning? What for?"

A longer pause, as if the hand didn't know how to phrase it. It floated closer to him, still offering itself to be held. Rowan grimaced at it. Last time, he found a snake crawling on his arm when he woke up. But if the message was a warning, perhaps he needed to take a chance. He took the glowing hand. It grasped his tightly.

"*Danger. Danger lurks in times we are most comfortable.*"

Rowan furrowed his brows. What kind of danger?

"*A familiar presence will come to disrupt the fabric of your reality. You must stay vigilant and be prepared. Do this, and you will surely succeed in keeping your life. If not…*"

"If not…" he repeated.

"Destruction." Its voice was distorted and haunting. *"Destruction shall haunt your days 'til you perish from this realm."*

Did that mean he was going to die? Would he cause the destruction?

Suddenly, the hand squeezed Rowan's even tighter. Its sparkling light spiraled around his arm once again.

"Wait! No, no, no! Don't go yet," he shouted. He still had so many questions, and yet the light persisted in leaving.

"What does that mean?" The light reached his left eye again. "What does that mean?"

His vision went black. Then he found himself lying on a firm mattress with soft navy bed sheets.

Rowan had never expected to have a new room. Sure, it was temporary, but until then, it was his room. Or at least his and Peron's room. A room that felt specifically tailored just for them. It had blue wallpaper and polished wooden shelves for clothes and books. He exhaled, relieved he hadn't woken up in that awful place again.

He tried shaking off his drowsiness, and more importantly, the strange feeling he had after his dream. That hand never answered his question. What danger could he possibly encounter? And just how could he stop it from happening?

Rowan squinted as daybreak shone through the circular window. Daybreak. Morning! It was already morning! If he didn't move, he'd be late for his very first lesson!

"Peron, why didn't you—" Rowan started to whine, until he realized the bed next to his was empty. Strange, Peron usually slept like a stone. Where had he run off to?

Rowan lifted the covers and strode barefoot along the cold hardwood, hoping he'd get to Linn the Moonstruck sooner. Also to give Peron a piece of his mind.

He opened the door and viewed the chandelier hanging in all its glory. Yet the second floor where he stood seemed a little…empty. Only a handful of adventurers sat at their tables. Rowan glanced over the balcony railing and observed the scattered few eating what smelled like heaven on a plate. He found Peron and Selah in a large booth surrounded by plates of glorious food.

The previous night, Linn the Moonstruck escorted Selah to a separate room from Peron and Rowan. Rowan had wondered if she'd be safe in a room by herself. But seeing Selah eating with pure joy, Rowan knew he had nothing to worry about.

"Morning Ro," Selah spotted him, waving cheerfully. "Come on down. We saved you a plate."

The young boy raced down the steps and met his friends half way.

"You remember what Madam Spehrow said?" Peron scolded. "You better eat something before she changes her mind."

Rowan scowled. "Why didn't you wake me?"

Peron chewed his scrambled eggs as he shrugged. "You're taking real lessons now. I'm not responsible for your schedule." But the young fiend still passed Rowan a plate of potatoes, toast, and five thick pastries with butter and syrup. The food made his mouth water.

"Rowan, you have to try these pancakes," Selah said, stuffing her mouth with a forkful of her own. "The Emphyrea's Lights party say they're the best in town."

He took a fork and knife and sampled a piece. He nearly cried from the sweet and fluffy texture. In between bites, he asked. "Wait, who'fs the Emphrea'v Lighfs?"

"Why, good morning, fellow champions." The purple fiend, Torrence, greeted them. The three men in white sat at the same booth as the children. Their tailored suits looked more pristine in the morning, with the addition of white capes and white gloves. They placed hot drinks on the table. "Good to see you all enjoying your breakfast. Hopefully, you all slept well last night."

"Hah, I'm surprised any of us could sleep after finishing that ridiculous quest," Master Avion, the long-bearded one, said, scooting into his seat.

"Oh, cheer up, old friend," the golden-haired one, Heziah added, sitting improperly in the chair he brought with him. "All that matters is we won. Besides, any quest is better than no quest at all."

Rowan snarfed down a chunk of pancakes. "What kind of quest did she give you?" he asked.

All three of them looked over their shoulders, then Master Torrence leaned in closer.

"You kids ever heard of the Forbidden Depths?"

The children shook their heads.

"What if I told you there was a secret lair of legionnaires beneath Venari's surface? One that even the Council doesn't want you knowing about. Apparently, it's the birthplace of the Legion of Khallus' strongest members. And what's more, their use of *virca*, the forbidden magic, is far more powerful than any other legionnaire known to man. Some say even the bravest parties haven't defeated them, yet."

"You think you guys can stop them yourselves," Rowan asked.

"But of course! Destroying secret lairs is child's play. It's nothing the Zealots of Paia can't handle. But I know some say no adventurer has ever entered the Depths…and made it out alive."

What a hair-raising quest. Possibly, it was just the quest he needed as a new mage. What a great way to start his first adventure.

"Do you guys need an extra hand?" Rowan asked. "I'm kind of new at magic, but I'm sure I could be of some help to you!"

The three men laughed at his question. Had he said something wrong?

"Oh, it's so good to see such child-like ambition," Master Heziah said. "Yet, a little too ambitious. Young man, this journey is far too dangerous. Besides, I'm not sure you'd want to travel with us. We're not those kinds of mages."

"But don't you guys cast a lot of fire magic? What makes you any different from other fire mages?"

"The difference is in our oaths." The three men showed off their white gloves. Each one had a diamond-shaped crest in the middle. Master Avion had golden-trimmed gloves and a flame stitched in the center, Master Torrence wore blue-trimmed gloves with a blue ax, and Master Heziah's had green trim with a small green tree.

There went that oath again, Rowan thought.

Heziah rubbed his gloves together until green flames enveloped his hands. A thin green vine sprouted from his palm.

Olivius and the footman had never done something like that before.

"Our oaths are dedicated to Caelum," Heziah said. "Whether it be healing, protection, or the blessing of the earth and soil, we help spread His gift of magic all throughout Pelle." He plucked the vine from his palm once the flames faded.

"So, if you wish to join us, be our guest to spend eternity at a temple in the mountains," Avion quipped.

Would eternity wait for destruction to fall upon him and his friends? No, he had to learn magic as soon as possible. Which meant he needed to leave his breakfast unattended and get to Linn the Moonstruck quickly. But when he scoped out the tavern, he found no sign of her. Only her waiters, Toby and Amori and…Mister Dre.

A heavily concentrating Mister Dre, preparing tea behind the counter. Rowan grabbed a bite of toast and strode towards him with a question on his mind.

"Good morning, Mister Dre," he exclaimed.

The stoic fiend tipped his head. "Good morning, Rowan. I hope everything is to your liking."

"Mm-hmm, it really is. Do you know where Madam Speh…I mean, Linn the Moonstruck is?" Rowan asked. Mister Dre raised a brow. "I just…didn't mean to keep her waiting, is all."

"Frankly, you'll have to wait for *her*," Mister Dre said, wiping his hands on his apron. "During her morning duties, our mayor came in to talk with her. Hasn't left her study since dawn." He gestured to the rounded door that clashed with the brick wall. Funny, had that door always been behind that shelf?

But the doors were slightly ajar. That gave Rowan the perfect way to sneak in for his first lesson.

"I warn you, though," Mister Dre added, "Linn the Moonstruck favors manners within her presence. Try to wait until she's done with her conversation." He left the counter with two shimmering drinks in his hand. It gave Rowan the chance to look to his friends for permission.

"Go for it, Ro," Selah cheered, raising a forkful of egg.

"If she changes her mind, I get all your pancakes," Peron added.

With that support, Rowan snuck over to the door until his back was pressed against the brick wall. He peeked in the dimly lit room, where Madam Spehrow—now Linn the Moonstruck—calmly sipped tea at a small wooden table. A tall figure paced past the thin slit in the door. Rowan cracked it open a bit more for a better look.

He saw Linn the Moonstruck staring dully at a thin, well-tailored man with skin that matched the night sky. His appearance resembled Linn, in the way his long, pointed ears twitched anxiously under his tan boater hat. He had a flustered expression, and the white specks on his skin flared like distant stars.

"Sire, there's simply no reason to worry about yesterday's incident," Linn the Moonstruck said. "From what I'm told, the border is in safe condition and the inqai at the Barrens were swiftly taken care of."

"And how would you know?" the mayor said primly. "You weren't even there when it happened."

"Perhaps but having your husband as an eyewitness certainly has its perks."

"Please take this seriously, Spehrow." The mayor harrumphed, pacing some more. "Do you know how it looks if we let another incident like this slip past us? Think of the reputation we must uphold. For the town, the island, for its humble leadership."

The mage could barely contain her eyeroll. "Sire, again, Dre and our zealous brethren defeated the inqai at the cusp of the Barrens. Even if they did invade, the border would surely thwart their advances."

"And what happens if those abominations do break through," the mayor demanded, slamming his palms on the table. "Are you willing to handle the strain if we lose more lives?"

Linn the Moonstruck clenched her jaw, trying to maintain her composure as the mayor glared at her. "If we worry ourselves to death over this, we'll grow madder than the Legion themselves."

Rowan let out a gasp. It was loud enough that both adults peered over to check out the noise. The mayor quickly disregarded it, straightening up and clearing his throat for a proposal.

"Be that as it may, I want you to do more regular inspections of the border," he said with an upturned nose. "Bimonthly visits apart from your quarterly ones. If you see anything out of order, report to me immediately."

"Anything else?" The exhausted mage placed a hand on her forehead.

The mayor continued in his snobbish tone. "Personally, if it were me, I'd check beyond the border itself. In the Barrens of Coriva, for example. Find out who might've aided Dremos in the beast's attack and bring them to justice."

Linn the Moonstruck's pointed ears perked up. "What exactly are you implying?" she asked.

Rowan wondered the same thing.

"Your eyewitness rode through the Barrens after another quest, correct," the mayor recalled. "After he told me, and he did tell me, I thought… his words seemed off. I'm not saying he's hiding anything, but you can't be too careful with these *Khallus spawn*, these deceivers and traitors of Caelum's gifts. And wouldn't it be a shame if someone was harboring a traitor in—"

"And that, *Oligio*… is where you've crossed a line," Linn the Moonstruck said with a hint of rage, rising from her seat gingerly. "I shall inspect the border tomorrow morning. However, I'd rather not have this conversation if it involves any ill will towards *my* husband and *your* best hunter. Or has the Battle for Nidas slipped your mind once again?"

Rowan let the long pause sink in, watching the two glaring at each other with deep disdain.

"We both know your magic has its limits. And that little Ataxia title you carry only gets you so far with the authorities. Take care of the border, or I'll have the Council do it for you," the mayor said, before he headed towards the door.

Panicking, Rowan pressed his back against the wall as the door swung open. The mayor stormed out of the tavern, leaving Rowan to process what had just happened.

He peered back into the doorway and was shocked to see the teacup, the chairs, and a multitude of books; all beaming stark white and spinning furiously around Linn the Moonstruck. Her hands tightly gripped the table as her dreadlocks floated upward. Rowan didn't want to know what would happen if he went in. Then suddenly, the objects all froze and dropped to the ground. The mage's hair lowered while she let out a long, shuddering sigh.

"You can come in now, Rowan," Linn the Moonstruck said calmly.

Rowan hid himself for a moment, then went into the room, where he looked sheepishly at the floor. "H-how did you know I was here?" he asked.

She turned around, smiling politely, and picked up the fallen books. "I'd suggest putting your ear closer to the door rather than your eye. That way you can eavesdrop more discreetly."

He helped pick up her books, until he noticed something amazing: dozens of massive bookshelves that reached the ceiling. "So many books," he whispered.

"Why, thank you for noticing," she said, putting her teacup back into place.

"Have you read all of them?"

"Not yet. But I do intend to read this section by the end of the year." She pointed to the row closest to the ceiling. It would probably take Rowan centuries to finish all those books. "Are you here for our lesson or did you just come to gawk at my collection?"

"I didn't mean to," he blurted. He lowered his voice. "I, uh…yes. Yes, I think I'm ready."

"Wonderful! Have a seat," she said passively, fixing the chairs upright.

He sat in the chair next to her, anxiously drumming his fingers on the table. He had just met her yesterday, so why did he feel nervous? When she sat down, his nervousness only increased as he avoided her gaze.

"Alright so, umm… Madam Linn the Moonstruck… S-Spehrow," he began. "I'm still pretty new to magic. I mean, I have a couple of spells that I'm kind of good at. But if I want to get better, is there anything I should know before I start some real spell-casting?"

The tavern owner chuckled lightly. Had he said something funny?

"First of all, dear, you don't need to keep calling me that," she said.

"Calling you what?"

"The Moonstruck title. A polite gesture, but highly unnecessary. I only went by that during my days with the Ataxia. You may call me Madam Linn, if you'd like."

"Oh. Alright… Madam Linn." Rowan felt so strange saying it. It would definitely take getting used to. "Where should we start?"

"Well, the best place to start is at the beginning. For instance, what are some spells you already know?"

"I know how to…make things float in the air. And I know how to make them come closer to me."

"Hmm. Interesting," she said, resting her chin on her hands. "If you were to cast such spells right now, how would you normally do it?"

Was she asking him to cast a spell? What a dream come true! He searched for something, anything to perform his next trick with; and then he saw it. It was perfect.

"I mean…it's not very good. But I guess I could show you something," he said softly. He pointed to her teacup. "May I?"

She shrugged and took the teaspoon out of the cup.

Rowan stared at it for a moment, anxious about his spell. This teacup… it was far more delicate than marbles. Still, he lifted his shaky hands and called out the spell.

Altsum.

The teacup swirled within a dark blue hue, trembling as it rose from its saucer.

Surprised, Rowan watched it float into the air with a wide smile plastered on his face. He'd done it! Excitement filled his spirit. All he had to do was make it float closer to him. Thankfully, he remembered the correct spell and said it proudly.

Corimani.

It stayed in place, still floating, but barely moving an inch. He cast it again.

Corimani. Nothing. *Corimani.* Same thing.

A lump formed in Rowan's throat. He glanced at Madam Linn, who furrowed her brows. He was making things worse. He repeated the same word, each time getting louder and more agitated until his entire form flashed blue, and he slowly levitated from his seat. *Not this again*, Rowan thought.

"*Diasare*," Madam Linn whispered, grabbing the teacup out of the air.

Rowan dropped back into his seat with an uncomfortable thump. His breathing grew heavy, and his head felt dizzy, just like it had back in the caravan. He only just cast that spell today. How could he already be tired? He peered up at Madam Linn, who calmly placed the teacup back on its saucer.

"So, um… what do you think?" Rowan asked breathlessly.

"Elven spells," she said, tracing her fingers along the cup's rim. "Do you practice them often?"

Rowan nodded lightly.

Madam Linn smiled nostalgically at the cup. "Those take me back to simpler times when I was a young half-elf. In my day, elders compared my spell-casting to yours. Calling it immature, untrained…sloppy."

Well, that was certainly rude.

"But that was a different time. I find your spell-casting to be quite charming. I know the rest of the Ataxia would enjoy it."

Rowan sighed. If Den Mother observed his spells, she'd only disdain for it in word and deed. It'd be nice to have someone encourage him, even if he felt exhausted.

"That heaviness you feel," Madam Linn said softly. "That's from casting your spell too many times."

"Oh," Rowan said, straightening up from her critique. "Sorry."

"It's not your fault. You didn't know. Oathless mages can only cast each of their spells once a day. Do it too much, and you'll run yourself ragged. I suppose before you take your oath, we'll find you a familiar like Sly."

Rowan raised his head in wonder. "Why would I need a familiar? Will it make me stronger if I have one?

"Why do you think I have one?" Madam Linn answered smugly.

To be as strong as Linn the Moonstruck. Rowan could see it now. He'd get something like a giant bear, a wolf, maybe one of those repha birds. One of those would make him practically invincible. But before he found his own familiar, something Madam Linn had said crossed his mind.

"What do you mean by 'take an oath'?" Rowan asked. "I didn't think I needed one. I thought I could just cast spells and be happy. I mean, do I really need one? Should I make one now? Because if I do, I guess I can promise to—"

"Rowan, it's alright," Madam Linn said soothingly. "It was just a suggestion. And to answer your question. No, you don't need to take an oath right now."

Rowan relaxed his shoulders. But if he didn't have to take an oath, it still begged the question. "Well, what happens if I do? Mister Dre said it would be the most important decision of my life."

"Yes, well, Mister Dre has very… strict opinions about oaths, so there's no helping that. The way I see it, if you take an oath, you'd simply be enhancing your spell-casting abilities."

"But I thought I did that through reading and practicing."

"That certainly is the ideal way." With the handle of her spoon, she drew a circle in the center of the table. A colorful string of lights emerged and illuminated them from overhead. "But if one wishes to make their name known, give reverence to their deities, or even protect the ones they love, one makes an oath to gain the power they need; and in return, one hopes to achieve the impossible."

The young boy marveled as distinct silhouettes appeared from the lights: a hero holding up a sword, a person kneeling in prayer, and someone embracing their loved ones.

"When you make an oath, however," Madam Linn continued, "you are forever bound to it. And sometimes an oath can feel limiting, especially for those who wish to know more."

Rowan squinted at the lights in confusion. "Didn't you say making an oath makes your magic perfect? How would it feel limiting?"

There was a pause before the glowing silhouette changed to a mage performing tricks. "Say you make an oath to use… floating magic to save the greater good." The mage started floating, then flying through the air. "Your powers are heightened, but you're only allowed to use that kind of magic. If you wish to use different spells to help others, then…"

"You couldn't," Rowan realized aloud. "You're not supposed to. Because you would be… breaking your oath?"

Rowan already had people he needed to protect. Should he take an oath to keep them safe? What would happen to them if he broke it accidentally? Madam Linn watched him for a moment, then waved the lights away. "I suppose that concludes today's lesson. Perhaps this was a bit too much for you."

He grew concerned as he watched her stand. "No, no, no! I-It's not really," he said, scurrying out of his chair. "I guess I'll… just have to get used to it. Maybe we can…try again?"

Madam Linn chuckled, but not in a rude or condescending way like the night before. It was more like she was amused by Rowan's innocence and determination.

"Have you ever officially met the Ataxia? The Stringed Siren, perhaps."

"No," he said. Unless meeting her daughter counted for anything? What was she suggesting?

"Tell you what, my Dre is managing the tavern for the rest of the afternoon, and I still have my morning duties to attend to. Why don't I have Amori purchase some new clothes for you and your friends, and you can explore the beach? Once I'm done, we'll go into town to meet Clascia, show her one of your spells, and see if she has any pointers for you. How does that sound?"

Under her poised smile, Rowan couldn't tell if she was serious or not. "You mean it?"

"But of course. After all, mages never break their promises," Madam Linn said, opening the door for him. "Now you go eat the rest of your breakfast and get prepared. We'll make haste at high noon."

Rowan couldn't believe it. "Uh… alright. I'll see you then."

He walked out of the strange room, hardly able to contain the smile on his face. But even as joy overcame him, he knew he only had so much time to prepare.

Chapter 18

I Should Have Known

Altsum, Rowan called out.

The clay marbles flashed blue and slowly hovered over the sandy beach. They lifted higher until they met Rowan's vision. He felt a thrill of excitement as he observed his success. But his excitement dimmed once he lifted off the ground.

"Not again," Rowan whined.

"*Diasare*," Selah and Peron grumbled.

The marbles dropped firmly into the sand, while Rowan landed and slumped over.

"Ugh, I really thought I had it this time," he panted, with only enough energy left to fling sand in defeat.

"This is the fifth time you've practiced that spell. You need to take a break," Selah reminded him as she helped him up.

"I need to keep practicing if I want my spell to be great," he countered in a sluggish tone.

"It won't look great if you keep tiring yourself out," Peron said, picking up a few marbles. "Why do you think we're at the beach? Come on, it's time to give it a rest."

Rowan looked out at the sea. He wanted nothing more than to jump into the ocean, but salt water wouldn't fix his spell-casting. "I'm fine. Let's just try it one more time."

Selah tilted her head at Peron, motioning for him to give Rowan his marbles. The young fiend sighed and placed them in the small bag. But before Rowan set them down, he scrunched his nose as he counted. Four red, three orange, four green and…only two blue.

"Where are the other two?" he asked.

"What other two?" Peron challenged.

"There were four blue marbles in here. I counted last night," he said, aggravated. He set the other marbles down and fished through the sand.

"I… guess the breeze must have blown them away," Selah speculated.

"Well then, help me find them," Rowan spat.

His friends glanced at each other in concern. Even so, they helped Rowan search the sand. Not that he needed the marbles. But they were special to him. They were his new toy to cherish forever, and the one demonstration that proved his worth as a ward.

Rowan's search ceased when he hit his head on a stone. He heard a high-pitched chirping sound; he must've had a concussion. But then he looked at the top of the large stone, where a small, brown bird was perched, singing. Its black beady eyes stared blankly at Rowan. Its head tilted from side to side, revealing a long stripe on its neck.

Chirrup. chirrup, it sang. Then suddenly, it flew onto Rowan's head, nestling itself in his coils.

"Hey, shoo," Rowan exclaimed, trying to swipe the bird off his head. But each time, it flew back to perch again, making itself comfortable.

"Rowan what happened?" Selah said.

"This stupid bird won't get off my head," Rowan griped.

"Don't hurt it. It might just fly off on its own," Peron pleaded.

Rowan ignored him and kept trying. On the last swipe, the bird flew away and landed on the sand. Rowan thought himself victorious, but it still kept spying on him. He almost smacked it until he noticed a hint of blue paint under the bird's talons.

Could it be?

The bird flew away as Rowan stooped over and dug out a blue clay sphere.

Chirrup.

The chirping resumed by the shoreline, where the bird hopped along the wet sand. The orphans raced to the shore. The bird leaped up to reveal the second marble.

"Thank goodness we caught it before it washed away," Selah said.

Rowan's heartbeat slowed. That is until the bird flew onto his head again. "Aww come on!" he exclaimed.

His friends did nothing to help, laughing at Rowan's desperate attempts to shoo the bird. In doing so, he tripped over himself and fell on the sand. Only then did the bird finally leave him alone.

A shade covered Rowan, blocking out the bright sun. He gasped at the sight of Madam Linn peering down at him.

"My, my, my. Practicing a bit early, aren't we?" she said.

"Madam Linn," Rowan cried, swiftly standing up to meet her gaze. Although she looked a bit different. Her black and forest green clothing was the same, with her ladle at her belt loop and Sly casually draped over her exposed shoulders. Rowan wondered if he should've matched her, feeling out of place in his plaid shirt and dark slacks. Apart from that, he remembered her dreadlocks being painted a darker color. It was unlike the shades of highlights she wore outside, as if kissed by the sun itself.

He shook off his stare. "Um, yes…well. You said mages don't like to be kept waiting. So, I guess I just wanted to be early."

"A fast learner," Madam Linn said, making Rowan hide his smile. "Well then, are you ready?"

He glanced behind him. His friends gave him a thumbs-up.

"Yes. Yes, I am," Rowan said confidently. She rushed over to his side. But before they started walking, Peron stopped them.

"Rowan wait," he cried. He grabbed the bag of marbles and handed them over. "Whatever you do, try to relax. Only cast your spell if you're asked to. And don't—"

"Thanks, Per," Rowan interrupted softly.

Peron gave a half-smile while tousling Rowan's curls. "Just be careful, alright?"

Madam Linn and Rowan had already passed the Spehrow's Nest ten minutes ago. Rowan wondered how long it took to sift through the townsfolk just to meet the Ataxia. Also, if they were even going the right way.

"Um…are we still meeting The Stringed Siren?" he asked, catching up to walk by her side.

"Why, of course."

"Good! It's just we've been walking for a while. Surely she must be—"

"Patience, little prince," Madam Linn said soothingly. "The Stringed Siren isn't going anywhere soon. We'll keep walking until we find her."

Not liking his sudden new nickname, Rowan grimaced at the steep trail up ahead. Could he really manage another trial like the one from last night? Madam Linn observed his distress and sighed.

"I suppose the journey is a bit far. But it's nothing teleportation can't fix." She loosened the beltloop of her black skirt and revealed her silver ladle. Sly slid down her arm and wrapped around her newly crafted scepter.

Rowan beamed as he realized what his idol was about to do. "Wait, what's tele…*telepitation*? Does that mean we're going to—"

"Patience," Madam Linn shushed. "Now watch and learn."

She held up her scaled scepter and offered her arm to Rowan.

Who would reject the offer to travel with Linn the Moonstruck? Rowan linked arms with her, hardly able to contain his excitement. Waving her scepter overhead then lowering it to the ground, Linn the Moonstruck whispered a spell under her breath. To Rowan, the words seemed to echo slightly.

Metalauna K'vuldi

The road beneath them flashed a shimmering golden hue that traveled in all directions. The quaint Evermire street slowly disappeared and transformed into a vast sea of greenery. Never ending hills of grass spread across the lingering background of a rich forest. Each hill held small stands with merchants selling fruits and vegetables, fresh goods, and a few moving crates of fish. Among the stands, Rowan spotted children racing around, while grownups strolled along with parasols to block the blistering sun.

Rowan shook his head in disbelief at the scene; she really was Linn the Moonstruck. "Are we still in Evermire?" he checked.

"Naturally," she said. "That spell merely brought us closer to the person we need. I should've known. Clascia loves coming to the valley district on her visits."

"Can we travel back to the tavern with that spell?"

"Unfortunately, I can only cast that spell so many times. We'll have to walk back."

Rowan pouted. But he definitely wanted to learn a spell like that.

He heard the faint sound of a violin in the distance. Madam Linn chuckled to herself as she traveled towards the music. "Like I said: I should've known."

Rowan followed Madam Linn to the top of a steep hill. He looked down below, amused by the creatures big and small dancing in a lively circle.

Someone danced in the middle of it; an ebony woman with black, bubble-like hair and a violin. She pranced around as she played, accompanied by a band of fiddlers outside the dancing troupe.

"That's her," Rowan muttered. "Clascia Valdi. The Stringed Siren. I can't believe she's actually here!"

"And throwing a party without me, no less," Madam Linn said. "Let's get a closer look." She carefully descended the steep hill. Rowan tried his best not to slip and fall.

It was only when they reached the bottom that the dancers reached their finale. The Stringed Siren and her fiddlers finished their piece with a strike of their bows, and the dancing circle struck an energetic pose.

Applause rang among the performers. Rowan tried clapping the loudest of them all. As the dancers dispersed, The Stringed Siren turned to see Madam Linn clapping politely and greeting her with a wide smile.

"Linn, darling," the Stringed Siren exclaimed dramatically. Her voice was even more posh than Madam Linn's. After they kissed each other's cheeks, she said, "Oh, it's so good to see you! It's been ages since you danced with us!"

"It's good to see you too, Clascia," Madam Linn replied. "You should really stop by the tavern, dearest. We need more entertainment than a novice arm-wrestling competition."

Rowan couldn't believe it. Two of his biggest heroes in one place. He checked his pockets in a frenzy, hoping he hadn't lost his marbles again.

"Why don't you join us in the fun, darling," Clascia said, holding her instrument to her chest. "Show us that dance you love so much. We can all learn a thing or two from the master."

"Oh dearest, you know I only dance if there's something to celebrate," Madam Linn declined. "There's actually someone I'd like to introduce. He's been dying to meet you for quite a while."

Rowan realized the Stringed Siren was directing his attention to him. Madam inclined her head towards her companion, motioning for him to introduce himself.

"Pleased to meet you, madam," he said in an awkward bow. "My name is Rowan…Rowan the Brave. Pleased to meet you, madam."

Had he just said that twice?

"This is the Rowan my daughter's been raving about?" Clascia asked. "Honestly, ever since I grounded her last night, she hasn't stopped talking about him. *Ahrrria!* Come here at once!"

Ahria sat on a rock slab amongst the fiddlers playing her lute. Her clothes matched her mother's, an orange blouse with dark trousers and a matching cap. She turned to the sound of her mother's rolled r's. Seeing Rowan made her beam with glee. With one last strum, her lute disappeared. She ran over and embraced him tightly.

"I told you you'd see me again," she said looking up at Rowan. He felt uncomfortable. "Do you have any new stories for me to sing?"

Clascia cleared her throat before Rowan could answer.

"*Ahrrria* dear," Clascia crooned. "is this the… flying boy you told me about?"

Suddenly Ahria became self-conscious and let Rowan go.

"Y-Yes, madam," she answered modestly. "He was trying to get magic artifacts for Madam Spehrow. I helped him so I could make a story about him."

"My, a story," Clascia chuckled, placing a hand on her daughter's shoulder. "You'll have to forgive my *Ahrrria*. She tends to weave tall tales for her own benefit."

Rowan watched the young girl's expression change from victory to defeat in a matter of a mere sentence.

"A-actually madam, it's all true," Rowan corrected. "If she wasn't there to guide me through town, I would've never met Madam Linn… or you, of course."

Ahria smiled at slightly Rowan. Although it didn't hold the charm as it usually did.

"So, it would seem," Clascia said, sounding quite impressed. "Well, what are we standing around here for. Come, we have a feast prepared near the forest."

Rowan grabbed his stomach, already stuffed from breakfast. But he'd never decline free food, especially food offered by the Ataxia.

Rowan had only seen picnics on the cover of Selah's cheesy romance books: weaved picnic baskets with enough food to feed armies sitting under a tall oak tree with lovers' initials engraved in it.

Thankfully, none of that was present. It was just the celebration of the dancers and fiddlers dining together. Near the forest, however, Rowan noticed something interesting. Men in olive green uniforms guarded the forest's edge with tall spears, standing a yard apart. Den Mother's guards wore similar uniforms. How on earth did she lure such nice people to do her bidding?

"Rowan," Madam Linn called.

He turned toward his name. He couldn't believe he had fallen into a trance in front of the Ataxia. Were they talking about him? "Yes, madam?"

"I told them how you wish to become a great mage," she said. "Clascia wished to know more."

The Stringed Siren was spreading jam on her bread. "Yes, for instance, how long have you been training?"

"Um… Not that long. Since I was nine," Rowan replied.

"Oh, how cute. You must have quite the spells at your disposal. Why don't you show us one?"

Rowan registered her request. "Wait, you mean right now?"

"Yeah, right now," Ahria blurted. "I've wanted to see one since yesterday."

Clascia shushed her daughter, who went silent. Rowan also fell silent as well. He didn't think he'd have to show them so soon. He shot a nervous look at Madam Linn. She nodded and mouthed the words, *Go on*. Still nervous, Rowan got out his marbles, placed them on the ground, and gulped before calling out his spell.

Altsum, he strained.

The marbles turned a very dim blue. They lifted only a few inches off the picnic blanket before Rowan felt light-headed. He had to keep going. He heard Madam Linn's voice.

Diasare, she whispered.

The marbles dropped to the floor as Rowan panted in exhaustion. He peered up at the Ataxia and Ahria. They stared at him like a singer' whose voice cracked on stage, shocked and disappointed. Still, he smiled and said, "So…what do you think?"

The mages paused, unsure what to say, until Clascia broke the ice. "Well, it certainly is a work in progress." She waved off any negativity with her butter knife. "You're still new to spell-casting. Nothing a little extra training won't fix."

Rowan smiled, but only a little. At least the good advice masked his poor impression.

"Now that you mention it, dearest, he is taking a few lessons with me," Madam Linn said.

"You? Giving lessons?" Clascia said in disbelief. "Since when?"

"Since last night, when this young boy and his two friends requested my presence. It's only for a few days until they find a suitable home. But you know what they say: 'it takes a village to raise a child.' And what better village than the Ataxia?"

Rowan stifled a gasp. All the Ataxia teaching him magic? He nearly fainted.

Clascia narrowed her eyes at Madam Linn. "I suppose. Pray, why would you need my help if you're already teaching him?"

"Uh…well, Madam Linn told me it was because of her oath," Rowan explained. "It wouldn't… let her take anyone as a ward."

Clascia lowered her tone. "An oath? And what would that oath be?"

"Ah, ah, ah. We mustn't spoil the conversation with oaths," Madam Linn said, tapping her scepter to Clascia's nose. "Dearest, think of what two teachers could do for this child. He'd be on the same level as Ahria in no time."

Clascia crossed her arms at the mention of her daughter. "*Ahrrria* has been spell-casting since her primary years. You expect me to take time out of my touring schedule to teach not one, but two pupils?"

"Well, when you say it like that—"

"You also said he has two other friends in need of homes. That's four children and a string quartet…for five more months at sea. Are you sure you thought this through, *Kherolyna*?"

Madam Linn's poised smile melted upon hearing that name. Rowan and Ahria watched her gaze at The Stringed Siren with a downturned lip.

"*Ahrrria*, wait here," Clascia said, staring at Madam Linn. "I must speak with your Auntie Linn in private."

She headed for the edge of the forest.

Madam Linn looked at Rowan.

"I'll be back," she whispered.

Rowan simply nodded, nervous about the sudden dismissal. She followed her companion until they stood in between two guards.

Time passed, as the performers continued celebrating around the picnic area. But even the lively music couldn't erase Rowan's worries. The Ataxian conversation felt like an eternity, at least to him. He wondered what they were saying.

"Mama says you're a work in progress," Ahria broke in, watching the mages as well. "In my world, that's usually good news."

Rowan sighed. This charming girl wouldn't last a day in his world. "I'm going over there," he announced as he stood.

A tug on his pant leg stopped him. The annoying girl glared at him.

"Didn't your mama ever tell you it's rude to spy?" she said.

She had absolutely no idea. "I'm not spying. I'm just…listening from a close distance."

"Right, and you're also *not* stepping in jam."

Rowan looked at his boot and groaned at the grape mess. He sat down to clean it off. "You can't just walk up there rudely. If you are going to spy, the least you can do is spy like a mage."

"Oh yeah, and how do I do that?"

Ahria flashed her charming smile and displayed the pendant from under her blouse. She blew a soft and lazy tune on her whistle. It glowed teal, while emitting bright musical notes. They spiraled and settled on Ahria's lap in the shape of an animal. The bright silhouette faded, revealing a small, black cat yawning on her slacks.

"This little cutie is Lucky," she said, lifting her cat like a doll. "She's been my familiar since I was seven. You help me with my really hard spells don't you, girl?"

Rowan blinked in amazement. "I wish I could have one too," he said, still shocked by her spell.

"Well, if you haven't taken an oath yet, you probably will get one."

Ahria placed Lucky back on her lap. It purred and fell asleep.

"There's this one spell that Papa taught me," Ahria continued. "It allows someone to spy on people from a distance. It's super cool, but it weakens me if I use it too long." She looked up at Rowan with a straight face. "Are you sure you want to know what they're saying?"

Rowan nodded.

"Good." She gave her cat to him. "Why don't you try scratching her head? She really likes that."

Rowan hesitated, but he supposed he needed to get over that feeling. He ran his fingers through the thin fibers of Lucky's fur, comforted by its soft purring. Then Ahria closed her eyes and slowly pronounced one of the longest spells he'd ever heard.

O culo vu Taxieh da mahee

Lucky woke to the spell. Her eyes were coated with a mixture of moving colors.

"Uh, is that supposed to happen…?," Rowan asked Ahria.

But the young girl's trance had already begun. Her mouth hung open, and the whites of her eyes had turned the same colors as Lucky's. Rowan's body felt weightless, and only the purest of pigments reflected in his vision.

Prismatic colors faded in and out, in and out, until clear shapes of the Ataxia stood before him deep in conversation.

"**I have nothing to apologize for,**" Madam Linn's voice echoed. "**He knows he only has one lesson left. Why not find him a permanent teacher before our time ends?**"

Clascia scoffed. "**And what if he asks for more lessons, hm? What then? Are you just going to string the boy along until you ship him off with some riff raff?**"

"**Of course not.**" Madam Linn raised her voice. "**I know you, don't I? He deserves a better teacher. A proper guardian.**"

"**Linn, you arc a proper guardian. Or at least I thought you were.**"

"**Clascia—**"

"**You give the boy false hope, you pin your responsibility on me of all people, and then you lie?**" Clascia laughed. "**Lie about oaths, no less? Your oath? An oath you've never taken. Do you even hear yourself? No, let me rephrase. With how deceptive you've acted, I wouldn't be surprised if you started acting like Nov—**"

Clascia suddenly stopped, having worked herself into a fury. Madam looked away, guilty. Clascia calmed herself, placing her hands on Linn's shoulder.

"**I don't mean to lecture you,**" Clascia said. "**I know what it's like to start on a new path after a loss. It's downright frightening. But if this has anything to do with *Dorian*—**"

"**It has nothing to do with *Dorian*,**" Linn snapped, shrugging off Clascia's hand. That name made Linn's ears flare out in heated annoyance. "**I... have a tavern to run and a border to protect. I cannot afford any *distractions* right now.**"

"Darling, don't say that," Clascia said defensively. **"He could be a bigger blessing than you realize."**

Madam Linn shook her head. **"No, I will not let this boy's passion be snuffed out by my mistakes. I've already failed one child. I will not do it again."**

A pause echoed through the prismatic space. The image of the Ataxia blurred and faded away. The reflective colors disappeared and shot past his vision. With a flash and a deep exhale, Rowan found himself back on the picnic blanket; his hand nestled in Lucky's soft fur.

Ahria snapped back to reality as well; her body slouched forward.

"Sorry," she panted. "I told you…it's pretty draining." She waited for a response, but he didn't give her one. "Rowan?"

Silent tears streamed down his face. Only Den Mother had ever made him cry such tears, destroying his spirit since he was three. But this Linn the Moonstruck had managed to dismantle everything he'd strived for in the matter of a day. She could've at least called him a distraction to his face. Rather than make excuses, vow fake promises, and give him false hope that a mage like her could ever want someone like him.

Would anyone truly want him?

Ahria's hand rested on his shoulder. He didn't want her to do that, but he let her anyway. "I'm so sorry, Rowan," she said softly. "If there's anything I can do—"

"It's fine," Rowan sniffled, wiping his tear-stained face. "It wouldn't have mattered, anyway."

Just as he thought before: she wouldn't last a day in his world.

More time passed. Rowan didn't know how long. Long enough for Ahria to summon her familiar back to her pendant. Long enough for the children to sit in silence, simply waiting for the great mages to come back. Rowan didn't want them to. He shifted his focus towards the shorter hills, where a few dancers were running down in small groups. They were shouting.

"Let's get out of here!"

"Somebody do something!"

"We're all in Danger!"

More headed for the trail. Whatever was happening certainly made Rowan more nervous.

He heard a pair of footsteps approach. It was one of the olive-green soldiers who guarded the forest.

"What seems to be the problem, sir?" Ahria asked.

The soldier tapped the end of his spear twice and recited. "A monster has been spotted at the border. We ask that you evacuate immediately."

Rowan sat up. "A monster? Where?"

"Evacuate immediately. An inqus has been spotted near the border," the soldier repeated before marching off with the rest of the army.

Rowan's eyes widened. Did he really say what he thought he said? Those beasts. Rowan remembered leaving them behind in that barren land. No. No, surely the guard couldn't have meant those same beasts. Until a man's screams disproved all his suspicions.

"INQAI! INQAI AT THE BORDER!"

Chapter 19

We're Always Watching

A high-pitched ringing filled Rowan's ears. His breath was already escaping him. His body wouldn't allow him to flee; all it would let him do was stare at the curtain of trees across the hill. If he took his eyes off them, he felt something dreadful would pounce out of the forest.

A loud yell dissipated the tinny ringing. "AHRRRIA!"

The sharp cry shook Rowan awake. He turned his head side to side, desperately waiting for the nightmare to be over.

Ahria yanked at Rowan's shirt cuff. "It's Mama. Quick, she'll get us out of this mess."

Rowan looked back at the hill where the Ataxia stood. Clascia, The Stringed Siren ran down towards the children. Linn the Moonstruck was nowhere to be found.

She'd… left him behind.

Ahria pulled Rowan's sleeve and dragged him through the valley toward her mother. They met in the middle. Mother and daughter embraced in the midst of the chaos.

"Is everything alright? Are you hurt? Did you break any instruments," Clascia interrogated, scanning her daughter's frame.

"I'm fine, Mama," Ahria responded, gently swiping her mother's hands away.

Clascia sighed, carefully straightening Ahria's orange blouse. "Oh good. We wouldn't want that to happen, now would we?"

"Where's Madam Linn?" Rowan asked.

Clascia looked at Rowan, she'd forgotten he was there. Still, she answered him. "She's in the forest. She's meant to keep the inqai away from the border."

"We have to go after her," Rowan said, ready to sprint in that direction.

"Absolutely not," Clascia commanded, her voice resounding like cymbals. "You'll come with us."

"But she told me she'll come back."

"And she will. But you'll have to wait a little while longer."

"But I—"

"Linn made me promise to keep you safe. And mages never break their promises."

Yet all of Linn's so-called promises had only left him heartbroken.

"But first things first," Clascia said. "We need to get these people to safety."

Rowan looked at her in shock. "Did those monsters make it—"

"It's just an extra precaution." She summoned her violin with a swipe of her hand. "I'm only using my magic to calm down the masses. You two might want to cover your ears."

The children did as Clascia told them. Perhaps this was the spell that burst people's eardrums.

ZZiinnnn! went the violin.

A series of fast and intricate musical notes danced along the summer sky; the solemn key reverberated through the entire valley. As if hypnotized, the frantic crowds below froze and listened closely. With one look at The Stringed Siren, their frames pulsed a bright gold and floated in the air with each melodic line.

Clascia lifted her bow, allowing a pause to set in. She plucked a sharp, wistful chord, and with a loud snap, the floating masses vanished into thin air.

The spell nearly gave Rowan whiplash as he uncovered his ears.

"They should be in town by now," Clascia said. "Now it's our turn."

She placed her bow on the bridge of her violin, ready to cast her musical spell once more. Rowan supposed there was no other way. That is until he looked beyond the valley into the trees. Pieces of black and green fabric passed through his vision. The same of kind fabric that… Madam Linn wore.

Zzziiiiinnnnn! went Clascia's bow.

Rowan and the Valdi's frames glowed a stark gold and lifted off the ground. The mesmerizing melody was already affecting his emotions, but deep down he didn't want to listen.

Then he had a thought, an insane and ignorant thought. Perhaps, if he covered his ears again, he wouldn't have to.

So, he did precisely that. Rowan covered his ears, muffling the music. The teal pulse faded away. He dropped to the grass and ran towards the forest with his hands still blocking the hypnotic song.

"Rowan!" Ahria shouted. "Rowan, what are you doing?! Come ba—"

SNAP!

Rowan didn't look back. He already knew where they'd gone. He needed to stay focused and get some answers. Rowan needed to find her.

He dashed into the thick forest, running through sharp twigs and branches. He called out her name. "Madam Linn! Madam Linn, where are you?"

No one answered. He kept moving forward, hoping he'd find her if he just kept running. But soon he had to stop to catch his breath. His hand brushed against a thick layer of bushes with rogue leaves sticking out. He heard branches break close by.

Crunch! Crunch! went the noise. Coming from beyond the bushes.

He peeked through the shrubbery, noticing the black hue he'd been searching for.

"Madam Linn! There you are," Rowan called, cramming his way through. "Why would you leave me here all by my—" Rowan stopped. Cut short by the smell of decay and a low, familiar grumble.

The inqus' soulless eyes gazed at Rowan like meat on a platter. The smell of rot secreted from its oozing black flesh.

He wanted to scream or flee, anything to get away from the horrible nightmare before him. But his legs wouldn't move. His feet, however, slightly shifted backwards. Perhaps if he went slowly, the inqus wouldn't notice.

But it did. As Rowan shifted back, the monster shifted forward. He swallowed his fear and tried again. He kept trying little by little, his back hugging the shrubbery.

The inqus kept stalking him. Rowan's only option was to cram through the bush, dart out as quickly as possible and maybe, just maybe leave the forest alive. Just as he turned to do so, he heard a loud *Boom!*

Rowan ducked to the ground.

Boom! Boom! Boom! it went again.

Rowan shakily looked up. Bright, purple fireworks flashed high above the trees. Wherever they came from, they certainly distracted the inqus, whose eyes were plastered to the explosions above.

Boom! Boom! Boom! Boom!

The explosions traveling farther from Rowan and the inqus.

Shriek! went the inqus, as it chased the purple flames.

The monster. It was gone.

Rowan still needed to find her. He crammed his way out of the bush and darted back to the trail. Minutes passed, and he still couldn't find Linn the Moonstruck. He came upon a stone wall with an archway. The town entrance. She couldn't have left town, could she?

He ran close enough to make out the archway's engraving: *FROM EVERMIRE, FAREWELL.* Trees rustled, and leaves fell on the archway. A shriek rose within the forest, and a growling inqus leapt on top of the stone fixture.

Rowan fell on his back in surprise, then tried to scoot away as fast as possible. The beast pounced off the archway toward Rowan and crashed into the lavender rays of the border. It whimpered as it fell to the ground with an enormous thud. Rowan regained control of his legs and stood up slowly to survey his surroundings.

That border kept the monster away. Just like Mister Dre's story, Rowan thought. *But how did that other one get in?*

He turned around. There was nothing but a vast layer of trees behind him. He almost headed back into the depths, but a low, distorted voice slithered its way into Rowan's ears.

I Fffoouunndd Yooouuuu, it said.

The grumbling sound rattled Rowan to the core. What kind of creature spoke with such horror?

Urchin, I Foouunnnd Yoouuu.

Only one person called him that. The sound of cracking bones made him flinch as he slowly turned around. A faint growl followed.

The once collapsed inqus stood in the archway. Its mouth dripped black drool along the grass. Its eyes smiled wickedly at Rowan, like it was all too familiar with his presence.

"What are you?" Rowan asked, his eyes wide open.

"Aww, have you forgotten me alreeaady, child," the beast teased. "You'd think after I raised you for aallll those years, you'd be happy to hear my voice."

The beast's distorted voice shifted to the shrill of Rowan's nefarious guardian. Rowan's world closed in around him. An unbearable itch burrowed into his scarred forearms.

"Den Mother," Rowan whispered.

The beast's sneer grew wider as he answered correctly.

"B-but how are you…How did you get…" Questions flooded his mind until he settled on the simplest one. "How did you find us?"

The inqus, Den Mother's vessel, took a step forward. "Khallus is watching, child." It took another step. "We're alllways watching." Another step. "You think he wouldn't have spies within this wretched little island? You think they wouldn't tell me every inkling of your worthless little lives?"

The vessel's head clashed with the border, but the lavender rays didn't jolt it back. Instead, the light flickered as the inqus strained its way through. Then the purple barrier disappeared, and the monster's entire body came through the archway. Its blackened smile made Rowan fall back, leaving him completely unguarded. This was bad. This was really, really bad.

The inqus lunged at Rowan. Defenseless, he covered his eyes, awaiting the monster's attack. But it didn't. When Rowan opened his eyes, the inqus had its head lowered to him as if it were bowing.

"As much as your trembling amuses me, I'm afraid I am running out of time." A sigh lingered in the beast's voice.

Rowan furrowed his brows. What did she mean, out of time?

"I've been dishonest with you, Rowan," the inqus continued. "You cannot fathom how much I truly need you children."

Den Mother hardly called him by his true name. Despite that, Rowan carefully stood up. He blinked at the monster, confused by its humility.

"W-What are you talking about," Rowan managed to ask.

The inqus lifted its head and revealed its eyes. Icy, glazed over with despair as it stared at Rowan.

"My oath, Rowan," it whimpered. "My oath to Khallus hinges on you, Selah, and Peron. If you all don't come with me now, I'll be ruined."

Rowan knew he should've ran away. But she mentioned Selah and Peron. And talks of oaths only made him curious about Den Mother's own. The monster bowed its head again.

"For every oathless in your care, may Khallus grant you higher power. For every young one given, may you find the chosen vessel and aide in his return. Should the last of your attempts fail, may Khallus extinguish your life like the fire you conjure."

He analyzed Den Mother's oath and applied it to his own experiences. That last line he paid attention to the most. She took care of so many orphans. Would she really die if he and his friends didn't come with her? He should've left when he had the chance. He turned to leave. But Den Mother had other plans.

"Don't you see, Rowan? You're special," the inqus said swiftly, leaping to block Rowan's exit.

Rowan gulped. "S-special," he asked. Asking questions was the only thing he could do, if he didn't want to become dinner for the beast.

"From the moment I took you all in." The inqus circled Rowan like a famished vulture. "You three are the last in my care. You have just the chance to become something greater than yourselves. Becoming one with Khallussss, is the highest honor anyone could ask for. Your loovve of magic, combined with your suffering, pleases him grrreatly. That's why I've been preparing you for so long. So that one day, you'll finally receive your heart's desire."

Rowan scoffed. "What do you know about my desires?"

"Why else would you request my teachings all those years ago?" The beast stopped a foot from Rowan's face. He avoided its glare, knowing full well it was right. "You knew if you became a mage like me, your powers would be limitless. Well, I'm willing to bring you back. Surrender yourself and your friends to me, and we both get what we want. I keep living for Khallus' cause, and you become the greatest mage to ever live."

Surrender? That's all they ever did in the orphanage. Would fulfilling his dreams really mean reverting to old habits?

No. He'd said that word to her once, perhaps he could say it again.

"And if we don't? What happens if we don't surrender?"

A low grumble left the beast's dripping fangs. "Oooh, I wouldn't tesssst that theory."

"Why not? You don't know what we're capable of."

"Hmmmm. And what are you capable of?"

"Stealing your things. Standing up to you. Stabbing you in the eye."

The beast grumbled. He'd never heard Den Mother so flustered, no matter what demonic form she took. It was liberating.

"And we'll do it again too! So just try to find us. We'll even fight back if we have to. We'll stop you. I'll...I'll stop you." The corners of Rowan's lips curled up. He'd never felt so confident. "I'll stop you if it's the last thing I do!"

Shriek, went the beast.

The inqus' massive claw smacked Rowan in the stomach. It knocked the wind out of him and sent him slamming into a tree. His whole body went still. His vision spun until he saw the beast snarling at him in fury.

"I TOLD YOU NOT TEST THAT THEORY, BOY," the beast exclaimed, towering over him. Its claws pinned his long sleeves, tearing through the fabric. Rowan howled in pain as its claws dug into his scars. Bits of ink flew onto his face as the inqus lowered its snout to his ear.

"Know thissss, urchin. If you truly believe you can stop my wrath from breaking you and everyone in that little town of yours, think again. No matter where you hide, no matter how fast you run, no matter how strong you think you are, there is no escape. And by the time the second moonrise approaches, you will be in my gra—"

A slicing sound cut Den Mother's proclamation short. Rowan's eyes went from the beast's face to its spear-protruded torso. The silver blade sliced downward, and he heard the sound of its sternum snapping in two. Den Mother's scream came out ragged as the inqus body faded into golden cinders.

Madam Linn knelt in the beast's place, hovering over Rowan in a warlike daze. She stared at him as he backed away.

"Rowan," she said. Realizing her position, she dropped her scepter. "Rowan, what are you doing here? I thought—"

"She found us," Rowan uttered, his eyes fixed on the ground. "She found us. She found us, and she's coming back for us. What do I do? What do I do? What do I do?"

"Rowan, it's not safe here. We need to leave as soon as possible," Madam Linn said. She went to grab his hands, but the young boy snatched them away.

"No, please! I'm sorry," he shouted, covering his ears and bringing his head to his knees.

Madam Linn brought her hand down, distraught by his reaction. Scanning him for injuries, she spied his exposed forearm. The claw marks were fresh. The dull branding scars were another story.

She scooted away from Rowan and picked up her scepter, waved her hand over the silver serpent's head, and whispered a spell.

Pethsana

Rowan felt a calm rush over him. He lifted his head and glimpsed green smoke emitting from Madam Linn's body. He peered at his forearms. The smoke enveloped the claw marks and bruises on his skin and evaporated them into thin air, like they'd never been there to begin with. Rowan felt his newly smooth skin. He'd never seen it so clearly.

"I assume *that* was all your last guardian's doing?" Madam Linn whispered.

Rowan noted her sympathetic gaze. She glanced at his healed arms. In response, he hung his head and nodded.

"And Selah and Peron, were they given similar treatment?"

He nodded again.

Madam Linn sighed. A sigh of regret, it seemed. But to Rowan it didn't matter. Soon, he and his friends would be out of her hair, once again searching aimlessly for a new home.

"You don't have to worry about us," Rowan said. "Once our last lesson finishes, we'll-."

"When…" Madam Linn's voice faltered. She hung her head. "When will she be back for you?"

Her question confused him. What did Den Mother's presence matter to her? He answered anyway. "Tomorrow…tomorrow by moonrise."

Madam Linn bit back tears before giving Rowan a serious look. She twirled her scepter overhead. "Well then. It appears only one lesson will not be enough."

"Wait, what does that mean—"

Metalauna N'spiro

Chapter 20

The Light of A Thousand Stars

Rowan's world changed before his very eyes. Flashes of golden light spread in all directions. The clear sky turned into a large chandelier. The trees became a brick wall painted red and black, the trunks transformed into a crowd of patrons nervously discoursing. The stone archway faded away to reveal the swinging doors of the Spehrow's Nest.

They had made it back safely after such a terrible nightmare. All because of Madam Linn. Still kneeling, she bore a worn expression as she limply dropped her scepter.

"I thought you said you couldn't use that spell a lot," Rowan mentioned.

"Yes, well," she responded, using her scepter to stand. "A mage must take risks once in a while." She stretched her hand out to Rowan. He took it, and she carefully lifted him to his feet.

The tavern, he noticed, had more patrons than the night before. A mixture of adventuring parties and innocents from the valley. Men spoke with a few soldiers searching for eyewitness reports of the inqai. Women distracted their frightened children by playing with them or feeding them from their packed picnic baskets. Merchants hung their heads in despair at how much of their imports they'd left behind. Madam's waitress, Miss Amori, managed to comfort some of them with warm tea and good conversation by the fireplace. Her waiter, Toby, and Mister Dre did likewise, both them trying to soothe the defeated Peron and Selah. Mister Dre had his hands on their shoulders as they slouched in a booth.

"Selah! Peron!" Rowan exclaimed. His friends shot up at his voice and jumped out of their seats. Their once drained faces came back to life upon seeing him. They darted for Rowan and held him in a tight hug.

Rowan almost cried as he hugged them back.

"I thought I told you to be careful," Peron scolded.

"I was, for the first few minutes," Rowan affirmed slyly.

He stopped himself from smirking. He knew his rebellion would be an act of boldness.

"Rowan," Selah said. "What happened to your arms?"

He lifted his torn sleeve. Thank goodness the gash in his arm had been healed before they saw it. The inqus might not have killed him, but Peron certainly would have. He glanced at Madam Linn. Rowan watched Mister Dre stride over to her, holding her in his embrace and kissing her knuckles to ease her weary expression.

"Let's just say Madam Linn helped me, even when I thought she wouldn't," Rowan said.

His friends glanced at each other until Selah smiled warmly.

"Well, I knew she'd bring you back safely," she said, squeezing his hand. "Now all I need to know is what spell she used for your skin. It's never looked better."

They laughed at Selah's remarks, as if they had only endured a terrifying dream.

"Kherolyna Spehrow!" an upset voice bellowed.

All eyes turned to a disgruntled moon-elf sauntering towards Madam Linn. Most of the adventurers then went about their business, but the innocents bowed as he walked past him. Rowan remembered his star-laden skin, his platinum hair under his boat hat, and his eyes filled with contempt. The mayor.

"Ah, sire. To what do we owe the pleasure?" Mister Dre quipped, giving a brief bow.

"Children, come this way," Madam Linn announced. "Allow me to introduce Mister Vassile, the mayor of our fine town."

The upset mayor waved off her introductions. "Yes, yes. Charming, charming. Why are my guards sending me reports of inqai at Evermire's borders?"

The loud question garnered a few gasps and murmurs among the patrons. Madam Linn's jaw clenched.

"Sire, no such beasts made it in. I made sure of that," she replied frankly, before lowering her voice to him. "And this is neither the time nor the place to have this conversation. Perhaps we can meet in a more private—"

"I disagree! This is the perfect time to let the people know the truth," Mayor Vassile declared. "You ought to be ashamed of yourself, Spehrow. Arrogantly disregarding the security of our borders, when I specifically told you—"

"But it *was a secret*," Rowan blurted. Both Madam Linn and the mayor turned their heads.

"Secure," Peron corrected.

"Exactly! Madam Linn went to stop the monsters on her own. I saw it all myself. That border blocked one monster from entering. I mean…it broke through somehow, before it attacked me. But-."

"It did *what*," Peron said under his breath.

"What are you saying?" Selah whispered.

Before Rowan could answer, the crowd had gotten up in arms at the terrible news. "*How did it get in here?*" he heard, and "*Did it make it to the docks?*"

It was clear that nothing had escaped Mayor Vassile's sharp hearing. He squinted his pale eyes at Madam Linn. "You said no such beasts made it through."'

Madam Linn huffed at the rising chaos in her tavern. She gazed at the mayor, as if waiting for him to calm the masses. But his sly smirk only encouraged their gossiping further.

His focus turned on Rowan, who shrunk back at his professionally forced smile. "My dear boy, it must've been awful what you saw. You're quite lucky to be standing here with us. Tell us your name, son. Why on earth were you around such vile devils?"

Rowan held back a sneer. The mayor's grating voice reminded him of Den Mother and the way she used it for trickery and control.

"His name is Rowan, Mayor Vassile," Peron said. "My name's Peron, and this is Selah. We're not really from around here, but we apologize for our friend's actions. He obviously didn't know what he was doing." The fiendish boy glared at Rowan.

"Ah, so you're all new in town. Is that it?" the mayor asked.

"We just arrived here yesterday, sire," Selah interjected. "Mister Dre guided us to Evermire so we could meet Madam Spehrow. Rowan is a really big fan of her magic."

Mayor Vassile's brows rose. "Mister Dremos guided you all here? From the Barrens, I presume?" The children nodded. "Well, this day keeps getting better and better!"

Rowan gulped nervously at the mayor's excitement. As he started to pace around the children, Rowan didn't know whether to be amused or concerned.

"So, Rowan, you saw the inqai with your very eyes, correct?

Rowan nodded shyly. "Y-yes, sire. But the border blocked it from coming in."

"Yes, but I recall you then claiming it somehow broke through and attacked you," the mayor countered, stopping his pacing leaning toward Rowan. "Care to explain?"

Rowan would rather not, but he explained to the best of his memory. "It, uh…I don't know how, but I saw it try to, like…shove its way through. And when it did, some of those purple lights started fading away."

"Fading away?" the mayor repeated loudly. The crowd followed suit, their murmurings growing in volume by the second. Rowan caught the mayor glancing at Madam Linn and Mister Dre with hidden mischief. What was he trying to do?

"My dear boy," Mayor Vassile exclaimed, turning back to Rowan. "A fading border means that virca has been at play! A forbidden magic only the Legion of Khallus use to tamper with our protection!"

That was certainly new knowledge to Rowan. Everyone told him it was forbidden, but its use remained unexplained to him until now.

"And was Madam Spehrow with you when the inqus attacked?"

Rowan's hand brushed his healed forearms. He nodded once more and responded, "Not at the beginning. But she saved me just in time. Enough time for her to destroy it and heal me."

Mayor Vassile chuckled at his reply. "Ah yes. But not enough time to arrive by your side before the damage occurred."

Rowan's mouth went agape. He was about to come to her defense when the mayor interrupted.

"But that's just like the Spehrows." He faced their glares and walked slowly towards them. "Only saving the day after destruction occurs. Since the Battle for Nidas, we've given them far too much credit and control over our security. If they keep letting incidents like this happen, our island will only regress to what it once was: a playground for Khallus and his legionnaire's."

Rowan heard whisperings of *that's true* and *I certainly remember.*

"So, townsfolk and visitors of Evermire, I leave you with this word of reason. I urge you to let me seek aid the Council for our safety. If the Spehrows' negligence at the border allows this poor boy… or even their own *son* to be harmed by their inaction, consider what will happen to you."

"FILKUZTAC CANIL VE," Mister Dre swore with a throaty grunt. He gripped the mayor's dress shirt and wrenched him closer. The townsfolk wailed and the adventurers cheered,

expecting a messy fight to begin. Selah and Peron pulled
Rowan back to make sure he didn't find himself in the mix. But
all Rowan could focus on was Mister Dre's rage. The red-eyed,
hunter bared his canines to assert power over the mayor.
Rowan didn't know what to make of it, but he knew he'd never
cross Mister Dre if it meant avoiding his horrifying temper. His
fist almost met the mayor's nose, but Madam Linn's voice
halted the attack.

"ENOUGH," she bellowed. She slammed her scepter
into the hardwood. A blinding light shone between the two
men, exploding before them and shoving them backwards. The
light rippled through the tavern, making the ground shake and
the chandelier swing. The power caused the patrons to shout as
they fell to the ground.

Then the light snuffed out the candles, and the
earthquake stopped as quickly as it started. In the center of the
tavern stood Madam Linn, glowing with the light of a thousand
stars. Her freed dreadlocks floated midair, while the shades of
full moons eclipsed her golden irises.

Linn the Moonstruck, in all her radiant, terrifying glory,
made Rowan gasp in awe. She walked towards the fighters, the
only sound being the clop of her heels. She moved past the
fallen Mister Dre and stared down at the panting mayor.

"Now, sire. You know better than to provoke your
citizens. Look at what form you made me take," she echoed
with a purr.

Rowan heard the adventurers' whispering rumors. *The
Star of the Soliear. Oh, he's done it now*, someone said. *She's not even
in full form yet and she's still so powerful*, another mentioned. *That
mayor must have a death wish*, others chuckled. Rowan
remembered her glowing form in her study. He knew she was
powerful, but he had never imagined this.

Surprisingly, Madam Linn held out her hand to Mayor Vassile. With a grunt, he took it and allowed her to help him up.

"Sire," her voice echoed once again. "We're aware that Evermire's safety is your top priority. If virca was used to damage the border, we know it's the work of the Legion. Interrogating children will not provide you more answers than what we already have." Her eyes found the gaping orphans huddled on the floor. She smiled politely at them, then returned to the mayor. "To atone for my… negligence, I will take my wards with me, and I will inspect the border tomorrow, as promised."

Doubt raised the mayor's brows. "And the bimonthly visits?"

Madam bowed her head. "As good as done."

"Hmph, it's what you should have done in the first place," Mayor Vassile mumbled.

Madam Linn reacted to his complaints swiftly and calmly. "I believe the correct answer from you is 'thank you, Madam Spehrow.'" Her beaming smile blinded the mayor. "Thank you for creating the border all those years ago and protecting Evermire from the Legion of Khallus. Thank you for using your magic to stop them. And thank you so much for easing my suspicions to calm my restless paranoia."

Gasps and murmured oohs erupted among the audience. Rowan, Selah, and Peron were no better; hiding their snickering as the mayor grumbled under his breath.

The stars on Mayor Vassile's skin flared in embarrassment. He cleared his throat and fixed his hat, in an effort to maintain his dignity. "You have until moonrise tomorrow to give a good report," he said through gritted teeth. "Should anything go wrong because—"

"Sire, I believe the school bell will ring shortly," Madam Linn whispered. "We don't want to keep Onyx waiting, now do we?"

Mayor Vassile turned on his heels, and marched out the doors, which swung behind him.

Ring, went the doorbell.

Once the mayor left, the chandelier reappeared. The patrons exclaimed at one another, about the flaring centerpiece and the scene that had happened below.

Rowan's eyes shifted from the chandelier to Madam Linn. Her brightness dimmed and her dreadlocks dropped. She kneeled in front of Mister Dre, placing her hands on his face as he looked away in shame.

"Linn, I'm so sorry," Mister Dre whimpered.

"You're alright, Rose," she lulled. "I felt the same way."

As Rowan blatantly eavesdropped, Peron squeezed his shoulder and spun him around to meet his face.

"You better start talking right now," Peron griped.

"Look, I'm sorry," Rowan said defensively. "I just didn't know how to tell you guys."

"Tell us what? That you ran into a monster-infested forest? Or how you got attacked by one when you shouldn't have gone in the first place?"

Rowan pursed his lips in annoyance. "It's not like I wanted to get attacked. I was trying to keep up with Madam Spehrow. I would've left if I hadn't seen..."

He paused, knowing there was no going back if he finished his sentence.

"Rowan, what exactly did you see in that forest?" Selah asked calmly, placing her hands on his shoulders. She gave him half a smile, believing the next words to come out of his mouth wouldn't be so bad. She'd be terribly mistaken.

He swallowed his fear. "It's Den Mother. She found us."

Peron shuddered, Selah's smile faded. "What?" she whispered, taking her hands off Rowan.

"Those inqus monsters. Like I said, I don't know how, but…one of them spoke to me, and it had Den Mother's voice. She tried convincing me to come back, but I said no. Then she said she'd come for us herself by moonrise tomorrow."

"How did she even find us?" Selah wondered.

"Who cares how she found us. She's gonna make us sacrifices if we don't leave now," Peron stated.

"Sacrifices," Madam Linn repeated. The children looked up. Rowan didn't know how long she and Mister Dre had been listening. "Sacrifices for whom, exactly?"

She looked worried. He gulped, trying to swallow his confession, only for it to come out in stammers. "F-for Khallus," he confessed shakily. "Den Mother, she…she said he'll kill her if she doesn't make us sacrifices to him. She said it was part of her oath."

Fortunately, only Madam Linn and Mister Dre heard him. Dremos nodded at Linn as she shook her head to process.

"I never thought I'd see the day where those lunatics still practiced that," she said. "So all this time, this whole search for Linn the Moonstruck, was just a means of finding a new home?" she asked the orphans. "Escape for survival?

"Yes, Madam," Peron answered. "And it's exactly why we can't stay here anymore."

"If she finds us, she'll only drag us out of Evermire and take us back," Selah explained.

"But we can't just leave. That won't work," Rowan argued. "She said she'd find us no matter where we went. Even if we went to Venari or Mydion, she'll try her hardest to catch us again. We have to do something."

Peron scoffed at Rowan. "Yeah, and what are you going to do about it, huh? Fight her head-on yourself?"

"You say that like it's impossible," Mister Dre proclaimed.

His interruption startled Peron, who stuttered for a counter to the fiendish hunter.

"W-well, with all due respect sir, it *is* impossible. Rowan shouldn't be facing someone so powerful. He doesn't know a lot of magic yet," Peron stated frankly.

Rowan bowed his head. Another blow to his self-esteem, courtesy of Peron.

Mister Dre chuckled through his canines. "If I didn't face anyone powerful, I don't think I'd be a hunter, would I, Starlight?"

"I'd say not, Rose," Madam Linn answered. "I'd probably never be a mage if I didn't face any powerful foes." She gazed at Rowan with such poise. "Nor would I let lack of knowledge deter me from wanting to know more. And so I ask again, oh Rowan the Brave, why should I truly teach you magic?"

Rowan looked back at his friends; they waited in anticipation for his answer, hopefully one that involved fleeing than fighting.

Rowan straightened up, his voice trembling even in his boldness. "If you make me your ward…make *us* your wards, I promise I won't make things difficult, I won't be a burden…I won't even be a distraction. Teach me how to face powerful foes and defeat them once and for all. Please…teach me how to protect my family."

Madam Linn kissed her teeth as she nodded, contemplating his earnest request. "This changes everything," she muttered. "I believe now, Dre, is the time we make arrangements."

Rowan noted her mysterious tone. What was she planning for them?

Tss, Tss, went Madam Linn.

The snake slithered off her ladle and spiraled around her arm. "Have you eaten anything since breakfast?" she said as the snake reached her shoulders.

Rowan shook his head. He knew he should've taken something from that picnic.

"Good. Once we're through here, we'll have our own picnic in the forest. See if there are ways we can harness some new skills."

Rowan exhaled in disbelief. "Uh…yes, Madam. I'll be ready," he said, trying to contain his excitement.

She smiled at him and retreated, linking arms with Mister Dre. The brave fiend even brushed Rowan's coils in approval. Rowan watched them leave. But before he could celebrate, Peron groaned under his breath.

"All I wanted was a new home with peace and quiet," Peron grumbled. "The last thing we should do is stay in a place with neither of those things."

"We will, Peron. Don't worry," Selah comforted him, placing a hand on his shoulder.

Rowan almost did the same but wondered if words would soothe his nerves instead. "What if…what if this *is* our new home?" He watched Peron raise his head, with a very unpleasant expression. "Maybe the best way to get peace and quiet is by…getting rid of the loudness? Maybe we should fight for our peace, instead of run from it."

That had sounded a lot better in his head. It got a reaction out of Peron, but not the kind Rowan expected.

"Rowan! We're talking about fighting Den Mother," Peron raised his voice, looking down at him. "It's a seriously dangerous idea! I know it, you know it, the strangers on the street know it! You can't possibly think you're going to win against her, huh? What happens if something goes wrong and we're not here to help you?"

Rowan heard the tremble in Peron's voice. He'd never seen him so worried. But Rowan thought about Uncle Rog, and the advice he'd given him during his quest. "Something probably will go wrong," Rowan responded. "But Per, if I don't face her now, I'll never know if I can face anyone else in the future. And I don't know about you, but I'm tired of always running from the first sign of danger?"

Peron paced around in frustration, then fixed his eyes on his more reasonable friend. "Sellie, for the love of all things normal, please tell Rowa this whole thing is ridiculous."

Selah brushed her curls as she contemplated Peron's logic. Rowan supposed there was no use fighting it. She was bound to take Peron's side.

"I'm tired of running too, Ro," Selah admitted. "I also think Evermire could be our home if we wanted it to be. But if we're going to stop Den Mother from taking it away from us, we have to fight back." She smiled at her friend proudly. "Besides, Perry. Rowan should already know that we're coming with him."

Chapter 21

First Lesson of Spell-Casting

The late afternoon sun nearly blinded Rowan as he carefully searched beyond the treetops. Any small sound of nature made him twitch in its direction. If he didn't stay watchful, Den Mother and her monsters might jump out and take everything away from him. He couldn't possibly defeat her yet, not without learning an entire spell book in a matter of hours.

"I wouldn't travel down that path you're on, Rowan," Madam Linn said.

He winced at his own name. Madam Linn sat neatly against a tree, taking sandwiches out of her picnic basket and handing them to Selah and Peron.

He shook off his trance. "Um… sorry, Madam. What path should I not take?"

She tapped her temples. "Those gears are still turning as we speak. If they're too tightly wound, it'll only bring more distress."

The gears in Rowan's brain merely stopped as he tried understanding that metaphor.

"She's telling you to relax," Peron said, chewing his sandwich. He handed Rowan one. Perhaps his appetite would lessen his anxiety. He took a bite and simply melted at the taste of sharp cheese and sweet marmalade.

"This is really good," Rowan complimented.

"Now, that you have some food in your system, tell me, what's on your mind?" Madam Linn asked.

Rowan exhaled softly. Maybe sharing his thoughts might bring him some comfort. After all, he'd done it before.

"I guess I'm just… worried," he admitted. "What if I freeze up during the fight and I can't use any spells that work? Or what if the spells I learn aren't strong enough against Den Mother?"

"You're afraid of being unprepared," Madam concluded.

She could read him like a book. He nodded.

Madam Linn set her plate down and clapped her hands. "Well, I suppose the beginning is a great place to start," she said, rummaging through her picnic basket.

"By being… unprepared," Peron asked.

"Quite the opposite. We're simply starting with the basics," the charming mage replied, sounding slightly strained. She took out a heavy navy-blue book and placed in in front of the children. Rowan thumbed its faded cover, noting its outlined gold stars and a ringed sphere in the center.

"No way," Rowan exclaimed. "Is this an actual spell book?".

"Not just any spell book," Madam Linn countered. "The first to be crafted into existence. The Compendium is what they call it; a list of spells collected through generations.

Written for mages both young and old. And the same one I used in the Battle for Nidas."

The stars in Rowan's eyes matched the ones on the cover. "This book's going to make me the best mage in the world," he proclaimed, ready to turn the pages. But Madam Linn pressed her palm down on the cover.

"Not so fast, little prince," she said. "How are you going to be the best mage in the world, if you don't know how to perform certain spells? Which brings me to our next rule of magic."

Rowan leaned close in anticipation.

"In the heat of battle, a mage must always be prepared."

A breeze blew by as Rowan waited for more.

"That's it?" he asked bluntly.

Peron elbowed him, "Seriously, man. Have some manners."

"It seems quite simple," Madam Linn affirmed. "But magic is more than flamboyant tricks and explosions. A mage must learn, memorize, and carry his spells wherever he goes, no matter how dire the situation. Before I used the Compendium, all my spells limited my true potential. So, when the time came to fight a… rather unexpected threat, I had no idea what spell to cast. It almost cost the Ataxia their lives. So, I know what it's like to feel unprepared."

The children glanced at each other nervously before watching Madam Linn skim through its pages. "This Den Mother of yours. She taught you in the ways of Khallus, I presume?"

"Hmph, she tried to," Rowan murmured, taking another bite of his sandwich. "But it's a great thing I wasn't good at it. Guess I'm just too pure-hearted to be taught by evil people."

Selah and Peron groaned, while Madam Linn simply chuckled at his vainglory. "Aren't we grateful," she said sarcastically. "Fortunately, the Compendium will have what you need to defend yourself from the Legion and its monsters."

"Well, that won't be a problem, Madam. We already tried defending ourselves when we were with Mister Dre," Selah said.

"Oh please," Peron stepped in. "You two hit them with a heavy bag and a clumsy lightning spell. All of that was purely coincidence."

Madam Linn glared at the children over the book. "What's this about a lightning spell?"

"Nothing," the children blurted, trying their best to look innocent.

Perhaps Peron had a point. If Mister Dre hadn't been there, those inqai would've torn him to shreds. If Rowan couldn't physically fight Den Mother and her beasts, maybe he could use something that could throw her off balance.

"Are there any spells in there that could…I don't know, distract the monsters?" Rowan asked.

The poised mage lifted a brow. "Distractions, hmm? Like some sort of illusion?

"I guess that's what it's called."

Madam Linn thought about it, then skimmed through the spell book. "Illusion, illusion, illusion," she muttered until she stopped at the center of the book. She read it, smiled at it, then reached into her picnic basket.

"Illusions are a magnificent tool for combat." She took out her silver ladle and placed her book on the picnic blanket. "A false image, a cunning disguise, even the sound of a roaring lion is enough to confuse your opponent before you strike."

With both hands, she gripped her utensil tightly, passing it steadily over her face. Her hands wrenched apart, pushing outwards then back near her chest. In a soft voice, she whispered,

Coemsae Tophsu

An outline of stars twinkled around her as she shimmered. As the orphans gaped in awe, a harsh breeze blew the thick dust in their direction. They shielded their eyes from the sudden glimmer, only for the sparkles to fly into their mouths. The grainy taste left them hacking and heaving while Madam Linn delicately placed her ladle back in her basket.

"Now, Rowan," Madam Linn reminded them. "This spell is merely a demonstration. I'd like for you to look around this hill and see if you notice anything different."

Rowan searched for something spectacular: lights dancing before his eyes or even a giant dragon flying in the sky. But no, instead he found a small brown bird perched on top of his marble bag. It was the same bird from the beach that morning. He groaned at the annoying and surprisingly lifelike illusion. *Did Madam Linn just do this to tease me?* he asked himself. Only for the bird to pick at his sandwich.

"Hey! Not again," Rowan exclaimed, shooing the bird away. It dodged his hand and flew to his curled crown, making his friends laugh at him. "I don't think I like this illusion very much."

"That's not my illusion," Madam Linn's voice called. It was followed by a tap on Rowan's shoulder.

The children spun around and shouted at a chuckling Madam Linn staring down at them. Rowan looked back at the tree; she was sitting there as well. How had two Madam Linns appeared at the same time?

"You…b-but you were just…how are you…," Rowan stammered.

"Shh. Look," Madam Linn hushed. Rowan, Selah, and Peron slowly turned to the frozen Madam Linn. Her eerie expression made them shudder, until the figure fell forward and disintegrated into stardust. They continued their speechless stammering as the true Madam Linn whistled behind them.

The small bird flew up to her call and balanced on her fingers. "Aww, the same sea sparrow that helped you earlier," she realized. "It remains unclaimed, but you never know which animal will be your next familiar."

Rowan didn't know whether to be excited or afraid of Madam Linn. But he knew one thing for sure. "I want to use that spell!"

Madam Linn shook her head, lifting the sea sparrow to let it take flight. When she went back to the spell book, the bird returned to its post atop Rowan's head. *Guess this is my life now*, he thought as he frowned.

"That spell requires more concentration than most illusion spells. You'll hurt yourself if you don't cast it correctly." She grabbed the book and saw Rowan pouting. "But that's one of the few ways you can distract this Den Mother. We'll start with an easy one. What illusion do you think will distract her best?"

Rowan had a thought. Well, more of a memory. A memory filled with ravenous beasts and the lavender flames they desperately craved.

"I know they like fire. The monsters, that is," he said. "Purple fire, actually. I remember seeing purple fireworks go off in the forest. Those inqai ran right for them. You cast that spell, didn't you?"

Madam Linn smirked at Rowan's cleverness and flipped through the Compendium again. She placed her finger on a single page, then invited the children to sit by her and read it together.

Rowan's older spellbook paled in comparison to the Compendium. Detailed pictures glided on the pages like a flipbook. Each ritual showed the correct gesture, effect, and finally the name of the spell. A few illusions called for voices or objects appearing out of nowhere. Spells like Madam's showed two identical men standing next to each other. One clone pushed the other, transforming his other half into the dust.

Madam Linn's finger stopped on an illustration of moving hands. They cupped into place, dragged down the character's face, and pushed out above their head. A series of curved stripes burst along the parchment, creating a fabulous firework effect. Mid-spark, the lines of the fireworks curled into cursive foreign words.

Aercis

"Air… kis," Rowan pronounced.

Another word formed in front of the first one.

Coemsae Aercis

He said it all at once. "Cohm-say… air-kis? So… does Aercis mean something to do with fireworks? And the other word makes it an illusion?"

She shot him an impressed nod. "Well, look at that. You really are a fast learner."

He did a terrible job hiding his grin. But who could blame him when Linn the Moonstruck praised his pronunciation?

"I'm gonna try it right now," he proclaimed.

"If you feel you must," Madam Linn affirmed.

He excitedly rose and presented his audience with a powerful pose. With his best friends and Madam Linn watching intently, he felt like taking on the world. It gave him enough motivation to perform the same motions from the Compendium. His shaky hands cupped together, slowly hovered over his face, then pushed out towards the sky.

Coemsae…Aercis, he called out.

Sparks shot out from his palms, then stopped. It had happened again, exuding more scattered pieces that traveled to his fingertips. Energy coursed through his veins, as if ready to erupt and soar at just the perfect moment. But then that moment fizzled out. He turned his hands inward, staring at the thin trails of ash lining his palms and fingers.

"But I did everything right," he murmured, confused.

Selah and Peron almost dashed over to comfort him, but Madam Linn rose and stepped in. She kneeled down and gave Rowan a handkerchief from her dress pocket. Reluctantly, Rowan took it and used it to wipe his hands.

"How did you feel when you first cast that floating spell?" Madam asked softly.

Of course. Distracting him from heartache again. Selah had done it a thousand times. "Nervous, excited… but then once it failed, I got scared."

"A lot of emotions are tied to spells. I completely understand," she affirmed.

"You do?" She did?

Madam Linn took the cloth from Rowan's hands once they were clean. Then she placed it over her hand, snapped her fingers, and swiftly removed it, revealing a radiant orb of light hovering in her palm.

"Emotions are quite thrilling, aren't they? We get excited when we succeed, angry when we lose, or even anxious when we plan for future victories. They are important, and many of our spells respond to them. But we can never give them more power over our actions, lest the effects of our spells go awry." The light suddenly dimmed and descended into the center of her palm. "Which is why the second rule of spell-casting… is to always remain calm."

He groaned softly. "That's going to be difficult," he answered ashamedly.

"We tried to warn him earlier Madam, but he only worried himself sick," Selah said.

Madam nodded at Selah's truth and gazed at the shame-filled Rowan. "Staying calm can be quite difficult for a new mage. It means blocking out all distractions. Not letting fear hinder our progress. But luckily, there's always the chance to try again." She clapped her hands, rose to her feet, and said, "So, let's try again!"

"But I-I didn't get it right," Rowan protested.

"That doesn't mean we can't fix a few things," Madam Linn said, circling him. "For instance, while you used the correct motions, we can tighten your posture a bit." Rowan drew his shoulders back and lifted his head; he didn't know he was attending an etiquette class. "And though your pronunciation needs improvement, it's how we say our spells that gives them a greater meaning."

"How do I do that?" Rowan asked, his tense posture making his words strain. But Madam Linn gently shifted his shoulders to where he finally stood comfortably.

"Instead of shouting it out, try whispering," she advised. "Rather than thinking of how the spell might fail, think of something that gives you peace as you cast it."

That made no sense, Rowan thought. The mages in stories always proclaimed their spells loudly and proudly. Could he really trust her judgment? He heard confidence and faith in her tone, as if she actually believed in his abilities. Perhaps that was all he needed.

Rowan sighed, training his voice to what he should sound like. "Alright," he softened as he nodded. "I guess I'll try again."

Madam Linn smiled proudly, impressed by his boldness. She straightened up and sat against the tree, observing him. Doubt crept in once Rowan looked at his hands again. Would this spell really be enough to be a good mage? To defeat Den Mother?

"You can do it, Rowan," Selah encouraged.

"Take a deep breath," Peron advised.

Tranquility soothed Rowan's spirit. Through all the trouble he caused them, his friends— the source of his peace, still wanted to see him succeed. With that in mind, Rowan actually took Peron's advice to heart.

The young mage closed his eyes and took a deep breath. The longer the exhale, the slower he went through his motions. His hands hovered over his face, and weight pressed into his shoulders. A whisper removed that weight immediately.

Coemsae Aercis, Rowan whispered, shoving his hands out towards the sky.

Sparks jolted from his fingertips. Flares fired into the air. Purple explosions blasted off through the clouds.

Boom! Boom! Boom!

And for the first time, a stunned mage smiled in contentment, amazed by the works of his hands.

Chapter 22

Someone Like Me

*I*n a town like Evermire, fear became nearly unfathomable. After securing victory in the Battle for Nidas, the common townsfolk of the small seaport felt a sense of security when they walked the stone streets. By day, the fishermen filled their quota of sea bass and trout. All while their wives focused on the washing, selling, and keeping house. But in the dark of night, such tasks were abandoned to partake in the lively and beautiful splendor of the Nocturnal Market. Where the full moon above and the warm street lamps highlighted the city streets. Where Nidas natives and Mydion visitors greeted one another with open arms, shopping and eating to their hearts' content. Where the night creatures of old did their due diligence, providing support and aid against the Legion's advances.

Where three young orphans sang along in the streets, peacefully celebrating their friend's newfound magic abilities. Selah, Peron, and Rowan vowed to come back and explore the vibrant bustle of the Nocturnal Market. But of all the places they had discovered, Rowan knew he had to go and show a certain gargoyle his new powers. And in exchange, receive a fiery treat filled with chocolate and caramel.

The orphans raced around the square with the empty pedestal, past Tawnwell's closed toy store, and into the hazy smithing district. But the smog didn't deter their competition. They saw the vases and ceramics through the black smoke. In their final sprint, Peron jumped inside the tent to mark his glorious victory.

"No… fair," Rowan, the slowest runner, complained breathlessly.

"Yeah, you were… way behind me… just a second ago," Selah, the second-fastest, recalled through her coughing.

"Save your excuses, Sellie," Peron taunted, flexing his fake muscles. "I told you I'd beat you in a rematch one day."

Smoke seeped from Mister Rog's dragon-shaped oven, and the smell of warm chocolate awakened the children's senses. But as they weaved through the smoke, they found that not a single gargoyle occupied the tent.

"So, you actually did it, huh?" Truegug's voice called from above. The children searched and found him perched on the roof of a building behind the tent. "You actually became Linn the Moonstruck's ward?"

Rowan nodded. "You got any truffles you want to share with me?" he asked bluntly.

"Got any magic you wanna prove to me?"

Rowan's smile faded. He already felt Selah and Peron's stoney glares piercing into his back.

The gargoyle searched the area anxiously. "Well if you do, just take that ladder on the side of the buildin'." He pointed to a long iron ladder.

They ran around the tent, climbed the ladder, and walked onto the flat roof. Truegug leaned against a small brown cottage sitting atop the building. A tin tray of grey truffles sat behind his bandaged wing. They lunged for it, but Truegug snatched the tray away.

"Ah, ah, ah," he uttered, placing the tray in his lap. "I wanna see the magic first."

"Are you serious," Peron groaned.

Truegug shrugged. "Evermire tradition. What you desire in gain, you give in return."

"Never fear," Rowan proclaimed, sporting an actor's grin. "For I, Rowan the Brave, will cast the most glorious display of fireworks you've ever seen!"

"Honestly, I'm just really bored without my toolbox," Truegug quipped. "You could cast *acid rain* and I'd still be entertained."

"Please don't encourage him," Peron mumbled into his hands.

Luckily, Rowan didn't know that spell yet. His excitement made him shake off his nerves. He imagined the spell and performed its motions.

Coemsae Aercis…

He pushed his hands out towards the town. Sparks erupted from his palms. But what should have been a fabulous show of amethyst fire, only came out in short spurts popping above his head.

Pop! Pop! Pop! they went, surprising the children.

A few sparks made contact with a flying gargoyle, who snarled at the burning sting.

"Ow! Watch it, kid," the nocturnal being exclaimed.

"Sorry," the children said back, watching the creature fly away in a huff. He soared away and descended into the street to stand by an olive-green soldier.

"Well, I'm impressed. Go on and dig in," Truegug said, holding up the tray of truffles.

Selah and Peron snatched skewers off the tray, while Rowan slumped down to contemplate his spell's failure. When he looked at his hands, however, not a trace of soot covered his palms like it did the first time. A small victory he barely celebrated in.

"Cheer up, Ro," Selah said, gulping down a truffle. "You should be proud of yourself! You can finally cast a spell correctly!"

Rowan tightened his lips into a half smile. "Yeah, but it wasn't as big and bright as it was last time." He took a skewer off the tray and ate it to ease his mind. It didn't help.

"You spent the entire afternoon practicing and making yourself sick. I think you deserve to give yourself a little credit," Peron said, covering his mouth filled with the sweet treat.

"Den Mother doesn't care about credit. And her inqus things won't care that I practiced either. She won't stop unless I beat her once and for all. Maybe I should've asked Madam Linn to teach me another attack spell."

Truegug scrunched his green brows at the odd orphans. "I don't know who this…Den Mother character is, but if she has inqai at her side, it may take more than a couple attack spells."

Rowan frowned at Truegug. "But those are the only spells she'll respond to. It's not like I can use floating spells the entire time and expect her to be defeated." His voice rose in frustration.

Truegug shook his head at Rowan's reaction. "Th-that's not what I meant. I-I mean…I'm no expert. I only use magic for some of my inventions. What I wanted to say was, if this Den Mother of yours is really powerful, you'll need extra support to defeat her."

"What kind of support?" Selah asked.

"Mmm, some muscle power will do. Hasn't happened in my life, but Uncle Rog says if there's an inqus attack, the mayor will have the elder gargoyles on patrol with his troop. That's why my uncle is gone. He flew down to the square to practice at his post."

Rowan had wondered why that gargoyle flew off in such a hurry. He looked down at a row of soldiers marching in time and gargoyles levitating alongside them. But what if Den Mother easily defeated both of them? Who would stop her from taking him and his friends?

"Den Mother's not after the town," Rowan argued. "If she's coming after us, there must be some way I can get really powerful, really quickly."

Truegug glanced at his two friends. They shrugged at his gaze, knowing it took more than logic to convince the young mage. "I guess the only other way to do that is by takin' an oath," he said, rubbing the back of his neck.

"Again with this," Rowan groaned. "I know that will make me stronger, but what if I don't want to be bound forever?"

"I don't think it's about bein' bound forever," Truegug stated. "I mean, I wouldn't know. I don't have one of those. But Mister Tawnwell says good can come from takin' an oath. Back in his day, he saw a lot of oathless mages get weak after castin' one spell in battle."

Rowan remembered how weak he became after casting his spells. Truegug continued while chewing on a truffle.

"Basically, it's like this: if you take an oath, you can cast more than one spell at a time. You also won't get tired if you do, on account of Caelum or Cretia or one of them Creators blessin' you with the strength to cast it."

Rowan didn't respond. He merely slouched over in defeat.. "Just…somethin' to think about," Truegug added. He stuffed a truffle in his mouth to avoid the awkward silence.

Rowan leaned against the cottage wall in defeat. Truegug's words crept into his mind. If all that was true, would taking an oath be for the better or worse?

Selah's hand rested on his shoulder. "You have until tomorrow morning," she said. "Right now, let's just focus on you finally becoming a mage."

Rowan gave her a clipped smile to please her, but it didn't stop his mind from racing the rest of the evening. He stared at palms, imagining them caked in ash if he had one more failed attempt. Perhaps, being bound forever was worth the risk. All for the sake of the people he loved.

Tension tightened every limb in Rowan's body. No matter how hard he tried, his concentration lay beyond the stone archway. The forest: it taunted him. Its trees and branches intertwined into a single entity. A perfect hiding place for the Legion's monsters.

Rowan's hand hadn't stopped trembling since they got here. The wooden tea cup he held made no effort to stop his tremors. He would never have chosen the forest for their second lesson. But Madam Linn insisted, calling back to her duties as keeper of the border.

His eyes flickered to the archway, where Evermire would soon bid him farewell if Den Mother bested him. He stared at the teacup, worried about the damage he'd cause if it didn't work. The same damage he'd done to his beloved spell book as it burned in his sights.

But this was no spell book, and the mage sitting against the archway was not Den Mother. And whether the spell failed or not, he still had family to turn to. He gripped the rim of the teacup and took a deep breath.

Plastratsii, he muttered.

A wave of electricity pulsed at his fingertips and jolted into the grains of the cup. Sparks of heat and sensation forced him to drop it before he burned his hands.

"Ow," Rowan yelped. He stooped to pick up the teacup. The lightning had left the grains dulled and charred to a crisp. His eyes flitted between the woodwork and Madam Linn. "Um…I-I'm really sorry. I don't know much about wood. B-but I guess I can find some way to—"

"What do you need to apologize for," Madam Linn interrupted, taking the cup from him. The morning highlighted her sun-kissed dreadlocks, bringing out the proud expression on her face.

"But you looked so upset. I thought—"

"A simple attack spell like that takes a dozen tries to complete. You improved your casting by half of that. If anything, I'm more impressed. That ambitious mind of yours truly is something."

"Oh," Rowan uttered, nodding slightly. More praise in less than a day. A truly strange phenomenon. "But will it be enough to…you know, knock Den Mother down or something?"

"She'll be in for a 'shocking' surprise," Madam joked, putting the cup in her picnic basket. "But only if you maintain close contact; you can touch her garment, her skin, or even weapons she holds. Just as long you cast it on her and not yourself. Wouldn't want you to be electrocuted, now would we?"

Rowan nodded at her advice. She didn't see it, however, as she'd become more invested in the archway once she set her basket down. The lavender rays enveloped her, as she slid to one side of the stone fixture. She pulled her silver ladle from her grey belt loop. When she tapped it on the archway, it glowed a deep purple. She glided her hands along the stone, not letting a single dent or fragment slip through her fingers. She closed her eyes in concentration, even a chirping bird couldn't disrupt her.

"Is there really damage to the border?" Rowan blurted.

"It's difficult to say," Madam Linn said. "This process is merely a precaution. Mayor Vassile would be most upset if I didn't follow through." She made her way to the other side and repeated her motions.

"Well… yeah, but do *you* think there's damage to it?"

"Hmm, I think…if this Den Mother is so desperate to capture you, then checking for any flaws will benefit your defenses."

She proceeded with her inspection, leaving Rowan to ponder the inevitable. Based on Truegug's advice, perhaps he needed a bit more support to defeat Den Mother.

"Now that you've mentioned it, can I ask you something?"

"If you must," Madam Linn replied through her concentration.

He paused, regretting his next words already. "I've been thinking. If I really want to make sure Den Mother never comes back, I need to be much stronger. Sure, I still need to find a familiar. And I…I'm grateful you've given me lessons but…I'm just running out of time. What if the only way to be more powerful was by… taking an oath?"

Madam Linn's ears twitched at his question. "An oath, you say."

Rowan nodded.

Madam Linn stopped her inspection and sat beside Rowan. "And how do you feel an oath will make you more powerful?"

This was a trick question. Rowan could feel it. "Well uh…I always get tired after casting my spells so many times. My new friend, Truegug, says I'll have more energy if I take one. I can cast them as many times as I want."

Madam seemed to agree. "Truegug is right, in a way. But you are still learning, and that energy will develop over time."

"Oh," Rowan uttered. "Oh! Also, you said it yourself! Lots of mages took oaths to become more powerful and gain glory. I mean, taking out Den Mother with an oath would be the most glorious thing in my life." Madam Linn laughed at his exaggeration. Perhaps he was getting through to her. "Then when I grow up, I can use my oath to do more good. Have a lot more victories. I could…even become someone like you in the future."

The compliment appeared to tug Madam Linn's heart strings. But Rowan sensed an ache in her eyes.

"Someone like me, hm," she repeated softly. She inhaled deeply, as if preparing to let go of a heavy burden. "I'm afraid if you do that, you will also need to become *oathless* like me."

Rowan's smile dimmed as he stared at his teacher. Oathless. Linn the Moonstruck was oathless? How could this be?

"But I thought—"

"That I had an oath all along," Madam Linn finished. "I did at one point. But… I broke it. So, I believe the correct term for me would be, Oathbreaker."

She had mentioned the possibility of someone breaking their oath. It seemed much worse than being oathless. Almost criminal. But if this poised mage said it so plainly, was it truly a bad thing?

"How did you… break it?" Rowan asked.

Madam Linn's smiled sweetly at him. "That's a story for another time."

Rowan grumbled to himself. Hopefully, he'd know more about her one day.

"But I will tell you this," she continued reaching for her picnic basket. "Though I remain an oathless mage, there are benefits of being part of the Ataxia."

He watched her take out a leather booklet with an etched emblem of three circles twined together with different images in each one: a single flame, an ax, and a small tree.

"I've seen those symbols," Rowan blurted. "That *Im,* uh…*Impyria's* Lights party had them on their gloves."

"*Emphryea's* Lights are Zealots of Paia. Protectors and restorers of Caelum's gifts. If anyone, mage, hunter, or zealot wishes to take an oath, a High Patron, an authority of Paia's temples, must bless them." Madam pressed the center of the emblem, and it popped up. She grabbed it and revealed matted ashes packed in its center. "And as a Savior of Nidas and Keeper of the Border, I've been blessed with partial authority to perform oath ceremonies."

Rowan smiled down at the ashes. He didn't know what he needed to prepare for the ceremony, but if he helped defeat Mother once and for all, he'd gladly take that chance.

"But for you, dear child, this is one ceremony I cannot perform," Madam said solemnly. She covered the ash tray with the emblem cover.

Rowan shook his head in disbelief. "I know my answer for what I want to do with my oath was confusing. But I was just trying to impress you," he explained. "I really will take an oath to protect—"

"It's not about the oath you take, Rowan," Madam Linn interrupted. "It's about the price one must pay in keeping it."

"But I already paid that price back at the tavern,' he said.

"Like I told you." Madam held out a hand as she spoke, trying to calm him. "When you take an oath, you are forever bound to it. And oaths can be tricky. Say you did want to protect the innocent. Innocence has a different meaning for everyone, given the situation. If you were to blindly protect a foe of some kind, or use a spell that your oath prohibits, you'd be an Oathbreaker yourself. Which is something that our Council views as a stain on magic entirely. All mages, even the

Oath keepers, must know their limits. You are still learning yours."

"But I don't have time to learn all that," Rowan argued, towering the seated Madam Linn. "Den Mother's going to be here any moment now, and I can't waste any more time!" He felt himself yelling, but he didn't care. "Either you help me with an oath or—"

"Or else," Madam Linn raised her voice. "Is that what you intend to say? Well, what then? What could you possibly do?" She rose and looked down at the suddenly timid Rowan. Her dreadlocks blocked the morning sun, emphasizing the glint in her offended glare. "First, you *demand* my presence in my own home. You *ask* for my help, and I *grant* it to you. Now here we are again, little prince; demanding I give you a *blessing* that you have no knowledge of comprehending."

She sounded like Den Mother. All her talk of blessings and curses as she looked down on him.

"So, finish, oh Rowan the Brave. Or else… what?"

The past repeated itself no matter how hard he tried to avoid it. Rowan nearly froze, afraid of the consequences if he spoke. But he'd come too far to not speak his mind. "Or else I'll fight her myself."

Madam Linn scoffed. "With your novice spell-casting? If she's as powerful as you've seen, you likely won't survive."

"That's because you've only taught me two spells."

"Yes, because our time together has been so brief. I apologize for that. But an oath won't give you a Compendium's amount of knowledge in the span of an afternoon. And it most certainly won't make a difference in your skill level; Den Mother will see right through that."

Of course, she was right. He just hoped she wouldn't say it out loud.

"So, then what do I do?" Rowan asked in defeat.

"For starters, you don't need to fight this battle alone." Madam Linn held out a hand. "When moonrise approaches, I'll be right by your side. You, me, and Dremos. Just say the word and we'll fight alongside you."

He wanted to take her hand so badly; but he merely worried about his own weakness showing.

"Den Mother's coming after me, not you. This isn't your fight."

Madam Linn's gaze flared with sincerity. "Rowan, if it means protecting you and your friends, I will gladly be part of it."

She glanced away, then sighed. "Besides, you're mistaken. This is also my fight as well."

"How?"

Madam Linn turned towards the stone archway, her fingers scratching along the inside. "It appears I *have* been too dismissive about our borders."

Rowan leaned closer to see what had Madam Linn so downcast. Thin streaks tore into the edge of the lavender rays and the slabs of rock. As if someone had tried clawing their way through the border.

"Claw marks," Rowan said. "Do you think some kind of animal broke through or something?"

"This was no animal," Madam Linn countered, shaking her head. "And unfortunately, this was no accident." Her hand grazed the lines. "These marks are deeper and only a couple days old. And if anything were to claw through here, they would've done it outside the border; not inside. If our mayor's suspicions are correct, I believe there are traitors in our midst. Possibly from the Legion themselves."

Rowan's breath escaped him. First Den Mother and her monsters, now a possible spy in Evermire. There was only so much more he could take.

"What does that mean," he asked, shaken by her theory.

Madam inhaled sharply, as if bracing for what needed to be done. "It means there's much more at stake in this fight. Stopping Den Mother, fixing the border, and catching the traitor ourselves."

Chapter 23

Everybody Run

*F*or the first time in years, Rowan hadn't felt a single itch on his body. However, on nights like this, he certainly wished he did. It could have been something to distract him from the inevitable.

The view from his open window allowed him to do just that. But as Evermire's moon sat high in the navy sky, Rowan only envied its beloved people. How they roamed the streets, playing and shopping at their leisure. What it must've felt like, to live in blissful ignorance as destruction lurked in the shadows.

He recalled his dream. That hand said destruction would haunt him forever if he didn't succeed. He knew Madam Linn had tried to reassure him, but would these spells actually be in his favor? Or would they cause him to fail, allowing Den Mother to make chaos reign under her control?

Knock, knock, knock, went the outside of his bedroom door.

He went over and opened it. Standing in front of him were Selah and Peron, along with Miss Amori and her bird's-nest hair.

"Ah, there you are," she said. "See, dearies, I told you there was nothing to worry about."

"Thank you, Miss Amori," Selah and Peron said in unison. The children waited for her to close the door before pouncing on Rowan with a big hug.

"You can't just hide in here forever, dummy," Peron said.

"I wasn't hiding," Rowan countered. "Just hoping Den Mother wouldn't find me if I stayed in here."

Usually, he and his friends would laugh at that response. But not tonight. This time, the joke collided with a deep silence.

Finally, Selah broke it with a question. "Are you scared?"

Rowan almost masked his answer. But he couldn't hide anything from them. Not anymore.

"Yeah," he mumbled into her shoulder.

"Me too," Selah said.

Rowan pulled away from her, puzzled. "You? But you're not afraid of anything. What do you have to be scared of?"

She shrugged. "Come on, just because I'm stronger than both of you doesn't mean I don't get scared too."

It was so true that it garnered a chuckle from the boys.

"I'm scared of facing her too," Selah said. "Scared of how I'll react when I see her. I'm afraid of what I'll become if I try to stop her from attacking you."

"What do you mean, 'stop her'?" Rowan asked.

"You didn't think you were going to fight her by yourself, did you?" Peron asked.

Selah and Peron showed off the brown belts around their waists. Selah pulled a copper dagger from its sheath. Then Peron pulled one out too.

"You have a knife with you," he asked in disbelief.

Peron shrugged. "It wasn't my first choice, alright. When I picked the sword, Uncle Rog said it would tear me in half."

"We got them from the smithing tents about an hour ago," Selah said. "Had to trade a lot of seashells to get small weapons like these."

Rowan smiled at his friends. He truly didn't deserve them.

"I never really got to thank you guys," Rowan hushed. "I know you put up with a lot of what I do."

"Well, don't be modest now, Ro. Of course we're gonna help you," Selah said.

"We always have," Peron added.

"I know." Rowan's smile faded. "And that's the problem." He searched Selah's worried expression. Thoughts of Raegar crossed his mind; the last thing he wanted was to see her hurt again. "All I've ever done this entire journey is make mistakes. I just wanted to prove I could be brave and protect you guys without worrying you." He bowed his head in shame, thinking of Den Mother's words. "I know I can be a burden, but—"

"Don't you dare say that," Selah countered. Her hazel eyes froze him in place as she gripped his shoulders; not strong enough to hurt, but strong enough to keep his attention. "Now, Rowan, remember what I told you? We've always protected each other. You, me, and Peron, we all help each other in our own way, and that will never change. The only reason we do that is because we love you." Her hands landed on his cheeks. "You know that, right?"

In a house filled with hate, love never expressed itself with words.

"Yeah, I know," Rowan answered.

"Of course he does," Peron said, draping his arm around his friend. "We know you make mistakes. I mean, you've made a *lot* of mistakes."

Rowan rolled his eyes at the emphasis. Was Peron trying to make him feel better or worse?

"But that doesn't mean we're gonna stop helping you," Peron continued. "You're a lot of things, Rowa. But a burden is never one of them. You learn from your mistakes, and it makes you a better mage every time. And if anyone tries to tell you differently, have Selah punch them in the face."

"Exactly," Selah said. "So let us fight *with* you, Rowan the Brave. Let's stop that witch once and for all."

His reason for fighting and enduring for so long. His reason for the peace Madam Linn told him to find, standing before him with open hearts and open arms. The orphaned children gathered into another hug. Then Rowan had a thought, an anxious and sad thought.

Will this be the last time we get to do this?

Knock, knock, went the door again.

Peron opened the door. Madam Linn and Mister Dre stood in the doorway. For a moment, Rowan wondered if they would need to change clothes.

Selah's new lavender dress seemed far too flashy compared to Madam Linn's black dress and green vest. With Sly wrapped around her scepter, she looked so regal. And while Mister Dre was adorned in black as well, Rowan couldn't help but compare his own black shirt and its lack of purities. Peron, he imagined, was probably wondering how Mister Dre's hood actually fit over his horns.

"Wonderful, Amori told us you'd be here," Madam Linn said."

Mister Dre glanced at Selah and Peron's weapons. "Do you plan on slaying squirrels with those toys of yours?"

Selah looked at her dagger, then back at Mister Dre with a smug expression. "At least I'm holding it right this time, aren't I?"

He met her retort with a curt nod.

"We were hoping to use these when Rowan fights Den Mother," Peron said.

"We're going to fight right by his side," Selah added.

"Indeed," Madam Linn said. She looked at Rowan. "And just before we meet her at the border as well. It seems you have more support than you thought, little prince."

Selah and Peron linked arms with Rowan, making him shrink in embarrassment. This whole relying on others was a bit much for him.

With that, the Spehrows lead the way downstairs into the colorful tavern. Laughter and playfulness spread through the chandelier-lit space, making the children grin without realizing.

The Spehrows and the children headed for the entrance, where the skittish waiter, Toby, bided his time sweeping the floor.

Once Mister Dre opened the door for his wife and the orphans, Madam Linn said, "You'll take good care of things around here, won't you, Toby?"

"O-of course, Mistress," the lanky man responded. "A-anything for you."

Reassured, the Spehrows and the children went out to face the unknown.

Lilting strings had the power to make a grown man leap for joy. At least that's what Rowan saw with his own eyes. The town he'd envisioned with lights, streamers, and celebrations had finally come to pass. In the town square, citizens circled the stone pedestal to watch the Stringed Siren and her band of fiddlers down below. On their way to the border, the Spehrows and orphans' path was blocked by the audience around them. They clapped and cheered for the Stringed Siren as she danced atop the empty pedestal with her violin in hand. Ahria twirled by her side, shaking her tambourine to the fiddlers' jumping melodies.

Rowan saw Selah beam at Clascia Valdi as she watched from afar, basking in the hypnotic sounds of her violin.

"I can't believe it! It's the Stringed Siren," Selah exclaimed. "I've never heard her music so clearly before!"

"Yes, her sound is quite lovely up close. Clascia's music always brings joy to those in Evermire," Madam Linn explained. Then she sighed. "Shame she departs for Venari tomorrow. This is just a final performance to bid her fans farewell."

Rowan's ears perked up. Did that mean Ahria would leave, as well? Would this be the last time he saw her?

"Do you think we can go say hello?" Selah said, almost shoving through her friends.

Mister Dre stopped her way with his cape. "Our priority is the battle at the border, Selah," he reminded her. "Don't let yourself get distracted."

Rowan and Peron chuckled at Selah's brief pout. But it didn't stop her from trying to match the steps of a few dancing citizens. It only made the boys smile at her musical spirit. Perhaps once they defeated Den Mother, Selah could finally dance the night away like she wanted to.

Unfortunately, the audience and dancers were preventing them from fulfilling that destiny. If Rowan had his way, he'd make all of them move aside like Ahria did with her trumpet. He took a few steps back, just to see how far the audience stretched. As he did, he bumped someone's shoulders. An older boy with dark, star-laden skin turned around with a sneer. Rowan gasped at Nyx, who looked him up and down with pale eyes. A thick bandage covered the length of his nose. Rowan glanced at Selah. Her red-hot expression and balled fists made him nervous. Not for himself, of course. But for the injured bully, who eyed Selah with a snort.

"Well, look who it is," Nyx mocked in a nasal tone. "If it isn't the mu—." He stopped mid-sentence when he saw the Spehrows looking at him. He slouched forward in humility.

"M-Mister Spehrow. Madam Spehrow. A pleasure to see you again."

"And to you as well, Onyx," Mister Dre greeted him.

Seeing Nyx grovel before them made Rowan snicker. Selah and Peron, reacted similarly, leaving Nyx with flushed stars emitting from his skin.

Mayor Vassile walked up with a dignified stance, a quiver of arrows, and a bow hanging over his back.

"Ah, *Peravo Kalai*, sire!" Madam Linn greeted him. "Good to see you out and about. And I see you brought an army. How delightful. I'm surprised my reports of the border this morning didn't leave you huddled in your study."

Rowan squinted past the mayor and Nyx, noticing the olive-green uniforms and grey wings behind them. Dozens of spear-wielding soldiers were lined up with gargoyles by their sides. If anything, her reports had done quite the opposite.

The mayor harrumphed at her fake smile before adjusting his quiver. "Well someone needs to show Onyx how to be an exceptional leader. One who protects his people," he snipped, before glancing at the orphans. "I presume your wards are fighting in your place?"

"On the contrary, sire." Madam Linn said. "Our plans involve protecting my wards. The same way, they're meant to protect your son as well."

Rowan blinked from Madam Linn to Mayor Vassile, to a smug-looking Nyx. Did she just say "son"? *No wonder he teased Truegug like that. Look where he learned it from*, Rowan thought. Nyx stuck his tongue out at the orphans, then clutched his injured nose in pain.

Rowan, however, didn't hide his frown from the mayor and his son. "Yeah! And if anything, we're fighting our…own battle," he blurted. The mayor looked befuddled. It had sounded much better in his head. "I mean…we'll try our best to keep your town safe." He looked to Mister Dre for approval. The fiendish gave him a pitying nod.

Mayor Vassile chuckled doubtfully at the outburst. "Well, I certainly hope you're right, dear boy. Or else my soldiers will have to step in for her." He motioned to the army behind him. The soldiers slammed their spears twice at attention while the gargoyles flared their wings in unison. Rowan spotted Uncle Rog and Truegug in the formation. The smaller gargoyle popped his head out to wave at his new friend. But his crotchety uncle blocked his greeting with a swipe of his wing.

"Why, sire, I quite agree," Madam Linn said. "The more defenses, the better."

The mayor shrugged. "It's a precaution, really. Can't have your negligence rotting this town to the core."

"That would be the actions of your forefathers…sire. Or have you forgotten the Battle for Nidas again?" Dremos said through gritted teeth.

Mayor Vassile frowned and grumbled at the mention of his family; his hand gripping his quiver. Rowan gulped at the hunter's harsh words, hoping another fight wouldn't break out. Luckily, Madam Linn calmed Mister Dre with a hand on his forearm.

He cleared his throat to compose himself. "But let us not dwell on past mistakes. Why don't we work together, just as we did that fateful day? Have your armies guard the perimeter and we'd be eternally grateful."

The cunning fiend bowed respectfully to the mayor. The orphans bore Mister Dre the same stunned expression as Madam Linn did.

Mayor Vassile merely squinted at him in contempt. "Need I remind you, Spehrow's Eye, that I give the orders around here. But I suppose…" The mayor raised his hand above his head. When he circled his arm and pointed at the audience, the soldiers marched together, forming a circle on the cobblestone road. In unison, they all walked backwards, giving themselves space from the audience.

The mayor glanced at his son before making his proclamation. "Another lesson for you, Onyx. An exceptional leader takes his people's suggestions to heart."

"Yes, Pa. Understood, Pa," Nyx called at attention. But not before childishly bucking his head at Rowan.

Father and son paced around, checking the stance of each soldier protecting the square.

"Wait, does that mean the mayor's going to help us too," Peron asked.

Truegug clipped Peron's arm, as he, Uncle Rog, and a dozen gargoyles walked past the Spehrows. "What did I tell ya? Extra manpower," he told the orphans. It didn't take long before Uncle Rog dragged him away by the collar while the other Nocturnals flew up to the older buildings. "Good luck to you guys," Truegug managed to yell as he and his uncle joined the others.

Rowan watched the gargoyles perched along the edges of roofs, silently observing the masses while the concert continued.

The audience cheered as Clascia's music grew louder. Cries of "Hey" and "Hoorah" sounded from the fiddlers, with the townsfolk leaping on each word. Dancers joined in lively waltzes to the sound of Ahria's tambourine.

"Children, listen carefully," Mister Dre announced as he and Madam Linn turned to face them. "These dancers become maniacs when they gather in the streets. Fights have occurred because people don't pay attention." Rowan gulped. He thought he saw a fight almost break out.

"If you don't want to get lost, keep your eyes on us as we lead the way," Madam Linn advised.

The orphans nodded as they linked arms and followed the Spehrow's. Rowan gazed at Madam Linn's green vest, following it as she and Mister Dre dodged a leaping duo. He marked where their footsteps landed. Selah managed to dodge a man who moved to his right instead of his left. Peron clung onto Rowan to avoid knocking into a spinning female dwarf.

Even as they swerved through the crowds, the orphans laughed at themselves as they stumbled through the throng. Luckily, their clumsiness got them much closer to the pedestal this time. Close enough to have Ahria in their sights.

She spotted them and waved with her tambourine. Unfortunately, the Stringed Siren interrupted her daughter's greeting, using her bow to lower her hand. Rowan supposed every parent wanted their child to concentrate.

He tried searching for Truegug and the gargoyles, wondering if they found this scene amusing. But instead of laughter, soft growls rumbled from the roofs. They gargoyles stood on all fours, baring their teeth at the dancers. Truegug and Uncle Rog on the side braced themselves in the same manner. The soldiers reacted and slowly closed in on the dancing audience.

Strange; the soldiers had seemed more stoic than usual. Why the sudden change?

"Stay close! We're almost past the square," Madam Linn said.

In that moment of determination, Rowan noticed something in the circle of soldiers, a dark figure with a black uniform and a…raven beaked mask. Did he see that correctly? He shook his head, thinking his eyes were playing tricks on him. But no, the figure was still there, staring blankly at him.

Rowan looked around, wondering if his friends or the Spehrows saw the same thing. But as they stepped to the beat, he sensed an even darker presence. He turned to the left and saw another similar figure passing as a bystander. It had the same black uniform, and the same black mask.

His feet froze on the cobblestone, while his arms slipped through Selah and Peron's grip. They turned around, confused.

"Rowan, let's go. We don't have time for this," Peron said, shaking his shoulders.

"We're gonna lose Madam Linn if we stay like this," Selah reminded. She tugged at his arm to get his attention.

But it was no use. Rowan's mind was racing with a thousand thoughts. Surely, they wouldn't be here. Because if they were here, that meant *she* was here. His gaze flitted all around trying to find Madam Linn and Mister Dre. But they were nowhere to be found. He couldn't believe it. She had abandoned him, again.

A blood-curdling shriek startled the orphans, making them cover their ears and duck to the ground. The townsfolk did the same, their cries of joy warping into horrified screams. Rowan had muffled it; he recognized that noise. It had the same anguish as Den Mother's did, when Selah stabbed her in the eye. Everyone's eyes turned to the sky, where billowing black smoke rose above the evening sky and enveloped the moon like thick fog.

"Black Haze! Everybody run!" a citizen shouted.

But before people could disperse, the black haze descended into the square. Rolling smog smothered the townsfolk, whirling around like a deadly tornado.

Rowan squinted through the haze, barely made out the flying gargoyles, the escorting soldiers, and the fleeing townsfolk. Their screams drowned out his desperate apology to his friends.

"You're right, I'm sorry," Rowan cried. "I'll never freeze up again! Let's just get to the border before we—"

He looked to his left. Selah wasn't there. Then to his right. Peron was gone without a trace. Rowan found himself stranded in the street.

"Selah! Peron!" he called. No one answered. Not over the scores of frightened people. He yelled louder. "Selah! Peron!" Still no one. Rowan spotted dark figures on each side of him, inching closer with each blown cinder.

Rowan's breath hitched. He wanted to panic. But with all his might, he swerved past the escaping crowds and fled the approaching figures. He waded through the dark smoke, hoping to simply bump into his friends. Tears rushed down his face. How could his own friends abandon him? No, they'd never just leave him like that. It must've been something in the haze that had separated them; something…or someone.

He spun around. Through frantic masses, he saw the masked guards marching side by side. They eerily followed him as Rowan stumbled away. Just as he broke into a final sprint for his life, he crashed into another fleeing stranger.

Rowan landed on his side with a groan. As he checked his forehead for blood, a gentle hand reached out for him to take. He searched the face of his helper, but the haze covered it far too well. But it didn't shield the familiar black fabric of a long dress. One, he remembered from a very familiar mage.

"Madam Linn," he exclaimed, taking her hand. "Thank goodness you didn't really leave! I'm so happy I found—!"

Rowan gasped as the haze began to clear. The woman before him, he quickly realized, was not Madam Linn. Her hair was styled in a tight silver bun rather than brown dreadlocks. She wore a vestless black dress, the same dress that brought back horrible memories.

Rowan's worst nightmare stared back at him with a black patch covering her left eye. A wicked smile curled her lips. The smile villains always sported in conquest and victory. He knew only one person who smiled that way.

"There you are," the woman hissed, the smog from her breath staining her teeth.

"Den Mother," Rowan uttered helplessly. This was no dream, hallucination, or any spirit come to haunt him. This was a clear view of Den Mother herself.

A high-pitched ringing resounded in Rowan's ears. He was too afraid to do anything. Too afraid to move. Even when Den Mother's dry and calloused hands grabbed him by the neck and lifted him into the air.

Chapter 24

Bartered Wardship

Spiraling cinders halted in their movement and sunk to the ground. They spread along the entire square, sticking to townsfolk's clothes and adhering the gargoyles' wings. The mysterious black haze left not a single thing untouched. All except for Rowan and Den Mother. The haze had only dissipated after she brought her hand to his throat.

Had she always been this strong? And how on earth was she lifting him high above her head? Rowan's legs dangled off the ground. He kicked and clawed at her forearm, doing anything to shake off her grip. He even reverted to old habits.

"Den Mother, please," Rowan pleaded through gasps. But she held him tighter.

"*That's right, beg. It makes this moment more victorious,*" Den Mother hummed in her distorted tone. The stench from her blackened breath made Rowan gag.

"Selah! Per—" Rowan cracked. Den Mother dug her nails into his skin, crushing his windpipe.

"*Aww. No friends to save you, hmm,*" Den Mother mocked. She leaned to whisper in his ear. "*You are in the hands of the Legion, urchin. They don't come to your aid because they fear you the same way they fear me. This is what happens when you don't remember your place. But you will soon. Shame you'll never bid farewell to your friends once I offer them to Khallus.*"

Rowan wheezed harshly, glaring at her at the mention of his friends. Not Selah and Peron. Not them. Not while he felt his life slipping away. His fighting efforts slowed. Just before his vision grew dim, he heard a *whoosh*, and an arrow zoomed by his ear and into Den Mother's shoulder.

Den Mother's pained cry cut through his near unconsciousness. She released Rowan's neck, letting him fall to the ground. On his knees, he gasped for air, coughing through labored breaths.

Den Mother yanked the long arrow out of her shoulder. With a grunt she revealed the bloody arrowhead. She snapped her fingers. Fire emerged from her palm and burned the arrow to ash. Hunching, she bared her smog-stained teeth, scouring the square with rage and anguish.

"WHO IS RESPONSIBLE FOR THIS?" Den Mother screamed, her voice returning to its aggravating shrill.

Another arrow landed into her side. It pushed her off balance, but she didn't fall. She whipped her head toward the arrow as it passed behind Rowan. He turned around and wondered who shot it at her, hoping his face wouldn't be the next target.

He found Mayor Vassile kneeling beside the pedestal, holding his bow with another arrow ready to fly. Behind him stood Nyx, who peeked over the mayor's shoulder as he shouted out orders.

"Now, men!" Mayor Vassile shouted.

Scattered soldiers rose to their feet. Gargoyles on all sides flew at the command. They charged after Den Mother with loud cries, spears and claws aimed in her direction.

But the villainous woman jeered at their advances. "What nonsense," she said, before letting out another earth-shattering shriek.

Like a river current, the haze sifted through the cobblestones to meet the running soldiers. A rotten smell rose from the haze. Rowan recognized that smell. Then he noticed the soldiers halt where the haze blocked their target. From its cindered state, it warbled and shifted, transforming into thick black ink.

Rowan couldn't believe his eyes as the liquid twisted upward and shaped into the mayor's soldiers, all of whom wore black and stared back at their doubles with crow-like masks. With their spears, the mayor's men and Den Mother's guards carried out a messy battle. Mayor Vassile gave his orders from a distance, trying his best to aim away from his own soldiers. Gargoyles lifted a few of her guards in the air before they could attack the frightened townsfolk.

Rowan's head spun from all the chaos. *How could she let this happen?* he thought.

"Stop! Stop it, please! Why are you doing this?" Rowan begged hoarsely. Smiting pain from the chokehold lashed at his voice.

"I told you, urchin, my wrath upon this town shall know no bounds," Den Mother said, pulling the arrow out of her side. "And as for you!"

She launched herself at Rowan. He guarded his face against her attack. Just in time, someone jumped in front of him and said a simple spell.

Piresto

Streaks of sunlight shot in front of Den Mother and swiped over to her nearby guards. The blinding light forced her to the ground while the dark figures vaporized into thin air. Once the light faded, Rowan adjusted his eyes and saw the green vest of his savior.

Madam Linn had her back to Rowan as she protected him with a sunbeam from her raised scepter. Tears welled up in his eyes again. *She's here. She's actually here*, he thought.

"Madam Linn," Rowan strained, but he couldn't stop coughing.

His hacking quickly caught her attention. She knelt by his side to lift him up, apologizing while dusting off his clothes.

"Rowan, I'm so sorry," Madam Linn said. "The crowds became unruly, and then the haze began to form..." She gasped at the bruises along Rowan's neck. Not that Rowan could see much; his focus remained solely on her presence.

Frantically, she displayed her scepter again. Rowan watched her hand wave over Sly's fixed state as she spoke.

Pethsana

Green smoke surrounded Rowan's neck. The bruises disappeared without a trace. Madam Linn searched for other scars. "If only I'd been here sooner. This would've never have happened."

She looked worried, Rowan thought, *as if this had happened before.*

"Thank goodness you're here," he said normally, the spell already healing his voice. "I'm so happy I found you."

Madam smiled, and he wanted to hug her, if it weren't for the chilling truth plaguing his mind.

"Den Mother," he uttered. "She…she has Selah and Peron."

Her smile disappeared. She shot a fierce glare at the fallen Den Mother as she fixed her posture.

Den Mother staggered up, yowling in frustration. Madam Linn stood in front of Rowan, ready to guard him from another attack.

"How dare you interfere," Den Mother scowled as she stomped toward Madam Linn. She aimed her threats at Rowan. "Treacherous child! I'll see you rot in that cellar for the rest of your—!"

Madam Linn cut off Den Mother's threats with her scepter pointed at her neck. She halted immediately and stared at the weapon.

Madam Linn tilted her head to study the villainous woman. "My, my. So, you must be Den Mother," she purred. "I can see why the children wanted to escape. Word of your reputation travels fast in these parts."

"You don't know a thing about me, half-breed," Den Mother insulted her. "Who are you to meddle in my business?"

Madam Linn bowed her head slightly. "Linn the Moonstruck is what they call me. But enough introductions for now. Why don't I give you a choice? Show us where Selah and Peron are, or Sly will make that decision for you." She tightened her grip on her scepter, bringing it up to Den Mother's chin.

She glanced at the crowd and chuckled at Madam Linn. "Your empty threats won't stop my wrath from laying siege."

She snapped her fingers, summoning another blaze of fire. She aimed it at a few soldiers shielding a family from Den Mother's guards.

Rowan almost shouted for her to stop, but he noticed something move beneath her feet. The light from the streetlamps revealed Den Mother's shadow. The shadow fled the ground and morphed into a physical form. Its outline shaped the horns of a familiar fiend. The black silhouette faded to reveal Mister Dre, shielding his masked face with one sword in hand. The other sword was stationed an inch from Den Mother's back.

Den Mother felt Mister Dre's presence behind her. She concealed her fireball and arched her back away from his blade. Rowan recalled his shadowlike powers from days past, relieved to finally see him again.

"I suggest you make a better choice," Mister Dre stated deeply. "Show us where the children are."

Mentioning the children seemed to calm Den Mother's nerves; her lips curled into a devious grin. Her good eye flicked from Madam Linn to Rowan. He didn't like that look, not one bit.

"Very well," she agreed. She let out a strained squawk, prompting her blackened guards to cease fighting. They stood at attention in a circle, while the mayor's soldiers watched in disbelief. Two black guards pushed through them, holding the wrists of two squirming children.

"Selah! Peron!" Rowan yelled out, stunned. He fled Madam Linn's side and rushed toward his friends.

"Rowan, stop," Selah warned.

"Rowan, stay where you are," Peron ordered.

Rowan was halfway toward them when a burning pain seared into his ankle. A guttural scream left his lips, and he fell to the ground. He lifted his face from the dirt and saw the ember symbol burn into his skin.

He hissed in anguish. His gaze drifted to Den Mother's ring and the light flames swirling along her fingertips. Peron and Selah called out his name, but their guards pulled them tighter and placed hands over their mouths. Madam Linn and Mister Dre would've ran to Rowan as well, if Den Mother hadn't given them warning.

"One more step, and this entire town becomes a relic of history."

Rowan watched the Spehrows remain in place, glancing at each other nervously. "Den Mother," he called out wearily. "Let us go, or I'll—"

"Spare me your theatrics," Den Mother said, walking towards him. Another arrow shot from above the crowds buried itself in the road, cutting off her path.

"You heard the child, legionnaire," Mayor Vassile shouted, still in his archery stance. "Let them go and leave this town at once! Or I'll turn you into the Council myself!"

Den Mother bared her grin at the distant mayor and politely faced him. "You must be the leader of this land. Rest assured, sire, this matter is none of your concern. I'm simply here to take back what is rightfully mine. These children are in my care. And I fully intend to bring them back. They have a purpose to fulfill, you see. For their sake and mine."

"State your purpose, and I will reconsider."

Den Mother's chin turned up proudly, but she remained tight-lipped, as if harboring a secret. One that Rowan spoiled as he hauled himself up.

"You were…going to sacrifice us to your…stupid Khallus," he spilled out.

Horrified faces surrounded the square when he told the truth. Rowan spotted the Stringed Siren and Ahria on the other side of the pedestal. Clascia clutched her daughter in her arms.

"Blasphemous fools like you could never understand the means of my oath," Den Mother shrugged, jeering at the crowds. "And you certainly don't need to. Just know if you capture me, your wretched Council will wonder how a legionnaire of Khallus left the battle of Nidas unscathed. And who do you think they'll blame?"

Rowan gulped at her blackmail. Surely the mayor wouldn't believe her nonsense.

"But there is a solution. If you allow me the return of my wards, I will gladly meet your demands and never return."

The mayor turned up his brow. "And if we won't?"

Den Mother conjured fire from her hands, gesturing to the guards posted around the square. A long pause lingered. Long enough for the Spehrows to shake their heads at Mayor Vassile. And long enough for the mayor to lay down his bow and nod at Den Mother. The masses made their protests known after her fire ceased.

Dread engulfed Rowan's stomach. Sounds of his friends' muffled screams rang in his ear. Den Mother glanced at him with smug victory lining her smile. Rowan turned to limp away, but the guards holding his friends blocked his escape. Den Mother pulled at his arm, ready to drag him from the only home he'd ever known. Until Madam Linn's voice echoed through the square.

"Bartered wardship!"

Rowan gasped at Madam Linn's words. By the looks of it, so did everyone else in the square. Den Mother's good eye widened with shock. Once the gasps died down, however, she had a sly grin.

"Bartered wardship," Den Mother repeated as she chuckled. "Whatever do you mean?"

"Your mistreatment of Selah, Peron, and Rowan has made you unfit to raise them in your care," Mister Dre accused. "Grant us, Dremos and Kherolyna Spehrow, full authority over these children and surrender your own."

So many words, and yet Rowan focused only on Madam Linn's proposal. She wanted to adopt them. She wanted to take them away from Den Mother. A smile almost came to his face, but Den Mother released his arm with force, sending him sprawling to the ground.

"Dremos and Kherolyna. I thought I recognized those names," Den Mother said. "Who knew Evermire still harbored two disgraces after that needless battle?"

Rowan whipped his head toward the Spehrows. Did Den Mother know them in the past? Mister Dre and Madam Linn were clearly confused by the allegation.

"But besides the fact that an Oathbreaker and a coward desire to take my wards from my custody, there's an element to bartered wardship you are missing. What was the phrase my spy told me? *What you desire in gain, you must give in return?* So then tell me, what is it you're willing to give me?"

Murmurings about spies echoed throughout the square. The mayor tried to push past the blackened guards, but they blocked him. Rowan looked at Madam Linn and Mister Dre, wondering what they'd say. Instead, they silently held up their swords and scepter to Den Mother, who cackled loudly.

They can't give her anything in return, because the thing she wants…is us, Rowan realized. He huffed at her brazen behavior, remembering why he hated her so much. Then he had a thought, an insane yet regrettable thought.

"Me," Rowan blurted out. "You can have me!"

Madam Linn and Den Mother looked at Rowan, speechless. Rowan heard Selah and Peron's muffled screams but didn't turn back. He shouldn't have said that. He wished he could take it back, but he knew it had to be done.

"You said it yourself, Den Mother. I'm the only student you have left. Use me to fulfill Khallus' will. Force me to sacrifice myself if you have to. In return, you leave Selah and Peron out of this and give them to the Spehrows. They deserve a happy life… one without me burdening them."

"Rowan, what are you doing?" Madam Linn said.

He could ask himself the same question. Rowan heard the tremble in Madam Linn's voice. He bit his lip to stop himself from crying. Without another thought, he scrambled up, rushed to the Spehrows, and embraced them both.

"I can't thank you enough for rescuing us," Rowan whispered to Mister Dre, who peered down at him with suspicion. To Madam Linn, he whispered, "I'm so glad I got to meet you. Thank you for teaching me, at least for a little while."

Taken aback, Madam Linn gazed at Rowan as she returned his embrace. She shook her head. "Rowan, you don't have to do this."

"And you have no right to decide the boy's fate," Den Mother spat. She snatched Rowan away from the hug, taking his hand in hers. "If anything, that's my job." She shrieked at her guards, prompting them to release Selah and Peron. They pushed the children away, making them fall to their knees and gasp for air.

"Rowan, please! Don't do this," Selah pleaded through her tusks.

Hearing her voice made Rowan want to change his mind. But he needed to do it to keep them all safe. Den Mother yanked his hand to bring him close.

"I knew you'd make the right choice," she teased softy. "You've finally learned your true place: an offering for Khallus' return." Rowan stared at her hand, the same ringed one that had branded him moments before. All he had to do was hold it. But before he decided, Den Mother growled in his ear. "Your sacrifice will do him nicely. After all, Khallus favors the ones who suffer most."

Rowan stared Den Mother in the eye, facing her without fear for the first time.

"You know what, Den Mother? I appreciate you trying to teach me magic," Rowan admitted. A smirk lined his face. "Sure, I was pretty bad at it, and you really were a terrible teacher." He glanced at her hand, the one crushing his own. He placed his free hand on top of hers and matched her gripping force. "But that just means I'll get to show you the spells I've been dying to use on you. The kind I should've learned a long time ago."

"Unhand me, you wretched—"

Plastratsii, Rowan breathed.

Lightning struck. An electric burst of energy spread from Rowan's palm to Den Mother's. The shock jolted them in opposite directions. Rowan fell on top of Madam Linn and Mister Dre, while Den Mother toppled into her guards.

Even as he landed wrong, electricity bounced Rowan back to life. He couldn't believe what that spell did to him; what it did to her.

I can't believe that actually worked, he thought.

"To think I almost believed your tearful farewell. I knew you were up to something," Dremos chuckled, brushing Rowan's hair.

"You, clever child," Madam Linn said, looking just as stunned as he was. "What on earth were you thinking?"

Rowan shook his head as his smile crept in. "I thought I'd give her a…shocking surprise," he joked. A terrible joke, obviously, but still a joke.

Selah and Peron watched Den Mother struggle to stand. They took no chances, running towards Rowan and knocking him and the Spehrows down again as they hugged him.

"If you ever do that again, I'll kill you," Peron said.

The children didn't know whether to cry or laugh. As they savored the heartwarming moment, however, inqai shrieks called throughout the sky.

The Spehrows and the children watched the nearby guards screamed in the same fashion. Their gloves and boots shed off their persons, revealing dripping oily claws. Their bodies contorted uncontrollably, tearing through the uniforms Den Mother disguised them with. Their long masks flung off their faces, displaying the dreadful snouts of the inqai themselves.

"Inqai! Inqai in Evermire," Truegug called out. Uncle Rog shielded him with one of his wings.

A light bulb went on in Rowan's mind. Den Mother's control over the guards; how she possessed the beasts to her will and word; the way she formed them from haze to take any shape. She was far more powerful than he realized. Powerful enough to withstand his shocking spell. She stumbled up from her fall.

"I will not let my oath be tarnished by the likes of traitors," Den Mother's distorted voice cried. "You urchins could have returned to me willingly. And now, because of your foolishness, everyone shall perish by my hand!"

Dremos clashed his swords together in a defensive stance. Selah and Peron clung to Madam Linn, praying the approaching inqai wouldn't pounce on them. Den Mother's vulgar gaze locked on Rowan. Her sickening ways to control their lives baffled him as he stared back. All this chaos, all this destruction, just to drag him back to the repulsive orphanage beyond the border.

A memory came to mind; one of a simple snake, a caravan encircled with inqai, and the one spell that eradicated them all. Then Rowan had a thought, a brilliant yet…risky thought.

"Thirty seconds," Rowan muttered, maintaining his gaze on the monsters.

"What do you mean thirty sec…Oh," Selah said, realizing what he was implying. "Rowan, are you sure?"

He glanced at Madam for a moment, not sure if he was doing the right thing. "Not really," he said. "But if we did it once, we can do it again. I just need you to trust me."

Selah peered at Peron, whose twitchy focus shifted from the growling beasts to Rowan. Selah nodded at him, and he let out a disgruntled groan, knowing he had nothing left to lose.

"You have exactly thirty seconds," Peron grunted.

"Whatever you're planning, use your skills wisely," Madam Linn whispered as she stood her ground. "You don't know what she might do next."

"Neither does she," Rowan stated. He glared at the inqai, then took a deep breath. He let his hands hover over his face. And with all his strength and might, stretched his hands upward and whispered…

Coemsae Aercis!

Purple sparks popped from the center of his hand. Streams of fire flew into the sky.

Boom! Boom! Boom!

Like stars bursting in the sky, Rowan's fireworks display caused the masses to gape and marvel. He even caught himself in his own moment of awe until he remembered what he had made the illusion for. The ravenous inqai ceased their hunt as they gawked at the purple explosions above. Even Den Mother was distracted, as her snarl melted into a beaming smile.

Only twenty-five more seconds, Rowan thought. Then came the hard part. He gulped as he eyed Madam's scepter, already regretting his next act.

"I'm so sorry," Rowan murmured to Madam Linn. "But I really need to do this."

In a flash, he snatched the scepter from her grip.

"Rowan, don't," she exclaimed.

But he had already aimed the next spell at the beasts beside him.

Striatsi!

Chapter 25

A Plan in Motion

Zooom-CRACK, went the explosion.

Rattled townsfolk snuck a peek, finding a trail of smoke where inqai once were. Rowan panted from the rush of disbelief; he had just slain a bunch of monsters. His reaction was delayed, however, as he watched the sparks of his illusion fade into dark mist.

Oh no, Rowan thought.

His vision snapped back to the distracted inqai coming to their senses and turning their attention to him. There was a moment of silence, then Rowan looked at his nervous friends and said,

"TWENTY SECONDS! RUN WHILE YOU STILL CAN!"

At Rowan's voice, Den Mother snapped out of her trance. She growled at the running children and shrieked at the inqai. So focused on giving commands, Den Mother didn't see Uncle Rog, who swooped in and seized her by the shoulders. Her screams resounded in the air as he carried her around recklessly.

With the legionnaire out of sight, Dremos leapt forward and slew the inqai by the pedestal, giving the mayor another chance to aim his arrows.

"Men, take my son and gather everyone to the safehouse," Mayor Vassile ordered. The soldiers and gargoyles instantly obeyed, escorting Nyx and the townsfolk away of the battle.

Inqai pounced at Madam Linn until she called out her spell again with an outstretched arm.

Piresto, she shouted. Her sunbeam vaporized the inqai before her.

Den Mother watched it all from above, seething with rage. She summoned her fire and threw it in Uncle Rog's face. He grunted and shut his eyes, causing his claws to release her shoulders.

Den Mother descended, ready to throw an enormous bonfire into the town. Madam Linn saw, pointed at Den Mother and whispered:

Flonatvi

The villainous woman glowed brightly as she floated in place. Madam Linn whipped her hand down, forcing Den Mother into the pavement, snuffing out her fire.

Casting such remarkable spells made Madam Linn stumble. She collapsed to the floor with an aching hiss. But even in weakness, she cried, "Dre, follow them! Clascia and I will take her!"

He nodded at her command and dashed for the street corner. Clascia responded to Madam Linn with a stroke of her violin, while Ahria followed the soldiers to safety.

Den Mother emerged from the ruined cobblestone with a fiery, hysterical cry. A heap of smog unleashed from her breath as she shouted,

"GET THEM, YOU INSECTS!"

●　●　●

"Fifteen, fourteen, thirteen," Rowan counted as he clutched the scepter. Or at least, tried to clutch the scepter. If the heavy Sly hadn't attached itself to it, the precious antique might've slipped out of Rowan's hand.

"Rowan," Peron panted. "I swear to Caelum, if you don't have a good plan, I'll—"

"Peron, shut up and keep running," Selah yelled, fixing her glare at Rowan. "Ro, you're the one who stole Madam's scepter, so you better put it to good use."

"I didn't...I didn't steal it," Rowan huffed. "I'm just...borrowing it until—"

A deep thud interrupted Rowan and startled them all. The source: their fiendish savior, who leapt down in front of them.

"Until what?" Dremos demanded in a controlled tone.

Peron and Selah pushed Rowan forward to explain. But his response came out in stutters. "Uh... until I... until we defeat all the inquses!"

"And how do you plan to do that?"

"Uhhh...?" was his only reply.

Den Mother's shriek resounded through the square. Half the night sky was already covered in the smoky haze. Horrid inqai bounded down the path, destroying tents and terrorizing merchants.

Rowan scrambled with the scepter, ready to cast the spell, but Dremos zigzagged past him. He sliced through the inqai one by one, leaving them to choke and vanish into ash.

For a moment, the children thought they were in the clear, but a larger army of monsters appeared and ran through the streets. As more townsfolk fled, Rowan tried out the scepter again.

Striats—

"Are you insane?" Selah barked, tilting the head of the scepter away. "You can't do that now! You might hit someone!"

"If not now, then when, Selah," Rowan demanded.

"When we're not surrounded by innocent people," Peron said.

Rowan wrenched the scepter back from Selah in a huff. But Peron wasn't wrong. There had to be a way to keep everyone safe.

A pompous voice announced itself from the side of the street. "Free of charge, folks," it called. It was the lion-faced gargoyle, who yanked several coats off his tent display. "Take one of my claw-crafted coats and escape the mass hysteria! Everything must go!"

"I think I have an idea. Follow me," Peron said, running towards the creature. Rowan and Selah went after him, quickly understanding his plan.

"Wait! Don't go anywhere yet," Selah called. "Three. We'll take three."

"Young cubs," the gargoyle recognized them with a gasp. "Anything for my best customers! What would you like? Pigeon, hummingbird—"

"We'll take the fastest bird you've got," Rowan said, bouncing on his soles impatiently.

"Three falcons coming right up!" The gargoyle flipped through the pile in his arms and passed them three bluish-grey coats.

The gargoyle flew up high, while the children put on the large, heavy coats as fast as they could.

"Hey, let's fly there," Selah said, pointing at the building behind Rowan and Peron. "We can make it to that roof before the monsters get us."

"But what do we do after that?" Rowan asked.

Peron adjusted his collar. "*You* stole the scepter," he said snarkily. "That's for *you* to decide."

"Shut *up*! It's not sto-LEN," Rowan squealed. The feathers on his coat hurled his body into the air.

Selah and Peron groaned at Rowan. They saw Dremos, who was struggling against the inqus army.

"There's far too many," he called. "I'll follow you!"

Selah and Peron issued their commands: "Up." They soared above just as the inqai trampled through. They flew next to the shaken Rowan, who had kept the scepter intact. Their coats directed them to the top of the old building. Mister Dre summoned the chain from his hilt, threw it up high until it grappled through the brick wall, and swung forward to leap onto the roof. His heroic flair amazed the orphans. They gazed at him until he shot them an intense look.

"You're lucky those coats were available," Dremos said, sheathing his weapons. "Or else your boldness would be your downfall." His bluntness made them bow their heads in shame. "Then it's settled. I'm guiding you to the safehouse with the rest of the town."

Mister Dre went to grab the scepter, but Rowan held it closer to his chest. "Wait, no, not yet. I need to use it," he said.

"You three have been through enough. Right now, is the time to get you to safety. You'll do well to follow orders."

He almost snatched the scepter again, but Rowan quickly commanded his coat, "Up," and flew up with the scepter in his grasp.

"Rowan, enough of this. Get down and hand me the scepter."

He could hear the frustration in Mister Dre's voice. He stood his ground as he looked down at the hunter. "I'm not just going to give up and hide somewhere for Den Mother to find us again! You saw how many monsters there were. Without this scepter, none of us will defeat Den Mother and her inqai!"

Mister Dre took off his mask and glared at Rowan sternly. "You're correct. And without that scepter, Madam Linn will only grow weaker the more she fights your Den Mother."

The orphans gasped at his explanation. Rowan whispered, "down" and floated to the roof.

"What do you mean, 'she'll get weaker,'" Selah asked.

Mister Dre sighed heavily, as if this was hardly the time to explain. "She'll be alright. She's powerful enough to maintain her magic. But as an oathless mage, Linn uses Sly to strengthen her spell-casting abilities. And without her familiar…" He glanced at the frozen snake enveloping her scepter. "Each spell she casts diminishes her power by the second until she can no longer use the magic she's learned."

Linn the Moonstruck getting weaker? Heroes in stories never weakened; they get stronger by the hour. But Rowan remembered his hero was oathless. No, an Oathbreaker. And he'd just taken away her strength. He grazed his thumb along Sly's scales. He needed to make things right. Then an idea came to mind.

"When you and Madam were in the Ataxia," Rowan asked Mister Dre, "was there ever a time when…I don't know, when there were so many inqai that they didn't let you escape?"

Mister Dre stroked the hair on his chin. "Once, on an island near Venari. That spell you used was the same one she defeated them with."

"Did any innocent people get hurt?"

"Of course not. The island was a barren waste land. Far away from any villages."

Rowan continued to think. Selah had mentioned making sure no one got hurt. Perhaps they needed to gather them all in one place.

"Mister Dre, you told me on that caravan to let Sly be my guide. And he was. If he helped us once, I think he can help us again," Rowan argued. Mister Dre folded his arms. "Maybe…maybe we can lead the inqai out of town. We can use our coats to distract them, then… then take them somewhere we can use Madam's scepter… without harming innocent people."

Selah and Peron looked at each other, grinning lightly. They looked so proud.

"Oh, I know," Selah announced. "We'll lead them to the forest. That way when you use the spell, it'll only affect the inqai."

"Not the forest. We might destroy the border if we're too close," Rowan said. Then he remembered something. "There's a valley right next to it. We'll have them follow us. Then, when they're all gathered in together—"

"We attack them there," Peron interjected.

Mister Dre shook his head at the orphans, amazed. "Seems you stubborn kids actually have a plan." The children chuckled bashfully at his praise. He shrugged at them while placing on his mask and displaying his swords. "I'll fight alongside Linn. Go. Protect the innocents and defeat the inqai. Try not to make anything explode this time."

Rowan nodded at his quip. The fiendish hero jumped off the building and landed on top of an inqus, plunging his swords into its back.

"I think I see the forest," Peron said, pointing slightly to the left. Beyond the haze stood a field of trees on the dark skyline.

"Just before that is the valley," Rowan announced.

The orphans all commanded their coats together. Selah and Peron steadied themselves. But Rowan yelled and cursed as he soared; his mind already panicking mid-flight. He remembered Madam Linn's words: "Remain calm." Rowan slowed his breathing and flew for the valley with his friends above Evermire with his friends.

●   ●   ●

Rowan recalled that hand telling him of destruction, but it never described how lawless it would be. As he and his friends traveled, they observed the terror Den Mother had caused. Black haze polluted the summer air. Screeching inqai, roaring gargoyles, and wailing citizens resounded above the streets.

But there was a silver lining. Throughout Evermire, adventurers defended the town using their magic and skills. Zealots like the Emphryea's Lights conjured weapons and fiery vines to attack the inqai. Gargoyles tried intimidating the beasts to defend their young ones. Even hunters like Raegar, threw barrels at an inqus with his good hand, only for it to dodge and pounce on him. A faint melodic tone sounded from below. One with the smooth and fast vibrations of a crooning violin. Rowan knew only one mage with that instrument.

"Stop! Look, there's Mister Dre," Peron called out. His coat stopped on cue. Rowan and Selah followed him. Rowan scoured the streets for Mister Dre, as well as a certain musical prodigy. At an intersection of large tents, he spotted Clascia Valdi hypnotizing the beasts with sharp, dreary playing. On the last of her high notes, she swiped her bow along the side. A blast of teal-colored energy sent them flying. While they were still in the air, Mister Dre leapt over Clascia and slashed through the inqai in an instant. With each swift motion, his blades turned each vile creature into golden ashes before them.

The children spotted Madam Linn, surrounded by a dozen inqai ready to attack. Mister Dre swooped in from behind, scooped her up and soared above the buildings.

Madam Linn prepared a spell in her hand as the beasts ogled the leaping adventurers.

Mistio, she cried.

Thin red beams sprouted from her fingertips. In an instant, the blast burned the monsters to a crisp. The real-life Ataxia, slaying evil monsters like the ones in his stories. A sigh of relief escaped Rowan, thankful to see Madam Linn once again. But his mind was wracked with guilt when Mister Dre set her down and almost lost her balance.

Suddenly, the surrounding tents were set ablaze. A block away stood Den Mother, her hands emanating the same powerful flames. She aimed a fireball at Clascia. The Stringed Siren almost cast a barrier to stop it, but the fireball exploded in her face and tossed her across the street. Mister Dre threw his sword at Den Mother. She caught the blade in her hand. Blood dripped from her flaming palm. She set the steel on fire and flung it back at him. The burning sword pierced Mister Dre's shoulder, pinning him to a wooden booth far away from Madam Linn.

"Madam Linn," Rowan shouted. His voice reached her, and she turned to view them in horror.

Like her shrieking creatures, Den Mother ran for the distracted Madam Linn on all fours. Weakened and alone, she stretched out her arms. They trembled as she brought her hands together.

Vouconu, she strained, causing the burning tents between Den Mother to crash into each other. But even as the wood and fabric burned and splintered, the villainous mage surged over them. She summoned another fireball and hurled it at Madam Linn. Though she covered her face, the flames obstructed her vision, allowing Den Mother to pounce on top of her. The weakened mage had enough energy to cast another spell, but Den Mother thwarted her plans. She grabbed Madam Linn by the scalp and slammed her head into the stone path. One. Two. Three times, until she almost lost consciousness.

Madam Linn's gaze locked onto Rowan. She reached out and called with a rasped voice, "Leave. Now." She collapsed. A pool of blood streamed beneath her head.

"No! Madam Linn!" Selah and Peron exclaimed.

Something snapped Rowan's nerves. His voice escaped him. He wanted to wail in pain. But his chest heaved and his grip tightened around his scepter, until all he could do was scream a loud and angry, "DOWN! NOW!" commanding his coat to quickly descend.

"Rowan, wait!" Peron yelled. But it was too late. With swift momentum, Rowan pushed Den Mother out of the way and into a burning tent. His eyes set on the fallen Madam Linn. Before he could float to her, Den Mother recovered and bounded at him. In a flash, he used his scepter to shield himself. She grabbed it and pushed Rowan into a solid brick building. He tried pushing her weight off him, but she only pushed down harder. When she was about to punch him in the stomach, a strong presence lifted her off the scepter just in time. Rowan was shocked to find Selah holding Den Mother by the corset.

Selah heaved through her tusks, struggling to clench the heavy weight in her hands. Then, all at once, the whites of her eyes turned red, and a bloodthirsty bellow spilled out of her mouth. With all her strength, she pulled Den Mother off of Rowan and flung her into the air.

"Alright, Selah!" Rowan praised, bringing himself upright. But she ignored his comment with her own frenzied war cry.

"I'm gonna rip out your other eye, you witch," Selah proclaimed. Dagger in hand, she commanded her coat to fly up, while Rowan followed her worried.

Den Mother steadied herself and shrieked when Selah's dagger landed in her arrow wound. She frowned at the screaming girl, who continued to advance even without her weapon. Den Mother summoned a massive fireball and prepared to cast it down. Then another blade sliced the back of her wrist, dismantling her spell. She clutched her injured limb.

Rowan flew behind Selah, fastening his arms over his shoulders to calm her down. His eyes widened at Den Mother's attacker. Peron floated behind her with a dripping dagger.

"Oh no," Rowan whispered.

"Oh no," Peron said, dangling the weapon in his hand.

"You impish traitor," Den Mother cried. Her threatening voice made Peron hold his knife upright again. She swung her claws at him, but the frightened fiend commanded his coat to evade every advance.

"Left!" He dodged. "Down!" Dodged again. He swiped his weapon along her left forearm, but she didn't relent. She caught him by the collar. Her haze-stricken breath made his eyes water.

"I should have ripped those horns off your skull when I had the chance," Den Mother swore, raising her hand. Peron looked away and swung his blade. The sharp steel sliced from her forehead to the lid of her good eye. Den Mother let go of Peron and clutched it with a shriek.

"Rowan! Use the scepter! Use it now!" Peron hastened to his side. He helped hold Selah down, while Rowan scrambled with the scepter.

Once Rowan held it steady, he kept his eye on the distracted Den Mother. With a loud voice, he yelled, *"Striatsi!"* Sly's head developed a bright sphere of electricity. One that Den Mother sensed by her side. She reached for the children, but the lightning blasted her away and sent her soaring into the outskirts of Evermire's forests.

The orphans watched in shock, wondering if their nightmares had ended.

"Is she…is she gone?" Rowan asked softly. Selah's rage soon vanished, and her breathing calmed. Rowan and Peron went to check on her. "Selah, I'm so sorry. I just got so worked up over—"

"Madam Linn," Selah said wearily. Her gaze was fixed on the fallen mage down below. Mister Dre and Clascia Valdi were limping and sliding to her body.

The orphans commanded their coats, flew to the Ataxia, and knelt before Madam Linn. Mister Dre glanced at them as he rested her head on his lap.

"I thought you all were headed to the valley," Mister Dre questioned.

"W-we were," Peron said. "But then we saw…" He could hardly finish his sentence as he gazed at Madam Linn. She lied there still, with Mister Dre smoothing her hair gently. Clascia used her broken bow and violin to play a scratchy song. Musical notes jumped over Madam Linn's wound to heal her. The blood staining her hair began to dry up.

Rowan dropped the scepter to be closer to her. He scanned her body, hoping to find any semblance of life.

"Madam Linn," he whimpered. "Madam Linn, please. Open your eyes." He watched the musical notes fade. Clascia's song ended as she hung her head. Rowan held Madam Linn's cold palm with a shaky hand. Tears trickled down his face. "I did this. She's here because… this wouldn't have happened if I just—"

"Rowan, I need you to listen to me," Mister Dre instructed, his voice deep and level. "You and your friends must finish what you started. Go to the valley, take that scepter, and destroy the inqai for good."

Rowan and his friends stared at Mister Dre confused. How could he say that with his injured wife lying at his feet?

"B-but what about Madam Linn?" Peron asked.

"Madam Linn will be just fine," Mister Dre answered. "Clascia and I will be right by her side until she—"

"We need to find a healer or the mayor…or something," Selah interrupted, her voice choking up with each word. "Why are we sitting around doing nothing? We can't end it like this!"

"Then don't," Clascia Valdi chimed in, raising her head. "If you wish to help, you must complete the task set before you. Linn would want you to act and fight, not wallow in sorrow. Her life right now… is in the hands of Caelum and His Children. We mustn't let our emotions be the reason not to move forward."

All eyes looked at Madam Linn. A thousand accusations filled Rowan's mind. *This is all your fault. Your presence burdens those around you.* Voices that Den Mother once yelled in his ear were silenced when Mister Dre brushed through his coils.

"And that's precisely what we need you to do. To keep moving forward," Mister Dre said softly. "Can you do that, Rowan? Promise me you'll do that."

Rowan was speechless. How could Mister Dre ask so much of him? Soon his guidance flooded his memories. *It only takes one step.* Rowan exhaled, wiped his tears, and picked up his scepter, ready to face his fears for the last time.

Chapter 26

The Reason They Call Me Moonstruck

Letting go of Madam Linn's hand was the most painful decision Rowan had ever made. Forget the destruction of inqai; he and his friends should have stayed with her until she woke up. But he'd made a promise to Mister Dre. And mages never break their promises.

Selah, Peron, and Rowan floated above Evermire's desolation, staring at the inqai in a piercing silence. Their plan seemed utterly impossible to Rowan: three young orphans attempting to defeat hundreds of monsters just like the heroes in their stories. But in the back of his mind, only one reason forced him to overcome such danger.

"No matter what happens, let's agree to do this for Madam Linn and save our new home," Rowan declared softly.

Selah and Peron faced him with weary expressions. Were they willing to go with him after so much? Peron sighed. "She'd be really proud of you, Rowan," he said. "Let's finally end this."

The boys peered at Selah, who was viewing the broken city in quiet despair. Rowan never knew what went on in that head of hers. But he saw her fists gripped together while her brows furrowed in, looking more determined than ever.

"Cast your fireworks over the valley," Selah instructed. "We'll gather them all there once they follow it."

Rowan nodded. He found the horizon where the trees met the sky. With his free hand, he hovered it over his face, pushed it out, and angled his movement just above the forest.

Coemsae Aercis, Rowan whispered.

Pop! Pop! Pop!

Purple fireworks burst into the air. The sea of black monsters filling the streets ceased their terror as they gawked at the exploding flares. Calm washed over Rowan. No, not calm. Numbness. His whole body had gone limp. He almost sank from his flight until Peron and Selah caught him. His second use of that spell in one evening. What would happen if he used it again?

Rowan gulped and shook his head. He needed to stay focused. "Let's take them to the valley," he reminded his friends.

They commanded their coats to fly forward, as the inqai sprinted for the bright, purple light. The orphans flew past the terrorized town of Evermire until the streetlamps faded behind them, and they entered the dark-green territory.

Rowan recognized the hills of the valley, sighing as the cool breeze chilled his face. A moment of peace before the storm.

"You think you've got it, Ro?" Selah asked.

"I think so," Rowan said, grazing Sly's head. Selah's smile comforted him under the bursting light. Then the light faded, leaving only the glow of her hazel eyes. As the last of his fireworks flitted away, an army of noise charged into motion.

Shriek, went the inqai.

Entrances through shrubbery connected parts of the town to the valley. Scores of inqai trampled through the leafed ornaments and ripped the entrances to shreds.

"Selah, I don't think I've ever aimed it this far," Rowan realized.

"It's alright, Rowan," she replied, touching his face. She turned his head toward the raving beasts toppling each other. "Just make sure the scepter is steady, keep your eyes on the monsters, and—"

"Remain calm," Rowan finished.

Peron and Selah nodded one last time, then Rowan set his sights on the monsters. He pointed the scepter at an inqus who stared directly into his soul. It snarled and grinned its dripping grin, even with the weapon in view. With that motivation, Rowan took a slow breath and cast the spell.

Striatsi.

Energy expanded into a bright ball of electricity. The beasts below gaped at the spell, distracted from their own savagery. The weight of the lightning pushed Rowan off his course.

"Just hang on, Rowan," Peron strained, propping him up to keep him steady. Rowan held his ground, even as the lightning grew larger and ready for takeoff.

Zoom, the spell went into the valley.

CRACK, went the explosion.

A powerful force knocked the children off their flight pattern and struck the inqai where they stood. Their forms sparked and vaporized, leaving only a trail of smoke swirling in the breeze.

The rogue scepter and the orphans plummeted to the ground. Their soft coats saved them from serious injury, but they still suffered aches and pains. As they sat up, their eyes widened at the heap of ashes spread along the flowing grass.

"They're...gone," Selah said in disbelief.

Rowan shuffled towards the charred remains as the smoky air whistled past his ears. Sparks from Sly's head dimmed within the scepter, helping Rowan identify the clear-cut evidence of the slain monsters.

"We did it," Rowan said.

"We did it," Peron asked, still huddling on the ground.

A smile formed on Rowan's face as he leapt for joy. "We did it! We did it! We did it!"

Peron joined in his celebration, chanting with him as he bound him in a hug.

"Selah, did you hear that?" Rowan said. "It's over! It's finally..."

Rowan's smile dropped at the sight of a trembling Selah fixed to the ground. Her hands clung to the grass beneath her as she let out a soft whimper.

"Se, what's wrong?" Rowan asked.

"I can't... I can't move my leg," she mumbled through her tears.

Cautiously, the boys crept towards her. "Sellie, what is it? What's wrong with your leg?" Peron asked. But Selah ignored him and raggedly pronounced her trials.

"My leg. It burns," she cried. "It bur-AAAAAH!"

Her squeal made the stars bend to her pain. The boys rushed to her side. Peron swore in horror at the dark ember etched into her skin. Rowan gawked at the bright red mark appearing on the back of her hand.

A rasping scream tore through Peron. He sank to the grass, scarping furiously at the base of his head.

"IT'S ON MY HORNS! SHE GOT IT ON MY HORNS," Peron wailed.

He sobbed as he fell on his side, displaying the branded symbol on his chipped horns. If those embers appeared out of nowhere, that only meant…

"And just as foretold, Khallus has brought you safely into my grasp," Den Mother's distorted voice declared. Rowan turned to see her charred form limping in their direction. He glanced at the hot iron ring on Den Mother's finger, how snugly it stayed even as her skin peeled. Her melted smile made the gash in her other eye spill a pool of blood down her singed dress. Now fully blind, she scanned her head from side to side, using sound to locate the terrified Rowan. He kicked his feet to run but quickly tripped over himself, landing with a heavy thud.

Den Mother perked up at the noise and clenched her ring. Rowan strained as the sizzling heat branded his back and forearm. He let out a desperate gasp and rolled to his side, hoping to relieve the familiar sensation. Rowan heard her footsteps, then glimpsed her hovering over their tortured bodies.

"I ought to thank you, Rowan," Den Mother said. "You and your friends are helping me aid in Khallus' cause." She grabbed Rowan by the collar and pulled him. Selah and Peron called out his name, only for Den Mother to brand them again. Rowan sobbed under Den Mother's conquering gaze. His hopeless whimpering brought a smile to her face. "And since you're so worried about your friends' souls. I'll save you the pain of loss and sacrifice your life first."

With a forceful punch, Den Mother stamped another hot emblem into his stomach. Rowan's drawn-out scream echoed through the valley, as she dragged the burns up his sternum. Her ring reached the base of his neck. All the oxygen left his lungs. His eyes glazed over. The closer she traveled towards his face, the more life he felt being drained from his body.

A massive earthquake shook the ground beneath them and stopped the process from continuing.

Den Mother released Rowan as they both stumbled to the ground. As Rowan caught his breath, something strange caught his eye. In the distance, a blinding white light soared above the town of Evermire. It dispersed outward and rippled over the buildings, the valley, even the children themselves. The ground stopped shaking. Rowan, Selah, and Peron looked at the sky and shuddered.

A radiant mage hovered high above them, a crown of floating stars spiraling around her dreadlocks. She pulsed like the galaxies across the realm. Her eyes, like full moons, looked over the feeble Den Mother with rage.

Madam Linn. Linn the Moonstruck, surrounded by the heavens, surrounded by the heavens, floated down to where Den Mother lay. The legionnaire sensed her presence and staggered to her feet.

"I've only heard legends of a light such as this," Den Mother grumbled. "The Star of Soliear. Another stain on the ways of magic; come to lose another battle." Madam Linn only glared at her, staying eerily silent. But Den Mother took her chance and ran toward her, hands ablaze.

Madam Linn plucked two stars from her crown and flung them at Den Mother. The stars snuffed out the fire and burned her palms at the center. She screeched at her cindered hands. It allowed Madam Linn to swoop in, take Den Mother by the throat, and hoist her into the sky.

She pushed her free hand into Den Mother's stomach and left her floating aimlessly; her center of gravity disappearing. Madam Linn gathered more stars from her crown and hurled them at the villainous mage. Each hot flare scalded her body and evaporated upon contact.

"Lousy tricks," Den Mother cried as she spun. "Is this the best you have to offer?"

A question she knew better than to answer. Four extra stars burned into her wrists and ankles, freezing in place. Linn the Moonstruck brought her hands together and expanded them to create a bright transparent sphere encircling Den Mother. She pushed down the space between her hands. All at once, the sphere collapsed around her, suffocating her.

"Release me at once! I command you to stop!"

But Madam Linn ignored her pleas. She flew to the trapped Den Mother and shoved her into the ashes of the inqai. The orphans shielded their eyes from the blinding explosion. When they looked back, Den Mother was lying on her side, cradling herself and shivering.

Rowan peered up at Linn the Moonstruck, who was floating back down to the grass.

"My ring. Where's my ring?" Den Mother murmured. Even though all the heavens had cast down their fury, she still never gave up. She crawled through the grass like a spoiled baby, feeling around with her hand. "Y-you think s-stars can def-f-feat me?" she stuttered. Rough iron touched her fingertips. She scurried to put it back on her finger.

Before she burned it, a swinging black sword scraped her knuckles and plunged into the ground. Mister Dre stood in the shadows with his hand out and his red eyes shooting a deadly glare.

"Pity," Mister Dre said, walking out of the darkness. "I was aiming for the head."

Madam Linn and Mister Dre peered down at the helpless woman, who avoided their gaze.

"Now, let's try this again, shall we," Madam Linn told Den Mother. Her voice became a loud, but calm echo. "Under the terms of bartered wardship, your mistreatment of your wards, and the damage you've caused to Evermire make you unfit to raise them as your own. As of today, you will pay the price for your crimes, and surrender your authority over Selah, Peron, and Rowan."

Den Mother snickered at her claims. As if she'd still forgotten the main rule of bartered wardship.

"You say I have nothing to give you," Madam Linn said. "And you'd be correct. For I plan on forcing your surrender. Be it violence, persuasion, or madness itself, I will strip you of your pride 'til dishonor claims your very soul."

The tattered witch laughed to herself, then spat. "Oathless half-breed. You still think I'd give them up so easily? Well, think again. I didn't have my spies use virca on that border just for you to make demands of me. A mage like you doesn't have what it takes to force my hand."

The border. Someone had to have let Den Mother in just to get to Rowan and his friends. But what spies would be in Evermire?

"Do you hear that, Rose?" The adventurers smirked at one another. "Not only a challenge, but… two confessions. Tampering with our borders and the use of forbidden magic. Which now makes this all the more satisfying."

Madam Linn leaned down and ripped Den Mother's eye patch off, revealing a nasty scar. Den Mother cringed under Linn's wicked grin. Then she gently whispered a familiar and entrapping spell.

Silituum.

A series of golden chains sprouted from the grass. They wrapped around Den Mother's wrists and neck, slouching her posture. She tried to escape, but the chains would not let her budge. Mister Dre pulled Den Mother by the hair, wrenching her upward to view Linn the Moonstruck displaying eight small moons. They went from full, to crescent, to the new moon itself; each phase orbited around Madam Linn's palm in a bright array.

"Perhaps you should see the reason they call me Moonstruck," Madam Linn said.

This was a new spell. She'd never done it in any of her stories. How could she do all that without her scepter?

Den Mother's eye widened as she shuddered. "The Moons of Felandii. Impossible."

As Madam Linn stepped towards her, the madwoman begged for her life. "No, please don't do this! Without these children, my oath is incomplete. Khallus. He'll take my life if I don't offer a final sacrifice. I'll be ruined if I surrender my wardship. Please, have mercy!"

"Mercy?" The Moonstruck Mage sneered at the response, answering her in a low, gravelly tone. "You ruined your chance for mercy the day you laid hands on these children."

In a flash, the moons floated over to Den Mother's head. Mister Dre ordered the orphans to cover their eyes. They did, except for Rowan. He saw the moons spin around Den Mother's scalp. Her eyes rolled back in her head, and she began to choke, as the endless cycles circled round and round and round. Her wheezing turned into heavy wailing. The moons spun faster, making her hair turn whiter and her skin even paler. As if time itself began cutting her life shorter and shorter.

"Stop," Den Mother shouted. "Please, make it stop! ENOUGH!"

Madam Linn pulled her arm back. The moons wrenched away from Den Mother's head, and she leaned over as if plagued by a terrible sickness. Madam Linn held the moons safely in her palm and blew on them. They floated away into dust.

Diasare, she murmured.

The chains around Den Mother dispersed. She lifted her head toward the ruthless adventurers. Their night vision leered at her like lions in a den. Rowan had never seen her so drained of life. Whatever those moons did to her, must have held enough madness to make her surrender. Rowan had thought it was impossible. Until she brought up her trembling hands. She yanked off her ring, clenched it one last time, to no avail, and handed it to Dremos.

"Wardship granted," Den Mother strained in defeat.

Dremos retracted his other sword, tossed the ring into the air, and split it in front of Den Mother. The orphans' fresh welts disappeared in an instant, making them drop to the ground in relief.

Rowan felt at his neck and sighed in relief when he realized her emblem was gone. He caught Den Mother staring at him. Blackened cinders enveloped her lower body, which was ready to fade into the breeze. But even death didn't stop her from displaying a devious smirk.

"We are many, child," Den Mother grumbled, her torso turning to ash. "Khallus' Legion will continue his cause even after my death. You'll see us again. After all, we're always watching." Her last words echoed as she was swallowed up by her own demise.

Mister Dre helped Selah and Peron back to their feet. The radiant Moonstruck Mage held out her hand to Rowan. He allowed her to lift him back up. The children stared at the pile of ashes, wondering if it would come back to life.

"Is she really—," Rowan murmured.

"Yes, Rowan," Madam Linn affirmed. "It's finally over."

Soft tears welled in Rowan's eyes. He hid his face to muffle his sob, but Selah and Peron wouldn't let him. They gathered around him, crying the same tears of joy while wiping each other's faces.

Madam Linn's glorious form returned to normal. Her crown of stars disappeared, and her dreadlocks floated back down. She rested her weary head on Mister Dre's shoulder. All at once, the orphans embraced the two adventurers as their cries grew louder.

"Thank you," Rowan wailed.

"You saved our lives," Selah added.

"We can't th-thank you enough," Peron cracked.

A heavy burden eased its way off their shoulders with every tear. Peace chipped its way through their constant anger, worry, and hopelessness. They didn't know how long the peace would last. But they reveled in joy, cried in the arms of their saviors, and let peace make itself known in this one fact: that the young orphans were finally free of Den Mother.

Chapter 27

A New Home

"**K**nock it off, Rowan. You're going to make me drop it," Peron said, pushing him away as he held Mister Dre's folded cape. Rowan had been looking over his shoulder the entire walk through the forest.

"Calm down, Mister Responsible," Rowan said. "I'm just making sure none of it falls on the ground."

"That's why Mister Dre gave you your half of the ring," Selah told Rowan, holding up her half. "Focus on your thing. Let Peron take care of the ashes."

It felt like a bad omen, carrying the remains of your enemy through a dark forest. It wasn't the way Rowan wanted to celebrate his first defeated foe. But if it meant repaying his saviors for their freedom, he'd gladly carry anything they asked. Especially Madam Linn, whose strength renewed once Rowan gave back her scepter.

"How's your head?" Rowan asked, glancing at the back of it where Den Mother injured her.

She winced as she tapped it. "Still stings," she confessed. "But feeling better. Thank you for asking."

"I'm sorry for… stealing your scepter," Rowan admitted. "If I had known it'd make you weaker without it, I would've…well, I'm not sure. But I really am sorry."

Madam Linn glanced at him, and he avoided her eyes. He couldn't handle any scolding right now.

"Sly is a very merciful familiar," Madam explained, brushing off his silver head. "Lending strength only to those with potent exposure to magic. He doesn't let just anybody use him. You must be quite special if he allowed you to."

Even the frozen snake thought he was special. That's just what he needed.

"In the future, however, we must see about getting you your own familiar." Rowan gasped. "As well as your own artifact to store your spells in. So, we won't be needing my scepter, now, will we?"

From the way she grinned at him, Rowan knew that meant *Don't even think about looking at my scepter. Let alone use it.*

"Yes, Madam," is all he said.

After a brief walk, the Spehrows and the children were in view of the great stone archway. In moments like that one, Rowan really wished he had night vision, if only to see the stone engravings wishing him well.

Madam Linn went to the spot where the border was scratched. She skimmed the claw marks on the stone and sighed.

"Perfect," she whispered. "Nothing's changed. Which means the ritual should go smoothly."

"Will this really help repair the border?" Selah asked.

"If it's kept our foes at bay once, it can do so again," Mister Dre said bluntly. He took the ring pieces from Selah and

Rowan, as well as his cape from Peron's grasp. He went under the archway and dumped the ashes on the borderline.

He placed both pieces of iron in Madam's hand. When he backed away, she knelt down, set the halves at the bottom edges of the border, and dragged the ashes in a straight line with her thumb. Once the line reached both sides of the border, she spoke in a slow, mellow voice.

Caelum and His Children, Madam Linn started. Dim light faded in and out of the borderline.

May you guide my hand and make shelter for your people.

Caelum and His Children.

May harm come not to us and let the wicked be torn asunder.

With that phrase, a fiery essence issued from the two ring pieces. They flared until they reached the sides of the archway, crackling along the stone fixture. Despite the blaze surrounding her, Madam Linn continued as she held out her scepter.

Caelum and His Children.

May this border protect us. Let your perfect peace smile upon us.

The head of her scepter began to glow. She raised it above her head, and in a louder voice, called out another spell.

Mutel Sotear

She stabbed her scepter into the ash-laden grass. A harsh breeze snuffed out the flames. It pushed the children and Mister Dre off balance. But not Linn the Moonstruck; her hold on the scepter never faltered. Not even as purple rays shone through the cracks of the stone gate. They illuminated the entire forest and rose into the sky. Rowan beamed at the light above, at how its thin barrier stretched as far as the eye could see.

Soon the lights dimmed, fading as if they had never existed. The claw marks at the bottom of the gate smoothed out to match the stone surface. Madam Linn stretched out her hand from the other side of the archway. The lavender rays swirled around her until she pushed her whole body through, looking back at her work in contentment.

"Wow, so she's really gone," Selah discerned. "Does that mean that…the Khallus Legion is gone? We won't see those monsters again?"

Rowan noticed Mister Dre clench his jaw at her question. "Unfortunately, the inqai and the Legion are still out there. And they'll remain here as long as evil and hopelessness reign in the hearts of men."

Rowan didn't like that answer, but he swallowed the harsh truth. More monsters on other islands. More people who talked and acted like Den Mother. Would their suffering truly never end?

"But that's why we fight and use magic the way we do," Madam Linn interjected, picking up the ring pieces again. "To protect others from their sting and destroy their forces. Just as you all did this very night."

She took Mister Dre's hand and said in her poised tone, "And now that we've secured the border, I suppose it's time to head home."

Rowan's eyes grew wide. "H-home?"

The tension in his voice caught Madam Linn's attention. "Yes, dear," she said soothingly. "Home. Back to Evermire."

"Oh… right." The way she said it brought a smile to Rowan's face. Home. An actual home. Not a place he stayed to survive, but one where he could actually live. One where he was wanted. Rowan sniffed back his tears and took a breath of fresh air. "Alright, let's go home," he said. For the first time in a long time, he finally felt safe.

Once he straightened up, he walked beside Selah and Peron, ready to bask in the comfort of their new abode.

●　●　●

"Rowan Spehrow," he said, announcing it like a royal title. He nodded to himself. "I like it! Makes me sound super powerful—OW!"

A slight knock to the knee cut off Rowan's sentence. Courtesy of Master Torrence of the Emphyrea's Lights, holding a small reflex hammer in his hand. He and his party had volunteered to heal the wounds of every child in Evermire before they went on to Venari. The children sat in a straight line along the sidewalk of the town square, ready to be checked out. However, Rowan didn't realize that healing meant getting hit with strange instruments.

"Well, your reflexes are active enough to be in high spirits," Torrence chuckled through his canines. "I presume Madam Spehrow has welcomed you into her court?"

Rowan nodded with an excited smile. "Uh-huh. And now whenever I go on quests, I can say, 'Never fear! For I am a mage of the Spehrow line!'"

Peron and Selah rolled their eyes at his theatrics. The long-bearded man, Master Avion, made time to whisper a blessing over Selah's head, while Peron respectfully declined Master Heziah's offer to stitch up his chipped horn. Once Avion finished, he huffed at Rowan's exclamation.

"Ha! Young man, perhaps it's best you gain people's attention with your skills first," he advised.

"Yes, family names can only get you so far as an adventurer," Heziah said, tucking his needle into his suit.

"Whoa, family name," Rowan whispered in amusement. "I've never had a family name before."

"You've never had a family, period," Peron corrected sarcastically.

"What are you talking about, 'Peron Spehrow,'" Selah teased, latching onto his arm. "How can you say that when we've always been family?"

"Wait! Does this mean we're like…brother and sister now?" Rowan asked. Peron and Selah glanced at each other before answering.

"Honestly, I kind of felt like we already were," Selah admitted.

A brother and a sister. A new family. A new home. Everything Rowan ever wanted, right within his reach.

"I call being the oldest," Rowan said.

Peron pushed his face to the side. "Yeah, no, that'll never happen. We all know Selah's the oldest. She showed up first."

"Aw, Perry. Good for you, volunteering to be the youngest," Selah joked, prompting Peron to flick her on the forehead.

The Emphyrea's Lights bid the children farewell and shifted to help Nyx and his two friends, Loka and Sailo. They paid no mind to the party, only to the small familiar bird they practiced their magic on. The delicate sea sparrow flew over their heads to escape the twins shooting fire and lightning at it. Rowan frowned at their harmful antics and stomped over to them. The bird must've sensed him coming, for it flitted its wings and landed atop Rowan's head for safekeeping. Though he grumbled and the kids snickered, the young Spehrow boy had a trick up his sleeve.

"Say, Nyx. Do you think your father would allow you and your friends to harm other living things? Doesn't sound like an uh…*acceptable* leader to me." Nyx stood up to wipe the smug look off Rowan's face, but Mayor Vassile's hand gripped at his shoulder.

"You're correct, dear boy. It doesn't," Mayor Vassile agreed. His stern glare made Nyx hang his head. Rowan hid his gloating grin once the bird flew away and the Spehrows walked over.

After all the smoke and disarray, the mayor tasked them with overseeing the town's repairs. Madam Linn levitated large pieces of debris with the help of the gargoyles, dropping them into a giant pile. Mister Dre helped douse the fires with the soldiers and escorted citizens from the safehouse to the surface. When they came back to check on the children, bright but exhausted smiles were spread across their faces. Selah, Peron, and Rowan rushed up to hug them without another thought.

The mayor interrupted their tender moment by clearing his throat. "Well, I assume things are coming along nicely."

Madam Linn bowed her head. "Precisely, sire. With everyone's help, the repairs should be completed by high noon tomorrow. Everything's under control."

"What about the border? And the legionnaire?"

Madam Linn took something out of her dress pocket. In front of the mayor, she displayed the two halves of the ring in her palm. Rowan squinted at it, noticing the fire emblem erased from existence. *It must've happened during the ritual*, Rowan thought.

"Like I said, Oligio. Everything's under control." Madam Linn placed the ring in the mayor's hand and closed his fist around it. The mayor was taken aback by her response. He sighed, with a hint of regret as he looked at her.

"It seems I owe you an apology, Spehrow," he stated professionally. "While the border's not perfect, you still sacrificed your life for this town and for these new wards of yours. I can relate in a way. I'd do the same thing for my Onyx." He pulled his son closer to his side. "Though I still believe we should involve the Council, I suppose that right now, I am in your debt. Name your price, and it shall be given."

The Spehrows glanced at each other until Mister Dre stepped up. He whispered into the mayor's ear. Rowan leaned in discreetly but heard only a few simple words. *Spies… information…* and *orphanage in Faegan.* Words that made both Rowan and Mayor Vassile jolt back in surprise. So there really were spies in Evermire? And what did the old orphanage have to do with anything?

The mayor adjusted his boater hat and nodded. "I'll see what I can do," he whispered before dragging his son away.

Nyx complained in the distance. "But Pa, that kid was bein'—"

"No excuses, Onyx," the mayor interrupted. "An *exceptional* leader lets pride brace him by the shoulders."

They passed by the Emphyrea's Lights, who had transitioned to helping Ahria and Truegug while their guardians stayed with them. Uncle Rog tapped his foot impatiently while he stood by Clascia and her band. She leaned on her crutch as she talked his ear off.

"Truegug! Ahria! We made it," the children called. Their new friends heard them and ran over, disregarding the healing mages. Rowan cringed when Ahria gathered him in a big hug. He still wasn't used to the charming girl's annoying presence.

"I knew it was you guys when I saw flying coats in the air," Ahria admitted. Rowan scooted away, not wanting that to be the highlight of his night.

"Seems you both made it out unscathed," Mister Dre said. "How's your mother holding up?"

Ahria straightened up like a pristine young lady. "She's doing fine, Mister Spehrow. Just telling Uncle Rog about the new song she's writing about the battle."

"Well, I'd certainly love to hear more," Madam Linn said. She latched onto Mister Dre's arm, and they strolled over to greet the Stringed Siren.

"So that was Den Mother, huh?" Truegug said. "You guys said she was evil, but I never thought you meant burn-the-town type of evil."

"I thought we made that pretty clear," Selah said.

"Well, it's not like we told them everything about her," Peron corrected.

"Who cares if we did," Rowan added. "All that matters is we never have to see her again. We're the official wards of Linn the Moonstruck, now!"

"Really?" Ahria asked, amazed.

The children glanced at the Ataxia and Uncle Rog, who alternately laughed and sulked in response to Clascia's dramatic retellings.

"Wow," Truegug said in disbelief. "I guess I do have to start givin' out free stuff." He held a hand beside his mouth and mumbled to Rowan. "You better show me more magic from now on, you hear?"

The children exclaimed at his offer, all except Ahria. Her disappointed sigh caught the others' attention.

"That's really a shame. I at least thought you'd want to be one of Mama's wards. She could really teach you a whole bunch." Ahria said. "I was also …kind of hoping I'd have some new brothers and a sister."

Her glum expression made Selah hold her hands. "That's so sweet of you," she acknowledged. "Of course I'll be your new sister. I've always wanted one of my own. But I think after all we've been through, my brothers and I belong here. And I'm sure you'd agree, too."

"Sorry, you and your mama can't stay longer," Peron mentioned. "You sure you have to go back to Venari?"

Ahria shrugged at Selah and Peron. Their height forced her to look slightly up. "It's where *I* belong, I suppose," she said with a clipped smile. "Then again, there aren't many friends that I can make stories about."

Ahria hopelessly bowed her head. And then Rowan had a thought, a kind and generous thought.

"Do you ever write letters?" he asked. His question made Ahria scrunch her face in confusion. "You and your mama visit Evermire once a quarter, right? Maybe… while you're gone, we can tell you about our own adventures on paper. Then, when you come to visit… you'll have another story ready for us to hear. It'll be like you never left."

A warm smile crept across Ahria's face. She stared at him like he was the best person in the entire world. Rowan expected another hug after his speech. Instead, she nodded, saying. "I'd like that, Rowan the Brave. I'd really like that."

Rowan flushed at her bright smile, prompting Selah, Peron, and Truegug to hide their mocking glances.

A string quartet echoed across the sky, the music coming from the fiddlers attached to Clascia's hip. Townsfolk, children, and adventurers alike reacted to the music with dancing feet and clapping hands. They all gathered around the empty pedestal, continuing their lively fun as if time never passed.

Madam Linn and Mister Dre dashed for the children. "Come, we must celebrate your first victory," Madam Linn said, holding out her hand. "There's a dance I'd love to teach you."

Rowan chuckled at her excitement, placing his hand into her own.

Peron peered slyly at his siblings. "What do you say, Sellie? Best dancer gets the loser's pancakes tomorrow?"

"Perry, we all know you have two left feet," Selah said, elbowing him. "But don't worry, I'll help you catch up."

And just like that, Selah, Peron, Rowan, and their new friends, followed the Spehrows onto the dance floor.

They attempted Linn and Dre's experienced moves with clumsy footsteps. They twirled around in circles, swung arms with different dance partners, and clapped in time to the fast tempos. By the final number, the new Spehrow children had memorized all the steps, and they danced the night away as if they'd done it a thousand times over. It was a celebration Rowan had always imagined, now come to life.

In his rejoicing, Rowan couldn't help but bask in the scenery of Evermire, his new home. The way the street lamps gave warmth with their comforting light. How townsfolk found joy after times of devastation. Even the members of the Nocturnal Market, both mage and creature, welcomed him with open arms. It was in the last moments of the dance that Rowan smiled and let a new voice echo in his head.

"I think I'm gonna like it here."

Epilogue

Oathless Mages

<u>Two Weeks Later. High Noon in the Forest</u>

Tssssss, went Linn the Moonstruck.

Rowan studied the fluid motion of her fingers. The way they plucked glowing words out of the Compendium and slowly made their way to brush the scales of the resting snake. The hiss in her voice didn't cease until the same words left golden engravings on Sly's back.

Rowan leaned over the picnic basket to see, almost tipping over his marbles.

"Whoa, so that's how you carry all your spells," Rowan realized. "I should've known those storybooks were lying. It's way too heavy to carry a spell book everywhere you go."

Madam Linn chuckled as she petted Sly. "Stretching the truth, maybe. Most mages haven't carried spell books for a couple centuries."

"Oh," Rowan said, disappointed. "Well, I guess I have that to look forward to until I find my own famili—"

A chirping noise cut him off, followed by a stifled snort from Madam Linn. He saw her glance at the top of his head. It couldn't be.

The boy groaned when he felt a small little bird perched on his coils. "Come on, not this again," he said, shooing the bird as best he could. "I should've never helped you from getting fried by those bullies. Honestly, ever since it found my marbles on the beach, it's been watching my every move!"

He grunted and swiped, but the little sparrow dodged his attack and landed on a red marble. Right before Rowan thwacked it again, the bird glowed a bright golden color. It expanded its wings until it shrunk and inserted itself into the marble; leaving a stamp of its flying position on the rough paint.

Rowan's eyes widened as he held it up. He looked at the stunned Madam Linn and let out a small exhale.

"A selfless bond between man and beast," she stated. "The sparrow helped you, and you offered help in exchange."

Rowan blinked at her statement. "And that means…"

"Looks like you have yourself a familiar," Madam Linn winked.

Rowan laughed and fell back in excitement. He couldn't believe it! A real-life familiar! Now he'd be even more like Linn the Moonstruck!

"Oh, that reminds me," Madam said. "Perhaps we should work on your flying spells. The Patrons grant oaths to anyone willing to fly like their repha."

Rowan didn't know which word to focus on, but the word 'oath' caught his attention first. He lifted himself up with a glum look, sitting in silence as Madam skimmed the Compendium.

"Actually, I thought about it." Rowan broke in. "Maybe I don't really…need or…want an oath?"

Madam's eyes lifted from her book; astonishment mixed with her soft gaze. "Really?" she said.

"I realize that taking an oath would make me more powerful. I can help my siblings better with one. But then I think about the attack and with Den…" He stopped himself; he promised never to speak her name again. "That… woman, and I think about how you protected us. You did all that even as an Oathbreaker." He bit his lip, hoping the title wouldn't rile her up. It didn't. She just kept listening. "So, if one day, I can be as strong as you without an oath, I'll gladly take reading and practicing any day."

Madam Linn smiled warmly at Rowan, impressed by his progress. At his ambition in the face of trials. It made her proud to be called his teacher.

She scooted closer to him, Compendium in hand. She set it down on a familiar page. The illustration showed a character pushing his hands down, stomping his foot, and bounding into the sky like a bird. The character's outline soon crafted into a single cursive word.

Altseria

"Ahlt-seh-ree-ah," Rowan pronounced. "It's kind of like that one floating spell."

Madam nodded. "But before we do that, I propose we have our own oath ceremony."

Rowan looked taken aback. "B-but I just said—"

"Not an official one. I save those for Paian temples," Madam explained, sitting up on her knees. "Now, give me your hands."

Confused but still willing, Rowan placed his hands in hers and laughed as she straightened her poised form.

"Rowan… of the Spehrow line." She leaned into her smile. "A High Patron of Caelum would ask you this…What shall you use your gifts for?"

The thing he had always wanted. "I…I want to travel all of Pelle and use magic to fight any foe that comes my way."

"And what will you hope to achieve in this endeavor?"

"To protect my family. And be confident in knowing I can." He said it because he finally believed it.

Madam Linn held up two fingers. She lightly tapped his forehead, the middle of his collarbone, then his lower abdomen.

"In knowing this, Rowan," Madam Linn chanted. "The path of the oathless reigns within you. You are to use your gifts wisely. Persevere, even if you falter from your purpose. Do you swear to use magic to protect the ones you love?"

Rowan nodded. "I swear—"

"Remember, little prince," Madam cut off, making Rowan open his eyes. "If you swear, you're forever bound to this. No turning back. So, I suggest that your honest answer only be 'yes' or 'no'?"

He hesitated. Then ultimately smiled at his decision, knowing it would be the most important one of his life. "Yes," he stated.

"Now close your eyes." He did. "And when I let go, I want you to perform the motions and cast the spell you just read."

His heart started racing. He didn't know whether he was ready. But once she let go, he had no choice. Rowan pushed his hands down, stomped his foot, and with a shaky breath he said,

Altseria.

Rowan's form glowed blue, and his knees lifted off the ground. He opened his eyes, to see how far the spell had taken him. He smiled as his body soared above the lowest branch of the tree they sat under. But his excitement began to fade. He looked down, and the picnic basket below was getting smaller and smaller. His only comfort was the marble he clutched in his hand. His ears started ringing. He wasn't floating down. He should've ended the spell, but the ringing wouldn't allow him to.

"Madam Linn," his voice cracked. He almost started to cry.

But upon his call, her scaled scepter reached out for him. Rowan clung to it, feet dangling in the air. Even amidst his worry and the fading high-pitched noise, Madam Linn Spehrow dealt him the most loving and supportive smile.

"It's alright," she reassured him. "I'm right here with you."

Acknowledgements

An old colleague of mine told me that an idea for a story, is not yet a story. All it needs is to be written down first. Four years ago, The Tales of Spehrow was an idea held in my mind alone. Who knew that my colleague's advice would challenge me to create a story for everyone to read. First off, I'd like to give all glory to God for giving me the mind and spirit to write this incredible book. Through His will, I pray many young minds read this and are inspired to live in bravery and confidence.

I'd like to thank my family for supporting me throughout this whole process. Mom, you have no idea how much your attentiveness means to me. Every day I read my book to you inspired me to keep going. Dad, your critique helped shape the book to what it is today. I thank the Lord for you and your wisdom.

Thank you to my editor Devin of First Editing, and my cover design team at Miblart for all of their suggestions and patience that have made this novel something special.

To my best friends, I'm so grateful to you both standing alongside me. Whether it was writing together or giving godly counsel, I can never thank you enough. A special thanks to Lizzy Myrick, Greg Washington, Tori Roberts, and Rudi Sanon for being my alpha and beta readers for my debut novel.

And to the readers, I hope you enjoyed the first installment of the Tales of Spehrow. This story is just the beginning for Selah, Peron, and Rowan. Never fear, for more is still to come. See you on the next adventure.

E.L. Baldwin

Glossary

Altsum - [AHlt-sOOm]:

- An elven spell that makes objects float into the air instantly. Floating range is about 10 feet off the ground.

Aurego - [Ow - rEh - gOH]

- elvish informal farwell for "goodbye"

Corimani - [KOH - ri - mAH - nEE]

- An elven spell for "come hither." Flying range is 5 feet.

Diasare - [DEE- Uh-sAh-rAY]

- An elven spell that stops other spells from being cast.

Ulsgat- [OOls-gat]

- A forbidden spell that causes unexpected fire to appear.

Virca - [VEEr - cAh]

- the forbidden magic of Pelle's Isles. Used mainly by the Legion of Khallus to destroy all that lives.

Striatsi - [StrEE - AHt - sEE]

- Spell that produces a lightning strike instantly. Cast from either fingertips or any spell holder of choice. Lightning strike has a concentration of 1 minute.

Pera Kal - [PEH - rAH KAHl]

- elvish informal greeting for "Hello"

Peravo Kalai - [PEH - rAH - vOH KAH - lAH - EE]

- elvish formal greeting for "Warm Greetings."

Repmarchis parc braazi - [REHp - mAHr-kis PAhrk - BrAH - zEE]

- A Bardic illusion spell for "Duet March with Percussion and Brass." A combination of using any percussion and brass instrument of choice. Spell creates a copy of the mage to play either one of the casted instruments.

Phinivenic - [FI - nEE - vEH - nIk]

- A Bardic spell for "Dismissed Finale." Dismisses the instrument in hand, making it fade into celluloid dust.

Soteriparc - [SOh - tEH - rEE - pAHrk]

- A Bardic protection spell for "Percussion Protection." A combination of barrier magic using a percussion instrument of choice.

Thra'ill - [ThrAH - il]

- The depths of the underworld; a cold, dark abyss feared by many lifeforms. A common swear used amongst hunters to express the severe nature of their trouble.

Siliituum - [SIl - EE - tOOm]

- A Zealous spell for "Dragging Chains ." An ancient spell used by the Zealots of Paia. Used to bind rogues and prisoners who stand trial against the Council and the High Patron of Caelum.

Floatvi - [FlOH - nAHt - vEE]

- An elven spell for "Float and Repair." Has a unlimited amount of uses for the oathed mages. Oathless mages may use these spells once a day.

O culo vu Taxieh da mahee [Oh kOO - lOH VOO Taks-EE - AY DUH MAH - EE]

- An observer's spell for "Lend me your eyes and show the Ataxia." One of the more advanced spells within the spellbook "The Oculos."

Pethsana - [PEH - SAH - NAH]

- An Elven healing spell. Used to heal open wounds and forming bruises. Concentration level 1 to 5 minutes depending on the amount of injuries. Oathless manges may use this spell twice in one day on one person each.

Metalauna K'vuldi [MEH - tUH - lOW - nUH VUHl - dEE]

- An Elven Spell for "Send to Valdi." Spell sends you to location of the mage's desire. Has a limited range of 50 miles and can only be cast once a day. Mage must put the initial of the person or business they'd like to see, if there is more than one of the same name.

Metalauna N'spiro [MEH - tUH - lOW - nUH SpEE - rOH]

- A variation of the spell above. An elven spell for "Send to Spehrow."

FILKUZTAC CANIL VE - [FIl - kOOS - tAk KAn - Il VEh]

- A fiendish swear word for being dishonorable and sly.

Coemsae Tophsu - [COHm - sAY TOHf - sOO]

- A Compendium spell for "Illusion on Oneself". Takes about 15 seconds to 1 minute of concentration before casting.

Coemsae Aercis - [COHm - sAY AIR - KIS]

- A Compendium spell for "Explosive Illusion." Takes about 15 seconds to 1 minute of concentration before casting.

Plastratsii - PlAH - strAHt - sEE]

- A Compendium spell for "Shocking Grasp." The mage
  must hold the skin, garment, or metal of the desired
  object before casting.

Piresto - [PEE - rEH - stOH]

- A Compendium spell for "Burning Light." An instant
  spell used to shoot sunbeams that blind and/or
  vaporize the victim.

Mistio - [MI-stEE- O]

- A Compendium spell for "Disintegrating Rays." Thin
  red beams shoot out of the mage's fingertips. Beams
  travel at around thirty miles per hour. Spell must be
  cast at a maximum range of twenty feet.

Vouconu - [VOW - cOH - nOO]

- A Compendium and kinetic spell for "Moving
  Mountains". An two objects with weight minimum of
  100 pounds can be moved and pushed into each other.

Mutel Sotear - [MOO - tEHl SOH- TEEr]

- A Zealous spell for "Guard and Protect." The mage
  must call upon all the deities of Pelle for restoration.
  Must perform ritual exactly in order to create, secure,
  or repair an artifact of protection. Can be performed in
  any language.

Altseria [AHlt - sEH - rEE - AH]

- A variation of the Elven spell "Altsum." Floating range
  is about 20 feet in the air depending on the force placed
  into it. Spell slowly brings you back down after 10
  seconds.

About the Author

E.L. Baldwin is the author of the fantasy novel, The Tales of Spehrow. This is her first book, and it most certainly will not be the last. When she is not busy writing, she is teaching music to her students or sipping coffee at a local café.